First Experience

Experiences: Book 2

*The Introduction of a Young Woman to Openness, Trust,
and New Experiences of the Submissive Kind*

Simone Freier

OTK Publications
www.OTKPublications.com

First Experience

EXPERIENCES: BOOK 2

By Simone Freier

Published by OTK Publications
http://otkpublications.com

Copyright © 2014-2018 OTK Publications
All rights reserved

ISBN: 978-1-942054-03-0
v1.5

Manufactured in the United States of America

COVER DESIGN BY OTK PUBLICATIONS

This is a work of fiction. All names, characters, and incidents in this work are fictitious. Any resemblance to actual events, or to real persons is purely coincidental. No humans or animals were harmed during the creation of this work.

Caution: This work contains mature content, including graphic sexual descriptions and scenes, and is provided for adults only. Neither the author nor the publisher intends to encourage or promote any of the activities depicted in this work. Many of the specific activities and scenarios described in this work can potentially be dangerous, and should not be attempted without special knowledge or training and, as appropriate, use of sterile single-use supplies. No information contained herein is intended to constitute advice or serve as instructional material, and this work should not be relied upon to ensure safe practices in real life.

Table of Contents

CHAPTER 1: A SURPRISING DEVELOPMENT

It was really frustrating: I was 'healthy, wealthy, and wise' ... but I was not happy. My marriage to Sarah of more than 25 loving years had ended prematurely when Sarah was taken from me in a traffic accident in England, nearly five years ago.

Sarah and I had enjoyed an open relationship, the confidence in our own marriage enabling us to have intimate experiences with other partners. Sarah, of course, had understood me well – including my sexual preferences and turn-ons, most based on memories of experiences in my childhood.

My introspection over the past several years had revealed that my turn-ons included both very general things – such as openness and trust, and very specific things – such as spanking and 'medical sex'. All of these things related to women submitting to embarrassment or pain in their rear end. I could identify the experiences in my childhood where some of these turn-ons had originated, but still did not understand why they had stuck with me – and even grown – over the past decades.

I had lived some of my fantasies, including giving shots to and taking the rectal temperature of my neighbor Shelia. And the spanking experience with Liz had resulted in additional fantasies and my further interest in these fetishes. Perhaps they weren't fetishes in the dictionary sense – which often defined 'fetish' as becoming erotically aroused by inanimate objects, or by a non-genital part of the body.

But my Internet research had shown that there were entire communities of people turned-on by very specific and relatively uncommon things. These included the usual fetishes – such as shoes, pantyhose, or other clothing (panties, lingerie, stockings, leather and latex).

They also included various 'kinks', such as BDSM (bondage, discipline, sadism, and masochism), in its various forms (spanking, flogging, caning, whipping); body modification, such as tattoos and piercings; ass play, such as insertions (dildos, vibrators, fisting) and enemas; and more extreme activities, including needle play, hot wax, and electrical stimulation.

I found that some people are turned on by specific types of women: Big breasted women ('BBW'), hairy women, mature women (termed 'MILF', an acronym for 'mother I'd like to fuck'), women in specific roles (slut, whore, slave, nurse, secretary), and women with specific ethnic backgrounds. Other turn-ons include voyeurism, outdoor or public sex, orgies, threesomes, and gangbangs.

I was excited by many of these things, but certainly not by activities involving bodily fluids (golden showers, hot lunch), or age play (diapers, breastfeeding). The range of sexual turn-ons was amazing, and the Internet demonstrated that there were people 'out there' who are turned-on by things that I considered very strange.

Over the past couple of years, I had created my 'playroom' and 'exam room' in the basement, and collected a huge number of spanking implements and medical equipment and supplies, for use on adventurous young women. I had realized by now that women my age were usually not turned on by these things – as most of my fantasies, even by my own admission, were rather immature, having been established during my childhood.

But I became even more interested in sharing these fascinations with younger women: Women who might be open to new experiences, and strong enough to see something like spanking in a sexual way, and not demeaning or humiliating.

I was not turned on by conventional BDSM – for example tying a woman up, while I spanked her. My turn on was related more to openness or submission – someone allowing me to 'use' her body, either because she is very open, or because she is willing to do it for me, even though it may not be a turn on for her.

Anyone could be spanked hard while tied down; they would not have a choice. But it was much more exciting to me to have a woman get into a possibly embarrassing position and hold that position voluntarily while I thrashed her bottom. That would take strength, courage, and self-confidence.

Although I was interested in domination and submission, I did not consider myself a sadist, nor was I turned on by someone who was clearly a masochist. It was not about hurting someone, but seeing her respond in the face of potential pain. And it was not about someone wanting to be hurt – in which case, she would not be 'submitting' to something that she didn't want. It was complicated.

Now that I somewhat understood the origins and meaning of my fantasies, and had the time, place, and toys to share some of them with a partner, I just needed to find a young woman who would 'play' with me. Liz had been in her late thirties while I was in my late forties; but now, I was fifty years old, and my fantasies were of girls in their twenties; younger than my own sons.

It was about this time in the evolution of my thought process that I was invited to a party, given by a couple with whom my wife and I had been friends. They lived on the other side of town, in a tract neighborhood loaded with families and children. I hadn't been over to their house since my wife's passing, and mainly remember every room littered with kids' toys, and their two sons, with whom our sons played on the middle school soccer team.

I arrived fashionably late, around 8:30PM, with a nice bottle of California cabernet in a neoprene wine tote, and Darlene greeted me at the door, smiling broadly, and hugging me tightly.

"It's so good to see you again, Sam! How are you doing? You look well."

I kissed her on the cheek, and said, "I'm fine. It's great to see you guys again, too."

We walked into the living room, and Dave came over and shook my hand, "Hey, buddy! We haven't seen you at the country club ... or anywhere else, for that matter. What have you been up to?"

We had quit the club years ago, after my kids had gone off to college. "I've been around. Just puttering around the house. I built-out the basement, and have a nice ... theater and office down there now."

Dave put his arm over my shoulder and ushered me into the kitchen, where I opened the wine.

I looked back into the living room; there were only about a dozen people, talking quietly. "Looks like a nice, intimate party," I remarked, as I pulled the cork from the bottle.

Dave followed my eyes, and said, "Yeah, Darlene wanted to have a few old friends over – and I'm not talking about their age. You remember Pam and Bill, don't you? Pam's been a close friend of my wife, and we had kids around the same time – they were in soccer together when our kids were older. Bill is a real jock." That was quite a comment coming from Dave, who I considered the ultimate 'jock' – definitely not my style!

I looked through the kitchen door at Pam sitting on the couch, and smiled as I pictured her from the old days. I now thought about her in a new light. She was still a beautiful woman.

We had known her before she married Bill, and I now wondered if she would have 'played' with me back in those days ... which I'm sure my wife would have approved (as she would have heard every detail from Pam and I, and she trusted both Pam and I implicitly). Oh well.

As I turned back to Dave, and began to ask him about his golf game, a stunning beauty walked casually into the kitchen. She looked around, and then took a glass and poured some wine.

I couldn't take my eyes off her – she had long, dark auburn hair that reached nearly to her waist, a model's face – with large, sparkling hazel eyes, a small nose, and cheeks that were naturally blushed, with no need for makeup. In fact, I realized at that point, that she was wearing absolutely no make-up at all.

She seemed under-dressed for the party, being barefoot, in a pair of running shorts and wearing an oversized sweatshirt. I could tell that she was big on top, even with the very un-sexy sweatshirt hiding her assets.

As my eyes traveled down, I saw that her waist was small, and her hips widened in the lower half of the classic hourglass form. I could not see her bottom, but imagined that it would be very spankable. Her legs were long and slender, and it was obvious that she was an athlete; her muscles were alternately outlined, as she shifted her weight from foot to foot. She was a knockout!

I don't think my review and analysis of her body took more than a few seconds, but my mouth had dropped open, and I was completely at a loss for something to say – not a very common occurrence, as all of my friends well knew.

Dave smiled at the young lady and looked up at me, beaming. "You remember my daughter, Kelly?"

I was astounded! I looked back at the most beautiful girl I had ever seen, and said, "Wow! The last time I saw you, you were a little girl; now, look at you!"

And I couldn't stop staring at her. Kelly was probably immune to boys looking at her, and I'm sure she didn't even consider that an older man (like me) would look at her in any way other than as a daughter, or niece.

Kelly looked at me, and replied, "I remember you and your wife at some of the soccer meets when I was little." She stopped suddenly, looking up at me with large, sad eyes, and whispered, "I'm sorry."

I said, "That's OK. I have grieved and moved on with my own life."

Then she smiled, and giggled, "And I remember you guys coming here for a pool party; I was showing-off, doing back flips into the pool. In my wilder days, I had my own pool parties – skinny dipping style!"

I was a bit shocked to hear this from my friend's daughter, but bit my lip and kept silent. Dave jumped in, "That's enough, Kelly!" Dave just looked at me and shrugged. "Kids!"

But Kelly was obviously not a kid, anymore. Dave left the kitchen to go back into the living room with the other guests, and I poured myself another glass of wine. "What are you doing now, Kelly? You must be in college?"

Kelly smiled brightly at me, and my heart nearly melted. I was much too old for 'love at first sight', but given the chance, I would have taken Kelly on the dining room table. What was wrong with me? I had to stop thinking like this!

A flicker of confusion crossed Kelly's face, but she smiled again and said, "I'm in graduate school. Biochemistry."

I couldn't believe that Dave's little girl was nearly grown – actually, fully-grown. "That's great. What do you plan to do, after you get your Masters?"

She enthusiastically explained, "Well, I'm certainly going to go for a Ph.D. – which is what all the biotech companies are looking for. I'm really interested in medical applications of genetic engineering: In my generation or the next, most of man's diseases could be eradicated, and people could theoretically live much longer."

The mention of 'medical' brought a flood of fantasies, unwelcome, into my brain. I found it difficult to hold a normal conversation with Kelly ... and I think she was starting to notice. "Where were all the cute girls, when I took science in school?" I groaned.

Kelly laughed easily, and swept her long hair up and over her shoulders.

I then turned serious. "You knew that I was in pharmaceutical research, for years?"

Kelly looked directly into my eyes, with her eyes sparkling in a hypnotic way, and said, "No. I don't think Dad ever told us what you did for work. All we talked about around here was sports. My older brothers were real jocks. Hey, how are your sons? I remember them from the soccer games and we all used to swim at the club."

"They're great," I said, "on opposite sides of the country. The older one works at an investment company, and is married (but no kids of their own, yet), and the younger one is an artist, and has been living with his partner in New York for many years."

Kelly looked down, and seemed to be deep in thought. After about 30 seconds, I assumed that she was finished talking with me, and I was about to go into the living room, as I hadn't yet said hello to any of the other guests.

But Kelly suddenly looked up at me, and said, "Would you mind having coffee with me sometime? I'd really like to pick your brain ... about the best way to get into research, how to judge these companies – that are so small, yet could sell out for millions, and where I should focus my research interests. I've been studying automated DNA analysis systems for my Masters, but that field is already done – the entrepreneurs have made their money, and the little companies have been bought up by huge pharma companies."

I chuckled, and said, "You know, if I could tell you what the next big field will be, I would be making a fortune myself. But that's a difficult thing to foresee. However, you could get some good professional experience with a big company – they might even pay for you to get your doctorate – and learn what is interesting to them. You would then be well-positioned to find and join a smaller company, when the time is right."

"That's just the kind of advice I'm looking for! Do you think we could get together for an hour, so you could give me some career advice? I'll pay for the coffee."

I laughed, "I have plenty of time, and would be happy to help you. And you don't have to pay for the coffee!"

As I said that, my mind became a blur: The possibilities! The responsibility – it's my friend's daughter! The danger (at least she was well over 18 years old)! And, the excitement of being with this intelligent and beautiful young woman.

My mind turned to mush, but fortunately Kelly took charge, and said, "Great! How about next week?"

My eyes must have glazed over, and I felt like I was about to pass out; these were more like the feelings of a teenager than a mature man.

Kelly *had* noticed, "Is something wrong?"

I looked down and focused on Kelly again, reality and my fantasies blurring, while I made a conscious effort to push these thoughts out of my head (or, perhaps, just to the back of my head?). "I'd love to help you, and am free next week (I don't have to consult the calendar on my phone). How about if I take you to lunch on Thursday?"

Kelly's eyes widened, and she beamed, "Thanks! That would be great – and very generous of you. But please let me pay – you're already giving me your time and your knowledge. I don't know how I'll ever be able to thank you." All I could do was smile weakly at her. My mind was already forming fantasies that would last at least the next year or two.

I woke up at home the next day, lay in bed, and wondered, 'Did that really happen?' OK – nothing actually happened. But I think I really did meet the most beautiful girl in the world; I hadn't had much to drink by that point, so I don't think it was a drunken illusion.

As the memory of Kelly came back, my hand wandered down under the sheets and I began to stroke myself. This was very unusual – I was actually getting very turned-on just by remembering what Kelly looked like; I have seen lots of beautiful women, including on nude beaches, and not gotten turned on until I fantasized about doing something with them (usually, one of my favorite spanking scenes).

Kelly was a turn-on, physically and intellectually; and she was a 'young woman' – which I had been logically deducing is what I wanted, and what I had been fantasizing about for the past many months.

The perfect storm was now resulting in an oncoming orgasm of massive proportion. I thought only at the last instant before I came about bringing Kelly down into the playroom ... and the medical exam room. My orgasm exploded, and I continued stroking as my entire body shuddered.

As I made breakfast, I began thinking more rationally. Kelly is a nice young lady who I have agreed to help. She is my friend's daughter. She undoubtedly would not think about me as anything other than a kindly father-figure. And there was absolutely no indication that she would be interested in any of my fantasies.

It was a pipe dream (that night, it would be another wet pipe dream), and I had to be very careful to act appropriate with Kelly. I really am a 'kindly father-figure', although I am relatively handsome and very fit, and in my fantasies I'm neither kindly nor a father figure.

That thought yielded another flood of fantasies – Yes! I could be the scientist father she never had, and discipline her like her real father never had! This was getting ridiculous. Before I had even had a first bite of breakfast, I was heading back to bed; for a little more resolution of these new fantasies.

Over the next few days, I had innumerable fantasies – and orgasms – based on what Kelly and I would do together, *if* ... (if only!). I stayed in the house, only going to the market and post office once over the first three days of the week. I cleaned the basement rooms, and re-arranged the items in my medical cabinet. I took a couple of very hot saunas, but nearly passed out when the fantasies returned, and I ended-up masturbating in 190-degree heat.

We have an expansive back yard – in which I seldom spend time – but I put in a full day of hard labor on Wednesday, making things beautiful. I also cleaned the pool and jacuzzi, and brought it up to perfect condition. I cleaned the bathrooms, mopped the floors, and vacuumed the carpets. How long had it been? I kept a very 'neat' house, but not necessarily a very 'clean' house ... unless someone was coming over.

Why was I doing all this? Kelly wasn't coming to the house – we were meeting at a local bar-and-hamburger joint. What was I thinking? Why couldn't I *stop* thinking of Kelly? My mind was in a whirl by Wednesday evening.

Over the past three days, I had thought of enough things I would like to do with Kelly to last a lifetime.

What I hadn't been thinking about is what advice I would actually give her. I fired up the computer, and did some searching – biotech companies, the latest breakthroughs in DNA research, and the current job market, including what recent graduates were making in various job categories. Fortunately, I was able to focus, and learned a lot that would be helpful in our discussion tomorrow.

Time evidently flew; I studied, outlined, strategized, and further researched, and it was 4 hours later before I climbed into bed, and turned out the lights.

I couldn't help it: Visions of Kelly in the exam room entered my head. This was not the graduate student Kelly, but Nurse Kelly – with a big syringe in her hand, smiling at me, and curling her finger in a "come here!" motion. Needless to say, I slept great after an orgasm that came before I could finish the scene in my head.

CHAPTER 2: BISTRO LUNCH

Thursday morning, I felt relaxed, and much more focused – only masturbating once, as I took a shower and allowed my mind to drift. I had manicured my nails, and trimmed my hair. As I stood naked in front of the bathroom mirror, and pulled the brush through my hair a couple more times, I stopped and looked at the brush: I couldn't help putting it behind me, and bringing it down sharply on my own bottom. Yes, that would make a fine implement, too - although I already had several nice wooden hairbrushes stored in the playroom.

I dressed sharply in crisp gray slacks, a textured powder blue dress shirt, and a navy blazer. I picked up a small briefcase (provided at some industry show or another), and put in a few of the pages I had printed last night, regarding the biotech field and job market.

Wishful thinking got the best of me, and I went downstairs to the office, and printed the latest version of the "punishment agreement," stuffing that in the back file-compartment of the briefcase when I returned upstairs.

I didn't plan on anything 'happening' with Kelly today. In fact, I would never have allowed anything to 'happen', as the most important thing – if there was ever hope for my fantasy to come to life – was to develop a trusting relationship with Kelly.

Actually, I wasn't sure that anything would ever happen – not because of *her* (the most likely thing), but because of my own fears in approaching a young (but old-enough) girl, coming on to my friend's daughter, and betraying any trust that we do build up.

I was becoming quite confused – in terms of what I wanted, and in terms of what was reality, and what would probably never be reality.

I left the house early, drove to the restaurant, and took a nice table in the front corner, near the window. I put the briefcase down next to the chair, checked the time on my watch, and then looked out the window at people walking by on the sidewalk.

I didn't allow my mind to drift, but focused on the various pieces of information I had found, and what my recommendations would be to Kelly, regarding her career. I was determined to be the kindly father-figure, at least for this initial meeting.

That's when I saw her across the street, looking towards the restaurant, checking traffic, and then bounding across. Her hair was still long but tied (too long to be a ponytail; perhaps a 'horsetail'?) and bounced around, as she ran.

She saw me in the window, smiled, and waved. The beauty was real – even in the harsh sunlight of the street. Her energy level, vitality, sparkling eyes, and incredible smile were amazing to see, and my heart melted again. This couldn't be happening! I don't want this to happen! I have to behave myself!

Kelly walked up to the table, and I stood and hugged her briefly. She pulled out the chair next to mine and plopped herself down. As she pulled the chair in, she looked up at me, and gave me another heart-melting smile. "How has your week been?" she asked.

My mind reeled, as a looked upon Kelly's beauty. I am normally quite comfortable with women – even beautiful women – but Kelly had me thinking, and behaving, like an adolescent. It was her long hair ... and her rosy cheeks ... and her womanly curves. No. Actually, it was her bright personality, her poise and her self-confidence that was already causing a stirring below.

I finally answered her. "Not bad. The usual, which for me is not that exciting." As I said this, I was thinking of all the 'excitement' I had had in the prior 3-4 days. I smiled at her, and asked, "How are you?"

I could plainly see 'how' she was: a perfect vision of health and youth, vitality and youth, energy and youth ... I guess I was feeling a bit older than in my fantasies at that point.

But with the question as an excuse, I let my eyes scan her, from her lustrous auburn hair, over her clear facial skin, down her majestic neck, and to where the top button of her blouse had been left undone – exposing just a bit of cleavage, very fashionable, but confirming my suspicion that the little girl I had seen ten years before was now the full-figured, all-woman vision that now sat before me.

Kelly looked serious. Then she smiled, and said, "Well, actually, I've been a bit nervous about meeting with you today."

My heart sank. I really did become the kindly father figure in that moment. Could she have already sensed at the party my ulterior motives? Seen my lustful stare? Noticed the growing mound in my slacks? Don't be ridiculous! On the other hand, it would be really disappointing, if she is doubting me, already. I just nodded, enticing her to continue.

She explained, "I should have spent more time preparing for our meeting; I don't want to waste your time."

Is that why she was nervous? My insides were somewhere between aching and laughing (maybe an aching laugh?). I said, "That's OK. I prepared a little. Hopefully, I can point you in the right direction, and then you can do your own 'research'."

Kelly smiled broadly, "Oh, thank you! I don't mean to be a bother, and I really am serious about deciding which way I'm going to go professionally."

I looked at her with a serious expression, and said, "I know you are. I'm not bothered at all. In fact, I'll take any excuse to have lunch with a beautiful woman!" I was being honest, and I hoped it didn't come across as flirtatious. Kelly smiled. I switched gears, and picked up the menu, "Shall we make an executive decision about what we're going to have for lunch?" Kelly laughed, and picked up her menu, too.

It was a very enjoyable lunch. Kelly and I had detailed discussions about the state-of-the-art in DNA research, what types of companies to work for (or not work for), and how to build experience, advance, and then find your own direction – whether in academia, a large company, or small company environment. My hamburger was great, and Kelly had selected the Salade Niçoise, one of the unexpected specialties of this funky dive.

Kelly's enthusiasm was contagious; I am already a high-energy person, and with Kelly, the energy level at our table was over-the-top. We seemed to hit it off immediately, and I found that we had some common interests – including cooking, sailing, and downhill skiing.

When we had finished our meal, and I looked down at my watch, I was surprised to see that more than an hour had passed – and it seemed like only a few minutes! I asked Kelly about her personal aspirations, and future plans, whether she had a boyfriend, or was looking forward to having a family.

She scrunched her nose, and said, "Yuck! I might have a family someday, but not anytime soon. I'm interested in my career. And, maybe having a few adventures and 'flings' along the way."

I was surprised to hear this. I arched my eyebrows, "Flings?"

She quickly said, "Well, you know, I like to hang out. I also like sex. But I don't want to spend my life looking after someone else ... I guess I'm pretty selfish."

I gave her my best kindly father-figure smile, and said, "No, not at all. Everyone should be independent, adventurous, and find their own way in life ... before settling down (or being tied down) and partially living someone else's life."

She nodded vigorously, "Yeah – that's exactly the way I feel. My parents don't really agree – I think they want to marry me off as quickly as possible!"

"Do you have a boyfriend?" I asked, avoiding the subject of her parents.

Between bites of salad, she replied, "There are a couple of guys I hang out with ... they may think we go on 'dates', but we're just friends."

I looked at her and put down my fork; I couldn't help but ask, "Kelly, when we were at your parents house, you said that you used to be 'wild'. What does that mean?"

Kelly's eyes scanned the restaurant, and she leaned forward, her voice getting soft, "Well, I did a lot of drugs – I even dropped acid a few times, and had a lot of wild sex. You know."

I looked at her, trying hard to keep a straight face, "No, actually, I don't know. I have no idea what people your age consider 'wild'. Back in the early '80s ..." My voice trailed off, and I decided to listen, rather than relate how I considered those the 'hippie days,' although I had actually been a decade late for that.

Kelly looked down at the table, and I could see that she was blushing, "You won't tell my parents what I've said, if I share some things with you?"

"Of course, not! You are an independent adult, and your parents are no longer responsible for you. In fact, I doubt if I'll see your parents again, unless they have another party – we're not exactly social friends."

"Yeah, my dad only cares about sports, so he mainly hangs out with his macho jock friends. You don't exactly fit that mold."

I laughed, "Ha! I should hope not! As you can see, I stay fit, but I'm not obsessed with sports – especially not team sports."

She wiped her lips with her napkin, "Me, neither."

Kelly was still looking down at the table, and became quiet. She said, "I've always had a problem with sex."

I nearly fell off my chair, but composed myself, and said, "How's that?"

She replied, "Well, I like adventure, new things, experimentation ... but almost all the guys I've gone out with go through the same mechanical motions – feeling my breasts, putting their hand down my pants, and – if we do finally have sex – they are only interested in a few positions, and only care about getting themselves off – which always happens too soon. I have gone out with a few older men – like in their late 20's,"

I sank lower into my chair, and hopefully Kelly didn't see my face reddening,

"And some have taken the time to go down on me. But it still seems like they're all using the same playbook. I'm a creative person, and I have a lot of fantasies ... but none of the men in my life have come close to satisfying me psychologically, even if they do get me to come."

It was my turn to look down at the table, "That's sad. As is often the case, I think you're just more 'advanced' than boys of your age. How about teaching your boyfriends what you like, and giving *them* some new experiences?"

"Don't you think I've tried?" Kelly was starting to get upset. I held my tongue. She continued, "I've shown men how to finger my clit – but they kept insisting on inserting their fingers into me; I've asked men for 'rough sex', and they've thought I was a slut; I've asked some to go skinnydipping with me, but they were too hung-up to undress in public. I even offered one of my boyfriends the chance to spank me, when I did something I knew he didn't like; and he tried ... but didn't want to 'hurt' me, so the spanking ended-up being a butt massage."

I could only think 'those young and inexperienced boys had no idea of what they were missing'!

I told Kelly, "Actually, I've had the same problem for years."

She looked up, with true amusement on her face, "What do you mean?"

"Well, I was always more adventurous than my wife. We acted out a few of my fantasies. My wife and I were also very open, so we sometimes 'played' with other couples, and she eventually allowed me to have some female friends who would 'play' with me."

"Wow! Really? And I thought you guys were so straight! What kind of 'playing' did you do with your 'female friends'?"

Now it was my turn to be quiet. I looked up at Kelly, and into her eyes. "I'll share some of my fantasies and experiences with you, if you'll share some of yours with me."

Kelly let out an involuntary chuckle, and said, "That's pretty private."

I just said, "Yes, I know. That's why it's so interesting. If we get a chance to know each other better, you'll find that I'm a very open person, and willing to share my secret turn-ons. But sharing fantasies takes a lot of trust in each other. In fact, it is that trust that is the biggest turn-on to me."

Kelly looked confused, "I don't know what you mean."

I responded, "A lot of people wouldn't understand my fantasies, and might think I'm psycho. Although I'm retired, I have a reputation to uphold, and wouldn't want my fantasies and fetishes shared."

Kelly frowned, and asked, "Fetishes?"

I forced myself to ignore her remark and continued, "I can only imagine what some of my family might think, if they saw something published on Facebook! And, there's another aspect to trust that is essential to my fantasies ..."

I was reluctant to go any further with this conversation. Before Kelly could speak, I said, "Look, Kelly. I don't want you to think the wrong thing about me (or maybe the right thing); you might be shocked by some of the things I tell you. And, I just don't want to ruin the relationship I have with your parents by 'contributing to the delinquency of a minor'."

That hit a nerve. Kelly raised her voice, "My parents! What do they have to do with this? I wouldn't even think of sharing my fantasies with you, if I thought you might blab to my parents. And I'm not a minor!"

Before the situation could spiral out of control any more than it already had, I quickly said, "Kelly, I know that. I'm just in a difficult position. I think you're the most beautiful woman I've ever seen."

Kelly looked up at me in shock, and said, "What!?!?"

I continued, "and I like very much being with you. I hope that we can be friends, even close friends, but I don't want to be the 'dirty old man' coming on to a college student." I then felt compelled to add, "Even though I think we could have some fun times together."

Kelly looked directly at me, "I don't think you're a dirty old man. And I'd be happy if we could become friends. But I don't think that would include sex. How's that for a turn-down on the first 'date'?"

I leaned forward and said, "Kelly, this isn't a 'date', and I'm not looking for sex. Per sé."

She asked, "What does THAT mean?"

How much could I tell her? I knew not to take it too far, too fast. "Look, Kelly, I know that most of the young guys you've dated are just out for sex – like most of the male population of the world. But sex isn't everything."

Kelly looked even more confused, "You're not making any sense. We were talking about fantasies and sexual experiences, weren't we? Or am I suddenly in the wrong conversation?"

Sitting back in my chair, I looked at my watch again. The restaurant was empty, except for a busser cleaning the last tables, and nearly two hours had passed since Kelly had waved to me from the street.

I decided to share a bit of my philosophy, if not my specific fantasies. "Kelly, I love sex. And, of course, I would love to make passionate love to you – you're a beautiful woman ... and I'm heterosexual."

This caught her by surprise, and suddenly she was on guard. I quickly continued, "But for many reasons, I don't think we will ever have sex, so you can relax."

Kelly's mouth dropped open; I'm sure this is not what she had expected to hear. I continued, "But there are a lot of things two people can do together that are very intimate and don't require intercourse. I won't get into how I define sex right now, but I'd like to continue this conversation with you. Can I take you to lunch again? Perhaps in a couple of weeks? You can do your homework regarding career choices, and we can both decide if we want to share fantasies with each other."

I continued, "If you're not too shocked by my fantasies, and/or if I'm turned on by yours, then perhaps I'll make a proposal for how we might 'play' together. I assure you that I can be trusted – both to keep your fantasies private, and to introduce you to some new things, in a trusting and safe environment."

Kelly didn't know how to respond. "Playing together (whatever that means) sounds like fun, but 'safe environment' sounds like my parents' bullshit."

I was shocked to hear Kelly say that, and disappointed that she was equating me with her parents. "You said that you sometimes wanted 'rough sex' (whatever that means). There is a fine line between 'fun' rough sex, and 'unsafe' rough sex: You must feel somewhat at-risk for the 'roughness' to feel real and exciting, but you should also trust your partner to play safely, so that you won't really get hurt."

Kelly shook her head, "You're getting too technical for me. Can't we just share some of our fantasies, and see where that leads."

I smiled, reaching across the table, and putting my hand on top of Kelly's. "Yes, that would be great. How about if we have lunch again two weeks from today? You can pick the place." I removed my hand, and picked up the napkin in my lap, folding it before putting it neatly on the table.

Kelly relaxed, and said, "Yeah, that would be great. I really appreciate you advising me on my career. And, on my sex life! And you've really gotten me curious about your fantasies; you seem to keep giving me hints, but I can't decode what you're trying to tell me. Maybe next time, you'll be more straightforward. I'm sure I won't be shocked by anything you tell me."

I very much doubted that would prove to be true, but it was an exciting prospect just to share my fantasies, even if Kelly never acted them out with me. I had come to this meeting telling myself I would 'be good', and stick to the career script with my friend's daughter. But somehow we got caught-up in this sex conversation, and now my fantasies were a step closer to reality.

At least that was my current fantasy, sitting in a quiet bistro after a 2-hour lunch with Kelly.

We went our separate ways, agreeing to think both about careers in biotech and what fantasies we would share with each other. When I got home and walked into the house, I was impressed how well I had cleaned-up. The house smelled fresh, and was ready for a visitor, even a young girl wishing to experience some sexual excitement. I went downstairs and sat at my desk, thinking back through our lunchtime conversation.

Kelly had actually said that she had asked a boyfriend to spank her. I have to admit, that was probably the most exciting thing that I remembered from our lunch today. This was a delicate situation – what an incredible and unexpected opportunity this could be! I had two weeks to strategize how to make my fantasy come true. I was confident that if I came across the right way to Kelly in our next meeting, she would be adventurous enough to at least try some of the things that I was planning.

The two weeks passed quickly. I kept the house clean, and rearranged some of my toys in the playroom and exam room. I thought a lot more about how I would introduce my fantasies to Kelly. I usually go for the honest and direct approach, and thought about telling her how my desire to have a submissive partner had evolved.

I thought about showing Kelly some of the pictures and videos on the various websites, as I had done with Liz so long ago. I wondered whether she would want to play and, if so, whether I should be prepared with some form of legal agreement.

I decided that I would listen to her fantasies first, hoping for an additional resonance with my turn-ons. I thought again about her spanking comment. Maybe she was just desperate to have her boyfriend do something new, and wasn't really interested in having the intense spanking experience that I envisioned?

I wanted to get her excited, but not scare her away. Would there really be an overlap in our fantasies? I thought how lucky I was to even be meeting with such a beautiful young girl, and discussing these things. Perhaps I should agree to acting out with Kelly any fantasy that she wanted?

CHAPTER 3: SECOND MEETING

Finally, the day of our next lunch came, and I decided to try to relax, and roll with wherever the discussion with Kelly led. As I drove to the cute little bistro that Kelly had selected, I thought about the possibilities. I would be delighted to just have her as a friend; it would be a bonus if she were comfortable being nude with me. Perhaps I could share the pond that Liz and I had frequented? What a surprising and nice development that would be!

I arrived at the restaurant – amazingly without having an accident, as I was concentrating more on my fantasies of the coming lunch than I was on driving. It would be an interesting lunch, whatever happened. I was determined to at least remain friends with Kelly, and hoped that we could become close enough to have a few play experiences together.

When I walked into the restaurant, Kelly was already seated. As I approached her table, she hopped up and gave me a quick kiss on the cheek. That was a promising start to the lunch!

"Hi!" she said.

I guess I had forgotten how drop-dead beautiful she was, and I just stood there and shook my head, as I scanned her from head to toe. Her hair was in French braids, and her face looked as fresh and soft as I had remembered.

She was wearing a tight top that accentuated her generous but firm breasts, and my eyes dropped further to examine her small waist, somewhat larger hips, and nice butt shown off by the designer jeans that she somehow had poured herself into.

She wore high boots that had viciously-pointed toes, and I briefly wondered how uncomfortable they must be for her ... and how uncomfortable they would be for someone being ... I had to stop this line of thought!

"Hello," I finally said. We sat down, and looked at each other across the table.

"I hope you like this place!" she said in her usual bright and perky way.

I laughed, "Having you dining with me, how could I not like it? How have you been?"

She smiled, "I just turned in my research proposal; my advisor seemed happy with the subject that I selected."

"That's great. You'll have to tell me all about it," I commended her, "How about we order a bottle of wine to celebrate?"

Kelly looked at me, sat up straight, and in a mock-stern manner asked, "You're not trying to get me drunk, now, mister, are you?"

I laughed, and then said seriously, "Actually, I need you to be able to think today – I don't want you agreeing to something while you're in a drunken state!"

Now, Kelly looked serious, "First of all, mister, I don't know that I'm agreeing to *anything* today. And, second, I never get drunk. I've had some bad experiences with alcohol ... and drugs... so am much more careful in my 'older' age."

She smirked at me, and I called the waitress over to order the wine. When we were alone again, I asked, "Are you ready to share some of your fantasies with me today?"

Kelly smirked again, and said, "Are *you*?"

"Touché! Yes, I will share with you. But I'm pretty nervous about your reaction; as I told you last time, I don't want you to get the wrong impression of me. I even considered suggesting that we hold-off on this discussion, until we had spent some more time getting to know each other.

But, you know I'm not a 'normal' person, so I would have suggested that we continue the conversation at a skinnydipping pond, or possibly invited you into my 'boudoir' where I could share with you the wonders of a sauna, and then taking a shower together ..."

She bit her lip, "But you're not going to suggest that?" The waitress came with the wine, and I asked Kelly if she wanted to taste it. She told me to do the honors; it was a nice merlot, and the waitress poured our glasses while we sat silently looking into each other's eyes across the table.

Kelly really was a knockout! I just couldn't believe that I was sitting here with her, about to share some of my innermost secrets – and listen to hers. And, possibly, ask her to experience something that could jeopardize any future relationship we might have had.

I sat back and swirled the wine in the glass, looked up at her, and said, "No, Kelly. I got a very supportive feeling from you during our last lunch, and I think I've built up the courage to tell you today what I fantasize about. It is my dream to act out the fantasy – basically role play – with someone like you ... but I want to make sure that we remain friends, so I'll never pressure you to do anything you don't feel comfortable doing."

Kelly sipped her wine. "It's interesting that you are saying that ... because I got a very supportive feeling from you, too. At first I thought I might be responding to the father-figure in you," I groaned, but Kelly continued, "but

I realized that you are the first person with whom I've felt comfortable talking to about these things; I don't even share this stuff with my best female friends!"

We drank more wine, and both of us relaxed a bit, but there was still an air of tension and anticipation, as we each pondered what we were about to share with the other. Kelly suddenly put her wine glass down, clasped her hands on the table, and leaned forward towards me. I pulled my chair closer to the table, and leaned forward to narrow the distance between us – appropriate for sharing intimate stories, and not having other people listen-in.

Kelly began, "My fantasies are pretty simple. I sometimes have the usual female fantasies about finding the perfect man, who whisks me off my feet and onto the stallion that will take us into the sunset," I rolled my eyes.

"But, mostly, my fantasies are about having adventures. I guess that means there is some danger. My wildest fantasies include being taken off my luxury cruise by a pirate, who ravages me – in just the ways I like. I pretend to be afraid, but I look forward to each intimate thing the pirate will do to me. He thinks he is being rough with me, while inside, I'm wishing for more." Kelly picked up her wine and took another sip.

Given the opening, I said, "And the pirate makes wild passionate love to you?" Kelly looked surprised, and nearly spilled her wine. She put down the glass, and replied, "Maybe. Actually, we never get to the lovemaking part. I guess the fantasy is about someone having their way with me, while I secretly want them to be doing it."

"I like that fantasy," I said, as my mind spun.

We were interrupted by the waitress, and both realized we hadn't even looked at the menu. Kelly said, "I love the seared ahi salad here."

I closed the menu, and nodded, "That sounds good to me, also."

The waitress left, came back with some warm bread, and then retreated to the kitchen. I leaned forward again. "In your fantasy, what, exactly, does the pirate do to 'ravage' you?"

Kelly thought about this a moment, and said, "Well, I have a few different versions of this fantasy, but basically, he strips me, ties me to the mast, and alternately whips my breasts, and then sucks them ... and then whips me underneath, and sucks me down there, too. I don't know. It's the idea of giving in to someone who thinks they're doing something that I won't like, but that secretly, I'm wanting. Does that make sense?"

I took a deep breath, and let it out slowly, staring into Kelly's eyes. This convergence of fantasies was absolutely amazing, and I thought about pinching myself (or asking Kelly to do it) to make sure this wasn't really a dream. It was unbelievable, and I realized that my breathing was shallow, and had nearly stopped.

I picked up my glass of wine, and took a gulp. "Kelly, I think that's a great fantasy ... and perhaps I shouldn't have been so nervous today, after all. I think our fantasies may be very compatible." I put my wine down, and looked at Kelly; her face looked flushed, but she sat there confident and very poised. She looked more mature than her mid-twenties age would have suggested.

"So, do you fantasize about being a pirate?" she asked, quizzically, with her smile growing and her eyes twinkling.

"Well, not exactly ... although I wouldn't mind playing that role with you sometime – sounds like fun. I'll have to find an appropriate outfit, a big sword, and some rope." I chuckled, making light of what could be *very* interesting roleplay. This conversation was getting better all the time;

perhaps I would find some new things to fantasize about ... and act out with Kelly.

Kelly then put a strict face on and, shaking her finger at me, said, "Now it's your turn. I want to hear what has you so frightened or embarrassed that you have to drink a bottle of wine to get up the courage to tell me."

It was a fair comment, but I came back with, "I'm not embarrassed to tell you, but I am frightened that I might jeopardize our friendship by sharing this with you."

Kelly stopped and looked up at me, "This almost sounds like *50 Shades*," she said, with a cocked head.

I groaned, and said, "You're very close, but my fantasies are really quite different. I had looked forward to that book, but the theme was not carried through, and it turned out to be just a conventional romance novel, instead of an insight into dominance and submission."

Kelly sipped her wine and stared at me, the silence coercing me to continue on.

"Kelly, it's complicated. The first thing that turns me on is openness. As you know, I was a scientist, and I don't understand people and psychology very well – even at my age. I've always gotten in trouble because I was too honest – I believe in truth and honesty, and I don't understand politics, or the other games people play. In my opinion, a 'real' relationship is one where both people can be totally open with each other ... both physically and psychologically."

I took a deep breath and continued, "That's one reason why I like going to nude beaches, or the saunas in Europe, where everyone is nude and comfortable. If people are comfortable enough to let others see their bodies, there must be a certain degree of honesty and openness; it is no longer about the fashionable clothes or expensive jewelry that someone wears – you are seeing the 'real' person.

"Of course, I realize that people may go to nude beaches, and still not be open about a lot of things ... but I tend to associate casual nudity with openness, and openness with honesty."

Kelly cautiously said, "That doesn't sound bad."

I agreed, "It's not 'bad', but often not accepted, even by intelligent people. There are seven billion people on the earth, all with 99+% the same body ... and yet hiding our bodies has become a ritual. People aren't comfortable being nude in front of others, unless it's at the doctor's office or with their spouse and family." My mind sped along, towards the exam room, but it was much too soon for that. I had to control myself!

"It's amazing to me that even healthcare professionals are often embarrassed about their bodies being seen, even though they see nude bodies every day. Just as we look at a family of dogs, and can't tell them apart without looking closely, if aliens landed on the earth and looked at humans, we would all appear the same. Why do people make such a big deal about nudity?"

Kelly shrugged, and said, "Not everyone does, but that's how we were raised ... especially in the Victorian U.S."

I nodded, "Yes! I agree completely. It's social custom, moral beliefs, and *religion* that is mostly to blame for the way our society behaves. As I said, it's not like this everywhere in the world. Japanese men and women bathed together in the 'onsen' for centuries, showing everything and nothing but respect for each other.

"Most Europeans are comfortable with nudity – women go topless on all the beaches, and there are even parks with 'naturist' sections, where people sunbathe in the nude, right in the middle of cities – like the 'Englischer Garten' in Munich." I realized that I was getting worked-up. I stopped to have another swallow of wine, and the waitress came with our salads.

I speared a piece of seared ahi, and popped it into my mouth, "Umm. That's good!" I flashed on Sarah and I having a great ahi dinner at a small restaurant in Hanalei, on the garden isle of Kauai. I wiped my eyes and set down my fork.

"The next thing that turns me on is trust. It is a responsibility, but a great turn-on to be trusted, especially by the opposite sex.

"For example, I've traveled with female friends, with whom I had a platonic relationship only (I bet you thought those didn't really exist), and we shared a hotel room. I have done this with women who are too hung up about their body to let me see them nude, but who are trusting enough to share a bathroom – with each of us respecting the privacy of the other – and sleeping in beds only a few feet apart.

"I'm not sure how many men could be trusted in this situation, but I can assure you that few women have such trust in men who are not related or to whom they are married, or have a close relationship. My fantasies leverage this idea of trust to a much higher level." I took a forkful of salad, and awaited Kelly's response.

She seemed confused. "That's not bad, either. Is there really something that I might get upset about, or was this all a show?"

"I'm getting there." I had another taste of the ahi, which was superb.

"Another thing that turns me on is showing someone a new experience – especially one that they thought they would not enjoy, but turn out to love.

"One example of that is taking people to a nude beach or European sauna for the first time. They are nervous and afraid (especially men, who think they might become inappropriately 'excited'), but once they are there, and see everyone nude, they feel more comfortable taking their clothes off. Then, as they begin to enjoy the day – perhaps sunbathing, swimming and playing in the waves, they forget about their hang-ups, and start really enjoying the experience."

I continued, "Virtually all of the people I have taken to a nude beach for the first time have loved it, and it was nothing like they had expected – nothing sexual, everything friendly and natural. In Europe, people who enjoy nudity are called 'naturists', and camping venues that advertise as 'naturiste' accept open nudity.

"Many people are surprised that not everyone at the nude beach is 'beautiful'; but, in fact, there is the same distribution of good- and bad-looking people at a nude beach as anywhere else – but they are comfortable with their bodies (whatever they may look like), and unconcerned about what anyone else thinks about their looks."

I looked at Kelly, who was enjoying her salad, as she listened to what was becoming a boring story, and apparently not an exciting fantasy. I continued on.

"I get especially excited by introducing younger women to new experiences – whether it's a new sport, like SCUBA diving or skiing, or a new type of sensual (or sexual) experience. I am an honest, responsible, and trustworthy person, and have had relationships for years with female friends without creating any pressure regarding sex; in fact, I have learned it is often the best policy to agree not to have sex.

"As I told you last time, there are a lot of things two people can do without having 'sex'. And, yes, I haven't yet defined what I mean by sex, but I will."

Kelly was listening closely, and looked fascinated; I could tell that she had a lot of questions, but I was intent to complete the list of my turn-ons ... the next one being the zinger. I would just have to proceed, and see how she responds.

I made the mistake of taking another bite of ahi, and Kelly jumped in, "You haven't told me anything specific, yet, but everything you've said so-far sounds pretty normal. I'm still not sure what your fantasies are."

I put down my fork, and wiped my lips thoroughly with the pale yellow cloth napkin. "Kelly, along with all of the things I've mentioned so-far, my biggest turn on is having someone submit to something that they are afraid of – something that might be painful or embarrassing that they willingly do, just because I ask them." I thought for a few seconds about how detailed I should get.

Kelly took the opportunity to say, "Now, we're getting somewhere!"

I coughed, and continued. "Most of the specific things that excite me are either forbidden by Western cultural tradition, or something that I feared myself as a kid. Many women find some of the things I get turned-on by to be incredibly immature – especially for someone with my experience (note that I didn't say, 'for my age', but that, too).

"But I have to tell you, there must be a lot of immature men, because some of my fantasies are well-represented on porn sites on the web!"

Kelly gulped, and then asked, "Like what?"

It was time for sharing, but I was still nervous. "Like putting you over my knee, and giving you a bare-bottomed spanking."

Kelly's raised her eyebrows, and a strange smile began to form, "I *knew* it was going to be like *50 Shades*!"

"Kelly, it's not, really. We can talk about that later. Despite your pirate fantasy – which I would still be willing to try, anytime – my turn-on comes from my female partner willingly accepting the pain or embarrassment – obeying my command, even though I know they would rather not be. Just to make me happy, to satisfy my needs, at their expense of taking some pain, or accepting some embarrassment."

I continued, "I am not looking for a weak woman; actually, it takes a very strong and self-confident woman – both to agree to something like this, and to actually go through with it voluntarily. While there may be some pain and/or embarrassment, my fantasies – and those times when I've role played with a partner – generally end by the woman being highly turned on, and having an orgasm – sometimes by my hand, or with her masturbating while I watch.

"And I am NOT interested in actually hurting anyone. My female play partners have been close friends, who I've cared deeply for. Theoretically, I could just *scare* the woman, preparing her, putting her into a punishment position, and then ... not doing anything. Just the fact that she cooperates up to that point is an indication that she is submitting to me, and allowing me to do something that she fears or doesn't really want – for my pleasure."

I continued, "But, if I don't actually spank her (or do whatever is supposed to happen), then it would be a one-time only event; she would know thereafter that I wouldn't really hurt her, so she could cooperate without fear; that would ruin my fantasy ... and not be very exciting for her, either.

"While I think role-playing can be neat, my fantasy doesn't involve 'acting'; the pain must be real for the feelings to be real. In fact, as I told you, one of my turn-ons is to expose people to things they thought they would not enjoy; in nearly every case I've actually experienced, my partner really believes that she cannot withstand more ... but she does, and it is a relief and very rewarding for both of us to find that she was stronger than she thought, and was able to have enough self-control to hold herself in position, as I dispensed whatever pain or embarrassment we had planned.

"But, I do have quite a few different role-playing ideas ... such as the 'spanked schoolgirl' fantasy, or the 'naughty secretary' fantasy (portrayed somewhat humorously in the movie '*Secretary*'), or the 'jail warden who has to punish one of the female inmates' fantasy. It doesn't really matter to me which role we're playing, as they all have the same basics in common: the female is put in an embarrassing or painful situation, and cooperates fully throughout the 'scene'.

"Sorry I've been so long-winded, but you can see that my fantasies always incorporate a combination of things – openness, trust, introducing new experiences, and submission. Does any of this make sense to you?" I sat back, and breathed heavily; it was done – whatever Kelly's response would be, there was no way to 'take back' the information I had shared with her.

I closed my eyes, and again wondered how this all could be happening. Yes – it was my fantasy to 'play' with a strong, self-confident, younger woman ... but this was incredible: I was sitting here with my friend's daughter, a true beauty, who obviously *was* independent, strong, and self-confident. She had listened to my entire story without saying more than a dozen words; but she didn't appear to be upset.

Kelly had finished her salad, but mine was only half-eaten. I guess delivering my message to Kelly had lifted a huge weight from my shoulders, and I suddenly relaxed. I realized that I was famished, so I ate my salad with relish, looking up every few bites at Kelly, who was chewing on a piece of bread and deep in thought.

"I think you may be right," she said.

Now, it was my turn to be confused, "About what?"

She smiled at me shyly, and replied, "That our fantasies might be compatible."

I closed my eyes again, and opened them, staring directly into Kelly's large, hazel eyes. Again, I couldn't believe my good fortune in finding someone like this; someone who could listen to my fantasy, and not run for the hills. And, even better, someone who might get off herself, role-playing the fantasy.

It seemed surreal – more like a dream than the fantasies I have before I drift off to sleep every night. I now had a very definite face to go with my 'younger woman' fantasies ... a very beautiful, young, and innocent face. Well, perhaps not so innocent ...

We paid our bill at the bistro, and decided to walk for a while. It was early summer, and the trees had finally regained their leaves, the flowers were blooming, and the sky was incredibly blue, with just a few cumulous clouds – as in a painting. After delivering my soliloquy, and awaiting Kelly's further response, I kept my mouth shut. We walked towards the small park on this side of town.

Kelly finally began, "I think I understand most of what you told me, but I'm confused about a few things."

I looked at her, and said, "OK. What would you like to know?"

"Well, you keep talking about a 'sexual' experience, but say you don't want to actually have sex ..."

I interrupted, "Kelly, I told you that I would *love* to have sex with you. But for many reasons, I don't think that's a smart idea. Can we discuss that part later?"

"I guess ... but you kept saying you 'defined' sex a certain way. Isn't sex just intercourse?" A frown crossed her face, as she started to realize that such a definition isn't that easy.

I explained to her, "For practical reasons, I define sex as the transfer of body fluids. If there is no transfer of body fluids, there can be virtually no chance of contracting a sexually transmitted disease, and there is no chance of becoming pregnant. That eliminates two of the main reasons why people are not sexually 'free' these days.

"Of course, there can be the psychological/emotional attachment – one reason why I don't think it would be a good idea for us to have sex anytime soon. You should be holding-out for someone closer to your age ..."

I had hit a nerve, again. Kelly stopped in her tracks, and scolded me, "Don't tell me what I 'should' or 'should not' be doing! That is my decision. Please don't start acting like my parents!"

Again, I had not been sensitive to Kelly's needs. "I apologize. You're absolutely right. It's neither my decision to make, nor my right to tell you what you should or shouldn't do."

Kelly relaxed a bit, but was still frowning. "You think I have enough psychological control to submit to a spanking, but not enough to avoid falling for you?"

I was starting to get confused now, thoughts racing through my wine-muddled mind. "I don't know. It doesn't seem right ... but then again, my suggestion that you be submissive to me doesn't seem right, either. I warned you that this could be complicated ... even *I'm* not sure what is right ..."

We started walking again, and Kelly asked, "So what does 'transfer of body fluid' mean?" We were again on solid ground, with something I could easily answer, "It means genital-genital, genital-oral, genital-anal, oral-anal, or oral-oral contact."

She stopped again, "What!?!?"

I explained, "Any contact of body fluids or mucous membranes. You're a scientist and learning about the healthcare field ... and you're sexually experienced. I'm sure you know what I'm talking about."

"I guess so." She thought a moment. "Does that mean that kissing is 'sex'?"

"Absolutely," I said. "Even eating or drinking after each other would be 'sex', according to my definition. That's the 'bad' news. But the 'good' news is that everything else *isn't* sex! That means self-masturbation and mutual masturbation, and nearly anything else you can think of."

I didn't want to put any more specifics into her head. "I know it sounds strange, but it truly is 'safe sex', without so-called 'abstinence' – which nobody could actually achieve – and wouldn't want to, in the real world."

Kelly started walking again. "And, you want to spank me? Would you want me to dress-up like a schoolgirl?"

I chuckled, "Yes, Kelly, I would like to spank you, and introduce you to many other things that might be a new experience for you – at least from a sexual perspective. Dressing up like a schoolgirl would be a great idea.

"But there are lots of other roles ... including the *real* one: You submitting to a new experience, and trusting someone implicitly to deliver pain, but not go beyond your limits. To deliver a sensual – and perhaps sexual – experience, without taking advantage of you, or forcing you to do anything. Have you been spanked before?"

She looked at me and said, "Well, of course my parents have slapped my bottom a few times, but nothing serious. There was never a formal 'punishment', or anything."

I continued, "So that would be a new experience for you. You may not believe this, but every woman I have spanked has been turned on by it. I don't want to promise anything, but they have had some incredible orgasms, after letting-go and submitting to some of the things I've done with them." I looked at her, "And, as far as dress, it really doesn't matter to me, unless we're playing a specific role."

Kelly's eyes grew even larger than normal, and she smiled, "This is certainly different from the conversations I usually have with my boyfriends! As I told you, they never seem to care about me being sexually satisfied." I wanted to say, 'they're young', but kept my lips tight.

We turned into the park, and sat on a bench. There were a few moms (and re-expectant moms) with their small children, but nobody near our bench. Kelly seemed to have made a decision, and finally looked at me, her cheeks flushed again, and her eyes intently staring into mine, "So what's the next step?"

I nearly fainted! This was my fantasy come true ... or at least, it was within sight. Again, I couldn't believe it. It occurred to me that this was a one-time, serendipitous opportunity, not something that I could put into a formula and repeat. I also knew that the next step could end the entire 'adventure' before it started. But then, for some reason, something came over me (perhaps due to the wine?), and I decided to have a little fun.

"Well, young lady, the next step is for me to report my findings back to your parents. They have had some suspicions that you were taking too many risks, and now we find that you are ready to give yourself to an old man, who might do anything to you!"

Kelly's eyes clouded, and she suddenly stood up. "Noooooo! You can't be doing this. I TRUSTED you!"

I started laughing so hard that I started crying. "Sit down, Kelly, I just thought I would give you a good scare, before giving you some scary information that you will need before you really decide to do this."

Kelly stared down at me with amazement, a few tears dripping from her eyes, and yelled, "Bastard! That wasn't funny! I think I'm going to have to spank *you*, if we do anything together!"

I laughed again, taking her hand, and pulling her back down next to me on the bench. "I'm sorry, I just had to do it. And, yes – it would be OK if you want to spank me."

Kelly's eyes widened yet again, and a huge smile formed on her face, as she wiped the tears with the back of her hand. "Well, in that case ..."

I wiped my own tears of laughter, and said, "OK, let's get serious for a few minutes. I need to give you some important additional information, before you 'officially' agree to this."

Kelly's shoulders sagged, and she said, "OK."

"First, you will need to sign a legal agreement."

Kelly burst out again, "What?!!?"

I chuckled, and held her hand, "Calm down, Kelly. Let me explain everything. This is for the protection of both of us."

Kelly just stared at me; perhaps the shock of what I was proposing was finally dawning on her. "Before we do anything, I will review with you a simple one-page agreement. I doubt if it would stand-up in court, but it might help in the event you ever tried to claim that I was abusing you. I know it will help define the limits of what we will do together. It will list your responsibilities and my responsibilities.

"I won't go through them all now, but your main responsibility will be to obey me ... but use a 'safeword' if you ever want to stop the scene. I will explain that later. My main responsibility is to ensure that you are given an exciting, but safe experience. I will give you pain, but I don't want to really hurt or damage you.

"The agreement also specifies what you should expect, during your experience. I'll tell you now, that the main things to expect are some pain and some embarrassment."

I thought for a moment, "Actually, I don't need for you to be embarrassed, in order to get turned on. If you are open enough to accept what I ask of you, and to share your body without being embarrassed, that would be great – it would be another kind of turn-on for me.

"And, of course, when I say 'share' your body, I don't mean 'sex', but giving me control over some aspect of your body – such as letting me examine you or letting me touch you."

Kelly was listening intently, and nodded a few times. She finally said, "I think I can do that. It's the unknown that scares me."

I smiled, "That's exactly right! That is the reason why trust is the key to what we will do. You will, in essence, be giving me your body to me ... to do with, as I like, within the limits we have set (mainly, not having sex, and not harming you). And you must trust me to do these things to you and with you in a controlled way, almost up to your limit but not beyond.

"If you trust me, and I protect you, there should never be a need for you to use the safeword – it is a backup, in case fear overcomes you, or you lose trust in me, or you are having such a bad time that you just want to end the experience.

"That would be a failure for me — as it is entirely my responsibility to respect your limits, even those which you may not know you have." Kelly nodded again, but didn't say anything.

"And, speaking of respect, my concept diverges from your pirate fantasy in some very important ways. I will not treat you like my property (even though you will have given yourself to me). I will not treat you like a slut. I will not force you to do anything ... you will have to force yourself."

Kelly looked at me again, much more softly this time. Her eyes were clear again and, although we were both feeling the wine, it was obvious that she was listening closely and understanding everything I was saying.

"If you visit some BDSM websites, you'll find that much of what they show is nothing like what I'm describing — you will not be tied up, but will have to hold yourself in position. I will inform you of everything that I'm going to do, before I do it."

I thought a bit, and continued, "But I'd rather not share every detail with you now ... or it would spoil some of the fear of the unknown and the 'shock value' that will be useful to see if you are really giving yourself to me. Again, you'll understand this much better when we start the experience. If you knew everything that was going to happen, it would be neither realistic, nor as suspenseful for you or as exciting for me. Again, it comes back to trust."

Kelly looked down at her hands, and quietly said, "I trust you."

Again, I was torn between just accepting my good fortune and being quiet, or telling her honestly what I thought of her comment.

At the risk of screwing up the opportunity, I chose honesty. "Kelly, I was only half-joking before. Of course, I would never say anything to your parents about any of this

(I'd be in much more trouble than you!) ... but you really shouldn't be so trusting. You don't know me very well. I am a trustworthy and safe person to be with, but there is really no way you can be sure of that, after having two lunches with me – and my getting you drunk on only our second meeting."

Kelly objected, "But our family has known you and your wife almost all my life, and I know you're a nice person ... despite your ... 'fetishes'. And, I'm a pretty good judge of people: We may have only had a couple of lunches, but we've spent quite a few hours together. And, I'm *not* drunk!"

I felt compelled to look at my watch, and was shocked to see that it was nearly 4PM. "I'm not saying that you shouldn't trust me, but you need to be careful – especially with older men."

Kelly whined, "Pleeaase don't start acting like my parents!"

I sighed. "OK – sorry! Shall we start walking back to our cars?"

We got up from the bench, and headed back toward the restaurant. The sun was low in the west, rays of light filtering through the leaves that rippled through the trees on an unseen breeze. "So, Kelly, what do you think? You said you were adventurous and wanted new sexual experiences. And, you said that you trust me. Shall we just go for it?"

We walked another block in silence, and then Kelly stopped and turned towards me. She gave me a quick hug, and stepped back. Looking into my eyes, her face serious, and her cheeks flushed again, she meekly whispered, "Yes, Sir."

I kissed her on the cheek, and the first true smiles in the past few hours came over both of our faces simultaneously. Had Kelly reached down and touched the front of my pants, I might have had an instant orgasm on the spot.

Just having the conversation we'd had over the past few hours would give me months of new fantasies – each time re-writing the ending that was yet to actually occur. I had no doubt that this was going to be an epic event.

I took her hand, and we walked across the street, back to where we had both parked. I hugged her, and she thanked me for lunch. I avoided saying 'the pleasure is all mine,' as Kelly was obviously also excited by the prospect of our next get-together.

"When would you like to do this," I carefully asked.

Kelly smiled and said, "I was just thinking about that. We should probably do it soon, or I might back out ... I do trust you, but I'm a little bit scared."

I was very relieved, and said, "I think that's a smart idea. I think you should look at a few Internet spanking sites, but don't do too much research – I would still like this to be a new experience for you. Also, you may see some very severe punishments on the 'net, with swollen and blistered bottoms; that is not my style. I will give you a hard spanking, but I don't want to mar your beautiful body ... too much. Anyway, I can't be too hard on you, because I'm hoping that you'll come back for more."

It was Kelly's turn to chuckle, "We'll see about that. Let me get through the 'introductory' experience, first!"

I said, "Sorry, but I have to ask ... when was your last period, or when are you expecting your next period?" Kelly smiled but didn't laugh (she had probably already thought about this); she said, "I expect to get it next week. I'm pretty regular."

We agreed that her punishment would take place on a Saturday, in a little more than two weeks. I told Kelly I would send her an e-mail with detailed instructions a week before our get-together. We hugged again, got into our cars, and drove off in opposite directions.

Once again, I don't know how safely I drove, as I don't remember anything except re-starting the fantasy, with Kelly as my punishment partner. The fantasy rolled on, as if it were a movie, playing in my mind, and blinding me to anything else around me.

When I got home, I went down to the playroom, and lay back on the couch. I undid my belt, and let my hand slip down over the erection I'd had for most of the afternoon.

Over the next week, I re-cleaned the playroom and exam room, and the basement bathroom. I changed the sheets on the king size bed in the playroom, and smoothed the duvet before drawing the privacy drapes. I repositioned the spanking chair, and made sure the small drawer in the side table was filled with implements and supplies.

I went into the wine cellar, and selected a bottle of red, which I placed on the coffee table with a corkscrew and a couple of glasses; and a bottle of white, which went into the bar fridge.

I also put more thought into the 'agreement' that I would present to Kelly. I'd described the most recent draft (it had been several weeks since I had worked on it) pretty accurately during our lunch. I sat for hours staring at the agreement, and deciding how I would handle the delicate first stage of her punishment experience – when she had to agree to the rules ... and also agree to additional punishment if she broke the rules.

There were so many possibilities ... I could see repeating this experience many times, each time unique and more interesting than the last.

I based much of my plan on the experience I'd had with Liz, nearly three years ago ... with many changes per the evolution of my fantasies over that time, and counting on Kelly still being young, and relatively inexperienced, compared to Liz or the women my age I had 'dated' over the past couple of years.

While I knew that Kelly would do some research before coming over, I also knew that she would be shocked by a few of the things I had planned. As I had told her honestly, the 'shock value' was an important aspect of the experience, forcing her to agree instantly to things that she had never anticipated.

Once again, the time passed quickly. It was Sunday when I realized that Kelly's punishment experience was less than a week away ... and I had not sent her the e-mail on how she should prepare. I sat down at my computer and composed a short note. It was business-like and direct – providing specific instructions in a list:

INSTRUCTIONS

* You will arrive at my house promptly at 9AM (attached is the address and phone number, with a map)
* You may wear a dress (not a skirt and top), or jeans (it won't matter, as they will come off quickly!); you will wear a plain white bra, and plain white bikini underwear
* You will bring with you a bag containing several of your nicest bras and panties – also some sexy lingerie, if you have some, maybe a couple of

your favorite bathing suits, and a regular nightgown or whatever you normally sleep in; please also bring a light robe; you should also pack your favorite shampoo, skin cream, hair brush, and whatever cosmetics you might need, as you'll probably want to take a shower after your spanking, and before we go to dinner

* You will be careful of what you eat and drink on Friday night; I expect you to have a full 8-hours of sleep!

* You will have a good bowel movement on Saturday morning; if you're not sure this will happen, you should drink a cup of mild laxative tea on Friday evening

* You will trim your fingernails (or get a manicure), and take a long shower on Saturday morning before you come over; please make sure every 'nook and cranny' is squeaky clean; please either tie your hair up, or bring supplies to do so

* You may have a light breakfast, but please no more than cereal or toast and milk or juice – your stomach should not be full when you get here

* From the time you arrive, you will address me as "Sir"; I suggest you add a "Sir" to the beginning or end of most of your comments, answers or requests

* The above will be considered to be part of the 'rules' for your experience, and you can expect to receive additional punishment, if any of these are broken

I thanked her in advance for her cooperation, and said I looked forward to seeing her on Saturday. I signed the e-mail, "Sternly, but lovingly, ..." I read through it once more, and hit 'Send'. Now, I just had to wait another 6 days.

I did not count the number of times I masturbated over the next few days, but let's just say it was essentially continuous. As with my experience with Liz, I drafted a 'punishment script', and felt it was my duty to masturbate to each of the planned 'scenes', in order to anticipate any issue, lack of supplies, or alternative punishment that I might want to offer.

This was really no different than an athlete 'visualizing' the course before a race. As Kelly had said, this was intended to be an 'introductory' punishment experience, but I knew that this might be my only opportunity to 'play' with Kelly, so I had to decide what I would want Kelly to experience, at a minimum. I added and removed activities from the script, as my fantasies evolved.

By Thursday, I felt I had gone through as many iterations and variations of the script as I could imagine – and my right hand was getting calloused (I always wanted to be an ambidextrous masturbator). I knew that the actual event wouldn't follow any of my scripts, but I wanted to be prepared, whatever Kelly's response.

On Friday, I did some marketing, and then came home and spent an hour doing yoga – mainly to calm myself and take my mind off the only subject I had thought about for the past two weeks.

Was I becoming obsessed with Kelly? Could I really complete her punishment experience without exploding? I knew I could control my impulses and not have 'sex' with her – as we had defined it – but I was also certain that I would need release long before the experience was over.

This was about being open and trusting, so I intended to share my needs with Kelly, and be open about whatever happened. For example, I realized that I had never actually self-masturbated in front of anyone but my wife, although several of my female friends had graciously helped me to get off while we were on trips together.

I shrugged; this would – of course – be a new experience for me, as well as for Kelly. I spent the rest of the evening chopping vegetables, and doing some other minor preparations for our lunch tomorrow.

I slept soundly Friday night, taking my own advice, and following rules 4-7, just as Kelly would. I woke up early Saturday morning, and got myself off one last time before getting cleaned up and ready for Kelly. Surprisingly, I was not nervous. I had done all the planning I could, and just hoped that Kelly would take this experience with a positive attitude.

I dressed in a pair of running shorts and a 'Run Naked' t-shirt. I poured a quart of fresh orange juice into a pitcher, grabbed a couple of glasses, and put everything onto a lacquered tray, which I brought downstairs to the playroom, and set next to the wine on the coffee table. Around 8:45AM, I went upstairs and sat down in the living room – probably for the first time in more than a year – and awaited Kelly's arrival.

CHAPTER 4: THE CONTRACT

My mind was reeling again, and I did some slow breathing exercises to relax. I was suddenly startled by a quick knock on the front door, and looked over at the clock on the mantel: 8:57AM. Kelly had been prompt; no extra punishment for that!

I got up and walked to the door, taking one last deep breath, and running my fingers through my hair, before opening it. Kelly stood on the porch – as beautiful as ever. I scanned her – this time having a good excuse, to see whether she had followed my instructions – as she stood straight and looked down at her feet. "Hello, Kelly," I said.

Kelly looked up, her eyes not quite reaching mine, and said softly, "I've come for my punishment, Sir."

My knees became a bit weak, but I quickly recovered and invited her in. She carried a small purse, and a larger canvas bag, of the type used as a beach tote. I directed her down the stairs to the basement, and we entered the playroom.

Kelly glanced around, and muttered, "This is very nice, Sir." I looked around quickly to make sure I hadn't left anything out that might give Kelly ideas.

"Thank you, Kelly. Why don't you have a seat on the couch. Would you like some orange juice?"

Kelly sat down, apparently surprised that I was treating her as an honored guest, rather than as a misbehaving schoolgirl or a sex slave. "Maybe just a little,

Sir. My stomach is a bit queasy, as it is. I'm glad I took your advice, and had only a bagel for breakfast. Sir."

I smiled, and poured her a glass, and then walked over to the desk to retrieve a folder with the agreements. After I had picked up the folder, I stood by the wall behind the desk, and flipped a few switches on an electronics panel. Then I slowly walked back to the couch with the folder open, studying the agreement, and sat on the edge of the couch next to Kelly. I closed the folder, and poured myself some orange juice.

I looked at Kelly, and raised my glass, "To your 'First Experience' – which I hope will be the start of many adventures you and I will have."

Kelly picked up her orange juice and touched it to my glass, then took a small sip. "I hope so, too, Sir."

Kelly looked down at the coffee table, her hands folded in her lap. She was comfortably dressed in blue jeans – ones not quite as tight as she had been wearing at the restaurant; she obviously had chosen them so that they would easily come off.

She wore a designer t-shirt, black with little jewels on it in an abstract pattern. It didn't quite come down to her waist, and I was relieved that she wasn't wearing a long blouse that would need to be pinned up. Her hair was beautiful – still long, but tied in a simple ponytail, which disappeared down her back. Her cheeks were flushed, and a dark cast clouded her face.

I put on my 'friendly' face and said, "You should be nervous about what is going to happen here today, but try to relax, at least a little."

Kelly looked up at me briefly, and said, "Yes, Sir," and lowered her head again.

I reached over and lifted her chin gently with my right hand. "Have you thought about any particular role or situation for us to act out today?" The question came out as if I hadn't thought of this, but of course I had thought of almost nothing but this. I would be happy to let Kelly select a specific role, as the consequences would be the same, in any case.

Kelly replied so quietly I could barely hear her, despite the fact that we were sitting only a few inches apart. "Maybe you could punish me, rather than tell my parents, about my looseness with a dirty old man, Sir?"

I smiled; this was already going great. I glanced over to the panel behind my desk to make sure the recorders were going. "Very good!" I picked up my glass and finished the orange juice, putting it back on the tray, and opening the folder that was on my lap.

"Kelly, I'm going to explain to you the rules, and what to expect during your punishment today."

Kelly sat up straighter, and said, "Yes, Sir."

I pulled one of the agreements out of the folder, and put it on the coffee table, placing the folder over it just below the top line of text, which read 'OTK Agreement'. "Kelly, as you know, what we're going to do today could easily be (and probably would be) misconstrued by anyone else finding out about this. May I please see your driver's license?"

Kelly was startled, but reached for her purse, and pulled out her wallet. She extracted the driver's license, which had a picture of her when she was 21 years old. She had been just as beautiful then – with somewhat shorter hair, but a bright, self-confident smile, and an air of dignity and poise. I wrote down the information, and calculated her age in my head; as she had claimed, she was 24 years old, and would be 25 in mid-July.

I returned her driver's license, and continued, "So we need to take some precautions. I am especially at-risk, being the 'dirty old man', while you are the young, innocent college student."

Kelly giggled, and said "You aren't that old ... Sir."

"And you aren't so innocent!" I was about to laugh myself, and wondered whether we were ever going to get through the agreement without rolling on the floor laughing.

But this was a serious matter, so I continued, in a serious tone. "We are both going to sign this agreement which, as I said, may not be rigorously 'legal', but which at least will define our roles and relationship today. I am also going to record video our 'scenes'."

At that, Kelly, looked up with a pained face and said, "No! Please don't record us. Sir."

I had anticipated this, and taping the experience could prove more dangerous than helpful. But I had considered the trade-offs long enough and made my decision. "I'm sorry, Kelly, it has to be done. I never want there to be any question that you wanted to be punished, agreed to be punished, and cooperated voluntarily throughout your punishment.

"I'm also taping us now, so we have a record of our discussion, and the fact that I have carefully covered all of the rules and other terms of the agreement with you."

Kelly glanced around the room and up at the ceiling, and then shrugged her shoulders, looked down, pouting, and said, "OK, Sir."

I finally lowered the manila folder half an inch, exposing the first subtitle: 'Your Responsibilities'. "Kelly, I am going to explain to you your responsibilities during your punishment today. It is *very* important that you understand and abide by these rules. Do you understand?"

Kelly was staring at the line of text, "Yes, Sir."

In my stern tone, I said, "Good. Because you will receive additional punishment, for every infraction of these rules."

Kelly started to moan, but smartly stifled it, "I understand, Sir."

"Now, Kelly, I want to remind you of something. You might think that the rules are to be broken, and that I might be more turned-on by you breaking the rules, so I can punish you more. But you would be wrong. As I told you in the restaurant, my fantasy is for you to willingly submit to the punishment, and obey all of the rules, and things I tell you to do."

I looked up at Kelly to make sure she was getting my serious tone. I had no doubt she was, as her face was even more flushed. "If you disobey, then you will receive a 'real' punishment. In other words, I will be harsher on you than in the main punishment, because I will really be angry that you couldn't obey the instructions. I call this extra punishment 'Corrective Punishment', and it will be given entirely at my discretion. Do you understand?"

Again, Kelly said simply, "Yes, Sir." It seemed like this was going to go pretty easily.

I lowered the folder again, and said, "Kelly, your first responsibility is 'To obey all instructions quickly and quietly'. I don't want you complaining or arguing about something I've asked you to do, or said that I will do to (or with) you."

I lowered the folder several lines, and read from the agreement, "That means you will 'remove whatever clothes, as requested'. You will also assume whatever position is requested ... and you will learn each position, so that you can return to it, if asked, later. Do you understand?"

Kelly continued staring at the exposed portion of the agreement. "Yes, Sir," she said — seemingly with less enthusiasm this time.

"You may ask questions — if they are relevant to what we are doing. I will be very open with you, and tell you what is expected; I want to help you through this punishment. I think we could both be very proud, if we are able to complete the punishment experience without your using the safeword."

I lowered the folder to the second responsibility. "You are 'To remain in position until told to move'. If you get out of position, you should return to it quickly without being told. Of course, getting out of position would be breaking this rule, and grounds for some corrective punishment."

Kelly swallowed hard, and just nodded.

"You are never to attempt to hide your body — you are to be open with your body and bodily functions throughout this punishment session. Do you understand these rules, so far?"

Kelly looked up and said, "Bodily functions, Sir?"

I opened my mouth, starting to explain in detail, but thought better of it, and just said, "Yes, Kelly." I glanced at her, and she swallowed again, the darkness running through her face becoming darker, yet.

"And now for a very important rule; this is for your safety, Kelly. You will 'keep your hands in front of you throughout each punishment'. Do you know why this is so important, Kelly?"

I could tell her mind was racing, as she glanced at me, and said, "No, Sir."

I sat back in the couch, and put my hand on her back, and slowly massaged her tense muscles, as I spoke softly to her, "Kelly, as you will see in a few moments, it is my main responsibility today to ensure your safety. I may be using hard (I mean solid) implements today, such as a paddle or cane. And I will sometimes be spanking you regularly, like the ticking of a clock, and sometimes irregularly, to keep you off-guard, and not let you anticipate the stroke and move out of the way.

"Can you imagine what would happen if I swung the 'board' (a thick paddle used at some schools still today in many states), and you suddenly felt like protecting your bottom – or rubbing it? It could break all of your knuckles! That would be a disaster! I cannot ensure your safety, unless you follow these rules – especially this one. Do you understand?"

Kelly nodded, and confirmed, "Yes, Sir. I understand. I'll keep my hands in front of me."

I removed my hand from her back, and smiled at her, "Good girl! And, of course, you should realize by now that breaking this rule will certainly be met with corrective punishment."

Again Kelly nodded. I looked down and lowered the folder to responsibility number three. "Your next responsibility is 'To answer all questions honestly'."

Kelly looked up and tilted her head with curiosity.

"Kelly, I'm getting a little ahead of myself, but I am truly curious about what you think and how you will react to many of the things we'll be doing. I'm a scientist, and always looking for the data.

"If I ask you something, it's because I really want to know how you feel – I don't want you to make up an answer, or say something because it fits the role-play; I want you to answer honestly, so that I can get to know you much better, and tailor your punishment to your needs and responses."

This seemed to surprise Kelly, "Oh! That is interesting, Sir."

I continued, "Another aspect of this responsibility is that 'If you are given a choice, you will make the choice quickly and definitively'." I looked directly at Kelly, and explained further, "For example, if I ask whether you want a hard swat on your left side, or on your right side, I expect you to say 'Left side, Sir' or 'Right side, Sir.' If you say, 'I don't care' or 'Whatever', you will receive a swat on both sides."

Kelly swallowed.

"And, for example, if I tell you that you are going to receive two swats, and ask which side you want the first one on, if you give me a vague answer, I will give you both options: first swatting you on the left then right, and then again on the right and then left. Do you understand?"

Kelly looked like she was about to cry; I had developed the art of building tension, but she was about at the breaking point, and we hadn't even begun her punishment, yet. Kelly just nodded, and swallowed hard again. She was wringing her hands in her lap.

I rubbed her back for a moment, and consoled her, "You'll do fine, Kelly. It's not going to be as bad as you're imagining ... provided you behave yourself." She looked down and fiddled with the rings on two of the fingers on her right hand. My consoling her didn't seem to help.

"As part of your honesty, and in the spirit of communicating with each other with openness, you may provide feedback to me throughout the session.

"However, you may not complain repeatedly. In fact, I don't want to hear you beg for me to stop or reduce your punishment. Because once we have agreed on each portion of your punishment, it will be carried out, and no amount of crying or complaining will stop it … unless you use the safeword. We're getting to that in a moment."

Again, I lowered the folder; it sure seemed like a longer list of responsibilities as I explained them, than when they were written in a neat column on the agreement.

"This leads us to your next responsibility: 'To not complain, unless there are issues that aren't directly relevant to your punishment'."

Again, Kelly looked at me quizzically. "That means that I don't want you complaining that I'm spanking you too hard … but it would certainly be OK to tell me that I was standing on your foot; or that you were getting a cramp or a Charlie Horse, remaining in position.

"I will administer your punishment with respect, and I do not intend to cause you any more discomfort or pain than the punishment itself. In fact, for some of the punishments, I'm going to make you comfy, with a pillow to put your head on, while I thrash your behind."

Kelly started to smile, then gulped, and then coughed.

"Are you OK? I'm glad you're taking this seriously, but, seriously, you need to relax a little! Your punishment will hurt more, if you are tense. I would like you to accept what is going to happen, and take it in as relaxed way as possible."

Kelly stared at me, and said, "How can I possibly relax, when you're talking about thrashing me? … Sir."

I tried to explain, "That is part of the maturity, and control over your body that we discussed at the restaurant." Kelly looked down again, continuing to fidget.

"Two corollaries of this responsibility are 1) please try to be as quiet as possible, unless you are answering a direct question, or unless I have asked you to speak. This is a sound-proofed basement, but I wouldn't want the mailman stopping by to put a letter in the slot, and hearing screaming coming from my basement." Kelly started to smile, and then frowned and looked down.

"And 2) please let me know when your bladder is getting full." Kelly let out a nervous giggle. "I'm serious," I said, "I'm going to put you under some stress, and asking you to relax, and the last thing you're going to be thinking about is your bladder. I don't want any accidents in here."

Kelly stifled another giggle, and said, "Yes, Sir."

"We're getting to the end of your responsibilities." Kelly let out a short sigh, and I continued reading from the agreement. "Your most important responsibility (along with keeping your hands in front of you) is to use the safeword to end the session, if you feel you cannot take any more. I want you to understand that the safeword is an automatic 'Stop', and the session will be ended – at least for the day."

Kelly looked at me and gasped, "You mean, I can't just stop one part of the punishment?"

I looked at her with a serious face, and said, "That's right. You're here to take a 'level-100' punishment ... I'll explain in a while what that means ... and you are expected to complete the punishment."

I looked up, and Kelly nodded. "If you use the safeword, I will immediately end the session. We will have a debriefing, so that I can obtain your feedback, and better understand what happened ... as it is my responsibility to keep your punishment within your capabilities to take it. I will be basing that on your physical appearance (for example, the redness or welts on your bottom), and your psychological response.

"However," and I had actually just thought about this – an example of how you can never fantasize accurately in advance about doing something with another person, "I will give you two free 'time outs'. You will be able to pause a punishment for five minutes, while you stay in position and compose yourself. During that time, we can discuss the punishment plan, and possibly modify it, if you are having difficulty. And, if you don't use the 'time outs', I may reduce your punishment, or allow you to delay part until another time.

"As you can now understand, the flip-side of this responsibility is also very important: 'It is also your responsibility to NOT use the safeword, except as a last resort'. Do you understand?"

Kelly quickly said, "Yes, Sir."

"Kelly, what would you like your safeword to be? It should be something unusual enough that you won't be saying it, unless you really mean to stop the punishment."

Kelly looked into the playroom, and her eyes glazed over, "I don't know ... do you have any ideas, Sir?"

"Kelly, it has to come from you, but something unique that we can both instantly remember."

Kelly was silent, and I thought I would have to make some suggestions, but she turned her head to me suddenly, and blurted out "Horseradish!"

A belly laugh came rumbling up from my insides; I really did feel like rolling on the floor laughing, but I wasn't about to spoil the serious and tense atmosphere leading up to Kelly's punishment. "That's a great safeword, Kelly! Good girl!" I pulled the folder lower, and looked at the responsibilities typed on the agreement.

"We're down to the last two of your responsibilities (there are 7 in total, although it sure seems like more). We have already discussed this. You are 'To be open about your anatomy and physiology'. As you've taken biology, I assume you know that 'physiology' is the same as 'bodily functions', which I mentioned before."

Kelly looked up at me, "Do you mean, like peeing?"

I smiled, "Yes, Kelly, that's right. I will be treating you with respect, and will give you some privacy, especially near the start of your punishment. But as we progress, you will become more and more comfortable with me, and after you realize what I'm seeing when I put you in certain positions, I don't think you'll have a problem peeing in front of me. That is going to be the least of your concerns, when your bottom is as sore as it's going to be."

I poured another half glass of orange juice, and drank half of it in one swallow. "Would you like some more orange juice, or iced tea? It's a bit early to open the wine, and I want you sober to take your punishment."

Kelly looked at the pitcher on the coffee table, and whispered, "No thank you, Sir."

I looked at her, and then got up and went to the bar fridge, and poured a crystal glass of ice water. I returned to the table, handing the glass to Kelly, and told her, "I want you to stay hydrated." Kelly sipped some water, and put her glass down on the tray.

"Finally, we're down to your last responsibility ... and this just might be the most difficult for you."

Kelly swallowed, and reached for her glass of water. She took another sip, and waited for me to continue.

I chuckled, and said, "Your last responsibility – which I hope you will remember throughout the session – is ... 'To have a positive attitude, be open to new experiences, and try to have fun!'" I smiled at Kelly, and winked. I couldn't tell whether she was closer to crying or laughing.

She eventually said, "That seems totally perverted, if you don't mind me saying so, *Sir!*"

I started to laugh again, but restrained myself. This was taking more control over myself than I had expected. I wasn't turned-on a bit at that moment, but was having a great time watching Kelly squirm, anticipating her first spanking that was only a few minutes away. "Young lady, do you understand and accept your responsibilities?"

Kelly looked directly into my eyes, and tried to smile (it came out crooked). "Yes, Sir. I understand and accept my responsibilities."

I lowered the folder to the next major heading of the agreement – which was only 1/3 of the way down the page. Perhaps we should have gone through this at the restaurant? "Kelly, I will now describe *my* responsibilities. They are relatively simple, and you won't have to remember them, so I'll go through them quickly."

Kelly looked at the agreement on the coffee table, as I explained. "My first responsibility – as I've told you several times already – is to ensure your safety. That means that I will apply sufficient but not excessive force; I want it to be challenging for you, but not beyond your limits. My main goal is to take precautions to avoid any medical issues." I saw Kelly squirm.

She asked hesitantly, "What do you mean, 'medical' issues?"

I thought for a moment. Of course, I had strategized all week how I could segue part of Kelly's punishment to a medical exam, and this required precautions like using sterile needles and aseptic technique ... but I wasn't about to broach this subject with Kelly – as fragile as she now appeared – until we were well into the punishment session.

So I replied, "Well, if a stroke of the cane bites into you and draws blood, I would clean and dress it, and avoid any further damage or possible infection to the area."

I heard Kelly draw in a quick breath, and thought she might be about to faint. But she recovered, and just said, "OK. Sir."

I continued, "My second responsibility is to instantly respect your use of the safeword." Kelly's mouth dropped open, and then closed. I explained, "The safeword wouldn't be of much use, unless I immediately stopped your punishment, would it?"

Kelly sipped some water, and said, "No, Sir, I guess not."

"And my third responsibility is to inform you of everything I will be doing before doing it. Now, I'm not going to lay out the entire punishment plan, as I want to keep you in suspense," Kelly groaned softly.

"But I will certainly explain to you everything I'm going to do before I actually do it. I am not going to surprise you – you'll almost always know what's about to happen. Again, we're going to work together to get you through this punishment session." Kelly just nodded.

"And one more thing that I will take responsibility for: 'To ensure that there is no transfer of body fluids between us'. As we have discussed already, there will be no anal, oral, or genital sex, kissing, or blood contact between us, during your punishment today."

Kelly relaxed somewhat, and smiled at me, "And that means that I can't taste a little of your wine?" I smiled back at her, and said, "We could possibly make some exceptions in that area ... but I do believe in the 'germ theory of disease', and I really am more comfortable not eating or drinking after someone else."

Kelly was surprised. "Oh, OK." As a quick afterthought, she added, "Sir." I smiled at her again, impressed at how well she was doing; I just hoped she could continue this way after I had begun spanking her.

"And, finally, my last responsibility, and another important one." Kelly was all ears. "'To provide an enlightening and adventurous experience for you'." Kelly put down her water, then leaned over and gave me a quick hug, as we sat on the couch.

I hugged her back, and then gently pushed her away. "You may not feel as friendly toward me, after I explain what you should expect during your punishment!"

Kelly waited silently for me to continue. I lowered the manila folder nearly to the bottom of the page, exposing the 'What to Expect' section of the agreement. There were four items, and I read them quickly.

"First, you will most likely be embarrassed; that is meant to be part of the punishment. You should expect that I will see every part of your body."

I glanced at Kelly, who had not reacted to this; she obviously knew that she was going to be stripped, and I had already told her that she had to be 'open about her anatomy'. I continued reading, "You should also expect that I may touch every part of your body.

"As I told you in the restaurant, if you are mature enough to not be embarrassed, that would be great – it does not diminish my fantasy, although you would be getting off easy, as the embarrassment is supposed to add a psychological aspect to the physical punishment."

Kelly said, "I'm pretty open, and I know that I will be undressed, but I still don't know exactly what you're planning."

I smiled at her, and said, "And that's exactly as it should be!"

I read the next line on the agreement: "'You *will* have a sore bottom!' That is part of the experience. By way of full disclosure, I will tell you that you may expect redness, perhaps black and blue marks, maybe some welts, or other marks ... all of which will disappear within about 2-3 weeks." Kelly's eyes grew large, and I could see that she was about to object, but she calmed down, and just stared at me.

I read, "'You may experience pain in other parts of your body for 2-3 days'." Again, Kelly looked up at me, but she did not ask a direct question, so I offered no explanation of this last statement.

"The third thing you should expect – and we have already gone over this – 'You will receive corrective punishment, if you do not meet your responsibilities'. Such corrective punishment will be entirely at my discretion, and you will willingly and cooperatively take any corrective punishment deemed necessary. Do you understand, Kelly?"

Kelly meekly glanced up at me, and said, "Yes, Sir."

I finished, "Good. The last thing you can expect is that 'You may be surprised at some of the things we do'. Again, I will inform you of these things before they happen, but I don't want to spoil the suspense by telling you now."

Kelly looked at me and said, "The suspense is already killing me. I think the waiting and anticipation may be worse than the punishment is going to be!"

I smiled, as Kelly had hit on the truth – I was making it painfully tense for her, building up to her punishment. There was really no way that most of the punishment would be worse.

In fact, we would be starting with a simple over-the-knee spanking (called 'OTK'), and this would relax Kelly and lull her into expecting a more mild punishment. But the more severe implements would certainly correct her misimpression. I hoped that the flow of the 'highs' and 'lows' of Kelly's punishment would be interspersed to keep her properly off-balance, psychologically.

"Kelly, I hope that you will accept the punishment I have designed for you. If so, I'll read the last few points, and we'll sign the agreements. But, I'm going to give you the opportunity right now to get up and leave. I hope we will be able to see each other again – have lunch once in a while, and perhaps go skiing together. I would be happy to help you with your career. I won't hold this against you, but will – of course – expect you to honor the confidentiality between us."

I looked at Kelly, and she nodded, as I continued sincerely, "I really want you to try this experience, but I won't force you, or put pressure on you. If you decide that you don't want to be punished today, I'll invite you back some time for a more social visit – maybe I'll make dinner for you, and we can go in the sauna together?"

Kelly seemed to wake up, and quickly said, "No, I want to do this."

With that, I handed her one of the agreements and a pen. I then started to read the final section of the agreement: "You hereby agree ... 'That you are here of your own free will and volition, and are desirous of this experience'."

I looked at Kelly, and she said "I just said that ... Sir."

"OK, then please put your initials after the first sentence." I watched her do so, and continued reading, "You hereby agree 'To make a best-effort to complete the session without using the safeword'."

She nodded, and I pointed to the pen; Kelly initialed the next line.

"You hereby agree 'That some or all of the session may be recorded, but any such recordings in which you can be identified will never be released publicly without your written permission'." I could tell that Kelly was thinking this through.

She said, "What about non-publicly ... like sending a copy to my family?"

I just looked at her. "Kelly, as I told you, this session is about trust. You *know* I wouldn't do that!"

She responded, "Yes, Sir."

I looked at her sternly. "Then initial the next line." She did so.

I then read, "You hereby agree 'To indemnify me and never make an ethical, moral or legal complaint against me, provided I meet all of my responsibilities defined herein'."

I looked up at her, and she smiled and said, "I'm not sure what 'indemnify' means, but I think you know that I won't mention this to anyone."

I continued, "Furthermore, you hereby agree 'To keep my identity and details of the session strictly confidential'." Kelly initialed that line, as we had just talked about this.

"Finally, you hereby agree that you have read and agree to all of the points of this agreement."

Kelly just nodded, and I told her, "Now, you can sign on the dotted line, and put today's date next to your signature."

She signed her copy, and I signed mine, and then we swapped agreements, and each signed the other. I folded one of the agreements and gave it to her. "I suggest you don't lose this, or leave it lying around where someone might read it. I think it would be difficult for you to explain this to someone."

Kelly chuckled (a pleasant change from her stoic discomfort over the past half hour), and stuck the folded document into her purse. I beamed: Kelly was actually going to go through with this! I got up and walked over to the desk, putting my copy of the agreement in the bottom of my 'In' basket.

I sat down at my desk, and looked over at Kelly, still sitting on the couch. "Come here, young lady, and we'll begin your punishment!" I commanded.

CHAPTER 5: BOOTCAMP MORNING

Kelly slowly got up from the couch and walked over to the desk. I told her, "Have a seat." Kelly sat in the desk chair across from me to my right. I removed a few things from my desk drawer. "Kelly, I'm going to prepare you for your punishment, and then I will give you some specifics on the punishment plan." She nodded.

I was purposely drawing this out; I wanted this to continue as long as possible. But I knew the moment of truth was only minutes away; by this time, I had little doubt that Kelly would be completely cooperative – at least as much as she could control herself.

It takes energy to give a spanking, and it takes energy to receive one. I knew that we would both be exhausted by the end of the day. I glanced at the desk clock, and was flabbergasted when I saw that it was 10:15AM already; we had 'wasted' an hour, just going through the rules and responsibilities!

I looked up at Kelly, and said, "Now, young lady, I want you to stand up. Move the two chairs a little to each side." Kelly complied immediately. She was possibly more beautiful now, than any of the three other times I had seen her, as she stood vulnerable and anxious in front of the desk.

Her long, dark hair had a simple tie, and hung straight down her back. Her cheeks were unusually red, and her face clouded with concern – but at the same time, I could see the brightness and anticipation lurking below the surface. Kelly was nervous, but still self-confident. She may have been afraid, but she was adventurous enough to accept the new experience with excitement. And, she may have some doubts about the adventure to come, but showed enthusiasm and a spirit that I had seen in few women (or men, for that matter) in my lifetime.

"Please put your feet apart - a little wider than shoulder-width." She looked down at her feet and separated them about 24 inches. I then told her, "Now, stand up straight, and put your hands on your head or behind your neck."

She instantly straightened, and put her hands on top of her head. "Kelly, this is called the 'standing' position. You are to get into this position any time that I haven't told you to be in another position. Do you understand?"

Kelly said, "Yes, Sir!" smartly, and smiled, happy to finally be starting the punishment, and satisfying my every command ... so far.

I began my schpeil. "Young lady, you have been sent to me, because your family is very disappointed in you – for taking drugs, having sex with the entire football team," Kelly nearly cracked-up, but contained herself, and only emitted a series of breaths that I knew were laughs, while she smiled, and just shook her head.

But I continued with as serious a voice as I could muster, "and fooling around with an older man."

I laughed, and continued, "Your father was about to call the police when he found illicit drugs in your bedroom, but your mother pleaded with him to give you another chance. They love you very much, and want to see you improve your behavior. I'm told that they have spoken with you about this, and that you have agreed to take a professional punishment, as a demonstration of your good intent to change your wanton ways."

I was really getting into it, and on a roll; but I had difficulty stifling my laugh, and I swiveled my desk chair around to 'cough', then composed myself, so I could deliver a serious lecture to this young woman, who didn't look so serious herself at the moment.

I continued, "You have signed the punishment contract, and know what to expect. Do you have anything to say for yourself, Miss?"

Now, Kelly was nearly laughing, but managed to squeak out, "No, Sir."

We smiled at each other, and I got back into the role. "Having a professional punishment license issued by our great State, and with 20 years of experience spanking the bottoms of naughty girls, I have been asked, and have agreed, to administer a Level-100 punishment on your bare bottom. This is the most that can legally be administered in a single day, and you can expect it to be very severe.

"You will cooperate fully throughout your punishment, as it is you who should be the one doing the work here; it's just my job to see that you are really serious about improving, AND to tan your bottom so that you will not be able to sit down for a week. You will remember this lesson for a long time!

"While your Dad agreed not to be here today to observe your punishment, he did tell me that he would take a good look at your bottom when you got home, to make sure I had done my job." Kelly groaned, perhaps not remembering that this was just part of the scenario.

"I'm very good at my job, and I am always professional – that's why your parents have selected me ... plus, I'm insured and bonded ... to cover any 'accidents' that could happen when a young lady like you stops cooperating. I told your Dad that he would be happy with the spanking I gave you, but if he wasn't he could bring you back here himself for another dose, at no additional charge."

Kelly just stared at me. Her eyes and her smile were growing wider with each new tale that I smoothly told. I've never acted before, but I played it really well, I thought … especially considering the scenario had only been decided upon an hour ago.

I saw Kelly's arms start to sway, and spoke up, "Kelly, you may put your hands on your hips, if you're too tired to keep them on your head … but they should never be in front of you or behind you (either blocking my view, or my spanking access)."

Kelly put her hands on her hips, in a defiant-looking pose, and incongruously said sweetly, "Thank you, Sir."

It was time to spill the beans. "Young lady, as I just said, you will be receiving a Level-100 punishment. One 'level' is equal to just one hard swat with the 'textured paddle', so a Level-100 punishment could theoretically consist of 100 hard swats with that paddle.

"It doesn't sound like much, but that paddle is a very severe implement, and I cannot give more than 10 or 20 swats on the bare bottom, or the little studs on the paddle will eventually break the skin, opening you to infection, and possibly causing some bleeding.

"We don't want that to happen, so your punishment today will utilize a variety of implements, and generally only a 'level-5' or 'level-10' worth of each implement, so you will be able to remain in position, as you take each new level.

"It is necessary to begin with the milder implements – such as my hand – so your bottom will gradually get used to the pain, and able to take more pain with each implement. I will alternate 'soft' implements (like my hand or a strap) with 'hard' implements (like a paddle or a cane).

"I think you already know that all of your punishments will be applied to your bare bottom ... with the exception of a brief demonstration spanking, and a warm-up spanking that will prepare you for what to expect during your first level-10 punishment. It's not going to take you long to realize that I don't play around."

I laughed and coughed again, glancing up at Kelly's curious face. "Let me rephrase that ... It's not going to take you long to realize that I'm serious, and am going to give you a hard spanking."

I continued the detailed explanation. "Each level-5 or level-10 of your punishment will also include a 'corner time'. As I'm sure you know, corner time is when a person stands in the corner of the room, with her freshly-spanked bright-red bare bottom on display, and her nose to the wall – not being able to do anything but think of her misbehavior, and the spanking it earned her.

"We don't have time for a 'real' corner time – which could be an hour for each level-10 spanking – so I have developed a more efficient corner time when I provide my services. After each spanking with a different implement, you will assume whatever position I tell you – usually with your buttocks well separated and your anus exposed.

"I will then do a rectal insertion, which will remain in for a full 5 minutes. That way, your bottom will still be on display, you will still need to think about your behavior and punishment you just received, AND the rectal insertion will provide some additional embarrassment, to compensate for the shorter corner time."

As I had been saying this, I watched as Kelly's eyes grow wide, and then shut, and then she was shaking her head, 'No!'

"You're not complaining already, are you, young lady?"

Kelly scrunched her face, and opened her eyes; they appeared to be tearing-up again. Kelly stammered, "Sir ... I told you that I was an open person, but I didn't expect *that*!"

I sat back in my chair and smiled, "I know. That's the point. If you're really open about your body, you won't really be embarrassed about displaying your anus – and it's not like we had a crowd of people here ... although I did initially ask your parents if they wanted to 'observe' your punishment."

At this, Kelly broke-up laughing. I felt like joining her, forgetting about the punishment, and rolling on the soft carpet of the playroom, laughing until we cried ... then holding and hugging each other ... and finally making love to candle light ...

But, No!, I had been planning this, and wasn't going to give up this opportunity and go against my promise to avoid intercourse with her. I looked at Kelly sternly, and she stopped laughing, and put her hand over her mouth.

"Back in standing position!" I yelled. She immediately stood straight, with her hands on her hips, although I could see that she was still laughing. I took an 18" wooden ruler from the top drawer, and brought it down with a 'CRACK!' on the desk. Kelly jumped, and wiped the smile off her face.

"Now, young lady, just one more thing – and again, I think you know this already. The third part of each level-5 or level-10 punishment will be the 'corrective punishment' that you will receive for misbehaving. That means complaining, not fully cooperating and, especially, not holding your position, which is your main responsibility during your punishments. The corrective punishment may be given along with the main punishment – extra strokes with the same or more severe implement, or even re-starting that level again. After you've received 32 out of 36 strokes, you certainly aren't going to want to start counting the strokes over!"

Kelly's face was serious now, and she just shook her head, 'No'.

"I might decide to administer your corrective punishment during your corner time. This will be something special, which I won't share with you until the time comes; if you cooperate, perhaps you won't need to find out for a while."

Kelly just frowned at this – another 'unknown' to stoke her fear. She had been starting to relax, but now that I was talking about corrective punishment, she was getting nervous again about what was going to happen.

"As I said, punishments are usually given from mild to severe implements, as your bottom is able to handle increasing levels of pain. However, I need to give you an impression of what I mean by 'level-1'.

"I should give you one hard swat on each side of your bare bottom to give you a feeling (ha!) for what I'm calling 'levels'. But I don't think your bottom would take the textured paddle, without at least a little warm up. So, I'm going to make an exception, and give you the demonstration on your underwear."

I looked into her eyes, and commanded, "Drop your pants, now!" I watched, as Kelly quickly unbuckled her belt, unbuttoned and unzipped her jeans, and pushed them down to her knees. She was wearing plain white bikini underwear, as I had specified; I could see that they were Jockey's, the same brand my wife had usually worn.

Kelly was standing straight up, with her hands on her head again, and a smirk on her face. She was proud of herself for immediately obeying my command for her to undress.

I pulled the textured paddle from the second desk drawer, and held it up for her to see. It looked like a typical Ping-Pong paddle, but was made more serious for spankings by the little spikes sticking up from the rubberized surface. The spikes may be rubber, but they really stung!

"I consider that double-spankings are needed without a corner time, and quadruple-spankings are needed when taken just on the underwear. I told you that you should get two hard swats on the bare, which would be 8 swats on your underwear, four on each side. As you haven't received any warm-up, I will limit the demonstration to only TWO medium (not hard) swats on each side." Kelly's mouth started to open, but she just nodded.

"Regardless of your expectations, I think the first swat will be shocking, and a second swat is needed on each side to show that you are willing to cooperate and hold your position, in the face of unexpectedly severe pain. Not that this is going to be 'severe', being only medium intensity, and over your panties. Are you ready for this?" I waved the textured paddle back and forth, and looked at her.

Kelly was about to respond to my question, when I realized I had already made a mistake and gone off-script. I put the paddle down on the desk, and asked her, "Do you need to pee, before your demonstration swats?"

She looked relieved, and said, "Actually, that's a good idea, Sir. Thank you."

"OK, then. Pull up your pants, and you can walk to the bathroom that way. It's just outside the playroom. Please leave the door open a crack, and wash your hands when you're done. Then you can come back here, and I'll give you a small taste of what a paddle feels like."

Kelly bent down, and lifted her jeans; it had been a good decision to wear loose-fitting jeans, but I would still have preferred if she had chosen a dress – which I had envisioned pinning up, as I had done with Liz. "May I go now, Sir?"

"Yes, you may." I sat back in my chair, and watched Kelly hobble across the playroom and into the bathroom. I saw the light go on, and the door close partway. Early this morning, I had made sure the exam room across the hall was locked. It just looked like a utility closet from the outside.

I rocked in my desk chair, and marveled that I was really beginning the punishment training of a knockout-beautiful young woman – almost exactly as I had fantasized (but I never had a face to go with the bottom).

I heard the toilet flush, and the sink running. A minute later, Kelly came hobbling back, with her pants not quite pulled up to her hips. She got back to the desk, and said, "Thank you, Sir. I'm ready for the paddle, now."

It had worked with Liz, and now also with Kelly. I had *caught* her! I looked sternly at Kelly, and said, "You are? I don't think so!"

Her face contorted in confusion, and tilted, as she asked me, "What do you mean?"

I laughed inwardly, but kept my stern countenance in front of Kelly. I raised my voice, "Young lady! I've only taught you one thing today, and you've already forgotten that? I thought you were serious in cooperating with me to get this punishment over-with?"

For a moment Kelly still looked confused; then, suddenly, she pushed her pants back down to her knees, and shot up, straight as an arrow, and put her hands on her head. She frowned, gave a little shrug, and said, "Sorry, Sir."

I was ecstatic, but acted even angrier. "Well, I guess you're going to learn sooner, rather than later about my special corrective punishment. I will first paddle you, and then we will take care of this blatant infraction of the rules."

I picked up the paddle, and waved it at Kelly. "Keep your legs apart the same width, but move closer, so that you are about a foot from the front of the desk." She carefully moved herself into position, keeping her hands on her head, and her feet apart.

"Now, without moving your feet, bend forward at the waist, until your forearms are on the desk." Kelly bent over, taking her hands from her head, and putting her arms on the desk as instructed.

I was impressed that Kelly immediately put herself in the proper position, unlike Liz, who was up on her hands, until I told her to get down on her forearms. Kelly looked up at me, and her eyes diverted to the paddle; she wasn't smiling. "You will keep your eyes forward, and take your short paddling quietly, and with dignity."

I stood up and walked around behind Kelly, with the paddle in my hand. Kelly kept her eyes straight, and I don't think she noticed the slight, but growing, bulge in my pants. I stepped around to Kelly's left side, and placed the paddle gently on her left butt cheek that was covered by the thin fabric of her underwear.

I said loudly, "Are you ready?"

Kelly immediately replied, "Yes, Sir!"

Without further ado, I brought the paddle back, and swung it into Kelly's bottom, snapping my wrist at the end, and delivering a much stronger blow than I had intended. In one moment, a loud 'SMACK!' exploded in the room, and I watched Kelly's pantied buttocks ripple in waves, as she moved forward slightly, and screamed, shocked by the intensity of the swat.

I just stood behind her watching her still-quivering buttocks, as Kelly yelled, "Oh my God, Sir. That *hurt!*" Kelly sniffled as I placed the paddle on her right cheek and moved it back-and-forth in a rubbing motion. I brought it back, and after a slight hesitation, back down on her bottom, making another loud 'SMACK!', and resulting in Kelly standing partway up, before realizing her error and getting back down – obviously hoping I hadn't seen.

"Young lady! You were told to stay in position, and you were told what would happen if you did not comply with the rules. You will now receive an extra swat, and then we can do the 'second' swats on each side."

Kelly groaned, but didn't say a word. She pushed her bottom back to where it had been before the last swat. Without warning, I swung the paddle in an arc, from lower to higher, and it crashed into the underside of her buttocks, right in the middle. Kelly yelped, but stayed in position. This quick adaptation was impressive to see. Kelly was sniffling, and I could see that a couple of tears had dropped onto the desk.

I moved slightly to the left, and asked her, "Are you ready for your second demonstration swats?"

Kelly managed to get a "Yes, Sir." out between the sniffles.

I said, "We're going to do this quickly. I want you to concentrate on staying in position; you don't want any more extra swats, do you?"

Kelly was calmer, and said, "No, Sir. I don't want any more extra swats. My bottom is already stinging ... or burning ... anyway, the pain is not going away."

I chuckled, and positioned the paddle. I said, "Get ready!" and swung the paddle quickly – once on the left side, and once on the right side. These swats were much lighter, but still painful, as they were being given over the first set of swats.

Kelly screamed again, and was now sobbing loudly, but she managed to stay in position. Now, she lowered her upper body even further, hugging the desk with her breasts squashed, and her head turned to the right, tears flowing from her eyes. I walked back around to my chair and handed her a tissue, before I sat down.

"Kelly, you have just received a 'level-1/2' punishment. I will count that towards the level-100 that you will be receiving today."

Kelly got back up on her forearms, looked at me with her hazel eyes, and asked, "Sir, I'm not complaining … but how can I possibly take 200-times more punishment? I don't think my bottom can take it. Sir."

My fatherly kind-face was on again, "I know, dear. I probably shouldn't have let you feel the textured paddle before a good warm up. But you will just have to trust that I will give you a proper warm up, and gradually increase the intensity of your spankings, so that you *can* take it. I haven't looked at your bottom, yet, but I bet it's barely pink; you've got a long way to go!"

Kelly daubed her eyes with the tissue, and she reluctantly said, "OK, Sir. I'll try."

I smiled, and mumbled Yoda's saying: "Try, you will not! Do, you will!" I arranged a few supplies on my desk, looked at Kelly, who was watching me intently.

The bulge in my pants grew, as I remembered giving Liz her first corrective punishment, and the astonishment on her face when she saw the long hypodermic needle. I calmly opened one of the packages, and brought out a 1.5-inch long needle, which I uncapped and held less than a foot from Kelly's face.

Rather than complain, as Liz had done, Kelly just closed her eyes, and said, "Is this another one of your little 'surprises'? Sir?"

I laughed and said, "Yes, young lady, this is my special corrective punishment method that is quite effective, doesn't leave any marks, and is really more a psychological than a physical punishment."

Kelly opened her eyes, and looked at the needle again. "That thing looks pretty physical to me, Sir."

I laughed again, and re-capped the needle. This should never be done after giving an injection, but at this stage, if I had stuck myself, I would have disposed of the needle, and opened a new, sterile one to be used on Kelly.

I thought for a moment, and said, "Kelly, do you remember that I told you I'd like to get some data during this punishment? I would like to hear about your prior experiences, your expectations, and your judgment of how painful, uncomfortable, or embarrassing the various punishments are."

Kelly looked up at me from her bent-over position on the desk, and said, "Yes, Sir, I remember."

I took a sheet of paper from the top level of my in-basket that had a number of columns, and text down the left side. This time, I was really prepared! "Kelly, when was the last time you got a shot?"

She replied, "I don't know, probably when I started college – we all had to get checkups and updates on our immunizations."

I then said, "When is the last time you got a shot in the rear?"

Kelly thought a moment, and said, "It's been so long, I can't remember."

"OK. In a moment, I'm going insert these needles into your bottom; how much do you think that will hurt, on a scale of 0-100?"

Kelly gave a quick giggle, and said, "Oh, probably a 20, Sir?"

"And, how about if I actually gave you an injection, like penicillin?"

"I don't know, Sir ... I would guess maybe 40?" I looked up at her, "You really think it will be that bad?"

This was the ideal situation – with someone fearing that something will be painful, but submitting willingly ... and then finding out that it isn't that painful, after all. I smiled at Kelly, and remarked, "I'll bet you're going to be used to getting needle sticks and injections in your bottom, before we're finished here, today!"

Kelly closed her eyes, and groaned. I decided to go off-script again ... I just couldn't resist finding out what Kelly would decide when I gave her a choice.

"Kelly, you have misbehaved a few times today, and have only received one extra swat. I want you to know, right away, that I won't tolerate any more misbehavior from you, so I'm going to give you a more serious corrective punishment, and you'll have to make a choice."

I started pulling more supplies from the bottom drawer of the desk, laying them out in front of Kelly. I don't think she wanted to see what I was doing, but she was too curious not to watch.

I slowly assembled two 5 cc syringes with needles, and filled them each with 2 cc of sterile saline. I also unpackaged another half-dozen needles. I stood, and walked around behind Kelly taking her underwear on each side, and slowly pulling them down to just below her buttocks. I heard a sharp intake of breath, and Kelly put her head back down on the desk, and moaned softly.

I stood back, and admired Kelly's round bottom – which some might argue was too big; but for my use, her buttocks were beautiful, and – with her narrow waist – gave her a very feminine aura. I realized that I had never seen her in a dress. I then walked back to my chair and sat down.

Kelly opened one eye, and glanced at me, surprised that I wasn't still behind her and about to insert a needle. I clasped my hands, and thought about it for another minute, and then said, "Kelly, you have a choice. Now I don't want you to get any more corrective punishment; you do remember your responsibility regarding making choices, don't you?"

Kelly got up on her forearms, and looked at me, "Yes, Sir, I remember."

"Good. Here's your choice; I don't think you're going to like any of them, but that's why this is a good punishment. Your choice will involve getting injections, or stuck with needles for short or long times."

Kelly closed her eyes, and said, "I don't understand, Sir."

"Your first choice is to receive two small injections of sterile saline, one on each side. The needles will only be in for 10-15 seconds, but the injection is going to hurt a little. But not as bad as the '40' you estimated. And, you'll be done in about a minute.

"Your second choice is to get twenty needle sticks – ten on each side. But I'll make them quick-sticks – using a needle for each side, and leaving them in about 10 seconds, while I move the needle on the opposite side."

Kelly's mouth dropped open, and she closed her eyes again. I continued, "That will take about three minutes. Or, if you prefer, for your third choice, I will insert four needles, two on each side, and leave them there for a full ten minutes."

A groan escaped Kelly's mouth again, and she shook her head. "I really don't want an injection," she said, "I guess the needles won't hurt as much."

I looked at her and said, "That's true. I'm using very small diameter needles, and if I insert them quickly, they really won't hurt much going in."

She opened her eyes, looking up at me, and said, "I'll take the four needles for ten minutes, Sir." Her head sunk down to the desk, and she closed her eyes again.

"Good girl! That's actually a pretty good choice. You're almost certainly going to be getting injections later, but I can only inject a certain amount safely, so would rather just have you experience the needles first."

I quickly dashed off to the bathroom to wash my hands. When I returned, I went around the desk and picked up four of the opened needles, and two alcohol swabs. I neatly lined-up the needles on the desk in front of Kelly, where she could contemplate them as I prepared her bottom. Then, I walked around the desk again, with the alcohol swabs, and opened one.

I looked down at Kelly, and asked, "Which side would you like me to start on?"

Kelly promptly answered, "The right side, Sir."

I was impressed with Kelly's compliance, and told her so. "You're really doing well. Someday, you'll make a great sex slave!" Both Kelly and I chuckled, as I swabbed a spot high up on her hip.

I picked up one of the needles from in front of Kelly, and uncapped it. I held her skin taut, as I positioned the needle, and told her, "OK, here we go!"

The needle slid in easily, and Kelly made only a small grunt. "I want to hear you breathing." I told her, as I held the end of he needle. "How does that feel?"

Kelly said, "You're right. I guess it's really not that bad. Sir."

I swabbed the corresponding site on her left side, and picked up another needle. As I got ready to insert the needle, I said, "Good! Then you're ready for the next needle." With that, I plunged the needle into Kelly's left hip, until only the blue hub could be seen. Kelly whimpered a little.

I realized I had forgotten something ... "Kelly, I neglected to ask you to 'rate' the pain or discomfort of the first needle after it went in, so I'll ask you now to rate the pain or bother of the two needles that are in you now."

Kelly swayed her bottom left and right a few inches, then said, "It's not that bad ... maybe a '5'?"

I looked a the two small needle hubs against her skin on both of her upper hips, visualizing the 1.5 inches of stainless steel embedded in her bottom. "A '5' out of '100'?"

Kelly nodded, "Yes, Sir."

I leaned over the desk, and wrote the information on the sheet I had prepared. "OK, then you're ready to take the second two needles."

Without saying another word, I swabbed Kelly's right buttock, in the middle, but near the top, in line with the top of her butt crack. I quickly inserted the needle, then moved slightly to the left. I swabbed her left side in the same relative position, and pushed the needle a bit more slowly into her. Her head came up, and she emitted a soft, "Ah ...", but otherwise took her corrective punishment very well.

Now there were four small blue hubs. I decided to pull each needle out about ¼", so that some of the stainless steel shaft was showing. Kelly didn't feel anything as I did this, but when I stepped back, there were now four needles, clearly going through the soft skin of her bottom.

"If these needles start to bother you, you may ask at any time for me to move one or more of them – you'll get another stick, but the pain will get spread around a little."

Kelly's head stayed on the desk, and she said, "OK, Sir."

I walked back around the desk, and sat down. "Now, let's finish this first interview."

Kelly looked up and said, "First?"

I smiled, and said, "Yes, Kelly, we're going to do several of these interviews and questionnaires, and I'm going to get to know you, your body, your experiences and your sensitivities very well."

I continued asking questions about her medical experiences – if she had ever been admitted to a hospital (no), if she had ever had a bad disease that had to be treated over more than a week or so (no), and what she thought about getting shots (doesn't like them, but not too afraid to get them). As she was doing well with the needles in her, I continued asking questions about her prior relationship experiences.

"Kelly, how many men have you slept with?"

Kelly's head snapped up, and she said, "What? Oh ... I think six."

I looked at her, and said, "You think? Don't you remember the men you've had sex with?"

Kelly's rear swayed a bit, and she simply said, "Yes, it was six."

"OK. How old were you when you lost your virginity?"

Kelly answered, "When I was 15. I was a freshman in high school, and starting my 'wild' period."

"Was it a good or bad experience for you, the first time?"

She laughed, "I guess it was pretty good. I didn't know enough to rate the sex, but I felt empowered, and in control of my boyfriend. Sir."

I then got more specific, "And how many different sex positions have you tried?"

Kelly looked me and rolled her eyes, "I don't know, Sir. The usual – him on top, me on top, and from behind ... I guess that's about it."

I then asked, "And how many men have seen you nude?"

Kelly thought, and said, "Besides the times I went to a nude beach?"

"Yes, Kelly – just your dates, not doctors, or your close family."

Kelly thought again, and said, "I don't know. Maybe a dozen?"

I smiled, "And how many of those have seen your intimate parts – for example, while you were in a knee-chest position, and there was enough light to see?"

Kelly quickly said, "I don't really think anyone has seen me up-close, except my doctor and maybe a couple of boyfriends, when we were getting ready to make love ... but it was always pretty dark, so I'm not sure how much they saw."

I got up, and said, "OK, Kelly, that's a good start. Now, I'd like to show you a few videos." She hadn't complained about the needles, yet, and it had been nearly five minutes, already.

I swiveled my large computer monitor, so that Kelly could see it from her position bent over the desk. I had cued-up a half-dozen videos that I wanted her to see. They were all male-female spankings, in various positions, and using various implements, from the hand to the cane, and they were all quite intense.

"Kelly, in another 5 minutes, I'm going to take those needles out, and you will receive your first spanking. It will be 'OTK' – the classic over-the-knee position. But first, I want you to watch these videos, and there will be a short quiz at the end."

Kelly giggled, and said, "Is it a written test, Sir?"

I laughed and replied, "Actually, there is only going to be one question; I'll even make it an 'open book' test: I want you to watch these videos carefully, and I'm going to ask what you noticed in common with all the videos."

Kelly shrugged, and said, "OK, Sir."

I went around the desk, and bent over it next to Kelly, on my forearms, just like her. She turned her head toward me, smiling curiously, and I leaned my head over and kissed her gently on the tip of her nose. "Let's watch," I said, as I reached over and hit the key combination on the keyboard to play the videos in full-screen.

The first was a great example of a hand spanking. Almost immediately, Kelly glanced over at me, and said, "That looks like a really hard spanking, Sir."

I chuckled and said, "Yes – most of these are harder than the spankings I will give to you. And some of these are very long punishments. Just keep watching."

We both turned to the screen, as the hand spanking continued. I pressed the Forward key, and told Kelly, "We don't have time to watch the entire length of all of these videos– maybe someday you can come over, and we'll put some interesting videos on the big screen in the playroom, eat popcorn, and then we could 'play' a little?"

Kelly laughed, and said, "We'll see. I haven't gotten through today, yet." Kelly wagged her behind, and didn't seem to be too concerned by the needles.

The next video was of an older, mature couple. Without a word, the woman walked in front of the fireplace, lifted her skirt and slip, pulled down her panties, and bent over, holding her knees.

The gentleman positioned himself behind her, and began applying very hard strokes of a leather strap to her bare bottom. The woman yelped on nearly every stroke at the beginning, but settled down, and only made a few grunts and a couple of 'Ow!'s' as the strapping continued.

I fast-forwarded a few times, and Kelly's eyes grew wide as she stared at the poor woman's bright red bottom. The strapping went on and on, with every stroke being incredibly hard. I told Kelly, "I won't bore you with the whole thing, but she takes 200 strokes of that strap!"

Kelly swallowed, and looked over at me, "Oh my God! I could never take that much. Sir."

"We'll see how much you can take, young lady, in about three more minutes."

Kelly groaned, and I asked, "What's the problem?"

Kelly scrunched her face, and replied, "A couple of the needles are really starting to hurt, now. I guess I might let you move two of them, Sir. I don't think I can last another three minutes with them feeling like this."

I stood up and, in my fatherly voice, I told her, "I'm sorry, Kelly. You should have asked earlier." I walked around behind her, "Which ones are hurting the most?"

She immediately came back, "The left side in the middle, and the right side on the outside." I said, "OK. I will swab you first, and then I'll pull each needle out and do a quick re-insertion." Kelly was silent, while I reached over the desk and took a new alcohol swab. I opened it, and swabbed her left side far to the left, below the needle that wasn't hurting.

I grabbed the hub of the needle in the upper middle of her left buttock, and pulled it out quickly; then, within a couple of seconds, I re-inserted it in a quick thrust in the new location. Kelly let out a small, "Mmmm."

I did the same on her right side, swabbing about two inches below the offending needle, which was high up on her right hip, pulling the needle out, and re-inserting it in the new lower position. Kelly remained silent.

I bent over the desk again, next to Kelly, and asked, "Is that better?"

Kelly looked at me sweetly and replied, "Oh, yes, Sir. Much better. I didn't mind the needles going in, too much."

I nodded, smiled, and said "Good girl," as I started the next video. This one was of a very severe paddling with a large, thick board. There were only about eight swats, but the girl who was bending over and holding her knees had to take a step forward after each powerful swat, and immediately put herself back into position for the next stroke.

Kelly, just shook her head, and said, "Wow!" I nodded, and skipped to the final video, of a long and hard caning. The girl was bawling long before the end, but the cane strokes kept raining down, creating a white line across both her buttocks with each stroke.

I turned off the video, got up and walked around the desk, and sat in my chair. I surreptitiously glanced at my watch, and saw that Kelly's 10 minutes were just about up. It didn't seem she would mind an extra minute or two, while we talked.

I looked up at Kelly, and said, "Now for your quiz. I'll ask a few preliminary questions to warm you up. What did you notice most about these videos?"

Kelly looked at me and said, "How hard they were, Sir."

I nodded in agreement, "Yes, that's true. Those girls were really taking a beating. And what else did you notice?"

Kelly thought a moment, and asked in a questioning tone, "They were all crying by the end?"

I ignored her lack of 'Sir'; she was doing very well. "Yes they were. But there's still something else that you should have noticed. Now, I'll ask the 'official' quiz question: What did all of those videos have in common ... that should be impressive to you ... and that you're going to have to remember during your spankings today?"

Kelly had a blank look on her face, "Uh ... I don't know, Sir."

I looked at Kelly and said, "Think some more. And your corrective punishment time is up, so I'll take out the needles now."

Kelly closed her eyes, and said, "Thank you, Sir. Maybe I'll think better without four big needles in my butt! Sir."

I walked behind her, and wiggled each needle a little, and then slowly pulled them out, one by one, until all four needles were out. I opened a 2x2" gauze pad, and patted the tiny dots of blood where 3 of the needles had been, and then pressed and massaged the area a little. When I was done, I pulled up Kelly's underwear. Then, I walked around the desk, threw away the gauze, and dropped the needles into the sharps container.

"Now, Kelly, have you figured out what I wanted you to notice, in all those severe spanking videos?"

Kelly just shook her head slowly. "I don't think so, Sir."

I sat back in my chair, deciding whether this would merit some additional punishment. Kelly really was trying, so I decided to just let it slip. "Kelly, what is the most important thing for you to remember and do during your spankings?"

Kelly looked at me, cocked her head, and said, "Not putting my hands behind me, Sir?"

I laughed, "Yes, that's a good answer, but not the one I'm looking for. What else can you think of ... it would be good if you remembered, because we're going to begin your spanking momentarily."

Kelly stared at the items in front of her on the desk, and looked up, "Staying in position, Sir?"

I clapped, and stood up. "VERY WELL DONE! You must have noticed that, despite the incredibly hard and long spankings, with some severe implements, all of those women held their position – without ropes or chains, or six other people holding them down. And, if they got out of position, they immediately returned to it – without being told. I don't know about you, but I thought it was pretty impressive."

Kelly nodded, "Yes, Sir. I agree, Sir."

I finished, "So, I really want you to think about that; these women are getting a much harder punishment than you will receive, but they were able to hold their position. You're a strong girl ... I know you can do it, too."

I then walked around the desk, and commanded, "Standing position, Kelly!" She immediately pushed up from the desk, stood up straight, and put her hands on her head. Her jeans were below her knees, and she looked very cute, standing there in her white bikini underwear, with her short bejeweled t-shirt barely coming down to her navel.

"Come with me, Kelly, but leave your pants down. That will give me time to get set-up." I strode out of the office area, and halfway across the playroom to the armless chair, and small table, and pulled out a stool that was next to the wall, placing it in the middle of the room.

Then I opened the drawer in the small table, and pulled a small box from it, and put it down next to the right rear leg of the stool. I went back to the table, and took a smooth Ping-Pong paddle from the small platform underneath the table.

I sat down on the stool, facing the couch and coffee table, my back to the drapes hiding the bed. The small spotlight shining down on the carpet had confirmed exactly where to place the stool, for best centering on the video that was rolling.

I watched, as Kelly hobbled across the room, her pants now down around her ankles, and her hands still on her head. She finally got to the stool, and stood in front of me, looking down at her feet so they could be positioned properly for the standing position.

"Are you ready for your first real spanking, young lady?"

Kelly quickly said, "Yes Sir."

I smiled, and said, "Good girl! Now come over here," as I pointed to my right side, "and get across my lap." Kelly took her hands from her head, and slowly lowered herself into position, lying across my lap.

I told her, "For some punishments, you will be in this 'across-the-lap' position. But right now, I want you to slide forward and put your hands down on the carpet." I put my right leg out straight, which had the effect of having all of Kelly's weight on my left thigh.

Kelly wiggled around a little, finally settling into position, her hands on the floor, her head pointing nearly straight down, her breasts up against the outside of my left leg, and the rest of her body angling straight, with her toes resting on the floor. I put my right hand on the underwear over her right buttock, and massaged it a little.

"This is the 'OTK' – over-the-knee – position." I pulled up her underwear a little from each leg, and chuckled. "Your bottom did get a little pink from those demonstration swats."

Kelly chuckled, and said, "I can't believe I'm still feeling the sting!"

I smoothed her underwear, and massaged her left buttock a little. "OK, Kelly, we're going to start your punishment now. I will first give you a 'warm up' on your underwear. Since you also won't have a corner time for the warm-up, it will take 80 spanks for every level-1. We'll do a level-4.5 warm-up, which will be about 360 spanks."

At that Kelly groaned, "Yes, Sir. It sounds like a lot, Sir."

I reminded her, "Well, for your bare-bottom OTK level-10 punishment, you will be getting 200 spanks, plus your first corner time. That means each level-1 is 20 spanks. Spanking you on your underwear and no corner time means a factor of 4 more spanks, or 80 spanks per level-1. Do you understand, Kelly?"

"I guess so, Sir."

"Good. I will mostly alternate sides, but also give you some with multiple spanks per side – just to keep it interesting. 360 spanks, with perhaps one or two breaks, so I can rub your bottom and ask how you're doing, will take about 10 minutes. It will feel like a very long spanking, Kelly, but by the end of your warm-up, your bottom will be able to take much more pain."

"Yes, Sir," she mumbled at the floor.

"I think you've probably had enough needles for a little while, so your corrective punishment, should you get out of position, will be some medium swats with the smooth Ping-Pong paddle on your underwear. I'll keep track of roughly how many times your feet or hands come off the floor, you lift up, you make too loud of noise, or – God help you – you try to put your hand behind you. Do you understand?"

Kelly nodded, her auburn hair – now looking somewhat more red under the bright ceiling spotlight – falling over her face so that I could not really see her, "Yes, Sir," she said.

With that, I placed my left hand firmly on her lower back, and brought my right hand up, and then back down on her right buttock, making only a moderately loud 'WHAP!' sound, and Kelly reared up her head, and said, "Oh!!!" My hand came down on her left side, and then settled into a regular rhythm of about one spank every second.

Kelly crossed her feet at the ankles; I would not normally have allowed this, but it was her first spanking, and she was obviously trying very hard to behave. The spanking continued, and I could see that Kelly was adjusting herself, trying to keep her legs down, and occasionally reaching with a hand – I think, to remove hair from her mouth. She yelped when I gave her some of the harder spanks, but stayed relatively quiet and still.

When I had given her 100 spanks, I stopped, and rubbed her bottom with my right hand, still holding her back down with my left. "How are you doing?" I asked.

Kelly sputtered a little, pulled some more hair from her mouth, and lifted her head up as far as she could, "I'm doing OK, Sir. I think. It hurts more than I thought it would. I still don't know if I can even get through this part of the punishment." She hung her head back down, and shook it, probably unbelieving – as I was – that this was really happening.

I started spanking her again, mixing it up a bit – slower and faster, and a random number of spanks per side, rather than just alternating.

As I was approaching 180, and giving her some harder spanks, Kelly cried out, 'Ow!' and both of her lower legs lifted up – almost straight into the air for a few seconds, until she brought them back down. I spanked harder, and she started bucking. I said, "Calm down, Kelly, you've got to stay still!" She just nodded, and I realized that she was moaning or sobbing.

When I reached 200, I stopped again. I said, "Kelly, your legs have come up, and you were not staying still. You probably deserve more, but I know you're trying, so I will only give you one swat with the smooth paddle on each side, as corrective punishment. Then we will re-start your warm-up spanking."

Kelly just moaned louder. I reached back by the leg of the stool, and grabbed the paddle, and placed it on her left buttock.

"Are you ready, young lady? I expect you to take your corrective punishment without moving or making a sound."

Kelly sputtered again, and said, "Yes, Sir."

I brought the paddle back, and swung it hard, impacting her bottom with a loud 'SMACK!'. Kelly let out an involuntary yelp, but remained in position. I quickly gave her another hard swat, this time on the right side. After another yelp, Kelly sobbed.

"You're only halfway through your warm-up, Kelly! Try to relax, and take your spanking calmly ... you need to practice that now, before we start with the heavy implements."

Kelly, with her head still hanging down, said, "Yes, Sir. I'll try." Then, she tilted back her head, and asked, "People don't really get turned-on by getting spanked, do they?"

I laughed, and said, "Yes, actually many women do. But they first have to get beyond a certain point of pain, where – due to control or just exhaustion – they relax and allow another part of their brain to take over. I'm hoping you might reach that part by the end of your level-30 or level-40 punishment."

Kelly just shook her head, and groaned. I put down the paddle, and placed my hand back on her underwear. "OK, Kelly, I'm going to finish your spanking without stopping. I will alternate sides every time, and I'll keep it at about the intensity you have already experienced. So, let's get this finished."

I continued the warm-up, spanking her steadily, alternating sides, and covering all of her bottom. I could tell that her bottom was now turning a nice shade of light red, based on the color of her unclad upper thighs.

Obviously, I wasn't' spanking nearly as hard as we had seen in the video. That wasn't the point: Kelly was cooperating nicely, and submitting to a long spanking.

Having done this with a few other women, I was only slightly turned-on; this required a lot of stamina from me, also!

As I spanked Kelly's bottom, time seemed to slow down; it seemed like this spanking was at least 30 minutes long. Finally, we reached the 360th spank. We were both panting, and I rubbed her bottom gently with my hand. "You did very well, Kelly. I'm proud of you!"

Kelly took some deep breaths, and was finally able to say, "Thank you, Sir. It was challenging. I'm not complaining, but maybe it would be better to do a level-10 each day, rather than trying to do so much at once?"

"Well, Kelly, that's an interesting idea, and perhaps the *next* time we have a spanking experience ... if there *is* a next time ... we can do it that way. It would be a big turn-on for me to see you knocking on my front door, and requesting your 7th or 8th day of punishment. I think you would find that very challenging, also."

I then pointed out, "As you may have noticed, rubbing your bottom spreads and dulls the pain. That's another reason that I don't want you touching your bottom, unless I give you permission. If I refuse permission, you may ask me to rub your bottom for you. Does this feel good?"

Kelly moaned – but it was a different moan this time, more of a deep cat's purr. "Yes, Sir. But ..." She cocked her head, and looked up at me – as much as she could in her position.

"Yes, Kelly?"

Kelly put her head down, shook it, and looked back at me, balancing on her left hand, as she used her right hand to throw her long hair over her back, so that she could see me. "Sir ... I'm not getting turned-on by this." She giggled, and I was happy to see that she wasn't entirely depressed.

She continued, "I think I might get turned-on by spanking *you* ... I can really understand the power, the control, and the vulnerability of the other person, who has agreed to cooperate. But I'm not sure I can understand why I would get turned on by you hurting me." We were both silent, and I continued massaging her bottom through her underwear.

Stepping out of character, I said, "I won't force you to do anything, Kelly, you know that. And my purpose is not to hurt you." How could I explain this?

"I think you know that hot is very close to cold ... if an ice cube is touched to your back without you seeing it, you will feel like you're being burned. You've probably stuck your hand in a very hot stream of water from the sink, and initially it felt cold. Love is very close to hate – they are both strong emotions about someone, whether positive or negative.

"Similarly, pain and pleasure are very close together – they both are strong emotions that come from the same portion of the brain. Pleasure can become pain ... and *pain can become pleasure*! I would just urge you to relax, accept the pain, and perhaps – at some point – the pain will become pleasure.

"Now, I will divulge another of my secrets: I would get nearly as turned-on if you were spanking me, as me spanking you."

Kelly looked back, and said, "Huh? I don't get it."

I thought this would be easy to explain. "I'm turned on by the idea of submission – not really the giving-up of power (although that can be fun, too) ... but submitting to something that you know will be painful – or embarrassing – and doing it willingly.

"And I'm not talking about real-life medical situations, where your health is at stake; but situations like this, where you are submitting today, out of curiosity, adventurous spirit, openness, and your trust in me."

I continued, "You don't really understand this, yet, but for me to submit to you, requires that I let-go, and really trust you ... developing an instant bond and emotional closeness that I think ... may be the nearest thing to 'love' between two people – whether they have been partners for years, or just met."

Kelly laughed, pushed back her hair, and said, "OK, then let's switch positions – let me spank *you*, for a while!"

I laughed too. "Kelly, I plan to do just that – I had been keeping it as a surprise reward, when Kelly had completed most of her level-100 punishment – but I'll only let you spank me after you have truly experienced and cooperated through a full spanking and, hopefully, can see the turn-on in both the 'top' and 'bottom' roles."

CHAPTER 6: THE PUNISHMENT BEGINS

"OK, Kelly, enough stalling. Your punishment training is over – you have 'graduated' with honors. It took a little sweat and tears, but you are now into the 'big league', the 'OTK University'. You have a lot to learn, yet, but you have proven that you're willing to make sacrifices, to gain some new knowledge and experience. We're going to begin your 'real' punishment, now. You've already received a total of level-5 punishment, so you have level-95 to go."

I thought a bit, and made a quick decision ... again, off-script. "Kelly, I had thought about reducing your bare-bottom OTK spanking, but since you've completed your punishment training so well, I've decided to keep it at a level-10. Does that sound acceptable, to you?"

Kelly said, "Sir, if I've done so well, why would you give me *more* of the spanking?"

I said, "Giving you fewer spanks now may be an advantage in the short-run, but I don't think you realize that in your level-95 to go, an OTK spanking will be the least intense punishment you will receive. If you take a longer OTK, then you will receive fewer strokes of a more severe implement. Anyway, you should learn right now what a 'level-10' punishment feels like."

I thought for a moment whether I would rather Kelly to stand in front of me and remove her pants and panties; stand in front of me, and let *me* remove them; or just remove them while she was in this position. I decided on the expedient approach. "Kelly, I'm going to lower your underwear now; you can help me by pushing off the ground and lifting your middle."

She said, "OK, Sir." She adjusted herself a bit, as I reached across her, and took both sides of her underwear in my hands, and slowly lowered them ... below her buttocks ... down to her knees ... and, leaning over to my right, I pushed her underwear and pants as far down to her ankles as I could reach. There was a strategy in this: the clothing around her ankles would help prevent her feet from swinging wildly.

I sat back and looked down upon the most beautiful bottom I had ever seen (at this moment, at least, I was convinced of that). I was more smitten, than in love, but with each 'scene', I was becoming more impressed with this intelligent and strong, but willingly submissive young lady.

I felt myself getting bigger, and reached into my shorts to adjust myself. I then pulled Kelly a bit toward me, so that my hardening penis was vertical, being held against Kelly's bare thigh.

"Kelly, do you need to use the bathroom again, before we begin your punishment?" Kelly raised her head, and answered, "I don't think so, Sir ... but thank you for thinking of that." The time had come.

"OK, Kelly. I want you to take some deep breaths, try to relax yourself, and then request that I begin your spanking. You're going to get a hard, bare-bottom, over-the-knee, hand spanking – 200 spanks in total. But I'll stop every 50 spanks to check on how you're doing. OK?"

Kelly said, "Yes, Sir." She shifted a bit, but her thigh was still up against me, and her breasts (under her t-shirt and bra) were against the outside of my left leg. I felt her pubic hair on my thigh, and her slightly parted legs extended to the right of my left leg, and over my right, which was still extended straight out.

She pushed forward with her toes and, with her right hand, swept her long hair over her back and left shoulder. Her head went down, and it sounded like she was doing deep breathing exercises.

Finally, she was still and, with her head still hanging down, proclaimed, "I am ready for my spanking now, Sir. I will try to behave." After about a 10-second pause, during which Kelly took one more long breath, she said quietly, "You may begin, Sir."

I smiled – with my face, with my brain, and with my 'other brain'; this was getting more incredible by the minute. I was living my fantasy. How long could this last? Was Kelly going to resent me, afterward? I knew that Kelly and I would only be friends, but I really wanted to maintain our friendship.

On the other hand, this could be my only chance to share my fantasies, and hope that some of it became a turn-on for her. I took a couple of deep breaths, also, and then was ready to begin the first of many level-10 punishments. This was to be the lightest punishment, but it would not be the easiest.

Back into the role, I said, with as stern a voice as I could muster, "Young lady, you know you have misbehaved; you've done a lot of seriously wrong things, you have disappointed your family, and you've said that you would take responsibility for your actions.

"You have agreed to a severe punishment, to demonstrate your recognition that you misbehaved, and show your good intentions to improve yourself in the future. Do you have anything to say, before your punishment begins?"

Kelly breathed heavily, and in a whisper said, "No, Sir."

I rubbed her bare bottom for a few more seconds on each side. And then, without warning, I began spanking her hard, again alternating sides.

Kelly bounced around a bit – her legs crossing and uncrossing, flexing up, and again touching her toes to the floor and pushing herself forward. Her head bobbed back and forth, and almost immediately, she began softly sobbing again.

I spanked her bottom rhythmically, from the top of her thighs nearly up to her waist. I knew that I wouldn't be able to use the severe implements safely, this high up.

Kelly's sobbing seemed to stop, but I heard occasional sputtering, whimpering, and quite a few 'Ow!'s', 'Ah!'s', and 'Oh!'s'. But she controlled herself, and was doing all of this quietly – the main sound in the room being my hand slapping loudly on her bare bottom.

When I reached 50 spanks, my hand was stinging. One more thing I hadn't thought of – wearing a leather glove while spanking her! With all the time fantasizing about this, that had never occurred to me. Of course my hand was usually busy doing something else, and not getting sore actually spanking someone.

I stopped, and inspected my handiwork: Kelly's bottom was now a uniform medium shade of red. She was strangely quiet, although I heard a few sniffles. "Are you OK, Kelly?"

She said, simply, "Yes, Sir."

Then I asked her, "Kelly, how would you rate the pain of this bare-bottom OTK punishment so far – the first 50 spanks? On a scale of 1-100?"

Kelly sniffled again, and I asked her if she would like a Kleenex. She said, "Yes, Sir. Thank you, Sir." I reached down to the box, pulled out a few folded tissues I had stashed there, and gave one to Kelly. She wiped her eyes, and then rubbed her nose. Kelly then looked back at me, and said, "I don't know, Sir. It really hurts. But I guess it's not as bad as I was expecting."

I kept quiet, and did not spoil her positivity by informing her that she had only experienced the lightest implement; she would have to take much more pain to complete this session. Kelly continued, "My bottom is probably at about a 20 ... or 30."

I looked down at her, and said, "So, it not that bad, then?"

Kelly sniffled, and said, "Not yet, Sir. It hurts, but I can take it. But, ... but you were talking about whips and canes ... I really don't think my bottom is going to take all that ... and I'm not sure I want to have that experience." I kept quiet. "But, I'm willing to try, Sir."

I smiled with satisfaction. This really was a strong (perhaps also headstrong) and independent girl. Her experience so-far had shown me that she had the enthusiasm to persist, despite pain and fear.

"Are you learning your lesson, yet?"

Kelly responded – it seemed a little over-enthusiastically – "Oh, yes, Sir."

I said, "OK, here come the next 50." I began spanking her again, this time, a bit harder, and speeding-up until I had reached a total of 100 spanks. Kelly's bottom was bouncing and quivering – even when I wasn't touching her.

As I was spanking her, she rocked a bit back and forth, as my spanks pushed her forward, and she pushed herself back. Now, in addition to that motion, she was swaying left and right – putting slightly more pressure on the hardness beneath my shorts with each of her swaying movements.

It occurred to me that this motion might just be turning both of us on. At 150 spanks, I paused the spanking and rubbed Kelly's bottom with both hands, kneading her beautiful red globes, and moving them in circular motions. These circular motions moved her buttocks apart, and I moved my hands down lower, where her separated buttocks began exposing her anus.

I stopped, moved her t-shirt up a bit on her back, and put my left hand down again. I told Kelly, "We're going to do the next 50 without stopping, Kelly. The spanks will get harder and faster. I want you to concentrate on holding your position. Do you understand?"

Kelly seemed pretty calm now, as she tilted her head back to me, and said, "Yes, Sir."

Then, I began spanking her reddening bottom again, with a regular cadence, my eyes glued to her butt, and my mind becoming mesmerized by the vision in front of me.

Again, it felt totally surreal. I was counting sub-consciously, and by the time I returned to reality, another 40 spanks had been given to Kelly.

It was then that I realized she was silent. I hoped that she was OK, and hadn't passed out (I didn't think it would have been remotely possible for her to fall asleep!), but I could hear her breathing, and finally I heard a sniffle.

I made sure the last ten spanks were zingers, much harder than the rest, the entire 10 being given in about five seconds. Kelly squirmed a bit, and let out some squeals after the last few spanks, but really controlled herself.

Although I had seen this effect before, it was still amazing to me – how the human body, and especially the human mind, can adapt to harsh conditions or situations. Both protective psychological mechanisms and a flood of endorphins not only deadened the pain, but provided another type of energy and excitement.

I could tell that Kelly was at this stage: she kept moving – slightly, but rhythmically – even after I had stopped spanking her. And, while she had been quiet throughout the last several dozen spanks, she was now moaning as I rubbed her bottom.

"Kelly, you've successfully completed your first level-10 punishment! And I really don't have much excuse for giving you any corrective punishment."

Kelly quickly said, "Thank you, Sir!"

I continued, "But now, you will now experience your first corner time. I reached down to the box near the leg of the stool, and pulled out the rectal thermometer, that had already been lubed and wrapped in a tissue. "Kelly, do you remember what I'm going to do for your corner time?"

She thought a minute, and said, "Yes, Sir ... you're going to stick something up my butt."

I laughed, "Yes, Kelly, I am going to do a rectal insertion. This will be the easiest one, to go with your easiest level-10 spanking." I leaned over her back, and she angled her head back as much as she could, as I showed her the rectal thermometer.

She made a slight groan, and her head hung back down. I separated her buttocks with my left hand, and found her anus. I asked Kelly to push her bottom up, and relax her legs, and her anus became more accessible.

I positioned the thermometer over her, and slowly lowered it, first touching her anus – yielding a quick flinch and an 'Oh!' from Kelly, and then I continued to insert it slowly, until only about an inch stuck out from her.

"I'm going to ask you to be quiet now, and think about your misbehavior and the punishment you just received ... and the punishments you're still going to get. And I'll move the thermometer around to remind you that this is still part of your punishment. OK?"

Kelly quietly said, "Yes, Sir."

I held the thermometer with my right hand, as I slowly massaged her lower back and bottom with my left hand. Despite the spanking and redness, her skin was so soft! I moved the thermometer around slowly – first back and forth, then in circles, and then in-and-out, gradually increasing the motion, until the thermometer came completely out of her.

Her anus remained relaxed and open, and I plunged the thermometer back into her. She moaned, and then became quiet again. I had forgotten to start the timer, so I glanced down at my watch, and checked the time. It was already 11:30AM! We hadn't made it very far through Kelly's punishment; but we had many more hours yet to play.

Kelly and I were both nearly silent for the next few minutes. I held the thermometer deep inside her, but kept it still, only occasionally moving it a bit.

My left hand lightly massaged her lower back, and I slipped it under her t-shirt, and very lightly skimmed her skin up to her bra strap. My hand glided over Kelly's soft skin, and I lifted it – tenting her t-shirt – so that my hand was grazing only the few soft hairs of her back. I brought my hand out from under her t-shirt, and glanced again at my watch – it had been 4 minutes, and I decided to read Kelly's temperature.

"Kelly," I said softly, "I'm going to move the thermometer around for a few more seconds, and then take it out and read your temperature."

Kelly was very relaxed, her head, arms, and legs hanging – with most of her weight supported on my left thigh. She murmured, "Mmmm ... OK ... Sir." I twirled the thermometer a bit, and moved it around in big circles, as I slowly pulled it out most of the way, and then suddenly plunged it back into her. I then slowly pulled it all the way out, as I kept her buttocks separated with the fingers of my left hand.

I transferred the thermometer to my left hand, and reached down for another tissue, that I used to wipe the thermometer. I twisted the thermometer so that I could read it, the small spotlight in the ceiling strategically beaming down from above the 'punishment stool' allowing me to read between the tiny lines etched on the glass rod.

"99.2 degrees. You're probably a bit sub-normal. I mean your temperature!" Kelly giggled.

I wrapped the thermometer in the tissue and placed it on top of the small box that was sitting on the carpet next to the stool. Taking one more long look at Kelly's lower back, bottom, thighs, and long legs, I was compelled to rub her just a bit more along the entire length of her exposed flesh.

She quietly issued a few 'Mmmm's, and it seemed that she was quite relaxed. That was great, but I couldn't let up on the anticipation and at least some of the tension.

"Kelly, you may get up, now." I said softly, in a tone much more like someone waking his partner after a sound night of sleep than anything resembling a command. Without saying anything, Kelly pushed off the floor and, somewhat awkwardly, slid off my knee and stood up, her underwear and jeans a wadded mess around her ankles.

I was very pleased and impressed to see Kelly get into the standing position, and even more impressed when she raised her head and looked into my eyes, smiling, with only slightly teary eyes, and said, "Thank you, Sir."

We both smiled even more, and I got up from the stool and stood before her. "May I please hug you?" I asked, unnecessarily. Kelly didn't say a word, but fell forward onto my chest, putting her arms around me; I put my arms around her, and hugged her tightly, and she buried her head in the crook of my neck.

We held each other for what seemed like several minutes, while I lightly rubbed her back with my right hand. I slipped my hand down, and slid it lightly over her bottom, then I stood slightly back and looked into her eyes.

Kelly scrunched her face a little, and said, "That spanking hurt, Sir. My bottom is really sore. But it wasn't that bad – I tried to relax, and I think that helped."

At that moment, I started getting turned on. I pushed my lower body against Kelly's, and kissed her softly on the cheek. "I'm glad to hear that. You behaved very well – maybe you'll make a good submissive, after all! Maybe the role of 'sex slave' will be a turn-on for you?"

Kelly looked down and giggled again. "I don't know, Sir. I still think I would be more turned-on if YOU were the sex slave."

I laughed, and hugged Kelly again, and then stepped back and gave her a slow once-over with my eyes, from her head to her toes.

Kelly's hair was a mess – still tied with a small band at the top into a ponytail, parts stuck out to the left and to the right, and the hair on top of her head fell across her forehead and over one side of her face. She was watching me appraise her, and smiled broadly, appreciating that I appreciated her.

My eyes dropped to her t-shirt, which seemed to accentuate her C-cup breasts more than I had realized earlier; I could barely see evidence of her hardened nipples raising the fabric of her t-shirt.

As I continued my southward tour, I smiled at Kelly's bare midriff; her tummy was very trim but she was not underweight. I was a bit surprised – with her supposedly 'wild' background – that she didn't sport any tattoos or body jewelry.

I then looked at the triangle of dark hair – with only a slight auburn tint – that seemed quite far below her navel. I guessed that it was an extended Bikini wax – which would cover all but the smallest of her panties and bathing suit bottoms.

She stood as I had instructed her, with her ankles about two feet apart. The pubic hair covering her vulva was not waxed, but was very thin, giving a tantalizing partial view of her labia that slightly protruded and hung down between her legs.

Kelly had athlete's legs, and I had to remember that this girl was still in her twenties, and was probably in the best shape of her life. With her pants and underwear still around her ankles, her entire lower body was totally exposed, but Kelly stood there with dignity, poise and confidence.

"OK, young lady, step out of that mess around your legs." I bent down, and Kelly put her hand on my shoulder, as she alternately lifted one foot and the other, and I pulled her clothing aside. She stood back up, putting her hands on her head, and I grabbed her clothes, and stood up in front of her. I slowly untangled the pants and underwear.

I handed the pants to Kelly, and said, "Fold these nicely, please." She did so. I then handed her the underwear, and said, "Put these things on one of the chairs in front of the desk, then come back here."

Kelly walked over to the office area, carrying her clothes, while I watched her red, receding bottom sway with every step. I quickly picked up the things next to the stool, put the stool back against the wall, and walked into the bathroom to throw away the tissues, and clean the thermometer.

While I was washing my hands, I looked into the mirror, and a very self-satisfied face smiled back at me. I was living a dream – but it was better than any fantasy that I had ever had.

When I returned to the playroom, Kelly was in a proper standing position where the stool had been before, awaiting my return. "Kelly, are you hungry or thirsty? I know you haven't had much this morning."

Kelly watched me walk through the room towards her, and said, "I guess I'm getting a little hungry, but my stomach is still pretty nervous. Could I please just have some water, Sir?"

I backtracked to the coffee table, grabbed her glass, and went behind the bar to add some ice and fill it with purified water. I brought the water to her, and as she took it, and drank almost half in a few gulps, she looked sheepishly at me, and said, "Thank you, Sir. You're being very nice to me, considering you're also beating me!"

Her tone sounded nice, but that statement got me a little upset. I took the glass, and put it down on the table near the wall, and then turned towards her. She had put her hands back on her head.

"Kelly! First of all, I already told you that your punishment would be given with respect. Other than your bottom being sore, I want you to be comfortable. And I certainly don't want you to get dehydrated, or have any other health problem.

"Second, I'm *not* 'beating' you! I'm applying a measured degree of pain, taking care to let your bottom acclimate to the experience, and not taking it too fast for you.

"And, if you remember our discussion earlier – it is not about 'hurting' you, but about giving you the experience of feeling fear – and some pain – and being strong enough, brave enough, having enough control over your body, and wanting to please me enough to deal with it. As I said, you've done very well so-far."

Kelly looked down at her feet, thinking about what I had said. "I don't know, Sir. I'm trying to understand all this."

She looked at me again, with a child's face, "It's confusing ... one moment you're spanking me so hard, I don't think I can stand it ... and the next, you're treating me like an honored guest, making sure all of my needs are met. When you're spanking me, it feels like I should hate you, and when you're nice again, I almost think I love you. I'm on an emotional roller-coaster, and I still don't know if I could do this again." Kelly looked down again, with her face in a pout, her hands still on her head.

I gently lifted her chin, until our eyes met. "I told you that pain and pleasure, love and hate, are related feelings and emotions that are very close together. Your feelings and confusion are normal; please hang in there, and let's see how you do on your next two level-10 punishments – which we are about to begin now.

"After you have successfully reached level-30, we'll take a break and have some lunch. Then we can talk more about how you're feeling. Does that sound alright?"

Kelly looked at me, with tears starting to fill her eyes again. "Yes, Sir. I'm sorry, Sir, I didn't mean to complain ... but this is all so weird ... I expected this to be about the physical pain and doing simple things like undressing for you; I'm realizing it's not really about that at all.

"I'm sorry to tell you this, Sir, but it's not about *you* at all. It's much more about me dealing with my own feelings. And, I've never been very good at that." Kelly looked down again, and was silent.

In my most fatherly voice I said, "Kelly, it sounds like this experience may be good for you – to put you in touch with yourself, give you confidence that you are strong enough – emotionally – to do this, and give you some insight into the perversions that some of us 'old guys' have.

"We are still doing this only because you're willing to, and we can still stop the scene any time you feel it is getting too much for you. All I ask is that you give it a chance. Let's talk about this again during lunch. Maybe after another two level-10 punishments, you will have a better idea of what you think about all this. OK?"

Kelly mumbled, "Yes, Sir."

I didn't recall Liz having been on such an emotional see-saw, when we had our spanking session to fulfill the note she had given me. Of course, Liz and I had known each other much longer, and done many more things together (an image of us skinnydipping in the pond, under a blue sky drifted across my mind's eye).

I hadn't thought of this before, but wondered whether Kelly was going through something similar to the 'Stockholm Syndrome', where someone being held captive begins to empathize with his/her captor? I wondered how much psychological study had been devoted to BDSM, and similar fetishes – there was obviously a wealth of information that could be obtained.

I stood there, thinking these thoughts, while a beautiful woman stood in front of me, half undressed, in my playroom.

Into my mind came, unbidden, the mock scolding my wife would give me, when I paid more attention to math or science than life around me – even at someplace like the nude beach.

A Playboy-quality model could spread her towel on the sand and lie down a few feet from me – I always noticed, of course! But then I would continue my sundial experiment with a small twig stuck in the sand, or refocus my attention on the science book I was reading, pretty much ignoring the beauty beside me.

I refocused now on Kelly – who was watching me with a curious expression on her face – and I snapped out of my daydreams. I stepped over to the couch, and dragged the end chair over to near where Kelly was standing. She watched, with a blank expression on her face.

I picked up the paddle that I had set down with the stool, and told Kelly, "please step up to the chair, and put each of your feet outside the front legs of the chair." I walked around behind Kelly, as she dutifully did as I had asked. "Now, I want you to bend over and put your forearms on the arms of the chair – like we did at the desk."

Of course, I had carefully selected the chair for exactly my purpose, although it also had an overall style that matched the decorating of the playroom and a fabric that complemented the couch. I had bought it in the showroom of a famous high-end department store, and it had been challenging to find a moment when nobody was looking, when I could 'try the chair'; it would have been incredibly embarrassing, if the salesperson had seen me in any of these 'positions'.

It would be a great punishment chair – especially for the 'over-the-front-of-the-chair' position (OTFOTC for the OTK? ... I chuckled at the thought), and my favorite – the 'chair position'.

The main specifications for the chair had been the width of the legs, width between the arms, height of the arms above the floor, angle and height of the back, and softness of the cushioning on the seat, sides, arms, and back. It looked like, and was, a very comfortable chair ...

unless you were bending over it in the manner that Kelly was doing right now.

I watched Kelly get herself into position. With the arms of the chair low to the ground, it was nearly impossible for Kelly to get into position without bending her legs, and thrusting her bottom into the air. She put her weight on one foot, and then the other, leaning forward, and holding the arm rests of the chair.

"That's good, Kelly. I expect you to have to bend your knees; they can rest up against the chair."

Then, I explained to her, "Kelly, as I told you, these punishments are to demonstrate your cooperation, and openness – especially with your body. When you get in any position today where your legs are apart, I want you to reach under and separate your labia as much as you can, and make sure your buttocks are pulled apart so that your anus is well exposed. Without me having to tell you. Do you understand?"

Kelly giggled, and said, "Yes, Sir, I understand," as she reached under with her left hand, put her long fingers along her labia, and then separated them widely. They kept moving back together, but she left them displaying a thin line of pink, moist tissue in the midst of sparse, dark-auburn hair.

In that position, her buttocks were already about as spread apart as they could be, so Kelly didn't bother doing anything there, and put her arm back on the armrest of the chair.

Kelly had the top of her head against the soft cushioning of the back of the chair, and said, "I understand what you are seeing, Sir. I guess I am a little embarrassed by being in this position, even in front of someone as trustworthy and nice as you. Sir."

I laughed, but was impressed by her honesty and openness. "I understand that, Kelly; it is a big part of the submission, the vulnerability, and the trust. You know I've seen many women before, and all female genitals look pretty much the same ... so it is not about actually *seeing* anything, except how you react to these situations, and how well you submit to something that is embarrassing to almost everyone – not just being undressed, but being in such a compromising and vulnerable position."

I continued, "You are to keep your eyes down or forward ... so another part of this experience is the 'unknown' – you will not know exactly where I am, or what I'm doing. I have full control of the situation, and you have essentially given me your body, presented your bottom for inspection and punishment. I am getting turned-on right now, just watching you await your punishment."

Kelly finally settled into position. "That position is perfect, Kelly. I call it the 'over-the-front-of-the-chair' position."

Kelly chuckled, and said, "That makes sense, Sir."

I laughed, and thought of the '*50 Shades*' series, "I can't see your face, but you're not *smirking* at me, are you?"

I guess Kelly knew about the series, but had never read the books about Ana and Christian, "Smirking, Sir?"

I laughed more. I think we could have had a good time right now, if I let Kelly off the hook, and we undressed and rolled around laughing (and maybe doing other things) in the bed that was waiting just behind the drapes.

But I am a strong person, also, so I said simply, "Now I want you to remain still, and in this position. Remember, if you ever get out of position, it is your responsibility to get yourself back into position quickly. And you can expect to receive corrective punishment, for getting out of position, even if you do remember to get back into position. Do you understand, Kelly? I'm serious."

Unfortunately, my continuing laughter, as restrained as I tried to be, killed any hope of Kelly thinking I was actually serious. Well, this was a role, anyway. And, maybe, some of my humor would rub off on Kelly and relax her.

"Yes, Sir. I understand. And I know you're serious … or you would have taken me from behind already." Now she was laughing, her head pushing on the chair back, and her bottom bobbing up and down, and sideways.

I couldn't resist. I quickly walked over to the small table, pulled out the top drawer, took an item wrapped in tissue, and walked back to just behind Kelly. She was still laughing sporadically, but trying to keep herself still.

"Maybe this will convince you I'm serious," I said, as I opened the tissue, pulled out the small, black already-lubricated butt plug, and plunged it into her behind.

"Oh! Sir!" I walked over to the desk, retrieved the pad and pen, and rolled the desk chair that didn't have her clothes on it over behind Kelly, and sat down. I had a great view of Kelly's rear; her long hair hung down on her left side, reaching the seat of the chair.

I slipped my right hand under my running shorts and adjusted myself. Considering that a beautiful young girl was bending over naked in front of me, I wasn't very turned-on.

That could be remedied, I thought. I considered taking a few minutes to masturbate right now. Would that be a turn-on or turn-off for Kelly? I decided better of it; we were still early into the experience, and I did not want to transmit too strong of a sexual overtone.

I still had hope that Kelly would let go, and eventually be turned on by this experience. I knew she was trying ... perhaps too hard.

I briefly stepped out of my role: "Kelly, I have asked you to try to have fun ... and I'm certainly not going to spank you or stick you with needles for laughing. So I'll just use the butt plug as a 'place-holder', and let you calm down, while we continue your interview."

"It feels big, sir."

"Kelly, it's barely larger than my finger – it's the smallest rectal insertion you're going to have the rest of the day. It's just to remind you that you are in the middle of a punishment session. And you've agreed to answer all of my questions quickly and honestly."

Kelly swayed her bottom left and right, and her head came off the chair back, and hung down, "Yes, Sir."

I swiveled my chair back and forth, and began the next line of questioning. "Kelly, when I first asked you to pull your jeans down, and you were standing in front of me in your underwear, how would you rate the embarrassment or discomfort you felt – again, on a scale of 0-100?"

Kelly turned the start of a laugh into a cough, "Zero, Sir ... well, I'll give it a one, for the nervousness I was feeling."

I looked up at her, and noticed that the thin pink line underneath her had actually widened.

"When you first went over my knee, how would you rate the experience?"

Kelly said, "Maybe a 5. Sir. But I probably had enough butterflies in my stomach to rate it a 15 or 20 for a few seconds, as I realized you were about to spank me."

I continued, "OK, thinking back on it, how would you rate your warm-up and level-10 spanking (all 560 spanks)?"

Kelly thought a moment, and said, "At the time it seemed pretty bad – I might have said a 30 or 40 ... but thinking back, I can't say that it was much worse than a 15-20."

My eyebrows went up, "That bad?"

Kelly breathed out heavily, "Sir, this isn't really very scientific. I'm just guessing, and you're asking me to give a numeric value. I'm doing my best, Sir!"

I sat back, "I know you are, Kelly. I'm not upset, but these numbers aren't going to make much sense later if I don't ask you what they mean now. OK, when I had you stand up from your spanking, in front of me, with your pants and underwear down around your ankles, how would you rate your discomfort or embarrassment?"

Kelly began to laugh again, and then seriously said, "About a 3, Sir."

I lifted the pen from the pad, "Out of 100?"

Kelly wagged her bottom a little, and said, "Yes, Sir."

I looked down at the numbers I had written on the pad. "But you just told me that you had a level 5 discomfort just going over my knee in your underwear?"

Kelly sighed, as if this was obvious ... and it probably was. My mind was not focusing entirely on the interview itself, but more on the interviewee, the taut muscles of her long legs, as she tried to straighten them.

But the requirement to keep her forearms on the armrests of the chair foiled her plan. She settled back down, her legs bent, and her buttocks separated wider, clearly displaying the black disc that was the end of the butt plug.

"Sir, by the time I got up from my spanking, I wasn't thinking about embarrassment, just the pain in my butt. I knew I would be undressing in front of you, and I knew from your experience that your goal wasn't just to see me naked. I'd say the discomfort of having you look at my bush was a 2, at most, insignificant, compared to the discomfort of my spanked bottom. Sir."

So I continued, "And, finally, Kelly, what is your discomfort level now – in this position, with the butt plug in you, waiting for your paddling?"

Kelly did not restrain her giggle. "Well, Sir, when I first was getting into position, I didn't think about it, but when you finally sat down behind me, I realized exactly what you were seeing.

"With everything we've done – and as I was expecting that you would see me nude – it wasn't, and isn't, that big of a deal. I'm not embarrassed of my body, or of being a woman. You, yourself, said we all look alike, and shouldn't make a big deal about seeing each other – even intimately."

I beamed – she had been listening. Perhaps she had always had this attitude, and I agreed that it was no big deal, but I really doubted that many women could be comfortable doing this with a strange (?) man they had just met, down in his basement 'playroom'.

I got up and put down the pad and pen, leaving my chair placed about 6 feet behind Kelly's rear. I walked over to Kelly and stood directly behind her. I gently massaged her bottom with both of my hands, and said, "OK, Kelly. Very good. How is the butt plug feeling?"

Kelly signed again, and said, "It's getting annoying, Sir."

I laughed, thinking what was to come later in the day. "I'll take the butt plug out now, and then we'll begin your paddling. It's going to be pretty intense, but I know that you will cooperate and hold your position. I will count the swats, and I'll let you count the number of times you misbehave. You will keep a running total.

I explained to Kelly my 'point system', with minor infractions – such as raising a foot, or bringing forearms off the chair, and major infractions – such as reaching behind, trying to shield the spanks.

"This is getting complicated, sir. I'm not sure I can remember all that. And, what do those numbers mean, anyway? Sir?"

I smiled, as Kelly provided the segue for me into the next explanation. "Those numbers will determine how much corrective punishment you will receive during this level-10."

Kelly groaned loudly, and involuntarily said, "Ooooh!" and then a quick "Sorry, Sir."

"I will give you some choices. Here they are: Each time you reach 10 points, you will inform me, and tell me if you would rather receive your corrective punishment as one hard swat, or a one-cc saline injection in your bottom."

Kelly gasped, and moaned again. I quickly added, "I'll give you the shots on your hip – not in the middle, where you're getting paddled."

I heard Kelly mutter under her breath, "That's a big help!"

In my sternest tone, I loudly asked, "What did you just say, young lady?"

I heard Kelly gulp ... a few times ... I wasn't sure if she was still breathing, but she said, "Sorry, Sir. I appreciate that you would not give me the shots where I was sore from the paddle. Sir."

I laughed, "OK, Kelly. I'm not going to be too harsh on you now, but I certainly will be, if you require corrective punishment. You may chose to take any corrective punishment immediately, or take it during your corner time.

"I'm going to take the butt plug out ... after I play with it for a minute." I grabbed the end of the butt plug, and told Kelly, "Give a little push, please, Kelly."

She did as she was told, and the butt plug popped out enough for me to slide it in and out a few times. I slid it all the way out, and then plunged it back in – and repeated this two more times. Kelly was squirming, but didn't make a sound. I took out the butt plug, and re-wrapped it in the tissue, placing it under the chair.

"OK, Kelly, it's time for your paddling. A level-10 paddling with the smooth Ping-Pong paddle is 24 swats. Don't forget to keep track of any corrective punishment you've earned, or I will give you double what I think you would have had.

"More importantly, STAY IN POSITION, and *never*, *ever* put your hands behind you. OK?" It sounded like Kelly was doing deep breathing exercises. "Kelly?"

She responded immediately, "Yes, Sir. I understand, Sir." After she took one more deep breath, she turned her head back slightly towards me, and said quietly, "May I please have my punishment, now? Sir?"

The slight bulge under my pants suddenly grew. I reached down, and stroked myself a few times, my erection now sticking straight up, with the head of my penis sticking out of my running shorts. I tucked it under my shirt, and re-tucked the shirt.

"Here we go, Kelly." With that, I brought the smooth Ping-Pong paddle back, then accelerating forward in an underhand path that ended in an upward arc into the lower part of Kelly's left buttock.

There was a 'CRACK!' of paddle against flesh; it echoed in the room ... or perhaps it was just echoing in my head. But it wasn't an echo. I kept up the regular motion, swatting each side alternately,

Kelly pushed forward, her head on the soft chair back, and her legs flexing and then straightening with each stroke. 'CRACK!' on the left side, and 'CRACK!' on the right side; the swats coming about once every 5 seconds.

To her credit, Kelly only emitted a few grunts, and soft 'Ow!'s, and pushed back into position, with her bottom high in the air, ready for the next swat.

She was doing well enough that I decided not to stop at the halfway point, as I had planned. In fact, the 13th and 14th swats came down quickly, one after the other on her left cheek, and the next two on her right cheek. Kelly was sniffling, and breathing very heavily. After each of these double swats, Kelly said, rather loudly, "Sir! Sir!"

I stopped the paddling at 14, and said, "Yes, Kelly, would you like to tell me something?" Kelly's panting was the main sound in the room. I reached down and re-adjusted myself again. Kelly sniffled once more, and said, "No, Sir. I couldn't help it, Sir."

"Kelly, I had to stop your paddling, because you might have wanted to use your safeword."

Kelly quickly said, "Oh, no, Sir! I'm not ready to quit ... yet."

I explained, "I'm very pleased to hear that ... but it was my responsibility to respond instantly to you ... just in case. I don't think you really understood in the restaurant, but I told you that you would ultimately be in charge of what happened here today."

Kelly sheepishly said, "I'm sorry, Sir. How many points should I add?" Once again, my erection grew.

I was going to let her off the hook ... but said, "I would say one point for each word, that's two ... and as you interrupted the flow of the punishment, you will get another 6 for that. You'll be at 8 points, so won't have earned any corrective punishment, yet ... but the next time you misbehave, you can be pretty sure you will reach ten points, and be punished."

Kelly gulped again, and said, "OK, Sir. Thank you, Sir."

Kelly really was getting into the role, and behaving very well. Very few people can take these kinds of punishments without getting out of position. Of course, I could have bound her in position, but then she would not have been voluntarily submitting.

On the other hand, I considered the idea of offering her to be bound – but at a cost of receiving 25% more strokes of whatever punishment was being given. She would then need to decide whether she would do better by being bound, and not getting any corrective punishment, or whether she could behave well-enough that she wouldn't get more corrective punishment than the premium she had to 'pay' to be bound.

But this was getting ahead of myself. The goal today was to see if Kelly would submit and, if so, whether she would get turned-on, once she let herself go, and was 'beyond pain'. "You have eight more swats coming, Kelly. They will be given quick and hard, and I'm going to give you several double-swats again, just to make sure you've learned. Are you ready, young lady?"

Kelly promptly said, "Yes, Sir."

I began paddling her again, giving her one swat on the left side, then two on the right, then two more on the left, and another on the right. The swats were raining down on Kelly's bum about every two seconds, which might have been too fast, because after the 6th stroke, she yelled, "Ooooow!!!" and quickly stood up letting go of the armrests of the chair.

She immediately realized her mistake, and before she had stood up completely, she was back down in position. She was silent.

"How many points was that, Kelly?"

Kelly wagged her bottom again, and said, "Umm ... Sir, could you please help me with that calculation ... Sir?"

You've earned either one swat or one cc, so far."

"Yes, Sir," she answered, and then asked, "So I have to chose, now?"

My flagging erection started to grow again. "Yes, Kelly, you may take one swat or shot now, or during your corner time."

Kelly groaned, "I guess I'll take the shot ... during the corner time, Sir."

I reached down and stroked myself a few times. "That's a good choice, Kelly. Now can we finish this paddling without another interruption? If you get out of position, just get back in place, and keep count of the corrective punishment."

Kelly said, "OK, Sir. I'm ready." It didn't occur to me until that moment that Kelly had not been sobbing, crying or even sniffling, much. And I was giving her very hard swats, all on the lower portion of her bottom, only varying a bit left and right, to cover all of the area.

I commanded, "Hold your position!" and began the paddling again – only 5 strokes left, but I gave them almost as hard as I could, alternating sides until the last swat, and giving it in the center of her bottom.

I was surprised to see Kelly rock left and right, raising one foot and then the other – twice, and then she said, "Ow! God! That really hurt!" Kelly suddenly stopped moving, and quietly said, "Sir."

"Kelly, Kelly. You were doing so well.

Now, you've earned another swat or 1cc shot; but if you don't earn any more corrective punishment, I will give you a single 2-cc shot during your corner time."

She just said, resignedly, "Yes, Sir."

I then instructed Kelly to get into the chair, with her knees about halfway back on the bottom cushion, and against the side cushions. She did this, and I told her to put her hands on the top of the chair back, and put her head down on them.

The chair was modern, with quite a low back, putting her nearly into a knee-chest position, only a bit more comfortable. Her bottom still stuck up in the air, and her anus was relaxed. She wagged left and right, settling into position. I told her, "This is the 'chair' position. You will remember this position, as we will probably come back to it; it's one of my favorites"

I went to the small table, and opened the drawer. I took out a three quarter inch diameter vibrator, a tube of KY, and a pair of exam gloves, and then went over to the desk and picked up one of the syringes I had already filled with saline. I returned to Kelly, and rolled the other chair over, so I could put the supplies on top of the pad and pen. I put on the exam glove.

I looked at Kelly's rear, my eyes traveling down to her genitals; her lips were slightly parted, and appeared to be quite moist. I then noticed a quite a few drops of liquid stuck among the few pubic hairs that grew around her labia.

I asked Kelly, "Have you forgotten something, young lady?" Kelly was quiet. "Do you want to think about it, or should I just tell you, and give you another 2 cc shot?"

Kelly moaned, "Sir ... I just don't know what I forgot ..." I waited. She said quietly, "I guess you should tell me. Sir."

"Kelly, when you get into each position, I want your anus exposed and relaxed, and your labia widely separated."

Kelly, yelped, "Oh! Yes, Sir." She reached down with her right hand, and used her long slender fingers to spread her labia.

I was watching closely, and was sure that she brushed her hand over her clitoral hood when she pulled it back from her lips, and out from under her. It was impossible not to notice that she was getting wet, now.

I informed her, "Kelly, as you know, each corner time includes a rectal insertion. For this level-10, it will be this vibrator." I reached around and showed her. She moaned softly. "Have you ever had something like this inserted in your bottom?"

Kelly shook her head, "No. I've played with a vibrator ... but not there."

I smiled, and would have to remember to ask her about her masturbation techniques. "Well, this is still not a very big insertion – your anus can expand much farther than you think." I decided it was premature to explain 'fisting' to her.

"I think you'll find that some of the modest butt plugs I'm using will still be pretty challenging. In any case, I won't insert something this long, until I make sure you are fully lubricated, relaxed, and do not have an obstruction, or something that would prevent the vibrator from going in. So I will use my gloved finger to lubricate you, and give you some practice relaxing your anus, so that the vibrator will go in smoothly. OK?"

I fully expected to hear Kelly make another snide remark, like 'Do I have a choice?' ... but she just responded simply, "Yes, Sir."

I then squirted some KY onto the middle finger of my gloved right hand, and placed my finger on Kelly's anus. She jumped, and then giggled, "That's cold, Sir."

I chuckled, and began moving my finger in a small circle, around her anus, and then centered it, inserting the tip slightly into her. I continued moving my finger in a small circular pattern, as I pushed gently, and my finger slipped into Kelly's rectum. Kelly gave a grunt.

I moved my finger in and out, going slightly further in each time, until the entire length of my finger was inserted, and my other fingers rested on her perineum.

I held my finger still in her for half a minute, using my left hand to lightly rub her very-red bottom. I then began moving my finger in and out, and swirling it around, coating her anus and most of her rectum with KY.

Kelly was quiet, but I felt her pushing back on me a bit, each time I pushed my finger back in further. Again, I inserted it fully, and held it there.

"Kelly, we're going to do a few squeezing exercises – similar to 'Kegels'. I want you to squeeze your pelvic muscles, and close your anus around my fingers as tightly as you can. Then you will hold the squeeze until I tell you to relax."

I waited, but there was no response. It sounded like Kelly was breathing a bit harder. I said, "Go ahead and squeeze." Her anus closed around my finger, and squeezed with moderate pressure. I tried moving my finger, but it was pretty well held in place by her anal muscles.

"Hold it." After a few more seconds, I said, "Good. Now relax." Kelly relaxed her anal muscles, and I slid my finger most of the way back out, and then back in. I said, "Do it again. Hold for a count of 10."

Kelly complied immediately, squeezing my finger and, after about 10 seconds, relaxing again. I moved my finger in and out, as before.

I then said, "Kelly, you're doing very well. Your anus is almost ready for the vibrator. I'm going to have you make three more squeezes. Each time, you will hold the squeeze for 20 seconds, and relax, and then, I will slide my finger completely out of you, and then push it back in all the way. When my finger is all the way in, I will hold it still, and you will then squeeze again. Do you understand?"

Kelly said, "Yes, Sir."

I said, "Good – then you may start the first squeeze, now."

Kelly squeezed her anal muscles, and I watched her rosebud tighten around my finger. She squeezed hard, and held it for the full 20 seconds. Then she relaxed, and I slid my gloved finger all the way out – moving it around a few times on the way – and then re-inserting it, and quickly sliding it all the way in.

I held my finger still, and Kelly dutifully squeezed again. We did this three times, and then I pulled my finger out, and removed the glove, inside out, placing it under the chair.

I placed the vibrator on her dilated anus, angling it in various directions, then increasing the pressure, until she opened up and the vibrator slid in. I slowly moved it in and out, back and forth, and around, while lightly rubbing her bottom with my other hand.

After a couple of minutes, I pulled the vibrator out, and reached for another butt plug – this one about the same size as the vibrator, but with a flared tip, long straight shaft, and narrower near-end, so that her anus would hold it in place.

I showed it to Kelly, and said, "This is your corner time insertion. We'll get it in, and I'll start my timer for 5 minutes. I just want you to relax. Then, I'll give you your 2cc shot." Kelly groaned, but didn't complain or comment.

I placed the large tip of the butt plug on her anus, and gently pushed, until she dilated enough to allow the tip to pass, and then the shaft followed easily, sliding in the full length of eight or nine inches. When the narrower part reached her anus, her muscles 'sucked in' the rest of the butt plug, and it was now firmly in place in her rectum, with just a small round black disc visible from the outside.

I picked up all of the trash – from under her chair, and on top of the pad and pen on the other chair – and took it all to the bathroom. I cleaned everything up, and washed my hands twice.

Walking back into the playroom, I was delighted to see Kelly quietly waiting in the chair, her bottom in the air, with a circle of black and, below that, a wide strip of the moist, pink tissue of her inner labia. I picked up the syringe, and pushed some saline out, until I was sure there were no air bubbles left, and then opened an alcohol swab.

As I stood behind Kelly, shot in hand, looking at the droplets on the thin hair below her labia, I said facetiously, "It's too bad that this punishment isn't turning you on. I'm really sorry – I thought at some point, you might start 'enjoying' it ... not necessarily the pain, but the entire experience. I'll have to try harder on the next few level-10's."

Kelly was obviously getting quite turned-on, but she made no comment. I told her, "You behaved pretty well, for your first paddling, but you still earned 2 cc. I will administer your injection, now."

I swabbed the middle of her right buttock – which was the fleshiest part when she was in this position – and hopefully below the diagonally-oriented sciatic nerve coming from her spine, and traveling down the back of her leg. I held her skin taut with my left hand, and told her, "I'm going to insert the needle now," which I immediately did

"We've done this before. I'll let you get comfortable with the needle, and then you can tell me when you're ready for the injection."

I pulled back slightly on the plunger of the syringe to make sure I wasn't in a blood vessel. I heard Kelly breathing, and a few moments later, she turned her head, and said, "I guess I'm ready, now."

I began pressing the plunger, with the saline going in very slowly, as I was using a thin 25 gauge needle. I heard Kelly sigh, and when the 2 cc had been injected, I asked her, "So how would you rate the pain or bother of this injection right now, with 2 cc in you?"

Kelly gave a quick laugh, and said, "I don't like the feeling, the pressure, but it doesn't really hurt that bad. Maybe a 10?"

I said, "Good girl," and pulled the needle back half an inch. I let go of the syringe and stepped back, looking at the syringe coming out from her buttock, being held in place by the inch of needle that was still in her. I left it in another few seconds, and then pulled it out. I walked to the desk, and disposed of the needle and syringe in the sharps container.

When I returned to Kelly, I realized I had left the alcohol swab. I turned it around, and told her, "I'm going to swab your bottom – just to make sure it's clean, in case there are any tiny breaks in your skin."

Kelly said, "OK," but she didn't realize what this meant. I turned the alcohol swab over, and began swabbing large swaths of her bottom. Kelly shrieked.

"Yes, I guess the alcohol would hurt, with your skin raw from the spanking." I laughed and continued to swab her bottom. I glanced at my watch. "Have you had enough of the butt plug, now, Kelly?"

She cocked her head back, and said, "Yes, Sir!! I've had plenty. Sir." I asked her to gently push, as I grabbed the end of the butt plug and pulled. I saw her anus dilate as the shaft of the butt plug slid out, and the large tip dilated her anus further, and then popped out, with Kelly giving a grunt. Her anus remained dilated and open.

I brought the vibrator to the bathroom, washed it, and then washed my hands again, and walked back over to Kelly. I examined her buttocks, her still-dilated anus, and the territory below. I asked, "Kelly, may I please put my hand under you, for a moment?"

Kelly laughed, and said, "Of course, Sir. I'm surprised you asked me! But thank you for the consideration."

I laughed again, and said, "I don't feel the need to ask your permission for most things, but I want to be sure that you are OK, if we move beyond a certain point from sensual to sexual." I wasn't at all sure that she understood what I meant.

I had made sure to wash my hands with hot water, and they were still quite warm. I placed my right hand under her, and she flinched when I settled it across her vulva – from her perineum, to above her clit.

The tips of my fingers were in the triangle of pubic hair left from her bikini waxing, and my palm was over her labia. That positioned the base of my fingers over her clit, and I slightly spread my fingers, so that they were going around both sides of her clit. I then pushed my hand up a bit, and felt her hood lift, and her clit throb against the sides of my fingers.

Kelly moaned, and said, "That feels good." I moved my hand very slightly up and back – probably no more than half an inch, varying the spots where I put more pressure. If someone had been watching, they probably would have thought that my hand was not moving at all. Kelly purred like a kitten, once or twice drawing in her breath or gasping, as my fingers pressured their target.

My palm was getting wet, and I decided that this had been enough teasing. Kelly would have to wait until after the next level-10 punishment before I would allow her to find her release. The teasing, waiting, hard punishment on her already-sore bottom, and then gentle consoling afterwards would contribute towards an explosive orgasm. I hoped.

I removed my hand, and Kelly said, "Huh? Please don't stop!"

I smiled. Some things about women were at least a little predictable! I told Kelly, "Sorry, young lady. You're going to have to get through one more level-10 punishment. Then, if you still want, I will help you have a nice orgasm, and we'll take a break.

"I've made a light lunch, and we'll sit out in the backyard, and get some fresh air. You can update me about your studies and your career, and then I would like to hear what you thought about this morning's punishment session."

Kelly shook her head – I assumed in wonder, over the quick change of my demeanor, and her ongoing confusion of how I could make her bottom so sore, and then take such loving care of her.

"Kelly, you may get out of the chair, now." Kelly got out of the chair, turned toward me, and assumed the standing position.

"Good girl!" I said, as I walked around her and moved the chair back, next to the couch. I rolled the desk chair back to the desk, putting the pad and pen on the desk, and picking up a small remote control. I walked back into the playroom, and stood in front of Kelly. I raised the remote, and pressed the button.

With a slight hum, the drapes parted, and slid back to the wall on each side of the playroom, exposing another ten feet of length, with a king size bed centered on the wall, backed by an exotic bamboo-wicker headboard that went up to the ceiling. There were small dressers on each side of the bed, with large candles, in candleholders encircled by glass, rather than usual bedroom lamps.

Kelly's eyes turned as the drapes parted, and her mouth dropped open. "I thought ..." She looked at me curiously.

"No, Kelly, we're not going to use the bed to make love ... at least not today; we have an agreement, and a punishment to finish. But as your punishment progresses, and gets more severe, I will try to make you more comfortable, and give you more leeway, since you will have already demonstrated your intention to cooperate with the punishment, and keep yourself under control.'

I walked over to the bed, which was covered with a richly patterned, duck feather duvet, a couple of throw pillows, and one king-size down sleeping pillow with a satin pillowcase. I pulled the large pillow over, and left it about 3 feet from the foot of the bed. Then I said, "Come here, young lady, let's get you prepared and in position for your next punishment – the tawse."

Kelly walked slowly toward the bed, shaking her head, her eyes darting around this new portion of the playroom, and noticing the erotic art on the sidewalls. She stopped at the foot of the bed, and turned to me, again assuming the standing position.

"OK, Kelly. When we reach level-30, I require that the rest of the clothes be removed. Please take off your t-shirt and bra." She didn't waste time getting them off, placing each item on the bed next to her.

She got back into the standing position and, for the first time, I feasted my eyes on this beautiful, intelligent, strong female fully naked, in all her womanly glory – something that would have been impossible to imagine a decade ago, when this particular female was a little girl, playing soccer on Saturdays, and running around the pool at summer parties.

Kelly had relatively large breasts, which did not 'hang' at all, but instead leapt out from her body, with a double-arc, terminated by a darker areola, and pert nipples.

The overall sight of her standing there nude, was one of pure femininity – curves in the right places, slightly larger hips than her body would call for, but she was beautifully poised. Kelly had an air of confidence, independence, strength and pride.

As I scanned her body, finally arriving back at her head, she was smiling at me. I stepped forward, up to her, and asked, "May I please hug you, again?"

Kelly melted, and a tear appeared in her eye. I circled her with my arms, and hugged her. Her breasts pressed against my t-shirt, and she thrust her hips forward so that she was pressing against the once-again growing bulge in my pants. She leaned her head back, and I gave her a quick kiss on her exposed neck.

She laughed, looking down between us, and said, "Well, I guess at least one of us is getting turned on by this experience!" She laughed again, "Sir."

I arched my eyebrows exaggeratedly, "*Only* one of us?" Kelly just gave me a sweet smile. My knees became weak for a moment, and my heart melted again. I brought my arms back to my sides, and stepped back from her.

"Kelly, I want you to take those clothes," pointing at her top and bra piled on the bed, "and run over to the desk. Fold them neatly, and put them on top of your jeans and underwear, and then run back here."

I looked into her eyes and, much louder, commanded "Now!" I watched Kelly's cute, red behind bounce, as she skipped and then ran the length of the playroom, quickly organized her clothes, and then ran back toward me, her breasts – although firm – bouncing with every step. Another idea came to mind – regarding bouncing breasts – that I would have to remember later …

"I am now going to administer your level-30 punishment, a tawsing." I walked over to one of the bedside dressers, opened the second drawer, and pulled out a three-tailed, leather Lochlelly-replica tawse. I closed the drawer, and examined the tawse, as I slowly walked back to the foot of the bed, and stood before Kelly.

I had just bought this particular implement from a British spanking Internet store, along with a few other supplies, including some old-fashioned switches, whippy canes, and leather paddles.

I looked up at Kelly, who could do nothing but stare at the tawse. The leather was so thick and stiff that the tails hardly drooped when I held it out for her to see.

I explained to her, "This is a replica of a leather strap called a 'tawse'. It was traditionally used to discipline children and wives in Scotland, and later throughout Britain. This kind of strap was probably used for hundreds of years, and the Scottish schools only stopped using the tawse in the last 20 years.

In former days, girls might get this on the outstretched palms, but both sexes would often feel the sting of the tawse on their bare bottoms. It was usually the last resort, before the miscreant was caned, or expelled from school altogether."

Kelly just nodded slowly. I saw her gulp.

"You will receive only 18 strokes, but they will really sting. Normally up to 36 strokes would be given – and earlier, you remember, we saw a woman being strapped with more than 200 strokes. But we're going to do a special corner time, which will prepare you for the afternoon session."

Kelly scrunched her face, and looked down; I heard a very quiet whisper, "Oh, No!"

I laughed, "Actually, Kelly, I think you are going to like what I will offer for your afternoon punishment session."

I took a step back. Sternly, I commanded, "Kelly, please lie over the end of the bed." Kelly placed her upper body on the bed, with her pelvis at the end of the bed, and her legs sticking diagonally down, her toes barely touching the floor.

I pulled the satin pillow over, and said, "Lift your head. You can put your head on the pillow, and hold it during your tawsing." Kelly lifted her head, and I pulled the pillow underneath, straightening it, so that it was lying parallel to the foot of the bed. Kelly buried her head in the pillow, with her hands around it tightly.

I said, "Separate your legs a bit more." Kelly complied. I then said, "Kelly, this is the 'over-the-foot-of-the-bed position'." I heard a slight, muffled giggle emanating from the pillow.

"I often give this punishment, while the punishee has a butt plug in place. But you've just demonstrated your ability to hold a butt plug – and we're going to have a special corner time ..."

Kelly wagged her bottom a little. I then said loudly, "Hold your position!" and brought the tawse down across both of Kelly's buttocks. The bed bounced and, as the tawse came off her bottom, a wide, dark red strip appeared where the tawse had landed.

Kelly shrieked. Although we were the only ones in the house, I was glad that I had invested in soundproofing the playroom.

Kelly sobbed once, then cried, "Oh, Sir! That really hurt! Ow, ow, ow, ..."

While she calmed, I lightly passed my hand across the dark red band. It was warm, but there was no welt. Kelly sniffled.

"This is a severe punishment, Kelly, but your bottom is sufficiently warmed-up to take it. I want you to feel the exquisite sting, but I don't really want to hurt you ... that's why this level was reduced from 36 stokes to 18," I added, under my breath, "... plus the special corner time."

I asked, "Would you like to rub your own bottom for a minute?"

Kelly sniffled again, and said, "Yes, Sir."

I smiled and said, "You may do so. You'll see there is not a raised welt. Your bottom is taking this very well ... and so is your mind, Kelly."

While keeping her head on the pillow, and her upper body flat on the bed, Kelly reached back with both hands, and rubbed her sore bottom. "Oooh ..." she emitted a long moan.

I stood behind her. "I'm just going to check something, Kelly." I slipped my right hand back under her, as I had done previously. I didn't have to guess, this time – Kelly was palpably wet.

I held my hand still, pressing lightly up on her, and she started a very slow, very slight rocking motion. I pressed my hand up harder, and then pulled out from under her. "Well, you're either getting turned-on, or you have some stress urinary incontinence."

Kelly laughed at this, and brought her hands back up, holding tightly onto the pillow. "I might be a little turned-on, Sir." Then she couldn't stifle a laugh, as she continued, "That very hard stroke of the strap may have done the trick, Sir ... maybe I don't need the rest?"

I joined in her laughter, glad that she still had a sense of humor about this ... and, might finally be getting excited by the experience. "Sorry, Kelly, we're going to finish this level-10, and you'll take your corner time. Then, we'll have a nice lunch."

Kelly adjusted her position a bit, and buried her head further into the thick pillow. I heard a muffled, and stammering, "OK, Sir."

I flicked the tawse on my left palm a couple of times lightly; it really stung. Once Kelly had reached a certain stage in her punishment, I was planning to surprise her by turning the tables, and allowing her to give me a spanking or two ... provided she had cooperated thus far with the punishment, and had a good attitude.

I could not avoid my hand slipping down under my running shorts – just briefly. We will have done enough by lunch to confirm that Kelly was cooperating, and that we were both getting turned-on; I was now strategizing a new plan – off the script that I had so-carefully developed over the past couple of weeks.

I stood to Kelly's left, and stretched my hand out, placing the tawse across her upper buttocks; Kelly flinched a little. I made sure that the end of the tawse was not much further than the middle of her right butt cheek, to avoid the tails wrapping around her, and causing damage on her right hip. Kelly waited silently.

I said, "Kelly, I'm going to let you control this tawsing: when you're ready for a stroke, you will say 'Ready!' nice and loud. I will then give you the stroke, and you will immediately give me the count, and say 'Thank you, Sir'. So the next stroke would be 'Two, thank you, Sir'."

"Do you understand?"

Kelly sniffled, and tentatively said, "Yes, Sir."

I continued, "After you have called out the stroke and thanked me, you may wait, and calm yourself down, before letting me know you're ready for the next stroke.

"I'll let you wait a reasonable time – like 20 or 30 seconds. But if your break gets near a minute, I will tell you to say it, and you'll need to say 'Ready!' immediately. I'll give you the stroke either way, but if you don't say 'Ready' immediately after I have warned you, then that stroke won't count.

"And, I'll give you one more reward for taking this punishment well: you may ask me once, during the next 17 strokes, if you can rub your bottom. When you ask me, I'll ask if you just want a quick one-minute rub – which I'll allow you to do, and then your tawsing will continue. Or, if you prefer, you may request a five-minute break, during which you may rub your bottom or ask me to do it.

"But, if you decide on a five-minute break, I will re-insert the small black butt plug – just to keep you aware that you're being punished. OK, Kelly?"

She answered quickly and calmly, "Yes, Sir. Thank you, Sir."

I placed the tawse in position on her upper bottom again, and said, "You may begin any time, Kelly."

She took a couple of deep breaths, and said, "Ready!"

The tawse flew, and came down on her bottom with a 'CRACK!!!', immediately producing another dark red strip, about an inch below the prior stripe, extending across her entire bottom. Kelly yelped, but stayed in position. Within a few seconds, she remembered: "Two, thank you, Sir."

I placed the tawse back across her bottom. Kelly sniffled and, within about ten seconds, said, "Ready!"

Again, I swung the tawse, and again a red line appeared – this time partially overlapping the last line. I needed more practice! Kelly hollered "Oooooowww!" She was panting, but quickly said, "Three, thank you, Sir. That really hurt, Sir."

I stopped, and lightly rubbed the overlap area on her bottom; her skin was doing fine. I looked around, at her head, but couldn't see her face, with all the hair falling around it; I assumed she was doing OK. I readied myself for the next stroke, and so did Kelly. She sniffled again, and – after about a thirty-second delay, said, "Ready!"

The tawse and I did our job, and Kelly did hers, holding her position, despite the pain, calling out the count and thanking me, her bottom quivering and swaying. She sobbed quietly until she was ready for each stroke.

I did not let-up on the intensity of the strokes, but kept them all similar, covering her bottom in thick red stripes, from the top of her butt crack to the border of her upper thighs.

I considered tawsing her thighs, but continued up and down her bottom, the stripes necessarily overlapping, as her entire bottom had been covered at least by one tawse stroke. Kelly started to cry, and her bottom shook more, but she still maintained her position, and was able to sputter out the count in between racking intakes of breath.

After the 14th stroke, Kelly said, "That's 14 ... Thank you, Sir. Ummm, Sir?"

I answered, "Yes, Kelly?"   I had a sinking feeling that Kelly was about to use her safeword.

Instead, she replied, "Sir, I'll take that rubbing break now, if that's OK?"

I was relieved, and told her, "Of course, Kelly. You've done very well, and only have 4 more strokes. Would you like a quick rub, or take 5 minutes with the rectal insertion?"

Kelly wagged her bottom, and said, "Just a quick rub, Sir. I'd like to get this over-with."

I said, "I understand, Kelly. Go ahead and rub. If you would like me to do a little rubbing of your bottom ... or lower down, just let me know." I wondered if she would voluntarily ask for some stimulation.

Kelly immediately threw her hands back and rubbed her entire bottom, moving her hands in circles, along the tawse marks, and finally grabbing each buttock with a hand, and squeezing and pulling them apart and back together. It was a wonderful scene to watch from my vantage behind her.

Kelly had stopped crying, but I heard ragged breathing, moaning, and a few sobs, as her hands found a particularly sore area on her bottom. I decided not to be very strict, and I didn't rush her.

I then heard a quiet, "I would like you to rub me, Sir ... but could you do it after ... I don't want to be thinking about taking more punishment when you're doing it."

It was already getting late; I was ready to eat, and I was sure that Kelly would be quite hungry, after we had finished her morning punishment, and she could relax.

"Kelly, I have a suggestion. When you're ready, I will administer the last four strokes – hard and fast, without you needing to say ready, or call out the count, or thank me. You must stay in position, and keep your hands in front of you. They will be zingers, but when they're finished, I will immediately satisfy all of your rubbing needs. How does that sound?"

Kelly said, "It sounds good, Sir ... if I can make it through the last four strokes!"

I assured her, "You will, Kelly – it's going to happen very quickly."

Kelly finally brought her hands back to the pillow. "OK, Sir. I guess you can finish strapping my behind." She delivered this seriously, but I thought, for sure, that I had heard a smirking or mocking tone, as Kelly closed her eyes and turned her head, pushing it farther into the pillow.

I placed the tawse across her bottom, and held it still. I put my left hand on her lower back, and pushed down, into the bed. As I said, "Here we go, Kelly!" I brought the tawse back, and let it fly four times in quick succession into her bottom – sounding like the multiple 'cracks' of a machine gun.

Despite my hand holding down her back, Kelly bucked – her legs came up, and her head flew back, and then her body was convulsing in every direction, as she caught her breath, and said, "Oh God! Sir!!! That stings!"

I put the tawse down on the bed, and said, "You've done very well Kelly.

"We'll start your corner time in a few minutes, but first, just close your eyes, and relax. I want you to keep your hands where they are, and let me do the 'work'."

Between sobs and gasping breaths, Kelly said, "Thank you, Sir. And thank you for the punishment, Sir. I agree that was quite an experience. Maybe after lunch, we can just play Monopoly, or something?" She couldn't finish the sentence without cracking up, half laughing and half crying.

We both laughed, as I slipped my hand under Kelly, and began stroking her, putting pressure to keep my hand in contact with her skin, from her moist, pink lips below, to the neat triangle of hair above.

I slowly slid my fingers along her genitals, occasionally squeezing gently when her clit was between my fingers. I started moving with longer strokes, and increasing speed, although still very gentle and slow.

Kelly moaned, and turned her head directly into the pillow. She slowly moved in opposition to the movement of my hand. I would normally have inserted a butt plug – or at least the thermometer – but Kelly was going to get a good rectal experience for her corner time after she came.

As my right hand stroked her, my left hand lightly glided over her dark red bottom. My fingers settled in her butt crack, and slowly descended until the tip of my left pointer finger was placed directly on her anus.

By this time, Kelly was in the full throes of her sexual response, moaning, moving her body to push herself even more onto my hand, and apparently oblivious of the pain she had just received.

I kept my finger on her anus, just slightly moving it in a small circle, as my right hand continued stroking – and spending more time with her clit between my fingers, which squeezed and slid, back and forth, until her breath caught, she grabbed the pillow more tightly, and emitted a muddled, "Aaah!"

I slid my hand once more over her clit, and then pulled it back, and inserted two fingers deeply into her already-dripping vagina. I added a little pressure, and put just the tip of my left pointer finger into her anus, and held it there. Kelly's entire body tensed suddenly, and she emitted a high-pitched squeal into the pillow.

I felt her secretions squeeze onto my fingers, which I pulled back a little, curling them upward to put mild pressure on the famed, but ever-elusive, "G-spot". Kelly stiffened and relaxed several times, and I felt the creamy fluid of her sexual output fill her.

She turned her head to the left, facing me, and opened her eyes, smiling up at me, and again melting my heart. I slowly pulled my fingers out of her, and grabbed a tissue.

Kelly relaxed totally, all of her weight supported by the bed. Her chest was against the duvet, with her breasts bulging out a bit from each side. Her long hair was now a mess, covering her shoulders, and flowing onto the bed. And her arms circled the pillow. It looked like every muscle in her body had relaxed.

With a satisfied grin, Kelly said, "Thank you, Sir. That was wonderful!"

"You're very welcome, Kelly; it was only partial thanks to you for playing with me today. It looks like you may have finally 'turned the corner' from pain to pleasure."

Kelly laughed, and blinked her eyes, "I don't think the pain became pleasure ... I'm just feeling BOTH pain and pleasure, now."

We laughed, and I said, "Sometimes, you can't reach the height of pleasure, without some pain." Kelly just closed her eyes; she was so relaxed, I thought she might fall asleep.

As Kelly lay there, I walked through the playroom to the hall, and turned to the closed and locked door to the right, opposite the bathroom. I pushed a few numbers on a keypad, and the door swung open, the bright lights of the exam room shining through. The exam table looking perfectly ready for a patient, and gleaming stainless steel instruments were lined up on the shelf.

I grabbed one of the two IV stands – filled enema bags hanging from each of them – and carried it and a tube of KY into the playroom, setting it next to Kelly. I carefully lubed the nozzle, and made sure the valve was fully tightened. Then I uncoiled the tubing from the IV pole, and ran it under Kelly's leg.

I then turned to Kelly, and said, "As you know, corner time includes a rectal insertion. To prepare you for our after-lunch activities and, perhaps introduce you to a new experience, this corner time will include an enema."

Kelly lifted her head, and said, "A What!??! You're kidding ... Sir."

"No, Kelly, I'm not kidding. We need to make sure you're cleaned out properly. Have you ever received an enema before?"

Kelly said, indignantly, "No! Sir."

I smiled, as I leaned down, and separated Kelly's buttocks with my left hand. "Then this should be interesting for you. I know you're no longer embarrassed by what we're doing, and there should be minimal discomfort. You might even find it enjoyable."

Kelly couldn't help saying, under her breath, "Yeah, sure ..."

I pretended not to hear her.

I inserted the enema nozzle with no further discussion, lifting the hose and thumbing the valve open. I watched the flow of water begin. I had mixed-up a cleansing enema, and Kelly would need to get a rinsing enema after lunch. The water was slightly warm to the touch.

Kelly suddenly said, "Whoa! I can feel it!"

I lay down on the bed next to Kelly, my face only a foot from hers. I reached over, and stroked her hair, and then collected all of her hair, straightened her ponytail, and placed it over her shoulder on the other side.

"Kelly, you have been cooperating very well, and I think you have some insight into what my fantasies are, and what it means to submit to a spanking."

With her head still on the pillow, turned to her left facing me, she smiled, and said, "Yes, Sir."

"You're completing your level-30 punishment now, and I told you that you would be getting a level-100 punishment today."

Getting a bit back into my 'role', I chuckled and said, in a stern tone, "Young lady, your father has paid me to administer a level-100 punishment, and he will expect my report to say that it was done ... AND, he expects to see your punished bottom, as proof."

Kelly looked curiously at me. I tried not to laugh, as I continued, "I convinced him to accept some photographs that I will take – a few showing your entire body from behind – so that he can recognize you – and then some close-ups.

"Your father told me that I could give you the choice of taking the photos, or sending you home to him, where you will strip from the waist down, and stand in the corner of your parents' living room for one hour, for the family to admire my handiwork."

Kelly initially looked worried, not being able to separate fantasy from reality, but about halfway through my schpiel, she smiled, and started laughing. "I'll let you take the photos, Sir, rather than standing in the corner while my parents look at my red butt."

I smiled back at Kelly, "Good choice!"

"Now the reason I've mentioned the photos, is that you will need to leave here with a suitably-punished bottom," and since we were both laughing, I couldn't resist adding, "and I always stand behind my work."

At that Kelly cracked up, and started belly laughing and, just as quickly, her smile turned to a frown and she moaned. "I'm getting a cramp. Sir."

I got off the bed, and closed the valve in the enema tubing. I massaged her bottom, and told her, "You may rub your stomach. Let me know when the cramp passes."

Kelly put both her hands under her, and massaged herself in front, as I took care of her rear. Finally, she said, "I guess it's better now."

I opened the valve again, making sure the flow was a bit slower. I then squeezed the enema bag. "You've taken about one quart, Kelly, and you shouldn't have any problem taking the full two quarts."

Her head lifted up, still facing left, "Two quarts! That's half a gallon! No wonder my abdomen feels like I'm pregnant." She put her head down, closed her eyes, and moaned softly. "It feels interesting, but I wouldn't say it felt 'good'."

I lay down alongside Kelly again. "It will when you're cleaned out. We'll do one or two more after lunch."

Kelly's mouth opened and closed, and her eyes closed tightly. I could see that she was struggling, but she whispered, "Yes, Sir."

As the enema bag emptied over the next few minutes, we lay on the bed quietly; I lightly stroked her naked back, down as far as I could reach – just below the small of her back, and my middle finger just reaching her gluteal cleft ('butt crack' to those not medically inclined).

Most of this time, Kelly's eyes were closed, and she was silent, save a few moans and groans, as the enema found its way through her colon. I glanced back at the enema bag, and it appeared to be empty.

I got up and squeezed the bag once, and then informed Kelly, "Good girl! You've taken your 'half-gallon' enema."

I grabbed a small plastic sheet that was stored on the legs of the IV pole, and opened it. "Kelly, I need you to lift up a little, so I can pull this protective sheet under you; we wouldn't want you leaking on my new duvet!"

Kelly cooperated, lifting her middle and, together, we got the plastic sheet under her, from waist level to over the edge of the bed. It could still get messy ... "I'm going to remove the nozzle, now; don't squeeze your anal muscles – just try to relax." I closed the valve tightly, and pulled the enema nozzle out quickly.

Kelly gasped, but then relaxed. She lifted her head and asked, "What are we supposed to do now, Sir?"

I had the belly laughs again. "I'm glad you asked that, Kelly ..." Again, I felt like rolling around on the playroom carpet, laughing hysterically ... but my superb acting ability – and desire to get this done and have lunch – combined to restrain my actions. This was incredible ... better than my fantasies, and better even than if I had scripted a story for some trashy erotic novel.

Kelly groaned again, and shifted her position, rolling slightly to the right to relieve the pressure on her very-full abdomen. I explained, "For you, this is only a corner time ... but if you were getting a punishment enema, you would probably be asked to hold it for ten or fifteen minutes."

I had a sudden image of Kelly running back to me from the desk, and my fleeting thought earlier, "And maybe even doing jumping jacks – your breasts and butt bouncing, while the half-gallon of liquid inside you achieved its cleaning action."

Kelly groaned again. "But I think you've had almost enough now ... and I think we're both ready for lunch ... so I'll let you up now, and take you to the bathroom."

As Kelly carefully slid off the bed, and onto her feet, I said, "We're getting pretty 'friendly' and I know there's not much that will embarrass you now, but I'm going to spend a couple of minutes with you in the bathroom, and then leave you and prepare our lunch.

"I'll come back down and get you when lunch is ready. You'll need to stay on the toilet for 10 to 15 minutes, to be sure your enema has been completely expelled."

I held Kelly's arm, as we walked slowly across the playroom to the bathroom. I stopped her just outside the bathroom door, and said, "Kelly, the most important thing now, is that you not release your enema, until I give you permission." Kelly nodded, and massaged herself just above her pubic hair.

I directed her into the bathroom, and onto the toilet. "I've never done this before, Kelly, but I think this will be a bonding experience for us."

And it would be another attempt to provide some shock value and embarrassment to this confident, young woman, who had been looking for 'adventure' with her partners. Kelly sat down on the toilet, looking up at me questioningly.

When she had settled into position, I straddled her, and sat on her lap, my legs widely spread around her waist, and my arms around her back to stabilize my position. "This isn't too heavy for you, is it?"

Kelly just looked at me blankly – I knew she was experiencing another surreal moment. "No, Sir."

I held Kelly by the shoulders and looked into her eyes. "Kelly, I don't know how to say this – with all seriousness, but I feel very close to you; I care for you very much, and am so proud of you not only agreeing to play with me, but having done very well so-far."

I hugged her, putting my cheek on hers briefly, and feeling her breasts brush my chest through my t-shirt. Then I sat back and looked into her big hazel eyes.

Kelly had a strange expression on her face – perhaps a mixture of curiosity, questioning, amazement, and slight discomfort: she was sitting on a toilet, ready to expel a large enema that had been given to her by a 'strange' gentleman, who was now sitting on her lap

I continued to stare into Kelly's eyes, and said, "I'm going to stay with you for two 'floods'."

Kelly looked confused. I told her, "Please keep looking into my eyes. You may release your enema now, young lady!" A smile came across Kelly's face – I'm not sure whether it was due to being able to release the enema, or due to my sitting on her lap, while she sat on the toilet.

It took a few more seconds, but suddenly a flood of water came out of Kelly. It continued, as Kelly tried to maintain eye contact, but was sufficiently distracted, embarrassed, or uncomfortable with the feeling, that her eyes darted around, her cheeks flushed, and she frowned, dropping her head, and looking down. She let out a long groan.

I put a finger under her chin, and lifted up her head. The first 'flood' had stopped, and Kelly was breathing more rapidly. I kissed Kelly on the cheek, and then leaned into her, and hugged her, holding her loosely until – about a minute later – another flood started. Kelly groaned again, as the flow continued.

When it stopped I kissed Kelly again on the cheek, awkwardly got off of her, then stood at the sink, and washed my hands.

When I was finished, I looked over at her: She was sitting on the toilet confidently, looking up at me with a smile.

As her next flood began, I walked out of the bathroom, looking back and saying, "Take your time; I'll come and get you in a while when lunch is ready. In the meantime, there's an iPad in the magazine rack next to you, with hundreds of bookmarks of spanking, BDSM, enema and other websites that you might want to peruse, while you're sitting there."

I smiled and bounded up the stairs to the kitchen.

I had bought fresh vegetables, salad-makings, and a couple of small olive, onion and sun-dried tomato quiches from our nearby specialty market. Last night I had cut the vegetables, and made a dill-olive dip.

I had also cleaned the lettuce, and torn it into salad-sized pieces, storing it in a baggie. I had prepared baggies with sliced mushrooms, and other salad fixings, and I had also made a special dressing with a fine olive oil, fresh lemon, basil, dried mustard, and a dash of white wine.

I took all of the ingredients from the fridge, quickly chopping a ripe avocado, combining the ingredients, and mixing the salad. I preheated the oven, and unwrapped the quiches.

I took out a large smoked plastic dip tray, and put the olive dip in the middle, with vegetables around – carrots, celery, zucchini, green and orange peppers, cherry tomatoes, and broccoli florets. The oven dinged, informing me that it was pre-heated, so I put the quiches in, and set the timer.

I ran back down to the playroom to retrieve the white wine from the bar fridge, and wine glasses from the bar and, passing the bathroom, looked in on Kelly. "How are you doing?" I asked.

She frowned and said, "The water keeps coming out of me. I don't know when it will stop."

I laughed and said, "Just stay there and relax. I'll come and get you in a few minutes."

I brought the wine up to the kitchen, opened the bottle, and poured half a glass – as a 'taste'. It was delicious, as I already knew, so I refilled my glass, and poured a glass for Kelly. It was a beautiful spring day outside, sunny and warm, with incredibly blue sky.

I brought everything out to the patio, and set the table there. The oven dinged again, and I took out the quiches, and put them on trivets on the patio table.

I surveyed things, and remembered that I had bought a great seeded baguette, so I retrieved it from the pantry, cut it into diagonal slices, and stuck it in the oven, turning the oven off to make sure I didn't forget and burn them. I also had bought a small ceramic crock of fresh whipped herb butter, which I brought to the patio table.

I drank the half glass of wine, and refilled it. It had been an incredible morning. Even if nothing else were to happen, it would have been an epic day. I think Kelly was finally getting into the spirit of the experience. She hadn't used her safeword, nor even complained much. I had been impressed at her maturity and control over her body.

I put my glass down, sighed, and walked downstairs to see how Kelly was doing. I got to the bathroom door, and saw Kelly pulling toilet paper from the roll. She looked up at me, and I said, "Lunch is ready. Get cleaned up and wash your hands. I'll be in the office, but whenever you're ready, come on out, and we'll eat. I'm starving."

Before Kelly could respond, I pulled the door closed, and walked over to the desk. I did a quick check of the video taken during the morning session, saved the files, and reset the recorder for the afternoon session; I would only have to flick a 'Record' switch on the panel behind my desk, and all of the cameras would be put into action.

I sat back in my desk chair, and marveled at my good fortune – actually meeting a wonderful young lady, who was adventurous and willing to play with me, yet inexperienced and open to new things.

I realized that I hadn't been turned on for the past hour or so, despite the incredibly 'exciting' circumstances. I was getting to really know Kelly, and was now seeing her as a beautiful independent woman, rather than as the blank-faced submissive of my fantasies.

Kelly had brought humor to her situation, and had made the best of a challenging first spanking experience. I was getting much more turned-on by her personality, strength, openness, and trust, than I ever could have just looking at her naked body, or spanking her bare bottom.

Kelly came out of the bathroom, and walked over to the desk, taking the standing position, proudly and confidently, in front of the desk, nude, and giving me a big smile. "Kelly, did you bring a robe, as I requested?"

Kelly beamed, and said, "Yes, Sir."

I smiled, and told Kelly, "Please put on your robe. You may wear it during our lunch." Kelly rummaged in her beach bag, pulling out a nice, light satiny robe, and holding it up for me to see.

"Very nice!" I said, while she put it on, and half-knotted the sash.

I walked up to her, and said, "One more hug, before lunch?"

Kelly didn't require any more prompting, and leapt into my arms, surprising me. I hugged her gently, my hands sliding below her waist, and cupping her buttocks lightly. Kelly kept hugging me, and I heard a sniffle.

I kissed her on the neck, and we held each other tightly. Then we stepped apart and, taking Kelly's hand, I led her upstairs.

On the way up, I explained, "Since it is such a beautiful day, I decided that we should eat out on the patio." I opened one of the French doors leading from the kitchen to the patio, and Kelly stepped, barefoot, onto the cool flagstones.

I had been barefoot all morning, also, and followed her to the outdoor table, pulling out a chair for her, and then sitting down next to her, as she gazed into my park-like backyard.

CHAPTER 7: LUNCHTIME INTERLUDE

"Wow," Kelly said, "This is a beautiful backyard." She looked around, at the free-form black-bottom pool, Jacuzzi, and waterfall, leading to a large grass area, and dozens of large trees framing the back and sides of our acre lot. Kelly looked down at the table – evidently for the first time – and said, "Wow," again.

I started, "I knew we would be hungry ..."

Kelly interrupted, "Yes, Sir ... I'm starving."

I continued, "So I prepared some quiche, salad, and vegetable dip." I then realized I had forgotten the bread. With Kelly wondering what was so important, I leapt up, ran back into the kitchen, and ran to the oven, sliding the bread onto a plate – it was warm but not burnt; good thing I had turned off the oven! I then brought the bread and butter out, and put it down next to the rest of the food.

I ran back again, Kelly just staring, bewildered, and brought out the pitcher of iced tea that I had made last night, putting it on the table, next to a couple of water glasses on a small tray. Finally, I sat down and picked up my wine. Kelly picked up hers, and we silently toasted, clinking the crystal glasses together. We each took a sip of wine.

Kelly said, "Mmm! I like this wine!" I put my glass down, and said, quite seriously, "Kelly, I hope you also liked your morning punishment experience ... at least a little bit."

Kelly finished chewing a carrot with olive dip, wiped her lips with the pink cloth napkin that matched the tablecloth that I always used when dining outside in the spring, and sat back in her chair. She looked at me with bright eyes, and playful smile.

"Yes, Sir. It has been an interesting experience. So far."

Her eyes glazed over a bit, and I knew we were both thinking back over the morning's experience: needles, over-the-knee warm-up and spanking, rectal thermometer, paddling, butt plugs, tawsing, and enema. While it had been occurring, it had felt like slow motion; now, like a rocket takeoff after a long countdown, it felt like a whirlwind.

It was nearly 1PM, already, but I had decided on a slightly different script. Kelly had been so willing and cooperative, so far, I had to take this to the next level ... and finally give my exam room a 'live' test.

Kelly was eating her lunch silently, obviously thinking about the morning (or what was to come in the afternoon) – just as I was. I sat back, taking another sip of wine, and she looked up – startled that I had been watching her shovel the quiche into her mouth.

"I guess I really was hungry, Sir." she said, and continued, "This is really good. Thank you for making such a nice lunch for us."

I took another sip of wine; it was great, but I had to last the afternoon, so couldn't indulge as much as I would have liked. "You're very welcome, Kelly. Just because you're here for a spanking doesn't mean I can't treat you nicely and with respect when you're not being spanked."

Kelly took the wine glass in one hand, and twirled a finger of her other hand around the rim. "Sir, I think I'm beginning to understand." I held my wine glass, hardly breathing, and waited for her to continue.

She looked into my eyes, and said, "In thinking about what was going to happen today, I had a general idea – you were going to pull my pants down and spank me – but I couldn't really envision how we were going to spend a whole day together – what were we going to do?

"Also, I had told you I was looking for new experiences and you told me that you would share some with me ... but I really couldn't think of what I hadn't already experienced – I've done a lot ... I thought."

Kelly took a sip of wine, and put down her glass. She reached for a celery stick, dipped it in the dill-olive mixture, and held it up, as she considered how to say what she was thinking.

"I assumed this was just about getting an older man" I cringed ... "off, and hoped that maybe I would find it interesting, as a one-time experience. And, I knew that I could trust you ... we'll maybe I didn't KNOW, but you are a really nice person, and I could tell that from the first time we re-met at my parents' party."

She ate her celery stick, and looked around the backyard again. There was a squirrel climbing the nearest oak tree, and birds chirping all around. The neighborhood was very quiet, with large lots separating the homes, so there was no other noise than the natural sounds of wildlife in the backyard.

Kelly ate her salad and quiche. I know most people wouldn't understand ... here was the cutest girl I had ever met, sitting next to me wearing a light robe ... over nothing. OF COURSE, I could have ravaged her – with her full consent and cooperation – on the spot.

But I was determined to show her that we could be satisfied by just 'playing' with each other, and not turning it into an overtly sexual experience ... as with most of the young men she had dated. They had only one goal; I had been there and done that, and had other, longer-term desires – not instead-of, but in addition to, sex.

There are many ways to reach orgasm – in my opinion, the best is inside a woman you care for; but the orgasm happens for less than a minute, and even a reasonably long love-making session might be ten or fifteen minutes. And it can't be repeated more than once an hour ... or two.

But here, Kelly and I had been 'playing' for hours. I had expected to be turned-on throughout the morning session ... but I was so intrigued by the psychology of what was happening – Kelly's reactions, ratings, decisions, and questions – that I was literally mesmerized by the experience, the pressure of the fluid build-up in my prostate notwithstanding.

We were both hungry, and finished our plates. As Kelly swallowed the last of her wine, I appraised her condition. "Kelly, you may have more wine, if you like, but I want you to be awake and coherent for your afternoon session."

I thought – having had these kinds of experiences previously – that we could finish the wine, fall asleep together in the playroom bed, and then continue the spanking experience in the evening. But I have a strong and focused mind, and was determined to keep to the script, as much as feasible.

I then remembered: I was planning to go off-script after lunch, risking the whole experience to have Kelly try-out my medical exam room.

It was silly – I had already seen pretty much every part of her body, and she had demonstrated her openness, and lack of embarrassment. But I had fantasized about this for so long, set-up the exam room over so many months, and dreamed of what I might do, if I only had a young and willing partner...

Kelly woke me from my daydreaming, when she said, "No, thank you, Sir. I'm feeling the wine already. I'd also like to finish this punishment – whatever that means – and not wimp out or fall asleep." She laughed again. "Sir!"

I finished my second glass of wine, and looked up into the backyard – the grass green, the flowers blooming, the birds chirping, and the sky deep blue above. A perfect spring day.

It suddenly occurred to me that I had never actually finished any of these fantasies! It had always been about getting the submissive into the situation, preparing her for her exam, and then going into the exam room.

About that time, I generally would come, so the fantasy never really developed from that point on. After all the planning, I wasn't exactly sure what we were going to do, after lunch. A few minutes from now.

I got up, walked around Kelly, and poured a glass of iced tea, that I placed in front of her. I sat back down, and looked over at Kelly, who seemed relaxed and satisfied, as she took a swallow of the mango-infused tea.

I asked, "How was the lunch? Did you get enough? I do have a dessert that I was saving for later, but if you're still hungry, I can bring it out?"

Kelly sat back and laughed, and said, "I've had plenty. And I don't want my stomach to have a problem this afternoon. And, didn't you say we were going out for dinner?"

I answered, "Yes, I have reservations at a local French restaurant that has great food, and a chef who I've known for years."

Kelly said, "That sounds good!"

I told her, "I plan to drop you off after dinner, because I think we're both going to be exhausted."

Kelly gave me a mischievous smile, and said, "How about if I just spend the night here? Then we can fall asleep anytime we get tired? Sir."

I laughed. That actually had been part of my fantasy. I gave Kelly a non-committal answer, "We'll see, Kelly. You know we're not going to have sex tonight, so if you stayed over, it would just be cuddling, and maybe getting each other off, and then *really* 'sleeping together'. I need my beauty rest!"

Kelly laughed, and looked down at the table. I said, "Kelly, I'm having fun playing with you, but I don't want to 'come on' to you – you should be looking for a 'real' relationship, with someone closer to your own age."

At that moment, I KNEW I had blown it … talking without thinking first … and hitting Kelly's button. There was a brief moment – the lull before the storm – and then Kelly exploded, "How could you *say* that? How do you know what I *should* do? I thought we discussed this? I'm really pissed, now. SIR."

Oh no! How can I ever recover from this?

I sat there dumbfounded; everything had been going so well two minutes ago, and now Kelly was nearly in tears, and probably turned-off from doing anything else with me.

My mouth opened and closed, but there were no words that would magically recover the situation. I sank into the chair, and suddenly was no longer hungry. In fact, my stomach started aching, in a dull, and expectant way – that I had only experienced a couple of times before.

CHAPTER 8: THE TABLES TURN

I took control and commanded, "Kelly! Come with me, now!" Kelly looked at me unbelievingly, as if I hadn't heard a thing. She hissed, but put her napkin on the table, pushed back her chair roughly over the flagstone tiles, and stood up, pouting, and crossing her arms over her breasts, the contours of which creased the top of the robe she wore.

Now, I said softly, "Kelly, I apologize. I should have known better, but my mouth was faster than my brain. Please follow me, and let's see if we can do something about this."

Kelly just stared at me, but when I walked through the French doors back into the house, she followed me silently. I restrained myself from giving her grief over crossing her arms in front of her; we were having lunch, clearly out of our roles, and I was now the one in trouble.

We walked down the stairs to the playroom and, when Kelly entered, I asked her to sit on the couch. She plopped down, her arms and legs crossed, her robe now falling open both at the top and bottom.

Despite my nervous stomach, I couldn't help but enjoy the view, and appreciate my situation ... if I could recover Kelly's trust. Kelly waited, watching me pace around on the other side of the coffee table.

I realized what I had to do, and resigned myself to it. This was a matter of building (or re-building) trust, and I clearly had let Kelly down – falling back toward the role of her father, and not her sex tutor, playmate, or close friend.

I stopped in front of the coffee table, and assumed the standing position, looking down at Kelly's suddenly startled face. Her legs uncrossed, and her hands dropped into her lap; she leaned forward, awaiting my next move, and the top of her robe opened more, showing more of her full, but firm, breasts.

I looked up a bit – into her eyes, with tears filling mine, as I realized that this might be my last chance to save the day - literally! Kelly just stared at me, waiting to see what I would do next. She looked ready to storm out of my house – and likely not wanting to return. It had been my worst fear ...

"Kelly, I apologize for what I said. I know not to try to advise you on anything – except perhaps your career – and certainly shouldn't have spoken to you like that. We are going to continue your punishment experience."

I prayed as I said, this, but Kelly crossed her arms again, and frowned at me, as I continued, "... but fair is fair, and you deserve to have some retribution."

She looked at me with a blank face. "What I'm saying, Kelly, is that I am going to allow you to punish me. Something I know I deserve, after speaking to you like that. I will give you some ground rules, but once we agree on the punishment, I will be subject to the same conditions and rules that you have been all morning.

"You may give me a corner time, and even corrective punishment, if I don't fully cooperate." Her mouth dropped open.

I continued, "I'm a bit nervous about this. After spanking you all morning, I know you would like to get back at me ... but I'm taking this seriously. I erred, and I think it's right for me to delay your afternoon punishment a bit, and allow you to punish me.

"What do you think? Would that help convince you that I'm truly sorry about what I said? It was wrong, and I know I got you upset. I want us to be friends, Kelly, and I'm willing to take whatever I dish out ... if I think I deserve it. So, ..."

I waited, and Kelly sat back in the couch, looking up at me, uncrossing her arms, her mouth falling further open, and her eyes closing. My hands were on my head, and I think we might have been both becoming faint.

Kelly opened her eyes, and looked at me; I saw only a blank expression – her emotions difficult to analyze, until she suddenly smiled, and said, "That sounds like a good idea! You do deserve it. So how should I punish you? Sir."

My lower body stirred; it was difficult keeping my hands on my head, standing in front of this young woman, knowing what was happening down below, something that she was undoubtedly noticing. I had to think about this: I had planned to allow Kelly to spank me, once her punishment had reached level-70 or level-80 ... but that was after she had received many different punishments ... including a session in the exam room.

Just thinking of that brought a clear bulge to my pants. Kelly just stared at me and waited. "Kelly, it was only a few words – although I know they infuriated you; don't you think my punishment should only be a level-5 or level-10?"

Kelly blinked, and said, "I don't think so, Sir. I've already received a level-30 punishment – plus the demonstration with the textured paddle, *and* a bunch of corrective punishment. You've stuck me with needles and given me shots ..."

Now, my knees were getting weak, but my erection was continuing to grow, "What level do you think I deserve, and what type of punishment would you like to give me, Kelly?" I held my breath.

Now it was Kelly's turn to think; she crossed and uncrossed her arms and put her hand under her chin, in a classic 'thinking' pose. She said, "I think you should at least get a level-20. I want to put you across my lap and give *you* a good bare-bottom hand spanking, young man!"

She chuckled, but I didn't think it was that funny; I knew she wanted to make sure my bottom was as sore as hers. She continued, "And ... I think it might be fun to stick a few needles into *your* butt! Give you a taste of your own 'medicine'."

I had to smile, as I had expected this, based on some of Kelly's earlier comments. The sudden reversal of roles irked me, at first, but I realized I had to submit to Kelly, as much as I had expected her to submit to me ... at least until she was satisfied that I had been sufficiently punished for my faux pas.

I agreed with her that a level-20 might be about right. I suggested how we should do this, "Kelly, I am not going to allow you to punish me with any implement that you haven't felt, yet. And for some of the more severe implements – like the board or cane, you would need to be trained."

Her arms crossed again, and I continued, "But I guess I could do some 'on-the-job' training ..." This would be another re-write of the script that I had fantasized about for so long. But perhaps an even better one, I now realized.

"Kelly, here's my suggestion: I will first go over your lap for a bare-bottom hand spanking, as you suggested; a level-5 would be 100 hard spanks. Then, you could use the rectal thermometer for a corner time, while I am still across your lap. That would be an easy position for you, and comfortable for me. You may give me corrective punishment, if I misbehave during my spanking. Does that sound OK, so far?"

Kelly continued to stare at me, with her arms crossed, "I'm listening; go on."

I realized she was not looking into my eyes, but much lower. My groin stirred again, and I really wanted to stick my hand down there ... but I knew that Kelly would react, just as I would have if she had done something like that. I wanted to get back to her punishment, so wasn't angling for her to give me any more than necessary.

"When we're finished with my corner time, you may place me in any position you like, and I will hold that position while you give me 9 strokes of the tawse. And then, another position, where I will take 6 swats with the paddle. Those are each level-2.5, making another level-5. With the spanking, that would make level-10."

Kelly looked up at my face, and said, "OK."

I then proposed, "For the last level-5 I have an interesting idea. You wanted to stick me with needles, and I will let you insert a few needles into my bottom – with my guidance, as it must be done safely. A level-5 would need a dozen needles to be inserted," I realized I was looking at the ground, and quickly looked up at her, "and I'll let you do that, if you insist. But I have another idea ... that you might prefer."

Kelly uncrossed her arms, and reached for her glass, filling it with water, and taking a swallow. We had left the iced tea on the outside table, along with the remains of our lunch. Not my usual style, but then this was not my usual 'position'.

"May I please sit down on the couch, so we can discuss this?" I asked.

Kelly shook her head, "I don't think so. This is *your* punishment now. And I think you should be standing there ... without those running clothes."

I blinked, and quickly had another stirring down below; I wasn't at all concerned about undressing, but I was hoping that I wouldn't be standing here, in front of the coffee table, with a full erection!

I bent over, and reached down, pulling off my shorts, and dropping them on the floor. I then pulled off my top and, picking up the shorts, took a few steps to the end of the couch and folded my shirt and shorts, stacking them neatly. I then returned to where I had been, in front of the coffee table, and assumed the standing position.

All this time, Kelly was watching me intently, first with curiosity, then a quick giggle with her hand over her mouth as I pulled off my shirt, with my lower body naked, and my penis hardening, but at least still pointing down.

Kelly was about to say something when I approached the couch and folded my clothes, but just watched, and by the time I was in the standing position again, and looked up at her, she was smiling.

"That's better, young man. I notice that you're getting a little excited, waiting for your punishment; but if you point any higher, I'm going to give you some severe corrective punishment!" I looked down, and realized that I was getting softer already.

Kelly said, "Now, what did you want to discuss?"

I looked at her, and said, "Kelly, this is difficult, as I'm not sure what role to be in ... but perhaps just myself for a minute. You took a good punishment this morning. Your bottom's obviously not feeling that sore, or you wouldn't be able to sit down – even on the couch. And you're 'supposed' to get another level-70 this afternoon – more than double what you've already had. As much as I've fantasized about something like this, I'm realizing that I just don't want to hurt you that much."

I looked down and stammered (something I can't remember ever doing previously), "You are beautiful, and you've been so nice – you've taken your punishment, and you have even gotten turned on – at least a little." Kelly smiled, remembering how I had masturbated her, only an hour ago.

"And, I explained to you at the restaurant that what I consider 'punishment' is always a combination of physical and psychological pain.

"For example, just pulling down your pants and getting over my knee is a psychological stress – at least it would be for most people – but the main punishment is the spanking, the physical pain. Inserting a needle, or giving a shot, entails some minor physical pain, but is mainly a psychological stress – again, at least for most people."

Kelly looked confused, and said, in an annoyed tone, "What are you trying to tell me?"

I said, "Kelly, I thought that we could substitute a few of your level-10 punishments this afternoon – instead of hard spankings ... I would like to substitute some other, simpler things that are almost entirely psychological – in other words, embarrassment or fear.

"But I know that you are not going to be embarrassed by anything we do, at this point, so I think it will be easy for you ... and give you a break from your spankings – which *will* continue, but maybe only another level-30 or level-40 worth." Kelly still looked confused.

"My plan, before I earned my own spanking was to substitute a level-20 or level-30 of your afternoon punishment with some medical experiences: a medical exam – including pelvic exam, enemas, shots, and rectal insertions. None of this hurt much or is that uncomfortable, especially compared to the spankings with heavier implements you will get after that.

"Near the end, you will take a large rectal insertion, and get two big shots. I can use those shots to demonstrate intramuscular injection technique, and then I will get on the exam table: You can insert a large butt plug into me, and then give me two large shots (which I rate at a level-10).

That will bring my punishment to a level-20, in total. I will give you 'needle and shot' training some other time ... if you're game ... but today, I can walk you through the steps; I'm sure you'll do fine."

Kelly was smiling by now. She first said, "Thank you, Sir, for giving me a substitute punishment. I will cooperate fully with you during the medical exam." She was quiet a moment, and then said, "And I accept your proposal for your spanking. Shall we get started?"

I smiled, although I was nervous about Kelly spanking me – especially after what I had done with her this morning. I said, "If you will allow me, Miss, I will get some supplies that we'll need, and when I return, I will be ready for my spanking."

Kelly nodded, so I quickly walked to the small table in the playroom, and pulled out the rectal thermometer, small black butt plug, and a bumpy glass butt plug, along with the tube of KY. I also retrieved the smooth Ping-Pong paddle and the tawse – which stopped me for a moment, as I looked at the heavy leather implement: My bottom was already hurting!

I also pulled out a five-pack of 25 gauge 1.5-inch long needles, a couple of alcohol swabs, and a couple of gauze pads. My hands were full, as I walked back, naked, and deposited all of the items on the coffee table. I lined them up in various groups, while Kelly watched intently.

There was already a box of tissue on the coffee table, and I pulled this, and the tray with our water glasses closer to the edge of the table nearest Kelly.

I then got back into a standing position, next to the couch. I was entirely flaccid, now, and – although the prospect of going over Kelly's lap excited me on a theoretical basis – I wasn't too happy about taking a real spanking at this moment.

I looked at Kelly, and said, "Miss, let me explain what I've put on the table. After you spank me, you may use the rectal thermometer for my corner time – you'll have to lube it first.

"In case I do not behave and stay in position, I brought five hypodermic needles that I *might* let you use, under my direction. You'll need the alcohol swabs and the gauze pads for that. I brought the paddle and tawse. It's your choice, but you might want to put me in the chair position for those.

"And, I brought the small butt plug for use after the paddle, and the larger glass dildo for use after the tawse, for the corner times.

"When you're finished with my punishment, we will begin your medical experience. Is that acceptable, Miss?"

Kelly smiled at me sweetly, and said, "Yes, young man, that will do fine." She frowned, and suddenly asked, "Do you need to pee, first?"

It was funny: I hadn't peed all morning, and now that she had brought it up, I *did* need to go. I laughed, and said, "Yes, please, Miss." Kelly smiled, and got up from the couch, taking my shoulders and turning me towards the hall, and then giving me a sharp slap on my bare bottom. "Ow!" I uttered, involuntarily.

As we walked together towards the bathroom, Kelly laughed, and said, "Just wait!" She had learned well from her morning session!

When we got to the bathroom door, she said, "Me, first," as she walked to the toilet and sat down. She looked up and smiled at me when the tinkle of her peeing resonated in the tiled bathroom. Before the tinkling had stopped, she had unrolled some toilet paper. She wiped and was finished less than a minute after we had reached the bathroom.

She got up and flushed the toilet. As I watched from the doorway, she stood at the sink washing her hands, then dried them, turned to me, and said, "Your turn!"

I walked over to the toilet, and sat down. Kelly immediately said, "What are you doing? You're going to pee standing up, where I can watch!"

I shrugged, and got up. She was looking at me questioningly, so I said, "I always pee sitting down when I'm at home – or in a hotel room. It's more comfortable and not as messy."

She laughed, and I turned around, lifted the seat, and positioned myself in front of the toilet. As I started to reach down, Kelly said, "Keep those hands on your head!" She stood behind me, pressing lightly on my back so that I could feel her breasts through the light robe she wore, and she reached her arms around both sides of me. She took my penis in her hand, and aimed, roughly. I winced, and said, "This could get messy."

She wiggled my penis and said, "Then you'll clean it up. Pee!"

With the years of experience I'd had – with a wife, and several close female friends – this was the first time I'd had this experience. As I relaxed my sphincter and let the urine flow, Kelly competently kept the stream aimed into the toilet.

I am a very open person; I've peed in front of quite a few females before. And I fantasized for years about various things I could do with females who would be embarrassed or open – either way providing a turn on for me. In fact, watching Kelly pee at close range while I helped her with a 'clean catch' urinalysis had always been part of the medical exam plan. But, still, what we were doing now was somewhat shocking and embarrassing to me. To ME!!

I finished peeing, and Kelly duly shook the last few drops from me into the toilet. She then said, "OK, you can flush and wash your hands. I will be waiting for you on the couch. You will come back and get across my lap, with no more discussion or delay, young man!" She had said this in her sternest tone, and left the bathroom, and I heard her laughing all the way back into the playroom.

I finished, and walked to the couch and then around the coffee table. Kelly's robe had loosened, and the tops of her breasts were visible; and, as I put a knee on the couch, and started positioning myself over Kelly's lap, the bottom of her robe slipped to each side.

Her legs were apart, anticipating supporting me, and her well-groomed triangle of darkness seemed to say 'Hello' to me, as I got across her lap, adjusting and readjusting myself, with my penis on top of her right thigh.

My chest was on her left thigh, and my head was down on the couch, turned away from her, looking over the surface of the coffee table.

I felt Kelly put her hand on my bare bottom. She rubbed and squeezed, and then ... 'SPLAT!' – much louder than expected, and I realized that my right buttock was burning. 'SPLAT!' 'SPLAT!' 'SPLAT!' 'SPLAT!' 'SPLAT!'

Her hand came down on my bottom, alternating sides, and causing me to rock from side-to-side a little, as the momentum of her spanks shifted my position. I couldn't have been spanking her that hard! I tried to relax my bottom – and the rest of my body – as I had instructed her. It wasn't that easy.

Kelly had administered at least two dozen spanks by now ... and I doubt that 10 seconds had gone by. My bottom was starting to really smart, and I imagined what Kelly was seeing – my buttocks bouncing and turning red with each spank, and the rest of my body jerking around, my legs raising ... Oh! I pushed my legs down, and focused on keeping my body still.

As she continued spanking me, Kelly laughed, and said, "Yes, you WILL get corrective punishment for all that kicking you've been doing!"

I hadn't even realized I was kicking! I relaxed my head back onto the couch, and an involuntary groan came from my lips – it was like watching myself from above, my body seemingly taking the pain, but part of my brain far above, watching the scene in amazement ... and horror.

Well, not 'horror' ... but Kelly evidently required no training on how to give a hard spanking! I remembered that she was very athletic, and she certainly had the strength and power to make an impression on my bottom.

Kelly continued without stopping, and I could not help but lift my head, and kick my feet again. I wanted so much to reach back and rub my bottom – I had done that for Kelly several times throughout her spanking. But Kelly was only interested in me feeling the sting of the punishment ... and I was. I groaned again.

Finally, Kelly stopped spanking; she was breathing heavily, and said, "That's 100." She put her hand on my bottom, and held it, but did not rub. I was surprised how much a hand spanking could hurt, given by such a petite and beautiful girl.

Kelly then said, "So how many points did you total for your corrective punishment?"

I was laughing and groaning at the same time ... why didn't I even think of that? "I'm not sure, Miss."

Kelly was now laughing, and saying "Well, I didn't count either, but we both know you were kicking and squirming around. I wouldn't say that you were totally cooperative." She reached over my to the coffee table; I could only see her arm, and wasn't sure if she was getting her water, or what.

Kelly then said, "I'm going to first give you a 'demonstration' corrective punishment," she couldn't help but giggle, proud that she was patterning my short punishment after her morning experience, "and then I'll give you a choice. Now hold still – you're about to get two swats on each side of your butt with the paddle."

Before I could say anything, I felt two hard stings across my entire left buttock ... and then, just as quickly, another two stings on my right side.

A loud, "Aaaah!" came out of my mouth, and Kelly laughed, "I'm sure that didn't hurt much ... you're just a baby. Now, I will give you a choice of corrective punishment for your bad behavior during your little spanking."

She chuckled, holding her hand on my sore bottom. In a stern tone, she said, "One: You may take another 8 hard swats with the paddle; it will give me good practice for the level-5 paddling I need to give you. Or, Two: You may allow me to insert 4 needles – two on each side, for your 5-minute corner time."

I was stunned. Kelly was learning this stuff too well! What kind of monster had I created? I was laughing and crying inside, as I thought about the trade-offs. My bottom was already burning, but I knew we had a long way to go, to finish my punishment ... another eight swats was just too much – I was only supposed to get 6 swats as part of the punishment.

I sighed, and said, "I guess I'll let you stick me with needles. But I'll need to walk you through it, so it will be safe. OK?"

Kelly was quiet. She reached over me again, placing the paddle on the coffee table, and grabbing the needles and supplies. She placed the supplies on my back; now that was a way to make me anticipate what was going to happen!

Kelly was quiet, but I could tell she was doing something, and this was confirmed when she said, "I'm going to insert the thermometer, now." She parted my buttocks and inserted the thermometer, with no playing around. I felt it slide into me but did not mind the feeling. If Kelly would just move it around a little, so that it pressed on my prostate ...

She asked, "What should I do with the all this stuff on your back?" I started to laugh, but Kelly put her hand on my upper back, leaning over to whisper in my ear, "Stay still, I don't want this stuff falling off of you!"

I turned my head slightly to see her face, very close, with a smirking smile, and her hair tumbling over her shoulder. I put my head back down on the couch, and said, "You may open four of the needles. Just pull on the ends of the package that are separated."

Kelly fumbled around a little, but I heard the peeling sound of the needles being unpackaged. She put them down on my back, and threw the packages onto the coffee table. She said, "OK. They're ready."

I said, "Now, tear the end off one of the swab packages, and take out the alcohol swab." I heard a ripping sound, and the doctor's-office smell of alcohol reached my nostrils.

I said, "OK. Let's start on the right side. Take your right hand, and put your thumb in the small of my back, and your little finger on the bone that sticks out at my hips."

I felt her doing this, and continued, "Now, where your middle three fingers are sticking out, will be the injection site, although there's not going to be an injection, this time. Now, swab me with the alcohol under where your fingers are now, starting in the middle, and spiraling outward. You can swab me hard, but only once – don't go back over the area."

I started, as I felt the cold alcohol on my skin. Kelly swabbed in a circular pattern, scrubbing as hard as any nurse would.

I said, "Put the swab down on the package, with the side that you swabbed me with face down, and pick up one of the needles. I want you to CAREFULLY uncap it, holding the cap, and gently pushing on the hub ... but watch out that you don't push so hard that it rebounds and sticks you!" I felt Kelly moving a bit, and then heard the 'snap' of the cap being removed.

She gasped, "That's a long needle!"

I told her to put down the cap, and felt it drop onto my back. "OK, now you can find the area you swabbed, and hold the skin taut with the fingers of your left hand – but don't touch the skin that you're going to stick with the needle." I felt her stretching my skin.

I had a few butterflies in my stomach, but quickly said, "Now, position the needle, vertical to the skin, above the site and, when you're ready, you can dart it in ... but keep pushing until it is all the way in to the hub. Take your time, you don't have to rush."

Kelly got the needle in position, and said, "Now ..." and I felt the stainless steel prick my skin, and slide into my buttock. Kelly said, "That wasn't too hard. It's all the way in, now."

I told her, "That was very good; it doesn't hurt that much." We were both quiet for a moment. "Do you want to do the next one on the left side, or give me another one on the right?"

Kelly said, "I don't know, I guess we'll do your left side."

I said, "Then it will be exactly the same procedure, but use your left hand to find the injection site."

She said, "You're going to have to move a little away from me, so I can reach." I lifted my middle, and maneuvered myself to my right – toward Kelly's knees.

I felt my penis drag over her thigh, and realized it was getting hard again – mostly from being pressed against her; and, from the feeling of the thermometer in my bottom. And, by thinking of the beautiful woman whose lap I was lying across, nude.

"You can swab me with the other side of the same swab. You can do the whole thing by yourself, but if you have any questions, please stop and ask me."

Kelly proceeded to insert the second needle. It hurt a bit more than the first one – which now was also hurting a little. I took a couple of deep breaths.

"Very good, Kelly. Now you can insert the other two in the upper middle of my bottom – as high as the top of my butt crack, and about in the middle, left-to-right of each buttock." I didn't want to start explaining how the sciatic nerve cut diagonally across each buttock, and the need to keep the needle either outside, or inside of that line.

Kelly pushed on my right buttock with her finger, and said, "Here?"

I lifted my head, and glanced back, but couldn't see where she was touching. "That feels about right," I told her. We were both silent, as she swabbed me and inserted a needle on each side.

I was now lying across her lap with four needles in me. They hurt ... but not really that much. Without either of us saying anything, Kelly separated my lower buttocks, and started moving the thermometer in and out, mirroring what I had done to her.

I started getting turned on, and tried moving on Kelly's leg a little. I told her, "You can also move it up and down, back and forth, and in circles."

Kelly took the hint, and now the thermometer was stroking my prostate, and I closed my eyes, my fantasy of doing this to someone else flooding my mind. Of course, I realized that a female partner would not be having the same sensations as I was, with my prostate being stimulated.

After a couple of minutes, Kelly said, "You're getting me all wet. Stop moving around!"

I snapped into consciousness, and realized that I had been rubbing my erection on her thigh; I could have come within another minute, given the proper stimulation. This, despite the needles in my bottom; the pain was offset by the feeling of the thermometer moving around inside me.

Kelly pulled the thermometer out, "What should I do with this?" she asked. I told her to take a tissue from the box on the coffee table, and wrap it. I felt her leaning over me, across the coffee table, and I nearly fell off her lap. I held on to the couch, as she wrapped the thermometer, put it down, and adjusted herself as she sat back up.

With all the moving around, the needles were hurting now. I told Kelly, "since you're about to take out the needles," (I hoped) "it may be interesting for you to first pull each of them out about half an inch. They will stay there, stuck in me, and you'll see the stainless steel shaft going into my skin."

She did as I suggested, and sat back, looking at the four pieces of metal coming out of my buttocks. Under her breath, I heard her whisper, "That is neat ..."

She then asked me, "What should I do with the needles, when I take them out?" That was a good question. My sharps container was on the credenza, and I didn't want her taking a chance at re-capping them, and potentially sticking herself – thereby transferring body fluids between us – which, as I had explained to her, constituted 'sex'. I told her to just take them out, and drop them on the tray on the coffee table.

One by one, she slowly pulled the needles out, and dropped them, as I had suggested. She then collected the rest of the trash and supplies on my back, and put it all on the tray, again reaching over me, her breasts grazing my back. "Shall I take the thermometer out, now?" she asked.

"When you're ready. You can move it around a bit more, if you like."

I think that was when she realized that a rectal insertion was not a pain, but a pleasure for me. I may have blown it, as I certainly wanted her to stimulate my prostate with the larger insertions coming up.

I thought Kelly would immediately take it out, realizing that I actually want it to stay in. Instead, however, Kelly kept slowly moving the thermometer with her right hand ... and then with her left, she pulled her ponytail over her shoulder, and dragged it along my back and bottom.

It was incredibly stimulating, feeling the tickling of her hair, moving down my butt crack, circling the center of each buttock, and being pulled across my back again. I was close to having an orgasm.

Kelly flipped her ponytail back over her shoulder, chuckled, and separated my buttocks, pulling the thermometer all the way out ... and then plunging it back in! Oh! That was a surprise!

She then took it out, and wrapped it with tissue, placing it on the tray with everything else.

"You have completed your first level-5. Now, let's get you up and in position for the rest of your punishment."

I struggled – and failed – to get off her lap gracefully, but eventually stood up in the space between the couch and coffee table. Before I had stood up fully, Kelly said, "Oh boy, we're going to have to do something about this."

I looked down, and saw that my nearly erect penis was only a few inches from her face. Now wouldn't THAT be incredible ... if only I had told her oral sex would be OK!

Kelly reached up and circled my shaft with her left hand. She didn't rub, but just held her hand around me and squeezed lightly. It would have taken only a couple of strokes to get me off, but Kelly let go, my erection springing up and bouncing up and down a little.

She took a tissue and wiped her thigh, "You've been a bad boy, I might have to give you some extra punishment."

I groaned. I really did want to get her to the exam room ... before dark! But Kelly said, "I will take your advice: You may assume the chair position."

I made my way to the chair, and climbed into it, adjusting my position, with my bottom sticking high in the air. What a great view Kelly must have, now – my 'package' hanging down below me, dangling between my legs. I heard Kelly moving toward me and, suddenly, the tawse was being held across my bottom. I groaned. This wasn't exactly going according to my script.

Kelly said, "Nine strokes. Prepare yourself. You may count them, with a 'Thank you, Miss' after each stroke."

I couldn't believe this was actually happening, Kelly taking the part of 'top' seamlessly and seriously, and immediately falling into the role, as if it were real. Well, I guess it was real. While the tawse was still on my bottom, I wondered briefly, if Kelly really *could* be a 'top', just playing me, as a pool shark would – being naïve at first, and losing a little, while readying herself for the big kill.

I had barely completed that thought before the tawse left my bottom, and returned with a huge 'SNAP!' that sounded incredibly loud, and hurt like hell. I yelled, "Ouch!"

Although I had felt all of these implements, it had been a while, and I doubt that I had ever been struck by someone with Kelly's strength. I managed to hold my position, but my bottom was stinging. I finally remembered, "One, thank you, Miss!"

Kelly brought the tawse down again, and tears came to my eyes. "Ayeee!!!" I couldn't help it. She was giving me a hard tawsing, with the new tawse that I had just purchased.

The 'CRACK!' of the tawse resonated around the room. I was barely able to call out the count and a 'thank you', and I actually did start sobbing, as Kelly finally reached the 9th stroke.

I was sure that my bottom was as red as hers, now. A vision quickly passed through my mind's eye of Kelly and I standing together with our backs to a full-length mirror, looking over our shoulders, and comparing the result of our spanked bottoms.

My erection had faded by this point, but I had an incredible urge to stroke myself, despite the corrective punishment that Kelly surely would deliver. However, at that moment, Kelly began rubbing my bottom. "Shall I insert that black thing you brought?"

I laughed, "Yes, you may lubricate and insert the small black butt plug."

I heard her getting it prepared, and soon she said, "Here it is," as she pressed the cold tip onto my anus. I involuntarily clenched, and then relaxed, opening my anus, and allowing her to slip the butt plug fully in. She pushed on the end to make sure it was seated, my anal muscles holding it in place.

I said, "Aaaaah," and Kelly surprised me by reaching under and holding my penis again. As before, she did not rub me, but held me tightly, squeezing and relaxing her hand slightly. I was getting hard again, and wouldn't be able to last for very long.

Kelly said, "Let's get your punishment finished. If you're a good boy, and take it well, I'll help relieve your stress afterward. She let go and took her hand out from under me; another few seconds with her hand squeezing me, and I would now be cleaning up the back of my expensive punishment chair!

Kelly picked up the paddle, and positioned herself behind me. "I'm supposed to only give you six swats? I better make them hard!" With that, she brought the paddle down on my left buttock, causing me to lurch forward, my head hitting the back of the chair.

"That's too hard!" I complained, before realizing what I had done.

Kelly stopped. "Young man! You have just interrupted your punishment! And complained after only the first swat!?!? You're obviously asking for corrective punishment. Stay in place, and let me finish!"

I had tears in my eyes, but didn't say anything. I resolved to take the next 5 swats without moving or complaining. That was a bit optimistic, as on the 4th stroke, I again yelled, "Ayeeee!"

Kelly promptly gave me the last swat, and said, "What a baby!" She was telling me that I was acting like a baby, not able to take a little pain. But this didn't seem like only a 'little' pain!

She said, "How many more needles should I insert, now?" My knees got weak and I groaned. Kelly laughed, and said, "I'll only use one needle." I felt a cold alcohol swab, circling in the same two upper-outer hip areas where she had inserted the first two needles.

I said, "Kelly ..." but heard a stern, "Stay still!" I felt her fingers making the skin of my left hip taut ... and then a needle was inserted. I breathed in deeply. Then the needle came out, and Kelly thrust it back in about an inch over. I groaned. She pushed the needle in and pulled it out, repeating this six times before moving to my right side, and repeating the process. I felt faint.

Finally, Kelly dropped the needle onto the tray, and I heard her lubing the glass butt plug. I waited for the cold KY to touch my anus ...

Kelly asked, "Do you have any condoms handy?"

I was stunned, "What? Why do we need ..."

Kelly slapped me twice on the bottom, and said, "Where are they?"

While I had no plans for lovemaking, I did keep a box of condoms in the medicine chest in the basement bathroom. It occurred to me now that I would have to move them, lest someone innocently open the cabinet and find them. Not that anything was wrong with keeping a box of condoms in the house.

I still wasn't sure what Kelly was planning, but said, "In the bathroom."

She left me in the chair, and skipped over there, and came back a minute later, opening one of the small foil packages as she walked. While she was gone, my hand had slipped under me, and stroked my already-hard sex organ, and I had a full erection when she returned.

She walked up behind me, and said, "Here." She reached under me and expertly rolled the condom over me. She then picked up the glass butt plug, and pressed it hard against my anus.

The shaft of the butt plug was about the same diameter as the small vibrator, but the spheres of glass placed along the shaft were much larger – at least an inch in diameter. I grunted as the first sphere passed through my anus. I said to Kelly, "Slowly, please! Miss."

Kelly moved the glass device back and forth, slowly advancing it, as each sphere passed through my anus, dilating it, and then allowing it to contract back around the glass shaft.

While she moved the glass plug slowly back and forth and around with her right hand, Kelly stroked my erection with her left – first with the flat of her palm, and then circling my rock-hard shaft with her thumb and forefinger, the rest of her fingers lightly curled around me, slowly sliding along me, with a perfect synchrony of squeezes on each down-stroke.

I moaned, and she moved the plug more violently back and forth, around, and in-and-out several inches, producing incredible feelings in my fluid-swollen prostate. That was all it took. I exploded into the condom, and bucked my body.

Kelly's hands did not leave me, but continued to stroke and squeeze, until I had completed my release. I was panting. She moved the vibrator very slowly in and out, and allowed me to recover.

For not being inside a woman, it was one of the best orgasms I could remember. Then again, I wasn't remembering things very well at the moment.

As my breathing slowed, Kelly pulled the vibrator all the way out. A moment later, I felt her wiping me with one of the tissues.

"Come with me," she commanded, and I got off the chair, only now realizing how sore my bottom was. Kelly was already walking toward the bathroom, all of the trash in her hands ... except the four needles that were now lying on the tray. I followed Kelly into the bathroom.

After discarding the trash and dropping the plug into the sink, Kelly turned to me, and removed the condom, disposing of it carefully, without spilling any cum.

She then ran some warm water, and soaked a washcloth that she had taken from the shelf. She wrung out the washcloth, and then gently put it around my flagging penis, washing me slowly and gently.

It felt wonderful, and I looked down, watching her clean me, with her ponytail hanging between us and swinging around as she moved.

She rinsed out the washcloth and wrung it, then folded it and placed it on the tile counter. She looked up at me, "I guess the first part of your 'punishment' is over. How did I do?"

All I could do was smile broadly, and take Kelly in my arms, hugging her again. Standing in the bathroom, we hugged each other, our hands dropping down and rubbing each other's bottoms. I winced, but it actually felt pretty good. Kelly's bottom must be feeling OK now; I would have to do something to remedy that!

As Kelly stood in the bathroom doorway, I washed the glass plug, setting it on the counter, and then washed my hands again.

I told Kelly, "Wait here," as I walked quickly back into the playroom and put my running shorts and shirt back on. I carefully picked the needles up by their hubs, and carried them behind the desk, dropping them into the sharps container. I reached back and rubbed my bottom – it was still stinging. Then, I walked back to the hallway, where Kelly waited patiently.

I turned to the right, and punched the code into the electronic lock of the exam room. Kelly watched, with a questioning look on her face. The door swung open, the bright lights of the exam room streaming out into the hallway, and I stepped aside. "Kelly, it's time for your medical exam, now."

Kelly looked into the room from where she was standing across the hall, and her mouth dropped open. There were alternate waves of humor and fear on her face, and she looked over at me. I held my hand in a 'please, you first' gesture, and Kelly slowly walked past me and entered my *other* playroom.

CHAPTER 9: EXAMINATION

I said, "Go ahead and sit at the end of the exam table. We're going to start by taking your history and getting your vitals."

Kelly took a moment to close her robe and re-tie the sash, turned facing me, and then pushed herself up onto the table. She looked around the room cautiously, her feet swinging from the exam table, and her eyes growing wide, as she saw the instruments on the counter and hanging on the wall.

I picked up a clipboard and pen from the counter, and sat down on the side-chair, looking over the prepared sheet on the clipboard. I leaned over, and swung the exam room door mostly closed, putting Kelly and I together in a close environment. "Kelly, you're going to get a medical exam, now."

Getting out of role, I confirmed, "You know that I'm not really a medical doctor, don't you? And that I'm not going to 'diagnose' or 'treat' you for anything?"

Kelly looked down at me, and said, "Yes, Sir."

I nodded, "OK, I'm going to start with your medical history." Again, out of role, I said, "In order to make this more realistic, I'm going to do two things." I got up and went into the playroom, finding and bringing back Kelly's beach tote.

When I entered the exam room, Kelly was still swinging her legs at the end of the exam table. "Normally,

I would tell you to disrobe, but in this case, I'm going to ask that you put on a nice bra and pair of panties, and then you can put your robe back on."

Kelly looked incredulously at me. Why was I having her dress, when she would just be undressing in a few minutes?

I continued, "Second, I'm going to let you change, and wait for me, as you would for any doctor. You may read one the magazines in the rack, and I'll be back in about 10 minutes." Kelly cocked her head, and gave me a funny look. I smiled, swung the exam room door closed most of the way, and went upstairs.

I had some work to do, cleaning up the patio table, washing the dishes, and putting away what was left of our lunch – a few baggies of vegetables, the bowl of dip, and most of the bread and butter. I brought in the pink tablecloth and napkins, and threw them directly into the washer in the laundry room.

Then, I brought the pitcher of iced tea, and a couple of glasses downstairs on another tray, leaving it on the coffee table. I opened a small closet at the end of the playroom, and took out a white physician's coat, complete with "Dr. Johnson" on the name badge. I closed the closet door, and walked back to the exam room.

It appeared that nothing had changed; Kelly was still sitting at the end of the exam table, swinging her legs, and reading a magazine. When I entered, she reached over, and dropped the magazine in the rack, then folded her hands in her lap. She had a gleam in her eyes, and smiled – almost cracking up – when I walked in wearing medical garb.

She said, "Hello, Doctor. I'm here for my checkup."

I smiled, and sat down, with the clipboard on my lap, and swung the door mostly closed again. I read the form in front of me, and began asking Kelly questions about her health history. We went through the list of childhood diseases (chicken pox, measles, etc.), and some of her doctor's office experiences.

"When did you first see a gynecologist?"

Kelly thought, and said, "I was about 14 years old, and had gotten my period. I had some heavy bleeding, so my mother decided to take me. It was a very uncomfortable experience, but my mother stayed with me; I remember the doctor being very nice, but he was male, and I was at a sensitive age ..."

I asked, "Have you had any gynecologic problems?"

Kelly shook her head, "No."

I went on, "When did you first start using birth control, and what kinds of birth control have you used?"

Kelly said, "A year later. I was still in junior high school, but had started dating. My mother insisted that I take birth control pills. I've had a couple different types. When I was around 18 or 19, the pills were causing problems – making me gain weight, and my skin break out. I then got an IUD. I still have that in.

"My doctor told me that if I had a problem with the IUD, he would suggest taking shots of Depo Provera – you'll like this: a big shot in the rear ever three months! Fortunately, I haven't had any problems with the IUD ... that I know about."

I nodded, "And you've had annual gynecologic exams, since then?"

Kelly nodded, "I think so."

I followed-up, "And, of course you do self breast exams, at least monthly?"

Kelly looked at me strangely, "Well, not really. I know how to do it, I think, but it's not something I dwell on. My doctor checks every year." Kelly was too young to need mammograms, but she should be checking herself, regularly.

I got up and walked to the small sink and, while Kelly watched silently, washed my hands. I took the stethoscope hanging on the wall, and put it around my neck. I then opened a cabinet, and took out an oral thermometer.

When I showed it to her, she opened her mouth (I'm surprised she assumed it went there!), and I put it in. She closed her mouth around the thermometer, and smiled at me with her eyes. I glanced at my watch.

I took the cuff of the sphygmomanometer, and put it around her arm, pumping the bulb a few times, and feeling the pulse in her wrist. I released the pressure in the cuff, and it slowly deflated; I noted when her pulse disappeared, and appeared again, and wrote the systolic and diastolic pressures on the clipboard form.

I then put the stethoscope earpieces in my ear, and placed the other end on her chest, slightly to the left of midline. I had bought a nice stethoscope with a plastic sensor, so it was not cold, when it touched her skin.

She held the thermometer in her mouth, while I listened to her pulse, placing the stethoscope in various positions. I opened the top of her robe a bit, exposing her upper chest, and the middle of a black bra.

When I had finished, I left her robe hanging open at the top. I then went around in back of Kelly and, taking the robe off her shoulders, and halfway down her back, I checked her lungs, listening with the stethoscope, as I asked her to take some deep breaths.

After I finished with the stethoscope, I hung it around my neck, repositioned her robe on her shoulders, and walked back around to face Kelly. I looked at my watch, and pulled the thermometer from her mouth, reading 98.4 degrees, which was consistent with the rectal temperature I had taken earlier. I went over to the sink, quickly washing the thermometer, and then my hands, in warm water.

I grabbed an alcohol swab, test strip, and small meter, and explained to Kelly that I would be testing her blood glucose level. We had just finished lunch, so the reading wouldn't mean much, but this was the only time during Kelly's experience that I *planned* to draw blood. I took her left hand, and swabbed the side of her fourth finger. I then picked up a lancing pen, and placed it firmly on her finger;

I looked into her eyes, and said, "Here's a little stick." As I said that, I pressed the button on the side of the pen, and a lance popped out and into her finger.

Kelly said, "Ow! That hurt more than those big needles!"

I laughed, and said, "Yes, these are meant to tear your skin so that you bleed; the other needles are very sharp and thin, and are quite atraumatic when they go in." I placed the test strip into the meter, held the meter under her finger, and squeezed a drop of blood onto the test strip.

I opened a small gauze pad, and placed it on Kelly's finger, and put some pressure to stop any further bleeding. I told her to hold it there, while I pressed the 'measure' button on the meter and waited. Her post-prandial (after-eating) glucose level was a bit high, as expected.

I then asked Kelly to get off the table, and step to the wall, where I had a medical scale and height gauge. "I'd like you to remove your robe so I can I weigh you." I said.

Kelly undid the sash, and shrugged out of her robe, placing it on the exam table. She was now standing in the exam room, wearing only a pair of panties and a bra. However, these were not the plain underclothes she had worn this morning; her panties were small-cut bikinis, which were black with lace accents, and a thong back, and her bra was also black lace, with thin straps – appearing at least one size too small for her breasts.

I don't get turned-on by seeing a woman in a bra in general, but this one was quite sexy and, in combination with the panties, made her look much more mature and fashionable than she had seemed this morning. Kelly stepped onto the scale, and I slid the weight across the beam until it was balanced, then read her weight. I then extended the height gauge and measured her height. I wrote these down on the form on the clipboard.

I opened the cabinet and picked up a couple of things, and then walked past Kelly and sat on the chair. I asked Kelly to come over, and she stepped off the scale and took the few steps until she was standing in front of me.

"Would you like me to get in the standing position, Sir?"

I smiled, "No, that's OK, Kelly. When you're in here, you're just a patient; when we return to the playroom for the rest of your punishment, you'll have to get into the standing position again."

I took a caliper, and adjusted it, then pinched the small thickness of her skin and subcutaneous fat around her waist, and measured the thickness with the caliper. After recording the measurement, I did the same with the tissue under Kelly's upper arms and upper thighs.

Kelly asked what I was doing, and I explained that I would be calculating her body fat percentage – which must be quite low, as she had little extra fat on her lithe body – except in her breasts and hips.

I put the caliper and clipboard on the counter and, still sitting in the side-chair, asked, "Kelly, are you ready to do a urinalysis now, or would you rather wait for a while?"

Kelly stood in front of me in her sexy bra and panties, and said, without expression, "I can do it now." I stood up, and grabbed a couple of items from the drawer next to the sink. I swung the exam room door open, and led Kelly across the hall to the bathroom.

I said, "Kelly, this will be easier, if you take off your underwear." She shrugged, and removed her panties, placing them on the counter. I told her to sit down on the toilet, and that I would tell her what to do at each step.

"I'm sure you've done this before, Kelly. We're going to take a 'clean catch' urine specimen. That means that we will collect your urine without contaminating it, so that it can be analyzed properly.

"Go ahead and position your legs as wide apart as is comfortable; I'm going to be observing you, as I explain what I want you to do. Kelly sat on the toilet with her legs spread apart, and looked up at me for the next instruction.

I knelt down in front of her, and had a clear view of her genitals. "Now, please use your left hand to spread your labia apart as wide as you can." She did as instructed, and I saw an expanse of pink lips nestled in thin pubic hair.

I then opened an alcohol swab, and handed it to her, "Now, please make one 'swipe' of the swab from the top of your labia to the bottom." She reached under with her right hand, and swabbed herself in a downward direction, looking up and saying, "That burns!" as she dropped the swab in the toilet.

I said, "Keep those labia separated." I opened the cabinet above the sink, and took out a small plastic cup.

Kneeling back down in front of Kelly again, holding the cup, I explained, "When I tell you, you will start to pee; I'll then tell you to stop, and hand you the cup. You'll put the cup underneath you, and I will tell you to start peeing again. Then, when there are a couple of ounces in the cup, I'll tell you to stop again, and you will hand me the cup. At that point, I will allow you to finish peeing, but I want you to keep holding your labia apart, until you're finished. Do you understand?"

Kelly nodded, and said, "Yeah, I guess I've done this before."

I placed my hands on Kelly's thighs to stabilize myself, and watched closely, as I told Kelly, "OK, you can start peeing now." A few seconds later, her stream started, and a few seconds after that, I said, "OK. Now hold it." The stream stopped, and I handed Kelly the cup.

She put it under her, and I said, "OK. Put some urine in the cup for me." Kelly peed a few ounces into the cup, and I again told her to stop. She handed me the cup which, reaching up, I placed on the counter next to the sink while still kneeling in front of Kelly.

I then said, "OK. Keeping your labia apart, you can now finish peeing." Kelly finished, taking another 30 seconds to empty herself. She looked up at me, and I told her she could wipe.

While she finished up, I stood, and opened the medicine chest, taking out a small box of test strips. I dipped one of the strips into the cup for a few seconds, and then lifted it over the sink, shaking off a few excess drops. I watched, as the colors 'developed' on the strip, confirming that Kelly had no protein or blood in her urine.

I threw the test strip in the trash basket, and dumped the urine down the sink, throwing away the cup. As Kelly flushed the toilet, I turned the faucet to wash my hands. Kelly got up from the toilet, and stood next to me, and we washed our hands together.

I told Kelly she should leave her underwear off. She wadded them in her hand, and we walked across the hall, back into the exam room, and I swung the door closed. I told Kelly to get back on the exam table, and she complied, sitting there in just her black bra, and handed me her underwear, which I put on the counter.

"Please lie flat on your stomach on the exam table."

Kelly turned over, and made herself comfortable, with her head on the small pillow that I had placed at the end of the exam table. I stood next to her, opening a drawer, and taking out some supplies.

I said, "Kelly, I've inserted the rectal thermometer before, but I'm going to take your temperature again, now, while I do another measurement I'll explain in a moment." I lubed the thermometer, separated her buttocks, and inserted it fully, without any further delay.

She put her head on the pillow, turned to the right, watching me open the drawer, and take something out. She heard the ripping of a sterile package, and I turned around to face her, holding a couple of VERY large needles – a full five inches long but a thin 27 gauge: They were spinal needles.

I glanced at Kelly, and saw her entire body flinch, and she quietly gasped before closing her eyes. I said, "Kelly, I'm going to measure your body impedance now. That will require me inserting a needle into each hip, and connecting some wires. You'll have to lie there quietly for a few minutes. We'll be finished with the needles before the thermometer is ready to be taken out."

Kelly quietly said, "OK, Sir. I'm getting used to the needles, now. But I still don't like them! ... Sir," she said hesitantly. Then, opening her big, hazel eyes and looking up at me, she said, "You're really just trying to scare me ... you're not *really* going to insert those incredibly long needles into me! Are you, Sir?"

I had a belly laugh, and Kelly started convulsing ... belly laughing also, while she was lying on her stomach, but trying to hold it in, her round bottom jiggling cutely, and her eyes now betraying her fear. She took a breath, and said, "I'm serious, Sir. That thing looks too long to go anywhere in my body! Sir."

I couldn't stop laughing, I was having so much fun watching Kelly squirm, even after all of the things we had already done! I wasn't going to ding her for complaining, as she was lying there, being – I thought – very brave, under the circumstances.

I teased and then reassured her, "Yes, young lady, I am going to insert these needles," I paused, and Kelly groaned loudly, "but they will only be inserted about an inch or so, not even as far as the hypodermic needles used for the injections. I'm going to clip wires to them, and make a measurement that can be used to determine your body fat percentage ... or your level of hydration. They're only going into your fat ..."

Kelly harrumphed, "I'm not fat!"

I interrupted, "No, you're certainly not, Kelly! I'm not saying that," although the roundness of her buttocks wasn't all muscle, and I was sure she knew that.

I continued, "but, unless you're an Olympic athlete, at least 10-15% of your body weight is fat – more than 10 pounds! It covers your nerves, is part of your liver, and a thin (or not so thin), insulating layer covers just about your entire body, under your skin, and over most of your muscles." Kelly sighed. I don't think she appreciated the biology lesson.

I swabbed each hip, and inserted the large needles, with at least 4" sticking out from her skin. Kelly gave a small grunt when the first needle went in, but said, "Ow," when I inserted the second needle. These needles were much thinner, and should not have had as noticeable a feel, but I had pushed them slowly through the skin.

Although I did not intend to actually measure anything or hook up any equipment, I took some wires with clip leads from the drawer, and clipped a wire to each needle.

Kelly didn't know exactly what was happening, but felt wires sitting on her bottom, and I took a small voltmeter, and flicked the knob a few times, so that Kelly would hear that I was doing something. I then said, "OK, Kelly, this will just take a couple of minutes. Please lie quietly."

I stood at the foot of the exam table, and surveyed the room; my first 'patient' was lying on the table face down, wearing just her bra, a rectal thermometer in her, and two large needles sticking out of her butt, small wires attached to each. This was nothing different than we had done earlier, but in the different setting, with the larger needles and wires, it gave Kelly ... and I ... a somewhat different experience.

The scene caused my manhood to grow, and I reached down into my shorts, slowly stroking myself, as Kelly lay quietly on the exam table. She was really a brave girl, and was being incredibly cooperative; it was clear that she trusted me implicitly.

I stopped the stroking, and walked to the sink to wash my hands again. I then stood at the side of the exam table, and removed the clip leads and wires from the needles. I asked Kelly, "Please rate the pain or discomfort of these two large needles in your bottom."

Kelly thought a minute, and said, "They started as about a '5', but they're hurting more now – probably a '10'". This 'rating' of 10 out of 100 demonstrated that Kelly was not really in pain; just enough discomfort to ensure that she was challenged to cooperate and submit.

I told Kelly I would take out the needles, and pulled each one slowly out of her, depositing it in the sharps container mounted to the wall. I spread her buttocks, and slowly moved the thermometer around, as Kelly lay there quietly, finally pulling it out, and washing it in the sink. (This was probably the 50th time I had washed my hands today!) I told Kelly to get up, and said, "You can put your underwear back on for a few minutes."

She got off the table, put her panties on, and hopped back up on the table, awaiting my next instructions. I told her to remove her bra, and she handed it to me; I put it on the counter, but not without first glancing at the size on the label: a 34C, which is about what I had guessed.

I turned back to Kelly, who was sitting on the exam table now, in just her black panties. Her hands were holding the edge of the table, and she waited expectantly.

I said, "Kelly, I'm going to do a breast exam, now. First, I will look at your breasts while you sit here – to assess their symmetry, look for any dimples or other indications of a problem."

I then examined each nipple closely with a small magnifying glass, making out the milk ducts at the tip of each nipple, and squeezing them gently, to see if there was any discharge.

I then asked Kelly to lie back on the exam table, and by the time she was in position, I had grabbed a small blanket from the shelf, and covered her, from toes to just under her breasts. I also put a small folded blanket under her right shoulder, which raised her upper arm and chest off the table.

I started on her right side, pressing the soft tissue in a radial manner, deeply – down to her chest muscles, to search for any lumps or bumps. Of course, at her age I did not expect to find anything, and I didn't. I palpated the lymph nodes under her arm, and down to the upper portion of her breast. Then, I repeated the process on her left side.

Kelly lay there quietly and, when I was nearly finished, she said, "This is pretty comfortable – the pillow is soft and the blanket warm. Maybe, I could take a nap for a while?"

I laughed, but imagined Kelly and I taking a nap together in the playroom bed. When I felt a stirring below, I decided to get my mind onto the next phase of Kelly's exam.

I pulled the blanket up to her neck, and moved to her feet, where I folded the end of the blanket up, so that it came down only to her upper thighs. I said, "Kelly, it's time for your underwear to come off. I'll take care of it."

Reaching under the blanket on both sides of her, I took the waist of her panties in each hand, and pulled them down slowly, all the way to her feet, and then off, placing them with her bra on the counter.

I then raised the stirrups, which had been folded down along each side of the exam table. They clicked into position. I opened a drawer, and took a pair of First Class socks from a major airline, and pulled them over the stirrups. I asked Kelly if she was cold, and told her that I could put some socks on her, but she said she was feeling fine. I think the wine had slowed her down a bit; she probably *could* have taken a nap, if I had let her.

I asked her to scoot herself down the table and put her feet into the stirrups. She did this, and then I instructed her to scoot a little further down, so her butt was just off the end of the table.

When she was in position, I straightened the blanket, keeping her covered from her neck to just below her waist. I pulled on a pair of exam gloves, and stepped around to the foot of the table, between her legs to begin her pelvic exam.

"Kelly, I'm first going to examine your vulva – the outer genitals." I started superiorly, lifting her clitoral hood, and watching her response as I put a finger lightly on her clit. I examined her outer and inner labia, and then held them apart to find her urethral os (opening where she pees), and the entrance to her vagina. I was planning for her afternoon punishment corner times to include vaginal, as well as rectal, insertions.

"I'm going to insert my finger now, and palpate your cervix." I inserted the middle finger of my right hand, pressing until I could feel the convex surface of her cervix. I then pushed up and to the left and right, while I pressed down gently with my left hand on each side of her lower abdomen to feel her ovaries, and determine if there was any sensitivity or pain there.

I took my finger out, and squeezed a bit of KY on my third and fourth fingers, and told Kelly, "It's time for your rectal, now."

I inserted my fingers simultaneously into her vagina and her rectum, feeling the tissue between. In a divergence from a 'real' medical exam, I slid the third and fourth fingers of my right hand in and out slowly, filling both of her openings, as I casually rested my left hand on her, with my palm pressing lightly on her clit.

Kelly raised her head slightly, and looked down at me, between the 'V' of her legs. I pretended to be seriously assessing her recto-vaginal wall, and not noticing where my left hand was resting.

I leaned a bit over, and my left hand rested harder on Kelly's clit. She let out a small breath, and put her head back down on the pillow. I smiled, and slowly pulled my fingers out of her. I pulled off the exam gloves, inside out, and threw them in an old-style trash container that opened when you stepped on the pedal at the bottom.

I then pulled on a clean pair of exam gloves, and told Kelly, "Well, you appear to be in good health, so far. I'm just going to look a bit closer at your cervix, and take a swab for a Pap."

Kelly groaned, as she watched me take a metal speculum from the shelf. I chuckled, and said, "I might get to 'know' you almost as well as your doctor!" Kelly laughed, the blanket rising and falling, until I walked to the foot of the table, and told her, "I'm going to insert the speculum, now." Kelly just stared up at the ceiling.

I loosened the central screw on the speculum to allow the blades to come together completely. I smeared a dab of KY over the end of the speculum blades, and carefully inserted the device into Kelly's vagina, with the blades in a horizontal orientation.

When the speculum was all the way in, I rotated it 90 degrees, so the blades were vertical and, holding it in place, turned the thumbscrew to separate the blades to hold Kelly's vaginal canal open, allowing an excellent view of her cervix.

I thought that another time, if there was one, I would have her douche with a mild vinegar solution, and then about 45 minutes later, I would do a speculum exam, and use my USB digital microscope to closely examine the surface of her cervix. Of course, I did not expect to see anything unusual, but it would lend an additional air of realism and unexpectedness to the exam.

Kelly yelped, and I loosened the thumbscrew a little. I did examine her cervix, holding a small fiberoptic light source at the entrance of her vagina to illuminate the pink tissues far below. However, I didn't really do a Pap smear, although I did have a good research microscope with which I could have examined her cells. Perhaps the next time ...

I left the speculum in place, and walked around to Kelly's side. I leaned down, with my face close to her, and stroked her beautiful auburn hair; her ponytail was hanging off the exam table. I asked, "How are you doing?"

She replied in a bored voice, "I'm fine ... but this isn't very exciting. It feels like I really am at the doctor – not something that I look forward to."

I laughed, "It's supposed to feel real, Kelly. I realize that it's not a big deal for you, or any other woman, who gets regular check-ups ... but it's still exciting to me. I know it's immature, and not entirely logical – I've seen plenty of women up-close ... but my fantasies are mostly stuck in my pre-adolescent years."

Kelly looked at me, and I thought she might say something philosophical ... but she said, "Can you take that thing out of me, now?" I laughed, and walked to the foot of the table, loosened the screw, and pulled out the speculum.

Kelly raised her head, and said, "Are we done, now?" I laughed again, and said, "Are you that anxious to get back to the playroom for your punishment?" That quieted her down. She dropped her head back to the pillow and stared at the ceiling again.

I said to her, "We're going to do a rectal exam with the anoscope," Kelly raised her head, and gave me a 'look', as I continued, "and then you'll get the large butt plug and your two big shots." Kelly groaned, but I quickly reminded her, "And then, you will insert a butt plug in me, and give me my shots ... the end of my earlier punishment." Kelly laughed softly.

I had an idea – it was dangerous (for me), but I thought it could be interesting. "Kelly, what if I offered you 'double-or-nothing'?"

Kelly said, "What?"

I looked at her from the foot of the exam table, between her legs, "We could play 'rock, paper, scissors and whoever wins 2 out of 3 will get two sets of large shots, and the other person won't get any."

Kelly sighed, "You make everything so complicated. No, I'll go with the plan you outlined. I'm not excited to get shots, but it was kind of fun sticking you with needles, and I think you deserve your big shots." I was actually relieved – I could have been the one to get four big shots!

"As I told you this morning, in order to prepare you for your anoscopic exam and large rectal insertions, you'll need to take another enema."

Kelly groaned, and said "Aren't I cleaned-out enough already?"

I ignored her question, and said, "We'll do this quickly, and in a slightly different way." Kelly groaned again. I opened a drawer and pulled out a long object. Turning to Kelly, I said, "You'll take this enema in a knee-chest position here on the exam table. I *could* use this ..." And I raised the turkey baster for her to see.

She nearly became apoplectic – she laughed so hard, that I thought she would fall off the table. She restrained her laughter enough to spit out, "You *are* perverted, aren't you?"

Her laughter was contagious (appropriate for a medical exam room!), and I started laughing also. I put away the turkey baster, and pulled out a huge 200 cc pressure syringe, and closed the drawer. I turned around and held up the syringe, and Kelly's eyes widened; the smile left her face, and she said, "You're kidding!"

Kelly plopped her head back on the pillow, and closed her eyes, but she was still laughing. I said, "This will make it quick. After I mix your enema, it will only take 6 or 8 quick injections with this syringe – see the little tip that fits into your anus? – and then I'll let you do your thing in the bathroom, while I make some additional preparations."

I put down the syringe, and walked to the foot of the table. I said, "Let's get you lying flat again, and these stirrups down."

I lifted each of Kelly's legs out of the stirrups, and she scooted back on the table, as I unlocked and lowered the stirrups to a horizontal position. I again covered her fully with the blanket, as I took a large open glass jar, and went to the sink.

This was going to be a rinsing enema, so I only added a couple of tablespoons of salt to the jar, and filled it with warm water. I used a glass stirring rod to mix the solution until all the salt had dissolved. I left the jar on the counter by the sink, and retrieved the large syringe.

I walked to Kelly's side, and said, "Let's get you into position now." I removed the blanket as she turned over onto her stomach, and pushed herself up into a knee-chest position. I told her, "Get down fully on your chest; you can put your head on the pillow."

She adjusted her position, pulling the pillow down under her head. I laid her ponytail alongside her on the exam table, and lightly stroked her back for a minute or two. Kelly was silent.

I then walked to the foot of the bed, and drew about 6 ounces of the enema solution into the large syringe. I tilted the syringe back and lubed the tip with KY, and then turned around, facing Kelly's upturned bottom. Her anus was relaxed, and her labia were slightly parted beneath. I said, "OK, Kelly, I'm going to insert the tip, and inject the first portion of your enema."

I positioned the syringe and slowly advanced the lubed tip through her anus. Kelly stayed still and quiet, until I suddenly pushed hard on the plunger, and the full syringe was emptied into her rectum in a few seconds; Kelly murmured "Oooooh!"

I removed the syringe from her bottom, refilling it and repeating the process of quickly injecting the warm saline solution into her. I had made-up a gallon or so (which would take about 20 injections), but didn't know how much she would be able to take. After 3 syringes of enema solution had been injected, I asked Kelly, "How are you doing?"

Kelly softly said, "I don't know. It feels pretty strange. I guess I'm OK ... but this isn't the way I usually plan to spend my Saturday afternoons!"

We laughed again, and I injected another syringe full of solution into her. It occurred to me that I should purchase some retention catheters, that are fitted with two balloons that can be expanded (one inside and one outside) to hold the enema in; I would have to place a few more orders via the Internet.

I put down the syringe, and rubbed Kelly's bottom – which I realized wasn't that red anymore. I then reached around, and put my hand on her belly, not really feeling the expansion that the few syringes of saline might have created.

I filled another syringe, and injected it into her, getting into a pattern of waiting a minute or so, then injecting the 200 cc syringe into her in about 10 seconds.

It took another 10 minutes, but Kelly took 14 syringes, which I calculated to be nearly 3 quarts. When I reached around and felt her abdomen again, it was clearly distended. Kelly was moaning now, so I dumped the rest of the solution down the drain, and left the jar and syringe in the sink.

I helped Kelly get down from the exam table, and walked her across to the bathroom. She walked over and sat down on the toilet and, standing at the door, I said, "I'll give you some privacy, now." Kelly just laughed, as I pulled the door nearly closed.

I knew Kelly would need at least 15 minutes in the bathroom, so I sat down at my desk, and carefully prepared four 6-cc shots, using standard 22-gauge, 1.5-inch long needles and 10 cc syringes. I brought the shots to the exam room, and lined them up on the counter. I took out some alcohol swabs and gauze pads.

Then I returned to the playroom, and took two large butt plugs from the drawer in the small table. I went back to the exam room and lubricated them well, placing them on paper towels on the counter. I then washed my hands at the sink in the exam room, and went upstairs.

The wine was still on the counter, so I poured a glass, and went out to the patio. The day was still beautiful – it was a shame that we had stayed inside almost the entire day, when we could have been out in the fresh air.

Well, it wasn't that much of a shame, as I was very pleased with how the day was going with Kelly so far. I sat back in the chaise, looking at the trees, now gently swaying in the breeze, and sipped my wine, wondering whether I would ever have a more perfect day playing out my fantasies.

I guess I'd never fantasized in the backyard. Now that my mind was drifting, the experiences of the morning began to blend in with my visions of the backyard, and I imagined several new things that a play partner (or 'partners') and I could do, while out in the beautiful spring weather. Incorporating the pool, Jacuzzi, soft grass and boulders decoratively placed around the yard, there were many opportunities.

An image flashed through my mind, of Kelly running around the pool at a warm summer evening party ... she was not the 11-year old little girl, but the fully-grown woman, prancing around the patio nude and teasing others at the party to join her skinnydipping.

The experience with Kelly would form the basis of many of my future fantasies, and I still wanted to get to know her better – including the life experiences that had molded her personality, morals, values, and beliefs. I finished the wine, and walked back into the house, quickly rinsing the glass and leaving it on the counter.

I walked down the stairs, and saw that the bathroom door was still swung closed. I stopped outside the door, and called to Kelly inside, "Everything OK?" She laughed and said, "Yeah, I think it's finished. I'll be out in a few minutes."

I walked into the playroom, and over to the office corner. I reset the closed circuit system, and restarted recording the images from a dozen high resolution cameras that I had discretely installed in the ceiling.

I sat down at the desk, and thought about the plan for Kelly's afternoon punishment session. We had already gone off the script, and I was still to get a couple of big shots myself – something that I had imagined for another day, but nothing that I had expected to occur today, as Kelly was supposed to be the 'punishee'.

I subconsciously reached a hand back and rubbed my bottom; although it was no longer stinging, I could still feel a dull pain across both buttocks. Maybe, it *would* be a good idea to end the session early, and ask Kelly to return for more – perhaps tomorrow?

As I was thinking these things, Kelly walked out of the bathroom, and stood at the doorway to the playroom – her nude body beautifully framed by the door, and a relaxed smile on her face.

"Do you want me to put my bra and underwear back on, or my robe ... or just stay like this?" She looked down at her body and then up at me, and her cheeks seemed to get rosier.

I replied, "Why don't you grab your robe and clothes – and the tote bag you brought – and come in here?"

Kelly disappeared into the exam room for a moment, and came back out carrying the tote bag, and a wad of clothing in her hands. She walked up to the desk, and put the clothes on the empty chair, and then got back into the standing position.

I asked, "How do you feel now, Kelly, after your second enema?"

She laughed, and said, "Cleaned out, Sir. I can't believe how much water came out of me!"

I said, "Being cleaned out will make it nicer, when I do the anoscopic exam ... and when we do some large rectal insertions later; remember, young lady, you still have a punishment to complete, along with a few more corner times." Kelly looked down, and shifted her weight, but didn't groan or complain.

CHAPTER 10: FASHION SHOW

I then shifted gears, "Kelly, since you brought a whole bag of clothes, why don't you model a few things for me? I'd like to see the kind of bras and panties you usually wear (or wear for 'special occasions'), and some of your sexier lingerie, if you brought any. You may relax, Kelly – you don't have to stay in the standing position during your 'fashion show'."

Kelly chuckled, dropping her arms, and reached over to the tote bag on the chair. She rummaged around a little, and pulled out a few things. With a tiny wadded piece of cloth in her fist, she looked up at me and said, "As 'less is more', and I'm already undressed, I'll model a few panties, then add bras, and then I'll show you a few other things I've brought – per your instructions. Sir."

I smiled, sat back in my executive chair, and said, "That will be fine, Kelly."

She put on the panties that she had been holding, and turned to face me, getting back into the standing position, with her hands on her hips. She smiled at me confidently, proud of her body – and, evidently, the skimpy clothing she had brought with her. The panties were a deep purple, nearly transparent material, with a pink lace waistband. They were stylish and sexy.

Kelly then turned around, with her hands still on her hips, and her feet set in a wide stance. The back of the panties continued the same thin purple material and pink lace waist, but were cut very high at the bottom, exposing the lower half of each of her buttocks – which seemed to protrude ... (I imagined the image upside-down), in a very similar way to the cleavage she showed with the small bra she had worn earlier.

Kelly whirled around, and said, "Do you like them, Sir?" She bent over the chair, and reached down into the tote bag, pulling out a matching bra. Standing up, facing me, and smiling into my eyes, Kelly put on the bra.

She was gorgeous, and I briefly considered turning the afternoon into a photo session. We could go out into the backyard, and I knew exactly where I would like to have her pose – so that I could get some fashion shots, and play – so that I could take some candid's of her ... although I doubted that I could capture the bright, perky, energetic, and humorous air that characterized her.

I re-focused on Kelly, and said, "They're beautiful, Kelly. I was just thinking that I would love to photograph you sometime – some portraits, fashion shots, semi-nudes, nudes, and candid's. Perhaps we could spend a full day outside – in the backyard," and then it hit me, "Or even at a small skinny dipping pond that is not far from here."

Kelly said, brightly, "I don't know much about modeling, but I would like that!"

Kelly reached behind her, unclasping the bra, and pulling it down her arms and off. Then she reached down and pushed her panties all the way to the floor, stepped out of them, and then bent over to pick them up and put the already-modeled clothes on the chair, next to the bag.

She reached into the bag and brought out a few more pairs of underwear, which she modeled – putting each pair on, standing up for me to see, and then turning around slowly – mimicking a fashion model. Then, I would nod, and she would remove that pair, and try on another.

The third pair was an interesting cut – the front being bigger on one side, and becoming smaller diagonally to the other side. When she turned around, I realized that these were thongs, with a tiny triangle of fabric sitting just above the cleavage of her butt.

Without a word, she pulled these off, and threw them into the pile, and reached into the tote bag again. She pulled out a skimpy bathing suit, holding it up for me to see, before quickly getting herself into it.

I couldn't help slipping my hand under my shorts, and doing some unobtrusive stroking – this was better than any *'Sports Illustrated'* swimsuit issue!

Kelly stood up, with her hands on her hips, wearing what was probably the sexiest bathing suit I had seen (of course, as I primarily frequented nude beaches, I seldom actually saw women in bathing suits). Kelly's suit was lime green, the front barely covering Kelly's dark triangle, thin strings extending from the top of the front, around her waist, disappearing behind her.

She turned around to show off the back of the suit, but I realized there was *no* back – just another string tied onto the string at her waist, and disappearing down between her buttocks.

She then bent over at the waist, putting her hands on her knees, and giving me an incredible view of her beautiful rear. Kelly turned her head back toward me, and said, "You don't need me to be entirely nude in order to spank my bare bottom, Sir!"

We laughed, and she got up and turned to face me again. "This is my Brazilian String." She looked down, and took the top of the front on each side, and pulled – it covered more of her front; then she pushed the fabric together, making a thin strip of what looked like pleated drapes. Now, it definitely didn't cover all of her pubic triangle.

Only now, did I notice her top – another set of strings, holding two, very small, triangles of lime green fabric. The top was much too small for her, with most of her breasts bulging out around the sides.

Kelly had tightened the top to pull her volcano-shaped breasts closer to her chest, squeezing them out around the triangle that was the Brazilian string top. I just shook my head, and said, "That's a very sexy bathing suit, Kelly!"

Kelly smiled, and batted her eyelashes at me a few times, "THANK you, Sir!"

I then had to ask her, "Kelly, have you considered removing all of your hair, down there?"

Kelly chuckled, and said, "Not really, Sir. This is my first Bikini wax – actually 'extended' Bikini wax – which I got a few weeks ago, realizing that summer was almost here."

I thought a few moments, and followed-up, "You would look very nice with a Brazilian wax, to match your Brazilian string; I really like the style where you leave a 'landing strip' of short hair."

Kelly laughed, "Yeah, I saw some of those 'styles' on a women's Internet site ... but I wasn't sure I was brave enough to actually look that way ... or brave enough to lie down in a 'butterfly' position for the beautician to do it."

The germ of another fantasy sprung to mind, and I realized that my hand was still around my hardening member.

I removed my hand, and leaned forward towards Kelly, "I would very much like to see you with a Brazilian ... or even 'Hollywood' wax."

Kelly cocked her head in a questioning way, and I guessed that she hadn't fully done her research into this area. "But I would like it even more, if I could watch you *getting* waxed. I would love to learn how to do it, but probably wouldn't get many women to volunteer to let me practice on them!"

Kelly laughed, and said, "I doubt it, Sir."

I continued, "But I do know someone who has done waxing for years; she's actually a close friend, and perhaps she would agree to come over here, and play with us? ... I mean, give you a full waxing experience, while I watch." Now we were both laughing.

She put her hands back on her hips, and said, "I'll consider that, Sir."

I smiled, and asked, "What else did you bring?" She turned to the tote bag, and I got an interesting side-view of her Brazilian string; it wouldn't take much Photoshopping, and she would look like she were standing there nude. It was very sexy ... even though I had been seeing her nude all day.

Kelly lifted more fabric out of the tote bag – it seemed bottomless ... which is exactly what Kelly was, a moment later, when she pulled on a string tied into a bow at the waist, and the Brazilian bottom came off. Kelly took off the top, and put the lime green suit on top of the growing pile of clothing.

I was then surprised when she put on a pair of pajamas. They were very nice, but ... now, I was the one with the cocked head.

As Kelly finished buttoning the pajama top, she looked at me and said, "Well, Sir, you did request that I bring whatever I normally sleep in ... and this is it."

I laughed, and said, "They're very nice, Kelly. I wouldn't mind snuggling with you wearing that outfit."

There was nothing inherently sexy about the pajamas, they were very standard; but Kelly's beauty somehow morphed from that of a sexy woman, to that of a teenage girl, and I pictured Kelly walking around her parents' house in those pajamas. That got me to thinking ... again.

"Kelly, how casual are you around your family – in fact how casual is your whole family – about nudity? For example, do you walk around in your underwear, in front of your brothers? Do you ever see your father undressed? Has your family ever gone to a nude beach, together?"

Kelly was shifting her weight, and I said, "Why don't you sit down, while we talk?"

She looked at the pile of clothes on the chair next to her ... and then the clothes she had worn this morning, neatly piled on the other chair. She walked over, taking the outfit she had stripped out of this morning and putting it on the floor, next to the leg of the desk. She then rolled the chair so it was centered in front of the desk, and sat down.

How could a person look so sexy in pajamas? Both the sleeves and legs were long, and with the top buttoned up, not much of her body was showing, other than her hands and feet, and her long neck rising from the 'V' of the pajama top. She settled into the chair, and looked at me.

"Well, Sir, when we were little kids, I guess we ran around in our underwear ... and I even remember going to the doctor with my brothers, and we watched each other getting checked-up. But, by the time I was around 12, my body was developing, and my brothers were much older – and already dating ... so I was pretty modest in front of them."

She continued, "Much more recently – in fact only a couple of years ago, my oldest brother and I did go to a nude beach. It wasn't a big deal, and he mainly played in the water, leaving me to get an all-over tan. My parents are open about nudity, I think, but they don't walk around without clothes at home ... as far as I know."

She giggled, perhaps imagining the scene of her mother at the stove making pancakes for the family and her father sitting at the breakfast table, reading the paper ... both of them nude?

Kelly went on, "My brothers were off at school, but when I was in my 'wild' period, I did go skinny dipping in our pool, and even invited some of my girlfriends to join me. Only once did my parents return home early from a movie, and walk out into the backyard, seeing us frolicking in the flickering blue light of the pool water. They weren't upset, just walked back into the house.

"But my girlfriends screamed and laughed, and weren't too pleased that my dad had seen them nude in the pool; they were probably 15 or 16 at the time, and pretty nervous about having a man see them undressed. In those days, I walked around in front of my father in my bra and underwear; I guess I was the typical rebellious teenager ..."

Kelly then looked at me and said, "Of course, most of my generation is pretty casual about nudity, and even all that bathroom stuff. You have to realize, I – and probably most students, these days – lived in a coed dorm; we even had coed bathrooms, one for every four rooms, with about an equal split of males and females. It was a shock when I first moved into the dorm, but I got used to it pretty quickly – probably within a few weeks.

"My entire four years as an undergraduate were spent sharing a bathroom with different guys and girls, as seniors graduated, and others moved into their rooms. We were still pretty private, and didn't just walk down the hall nude; at least not most of us," she said, her eyes glazed, and obviously remembering one of her dorm experiences.

She then looked confused, and said, "I guess I still don't really get it: You grew up at the end of the 'hippie' era of nudity and free sex; you were married for more than

20 years; and you've been with – and evidently played with – many women ... and you are still getting turned on by seeing women undress, or pee?" She was quiet, in thought.

I was a bit peeved, as I thought I had already explained this. "Kelly, you know that I don't get turned on just by seeing a woman nude. As you know, I've gone to nude beaches for years, and I've seen many of my close female friends nude – and even taken showers with them – without getting turned on ... much."

I looked into the playroom, and then back at Kelly, "But my turn-ons are all rooted back in my childhood, and are – as you know – based on things that I was afraid of doing, or that I thought other people should be afraid of ... but they were either open enough or brave enough to do it, or voluntarily submitted to embarrassment or pain.

"A woman undressing in front of someone who is not close to her, just because he asked – even though she knew she would be embarrassed; a woman submitting to a punishment, even though she knew that she would receive pain; or a woman willingly doing something new that she thought she might not enjoy (like going to a nude beach, or eating Indian food), but which she grew to enjoy.

"I know I'm repeating myself, but I don't know how else to describe it. Of course, through the years, my repertoire of turn-ons has expanded. But I'm still excited by many of the same scenarios that I fantasized about decades ago."

Kelly then asked, "But when you've acted out these fantasies, do you still have them? Does role playing your fantasies make them more or less exciting to you?"

That was a very good question – the answer to which I wasn't sure I knew.

"Well, Kelly, I've had a few prior opportunities to play out some fantasies – but my fantasies weren't detailed enough to know what I really wanted to do.

"The role play experience was fun, but it was after days, months, and even years, that I thought back on that experience, reliving it in my fantasies enlivened by many things that I know about now, or have thought about since then, but never considered during the real-life session. So those experiences contributed to years of additional, very detailed, fantasies."

Kelly sat in front of the desk in her pajamas, looking very cute, but also thoughtful – taking in my explanation, and pondering it, as I continued.

"In fact, I've always assumed that I just needed one or two of these kind of experiences to keep me loaded with fantasies. However, I'm not so sure what the result of our session today will be."

Kelly cocked her head, "Why would this be any different from your prior experiences?"

I thought, and answered, "I'm not sure – maybe because I've spent so long thinking of 'detailed' things to do ... and in our morning session, we've already done most of them! As we sit here, I'm re-thinking a bit what we should do for the afternoon session."

Kelly's eyes lit up, and said, "Go for some ice cream! Sir?"

I laughed, "I'll be glad to take you for some ice cream, but not until your punishment has been completed."

Kelly frowned and made a mock groan, then smiled again, and looked up at me with bright eyes, "I seem to remember that you still have some punishment left also ... Sir."

"Oh, that's right. Thanks for reminding me!" We both laughed. Then, more seriously, I faced Kelly, "While we're both comfortable sitting here, I'll explain my ideas for our afternoon session."

Kelly was confused when I got up and walked into the playroom, but just smiled and nodded, when I returned carrying the tray with the pitcher of iced tea – the ice about half melted, and two crystal glasses. Placing the tray on the desk, Kelly poured herself a glass, while I walked around to my executive chair. I then reached across and poured a glass for myself.

"Where was I? Oh, yes, thinking about the punishment plan for this afternoon." Kelly sipped her tea, looking at me over the rim of the glass; I could not read her expression.

"First, as I explained before lunch, we're going into the exam room, and I'm going to complete your medical exam by further dilating your anus, and examining you with an 'anoscope'. I'll then insert a large butt plug. The original idea was that you would then lie on the exam table, while I gave you two big shots – one on each side – that are left in for a couple of minutes.

"Remember, this was to be part of your punishment. Then, I would remove the plug, and you would do the same with me – dilating my anus, inserting a large butt plug and giving me two shots – under my direction – while I lay on the exam table."

Then, my mathematical mind took over. "You've completed a level-40 already – a level-30's worth of spanking, and a level-10 physical exam and enema. The shots will represent another level-10, and the butt plugs will be the corner time – just done at the same time as the main punishment.

"At the end of this, my punishment will be complete (a level-20, for misspeaking during lunch), and you will then have completed a total of level-50. That means you would be halfway through your punishment."

Kelly was nodding slowly until this last part, when she looked down and groaned.

"But here's where it gets strange," I started.

Kelly looked up and muttered, "Oh, no ..."

I smiled at her and said, "No – I don't mean we're going to do something strange ... well, maybe ... but I was thinking how strange it is how I'm thinking about the afternoon."

Kelly just stared at me and waited. "I *would* like you to experience a 'taste' of the spoon, hairbrush," Kelly closed her eyes, and I continued, "flogger, maybe the switch, possibly the board (also known as the 'school paddle'), and certainly the cane."

Kelly was breathing harder, and her eyes were still closed; I hoped she wasn't about to faint, and was glad that I had brought the iced tea into the office for us.

"But, I'm not sure I want to hurt you that much – I mean, give you that much pain. I'm not a mean or sadistic person, and you've cooperated so well ... that I would feel bad giving you a 'true' level-50 punishment, after what you've already taken this morning."

Kelly looked up at me questioningly, and her mouth opened slightly, but didn't say a word.

"That is why I'm not sure how, or even if, my fantasies will continue. They will probably morph into something else ..." I took a couple of swallows of iced tea.

"In fact, there's something else strange – most of my fantasies have focused on a girl's bottom, the position she took, how she reacted, and how well she held her position for a spanking ... or medical experience ... of some type.

"But spending the day with you, so-far, has me focusing on you – your beautiful face, your intelligent mind, your independence and strong will, *and* your beautiful body." I took another sip of iced tea.

"To be honest, and I don't understand it – after all this time fantasizing about doing something like today, I feel more motivated to cuddle with you right now, than I do to bruise your bottom."

Kelly was again the perky little girl, sitting with one leg tucked under her, and the other swinging from the chair, "Well, Sir, I would be OK with cuddling, if you think I've been punished sufficiently."

I laughed, "Nice try, Kelly, but I did make a commitment to give you the punishment of your life, and we're only halfway through it. And, your father will be expecting to see your bottom thrashed more than it is, right now!" Kelly laughed, and I joined her. We were very comfortable together.

"Here's what I have in mind: First, I will suggest a possible modification to what we're going to do in the exam room, in a few minutes. After that, we'll re-start your punishment, and I'll make some suggestions for giving you a sampling of the harder implements ... but suggesting some alternative 'punishments' that will enable you to more easily complete more levels.

"But I'm thinking now that perhaps your suggestion was a good one: we should delay some of your punishment for another day."

I thought about the 'modification' of our next scene in the exam room that I had mentioned to Kelly. I wasn't sure that the suggestion I was about to make for our upcoming shot experience was a good one, especially for me, but decided to change the script again ... adding something that might be a bit more fun and 'exciting' than the original idea.

I reached into the top desk drawer, and searched around in the back, pulling a couple of small objects out, and holding them in my fist. I asked Kelly, "Are you ready to continue?"

Kelly finished her glass of iced tea, and nodded, "Yes, Sir, I'm ready."

I sat back in my chair. "OK, then, get those pajamas off, and back into the standing position in front of the desk!" Kelly got up and immediately bent down, pushing her pajama bottoms down to the floor, and then off, standing next to the chair folding them, and putting them on the pile of clothes on the floor.

She then quickly stood back up and unbuttoned her pajama top and, as she opened it and took her arms out, I once-again realized how beautiful this woman was, and marveled that only a minute ago, she had looked like a little girl, sitting in her pajamas, perhaps waiting for me to read her a bedtime story.

CHAPTER 11: GAME OF CHANCE

Kelly got herself into the standing position again, totally nude and, obviously, totally comfortable. She smiled at me, awaiting my next instructions. I got up and said, "It's time for your anal muscles to stretch a little; then I'll explain how I think we should give the shots."

Kelly followed me across the playroom and into the exam room, where she hopped up on the table, without having to be told.

Kelly looked around the exam room again, staring at the various gleaming instruments on the shelf – most of which I had no intention of using – they were there for effect, only; exam-room movie set decorations. I dropped the contents of my fist onto a small metal tray, and then looked at the two large butt plugs that I had prepared.

One was a large glass butt-plug – with smooth, straight sides, but larger than any we had played with today, measuring about an inch and a quarter in diameter. The other was a red, hard rubber plug that was an inch and a half at the widest point – next to the narrow anal ring, so that it would sit just inside the rectum – and tapering down to a rounded half-inch tip.

I took the 'anoscope' from the counter, and lubed it well, placing it next to the butt plugs on the counter. The 'anoscope' (a straight metal tube, about five inches long) was actually a 'rectoscope' – a similar stainless steel instrument that allows vision inside the rectum. But the rectoscope is nearly ten inches long … although I would only be inserting it about six inches.

As Kelly watched, and mainly for show, I picked up each of the syringes I had filled earlier, and lined the shots up on the counter across from Kelly's head, so she would be staring at them. And, opening the drawer again, I pulled out a few alcohol swabs and gauze pads.

"OK, Kelly, here's what I suggest. If you would prefer the original scene – where we each get rectal insertions and lie down for two simultaneous big shots – we can do that. But I think my new suggestion will be a bit more fun, and put a little more 'chance and unknown' into the experience." Kelly listened intently.

"I will spend some time dilating your anus, and then insert the anoscope, and examine you. When I'm finished with your exam, I will insert that large red butt plug," pointing at the device on the counter, "then, you can get up (with the butt plug still in you, of course), and you will do the same to me – except for the anoscopic exam.

After you dilate me, you will insert this large glass butt plug into me. Then I will also get off the table." I thought a moment more about whether this was a good idea …

"Then, both of us with large butt plugs in our rear, you will bend over the exam table and throw one of these dice," picking up the objects on the tray. "I will then inject 6 cc into your bottom in divided doses, with the number of shots being equal to the number you rolled on the dice."

Kelly exclaimed, "What?!?!" She looked alternately at me, and the big shots sitting on the counter.

I continued, "And all of those shots will be given on your left side." Kelly closed her eyes and opened them; she stared at me opening and closing her mouth – looking like a fish out of water, suddenly gasping for breath.

"For example, if you roll a '1', you would get one big shot of 6 cc; if you roll a '2', you would get two 3 cc shots; and so forth ... up to a roll of '6', where you would get six 1 cc shots. Kelly was sitting firmly on the exam table, but she looked faint. She stopped swinging her legs, and looked over again at the four shots sitting on the counter.

I gave her a moment for the tension to increase still further, before I said, "And then, you will get up, and I will bend over the table ... and we'll do the same thing: I will roll the other die, and you will inject me on the left side with 6 cc in a number of shots based on the roll.

Then, we'll repeat the whole thing on the right side – with you first bending over, rolling the die, and getting 6 cc injected into your bottom, and then me doing the same."

I summarized, "You and I will each get 6 cc in each side of our bottom, but in an unknown number of shots, and alternating me giving you and you giving me the shots. When the shots are done, we will remove the butt plugs from each other, and go back into the playroom to complete your punishment."

Just to clarify, I noted, "We'll each get the same 6 cc on each side, as with the original plan, but it might be more fun to alternate giving each other our shots, and adding a little 'chance' to the mix."

Kelly slowly raised her eyes to mine, and her frown morphed into a crooked smile, "That sounds pretty perverted, Sir, if you don't mind me saying."

I laughed again, "Well, my mind is working overtime to make this a more interesting experience for you ... and not just a 'pain in the butt'!" Now, Kelly was laughing too, but nervously, and I noticed that she was staring again at the big shots waiting for us on the counter.

Kelly said, "I agree to your suggestion, Sir. I'm surprised that you even asked my opinion."

I just looked at Kelly. "I apologize for getting 'out of role' ... I'll correct that when we start your afternoon punishment session."

Kelly looked at me, very surprised, "Isn't *this* part of our afternoon session?"

I guess it was just a matter of semantics, "No, this will be completing your physical exam ... and the punishment I earned. Your afternoon session will be the rest of the spankings, as I mentioned; we'll have to discuss some of the alternatives before I get back into the 'professional spanking counselor' role."

I reached over and picked up an exam glove, and made a show of slowly pulling it onto my right hand, and flexing my fingers (exercising for the next event).

I asked Kelly, "So, shall we finish your physical exam, young lady?" I was trying to speak in a stern voice, but couldn't finish the last eight words without cracking up.

As I looked at the naked young woman - who I hadn't known until a few weeks ago - sitting on the end of the exam table, I couldn't help marvel that this was continuing to be a surreal experience.

"You could get back into a knee-chest position for this, but it might be more comfortable for you to 'take this lying down,' and get back into the 'lithotomy' position."

Kelly looked confused, "What's that? Sir."

I laughed, "It's the gynecology exam position – lying on your back with your legs in the stirrups."

Kelly said, "Oh!" and she lay back down on the exam table, while I put the stirrups into position. She knew what to do, scooting down so her butt was off the end of the table, and lifted her legs up into the stirrups. She adjusted her position a bit, and then said, "OK, Sir."

I smiled at Kelly's compliance, her nonchalance, and her spunk. I lubricated the middle three fingers of the glove with a daub of KY, and placed the tip of my middle finger on Kelly's anus. There was a slight flinch, and Kelly softly mumbled, "Oooh," but she quickly relaxed her anal sphincter, and I slowly advanced my finger into her.

Kelly stared at the ceiling as I moved my finger around in her, slowly slipping it out of her, and back in several times. I then pulled my finger out, and added a second finger on the way back in.

Kelly tightened a bit, and I heard, "Mmmm ..." as I moved the tips of my fingers slowly through her anal canal, gradually increasing their depth, but pulling back when I heard Kelly groan.

As two of my fingers finally entered her, and their full length slowly disappeared inside her, Kelly said, "They feel really big inside me ... it hurts a little, but I'm surprised that you could get two fingers into me."

I laughed, and informed her, "We're not going to go much farther today, but I have no doubt that you could take three fingers and, with some practice, you might even be able to try a 'fisting' experience."

Kelly raised her head slightly, looking down, between her legs, at me, "A what, Sir? I hope it's not what I think."

Laughing again, I pushed the two fingers fully into her, "Actually, Kelly, it is. We can watch a few videos another time – it's almost unbelievable, but the anus can expand enough to allow an entire fist to enter the rectum, with only the fister's arm sticking out."

Kelly groaned (this time I was sure it was a 'groan'), and said, "Yuck! That doesn't sound very enticing to me, Sir."

I had been holding my fingers still, but now started sliding them in and out a few inches. Kelly scrunched her face, and stared at the ceiling again. After a minute or two,

Kelly's anal muscles had relaxed considerably, and I said, "Kelly, I think you're ready for your anoscopic exam, now."

I slowly slid my fingers out of her, and removed the exam glove, dropping it in the trash, and washing my hands before I reached over and lifted the *colonoscope* from where it hung on the wall.

Kelly watched, nervously, as I held the four foot long, finger-diameter black tube. I held the distal (far) end of the tube, along with the near-end, just below the controls, in my left hand, while I twisted the large control knob with my right; the far end of the endoscope flexed up and down by more than 90 degrees.

Kelly's eyes grew larger, and it seemed like déjà vu (remembering the 5" spinal needle), when she exclaimed, "You're not going to stick THAT thing in me, are you? Sir?"

Again, I laughed, keeping my attention focused on the various controls of the scope. I had a surplus rack of electronic equipment, including a brilliant lamp that was connected to the scope through a fiberoptic cable, providing illumination deep inside the patient during the exam. Another portion of the electronics provided an 'insufflation' pump, that enables the physician to fill the colon with air, distending it sufficiently to enable navigating and viewing the mucosal surface.

The colonoscope is used – as its name implies – for colonoscopies, or deep endoscopic exams of the rectum, descending colon, and transverse colon. Navigation past the twisting 'S' of the descending colon can be tricky, and should only be done by professionals – which I wasn't. As Kelly had suspected – or was trying to convince herself – I had shown her the colonoscope only for 'shock' value, and had no intention of inserting this intimidating device into her.

As I hung it back on the wall rack, I reluctantly said, "No, Kelly, not today. We'll save the colonoscope for another time. Today, we're just going to do a quick 'anoscopy'." I took the already-lubed rectoscope from the counter, and showed it to Kelly, "This straight metal tube will easily pass into your rectum, and allow me to see inside you."

Kelly blinked, but didn't say anything, so I continued, "This thing," pulling a portion of the device from the outer tube, "provides a rounded tip for easy insertion, and then I can remove it in order to see through the tube. I have a fiberoptic light source that will illuminate the inside of your rectum. The exam will take only a few minutes, and won't be much more uncomfortable than having my two fingers in you."

As I lowered the stirrups, I told Kelly, "We'll need you in the knee-chest position for this part of your exam." Kelly turned over, and got up on her knees.

When Kelly was in position, I picked up the 'anoscope', and positioned it above Kelly's anus, with the obturator (part that goes inside, providing the rounded tip) in place. I warned Kelly, "It may feel a little cold, Kelly; just keep pushing a little, as I insert it."

With that, I pressed the rounded tip of the anoscope against Kelly's anus, and pushed gently. As she had already been fully lubricated, and somewhat dilated, the anoscope slid easily into her, going in nearly its full length – more than 8 inches. I moved it slowly back and forth a bit, and Kelly squirmed a little. I then pulled out the obturator, giving me a tunnel into Kelly's body.

I reached over to the counter with my right hand, and picked up the small fiberoptic illuminator, flicked the switch on, and inserted it partway down the anoscope. I could see moist, pink tissue at the end of the tube.

As I was not actually examining her, I moved the scope a bit, looking into it, and then sliding it nearly out. Finally, I slid the scope entirely out of her, while her anus remained wide open, her bottom sticking into the air. I brought the rectoscope to the sink, and did a quick rinse, leaving it there for further cleaning and disinfecting later.

"OK, Kelly, your exam is over. Let's get you back into the other position again."

Kelly lowered herself until she was lying flat on her stomach, and then flipped herself over on her back. As I raised and locked the stirrups, Kelly scooted down, and I helped lift her legs into the stirrups. I had Kelly move still further toward the end of the table, which had the effect of spreading her buttocks, and opening her anus, providing a perfect position for the next device.

"Now it's time for the big, red, butt plug," I explained, as I reached over, picking up the already-lubricated plug.

As I held it with the rounded tip pointing up, I realized that – had it been green – it would have looked like a Christmas tree; it would even stand up on its end – the portion that would soon be the only part of this large device outside of Kelly's rectum, sitting tightly against her anus, and holding the plug in place.

I put the tip against Kelly's anus, and there was no flinch, just a cooperative relaxing of her muscles. I said, "Good girl!" as I pushed the tip in, and the butt plug slid about halfway into her, her anus now expanded widely against the midpoint of the plug.

I began putting pressure on the end of the plug, and slowly pushed it in ½" and then out an inch; then in 1 ½ inches in, and back out an inch; then 2 ½ inches in, and back out an inch. When I pushed it back in, the widest part was only about ½-inch outside Kelly's anus, and Kelly groaned.

As I held the butt plug in place as far as it would go, I looked up at Kelly; her ponytail fell over the edge of the exam table, and disappeared below. "You know, Kelly, this is about as big around as any man's erect penis will get. Your bottom is certainly relaxed enough to have – and maybe enjoy anal sex now."

Kelly chuckled, "Probably. I let one of my boyfriends try anal sex with me and, with enough KY, he got into me, but it was painful the whole time. It was a turn-on feeling him come inside of me, and as he concentrated on thrusting himself into me, I got myself off with my hand. We almost had a simultaneous orgasm! But I don't think he was even aware of what I was doing; he probably thought he had gotten me really turned on!"

I kept pressure on the butt plug, and it advanced another quarter-inch. Kelly groaned again. I pulled it out about an inch, and pushed it back in to where it stopped; there was only a tiny push necessary to get the widest part beyond her anal sphincter.

"The neatest part about a butt plug like this – and I'm sure you felt it with the smaller ones – is that it 'sucks in' as the widest part gets past your anus," I pointed out. Kelly just nodded. "But this one is very wide, and has a steep 'lip', so two things are going to happen."

She groaned, and I continued, "First, it's probably going to hurt, but just for an instant, as I push the butt plug into you; I thought that with my two fingers in you, you would be able to take this more quickly, but the easiest thing for you now, will be to just get it in."

I continued, "And, second, it will feel very strange as it sucks into you, but then only a thin part will be going through your anus when it's in place, so it should be much more comfortable after it's in."

Kelly had her head in the pillow, and said a muffled, "OK. Sir."

I had built-up the tension enough. I told Kelly, "I'm going to move the plug back and forth a little, and the third time, I'll push it into you. OK?"

Kelly lifted her head to glance at me; even from where I stood at the foot of the table, I could see her 'Are-you-kidding?' face.

"OK, Kelly, here we go!" I did exactly what I had explained, pushing hard on the last time in. I knew that it would hurt a little, but her anus was almost dilated to the width of the plug, so it should not be dangerous.

As the plug took a second to get past her sphincter, I heard a high-pitch yelp from Kelly; a few milliseconds later, the plug had sucked itself into place, with just the thin, red, 2-inch diameter end-piece pressing against her perineum.

Kelly gasped for breath several times, then started panting, "That really hurt! And I'm not sure yet about how it feels now ..."

I massaged the sides of her legs, and then leaned forward between them, and put my hands on her sides, at her waist, and slowly massaged up and down, moving in towards her stomach, and eventually sliding them up, between and around her breasts. Her breathing calmed, as I repeated this several times.

Her eyes were closed, and a quiet moan escaped from her, as I continued my massage, up and over her breasts, including them in the territory I was massaging, but not focusing on them at all, sweeping smoothly from her navel nearly to her neck (as far as I could reach), stroking lightly, just grazing over her smooth skin.

I slowed down the motion of my hands, and finally ended holding her waist again. "How are you doing with the butt plug?" I asked.

Kelly opened her eyes, looking down at me, and chuckled, "Well, I guess it's not so bad once it's in. I'm sure it's going to get annoying, but I'm OK, right now, Sir. I think."

I smiled broadly at her, but wasn't sure which persona to use. "You're taking your punishment very well, young lady. I'm proud of you. Now you just lie there and think about your transgressions, and I'll be back in a while."

I left her, looking back into the exam room as I passed through the door. I saw the bewildered expression on her raised head, which, from my vantage, sat perfectly on her trimmed pubic hair. Which was, of course, above her genitals and, as my eyes lowered, the large, red disc of the butt plug between her buttocks.

I went into the playroom, crossed into the office to my desk, and poured another glass of iced tea. The ice had now melted, but it tasted wonderful; boy, this was hard work! I put the glass down, and a nervous shudder passed through my body, as I realized what was about to happen next: It was my turn to submit!

I took off my clothes, and put them on the floor, next to Kelly's. Then I slowly walked back across the playroom, and turned right into the exam room.

Kelly opened her eyes, and they sparkled as she saw me walking to the side of the exam table, nude. I turned to her, getting in the standing position, and said, "I'm here for my punishment, Miss."

Kelly was nearly apoplectic, but finally stopped laughing and said, "Then help me get off this damn table, so you can get up here yourself!"

I helped Kelly – lifting her legs from the stirrups and folding the stirrups down. Kelly then sat up, turning so her legs were off the side of the table, and hopped down. As Kelly stood at the side of the exam table, I hopped up on the end, pulling back up the stirrups and locking them into place, before I lay back and positioned myself with my butt off the end of the table, and my legs in the stirrups.

I rested my head on the pillow, and said, "I'm ready, Miss. There are exam gloves and KY on the counter, and the large glass butt plug is ready and lubricated for you."

Kelly donned a glove, and squeezed some KY on her fingers. She then positioned herself at the foot of the exam table, between my legs, and said, "Let's get started!"

I suggested that Kelly begin by inserting the middle finger of her right hand, and that I would teach her a little about a man's prostate gland. Kelly readily agreed and, after putting her gloved finger against my anus, and moving in a circular motion to lubricate me, she slipped her finger into me ... continuing to push as I gave a slight counter-push. Her finger was inside me fully, with the pad of her finger facing up.

I explained, "Kelly, I want you to press your finger 'up' (towards the ceiling, or my front), and push in even farther. If you move it around, you will feel my prostate – a gland about the size of a walnut, that makes much of the fluid in semen."

Kelly felt around, pushing in, and lifting her finger up and, looking down between my legs, I saw her smile, and say, "I think I feel it."

"Good," I said, "Now press your finger up into it – with a quick, poking motion." Kelly did what she was told, giving me a satisfying, but very brief, feeling. I told her, "Now, try doing that lots of times; you can vary the pressure, the position, and how often you press."

Kelly again followed my instructions, and a glorious feeling swept through my groin. I explained to Kelly, "This feels really good to a male – almost, but not quite, like the feeling of having an orgasm."

At this, Kelly cocked her head, and smiled, "That doesn't sound like a punishment, young man. But I can see that it is having some effect." I raised my head and saw that Kelly was looking down at my rapidly enlarging member.

I assumed that she would get back into her role, and not continue the turn-on, but she surprised me, and suddenly wrapped her left hand around me, and began stroking, even as she was pressing and massaging my prostate with the middle finger of her right hand deep inside me. I was in heaven.

Then, she surprised me still again, and stopped the motion of her fingers, but continued holding my penis in her hand, "I will reward you, young man, for taking your punishment, but not before you tell me how you like to be stroked."

I smiled – masturbation preferences and training was a subject that I had planned to introduce at some point, although I really hadn't thought we would get that far today.

"Miss, before I show you my favorite ways for you to 'do me', could you please show me what you already know about getting men off? I'm sure you already know some of the stroke variations that I will show you."

Kelly smiled and, with the finger of her right hand still inside me, she laid my hardening shaft on me – the tip already extending past my navel. Kelly said, "I usually do this," as she stroked me with her flat hand, from tip to base.

I closed my eyes, and said, "That feels very good, Kelly. I call that the 'flat-hand' stroke; it should start just below the tip, pressing harder initially, as your hand starts its slide down, and decreasing to the base. Never stroke back up – always in the down direction."

Kelly continued her slow flat-hand approach for a few more strokes, and then said, "And, I like to do this." She wrapped her fingers around my penis again, and made long downward strokes, again starting just below the head.

"That feels great," I commented. "Let's call that the 'wrap-around' stroke. Again, you should close your fingers more at the top, and open them a bit on the way down." Kelly continued, and I was now fully erect.

I said, "You can do almost the same thing using the 'Okay' stroke – in other words, just wrapping your thumb and forefinger around me – tightly at the tip, and gradually relaxing as you stroke down."

Kelly did a few strokes this way, and I closed my eyes again; my breathing was getting more ragged. I told her, "If you want to try a few more strokes before I come, you'll need to stop your 'Okay' strokes."

Kelly laid my erection down, but my penis lifted off my stomach and back down with regular pulsations, as I tried to control my breathing and prevent coming too soon.

I then told Kelly, "Now, take that excess foreskin on the underneath of my penis (on top, now, as it lays there) between your thumb and forefinger," which Kelly did, "and press your fingers together hard, and move them back and forth – like signaling to a waiter that you want the check ... but make these movements very slowly."

Kelly was a natural at this ... although I realized, of course, that she'd had some prior practice.

Kelly then looked down at me, and said, "OK, young man, I think I know what to do. Let's get you satisfied, and then I will insert the large butt plug."

As she started doing a variety of what we had discussed, I closed my eyes, and let my head push deep into the pillow. I pictured Kelly on the exam table, while I pushed the butt plug in, and ... passing from reality to fantasy (or current to future?), I could see Kelly bending over the end of the exam table, while I gave her several shots.

I couldn't really tell you exactly what Kelly was doing with my manhood down below, but the images in my brain took on a life of their own, and within a minute or two, I was coming over and over, spurting hot liquid over my stomach, while Kelly continued to stroke me.

I opened my eyes, and saw her looking into mine, and smiling broadly. "That's a good boy!" She put down my flagging member, and moved the finger of her right hand in and out, until it slid out of me.

Kelly went over to the sink, quickly washed her hands, and took a washcloth from the shelf above, soaking in hot water from the sink, wringing it out, and then applying it to my stomach, pubic hair, and penis, washing carefully, until the sticky mess had disappeared.

She dropped the washcloth in the sink, and then reached across to the other counter and picked up the large glass butt plug. This one wasn't quite as large as the red butt plug that was in Kelly, but the entire shaft was this size, and the tip flared a bit wider, before melding into the long thick shaft. It was definitely something that would be felt, once it was inside and filling the rectum ... and pressing against my prostate.

Kelly put the tip against my anus, and I tried to relax as she moved it around a bit, and then into me slightly –

moving it back and forth until the flared tip passed into my rectum, leaving my anus contracted tightly around the large glass shaft.

The butt plug was well lubricated, and Kelly had no problem advancing it – with long forward motions, and short retreating motions, until the butt plug was fully into me, and my anus tightened around the waist of the plug, with just a glass ball and integrated glass pull-ring sticking out of me.

The butt plug felt good, but had little effect, as I was already flaccid by this point, and had begun thinking about what was to come in a minute or two. I said, "Miss, if you are finished, I'll take my legs out of the stirrups, and you can fold them down … and then I'll get off this 'damn table'."

Kelly laughed, and looked at the base of the stirrups for the locking mechanism. As I lifted my legs from the stirrups, Kelly lowered them, and I rolled off the side of the table, and onto my feet. Kelly and I stood near the end of the exam table, in the small room, and I asked her, "Can we please hug again?"

Kelly melted, and we fell into each other's arms. After a minute or so of just holding each other, I leaned back from her and asked, "How's your butt plug doing?"

Kelly chuckled, and said, "It's a little annoying, but I guess it'll be OK for a while longer." I noticed that the butt plug in me was already becoming irritating, with my anus stretched around it.

"OK, Kelly, it's time for our shots." I opened a cabinet on the wall, and pulled down a shallow box, about 16x16" and a couple of inches deep. I took off the top of the box, and flipped it over, placing the top box and bottom next to each other on the exam table.

Kelly and I stood at the foot of the exam table, each of us standing before one of the box halves. I then grabbed the dice, and put one die in each of the boxes. "Let's both wash our hands again, first."

Kelly might think that I was obsessive-compulsive ... and perhaps I did have some of the DSM VI characteristics of that condition. But hand washing had been drilled into me, and believing in the 'germ theory of disease' made handwashing a simple and safe measure.

After that was done, I reached over, taking the nearest syringe from the counter, flicking it with my finger, and then shooting out a thin stream of saline, making sure there were no bubbles inside.

I said, "Bend over the end of the table, Kelly; we will now do the injections on your left side." Kelly bent over the end of the exam table, folding her arms, and lowering her chest down to the table, her breasts 'squishing' out from her on each side.

"Now, you're going to roll the die in the box in front of you. If it is at all tilted, you'll take the throw over. Whatever number is rolled will be the number of shots you will get; I will immediately begin, giving you the proper number of shots, and using the entire 6 cc of saline in this syringe. There will be no discussion during your shots."

Kelly glanced back at the 10 cc syringe, which was filled more than halfway, and the 1.5-inch needle, already uncapped, and ready to be stuck into her bottom. As she picked up the die, I tore the end off an alcohol swab, ready to administer the injections as soon as we knew how many she was going to get. Kelly threw the die into the box top, and it spun around, finally stopping with a "2" facing up.

I said, "Well, I guess you're going to get two 3 cc shots on your left side." I swabbed a site in her outer hip, just below the level of the top of her gluteal cleft, and then quickly inserted the needle fully to the black hub.   I let go of the syringe, and it stayed in place, the large plastic barrel of the syringe sticking out of Kelly's hip.

I held the syringe with my left hand, and pulled back slightly on the plunger, to make sure the tip of the needle wasn't in a blood vessel. I then squeezed the plunger with my thumb, my opposing fingers under the tab of the syringe.

Kelly was silent, as I watched 3 cc of sterile saline going into her bottom. Due to the larger gauge needle, the injection was faster, but still required quite a bit of pressure on the plunger, and took almost ten seconds for the injection. I thought about having Kelly 'rate the pain', but decided against it, as we had already agreed to give the shots silently.

I pulled out the needle, and repeated the process, swabbing her near the center of her left buttock this time (in the fattiest, roundest part), and held her skin taut, as I plunged the needle into her again. I did not hear a peep from Kelly.

Again, I slowly injected the saline, taking almost 20 seconds to empty the syringe. I then left the syringe in, while I took a step back, surveying the scene. The exam room looked like the real thing, and there was a beautiful, naked woman bending over the exam table, with a shot in her rear, waiting patiently for me to finish.

It had only been a few minutes since Kelly had masturbated me, but I felt a stirring, and could probably have been ready for another orgasm within a few minutes. In fact, my next vision was of me taking Kelly from behind, as she bent over the table, with a large butt plug in her rectum, and a shot still in her bottom.

I reluctantly brought myself back to reality, stepping up to Kelly, and pulling the needle out, then dropping the whole thing into the sharps container on the wall. I was going to put some pressure on the injection sites with a gauze pad, but saw only a couple of tiny needle marks where the shots had been given, and no blood.

I sighed, realizing that Kelly was half finished, and it was now my turn to bend over the table and get a shot ... or shots.

"Kelly, you may stand up, now." As Kelly stood, I bent over the table, taking the die in my hand. I said, "Kelly, I really should have given you some intramuscular injection training before we did this, but you have already inserted needles in me, and this won't be much more difficult.

"First, you will select the injection site (or sites). Although the 'upper outer quadrant' of each buttock is the safest, we've already stuck some needles there, and we'll need to use more of our butts for these injections."

Reaching back with my left hand, I ran my finger from the small of my back diagonally across my left buttock, to the center of the top of my left leg.

"This is where the Sciatic nerve runs; we really don't want to hit the nerve with a needle, so you want to either be outside of this line (toward the side of my hip), or inside of it (towards the center of my bottom). I'll let you do my shots anywhere you want that is away from that diagonal line ... preferably in one of the thicker parts of my bottom.

"After you've swabbed me, you'll hold my skin taut, and insert the needle straight in – all the way to the hub. You don't have to rush; if the needle doesn't go all the way in when you stick me, you can immediately push it all the way in. Give me a few seconds to relax – if it really hurts, you may have hit a nerve or blood vessel, and I would tell you to pull the needle out half an inch or re-insert it.

"Once the needle is in position, you will hold the syringe firmly, and pull back a bit on the plunger, watching for any blood that might enter the syringe. If you do see blood, please tell me, and I'll probably have you take out the needle, and re-insert it somewhere else.

"If you don't see blood, you can then press the plunger – squeezing against the tab, so you don't put any additional pressure pushing the needle into me – and inject the number of cc's we calculate. Each shot will be 6 cc divided by whatever number I roll. I will tell you the number of cc's and shots after the roll.

"The only thing I ask is that you place the shots at least an inch or two apart – not right next to each other. Once each shot is injected, you may leave the needle in for a few seconds if you like, before taking it out. Do you have any questions?"

I was bending over the end of the table, but had my chest lifted a bit while I spoke with her. Kelly said, "No – but I'll ask if I have a question while I'm giving you the shots."

I said, "OK. I guess I'm ready." With that, I threw the die into the box and it bounced off the edges and around, until it stopped. I cringed. Oh no! I groaned, and said, "Well, Kelly, I've rolled a '6' ... so you'll need to give me six 1 cc shots! I was certainly hoping that I was going to get a smaller number, like a 2 or 3 ..."

I thought quickly, and said, "Kelly, how about we forget about this, and go for that ice cream, now?"

Kelly laughed and, as I put my head down in my folded arms on the exam table, I felt Kelly poking a few places on my left buttock and hip, and I then felt the cold alcohol as she swabbed me. This was happening very fast – I had not planned on (or even thought about) rolling a '6', and was now going to get a half dozen needle sticks and injections, although a 1 cc injection doesn't hurt that much.

I felt Kelly holding my skin taut, and then the needle going in. I did not feel Kelly pushing slowly, nor did she ask any questions, so I assumed that the needle went in fully on the initial thrust. I felt the needle moving around – very uncomfortably – as Kelly checked for blood, and then I felt the pressure of the injection, but in only about 5 seconds, I felt the needle being slowly pulled out.

Kelly did not put the syringe down, but swabbed me with her left hand in another spot, and very quickly I felt the needle jabbing me. I didn't notice her holding my skin taut. This time the needle hurt a little more, but the shot was pretty quick, and Kelly had the needle out again within about 10 seconds.

She moved to my far upper outer hip, and swabbed again; this time, I felt her holding my skin taut, but the needle hurt as she placed it on my skin and pushed; I realized that she was doing a slow insertion, as I had done with her this morning. I hadn't said anything about this, so I couldn't complain, but it seemed like Kelly was having fun trying different kinds of insertions, at my expense, as long as she had so many shots to give.

Finally, she gave me the last shot, injecting the 1 cc slowly, and then leaving the syringe in me. I heard her step back, as I had, and she said, "This is pretty fun! It's an interesting sight, seeing you bent over with the shot in you; I might let you give me the full 'shot training' sometime."

I wasn't sure she needed much more training, but still had a few things to share with her ... next time. She then pulled the needle out, and told me that I could stand up. I stood, and pointed at the sharps container, "Just drop the whole thing in there."

Kelly did so, and asked, "How did I do, Sir?"

I smiled at her and said, "You did great – a couple of the needles hurt ... and my left buttock felt like a pin cushion, but you did a very professional job. Actually, that's the most shots I've ever gotten at one time."

Kelly beamed, then frowned a little, saying, "I guess it's time for my right side, now?" I just smiled and nodded, picking up the third already-prepared syringe on the counter. Kelly shrugged, turning toward the exam table, and bending over it as before.

Kelly picked up the die in the box top on her side, and rolled ... a '1'. Kelly said brightly, "That's good – I only get one more shot!"

I smiled, and said, "Yep, only one shot ... but it's going to be 6 cc – about the biggest intramuscular shot you can get."

Kelly calmed, and said, "Oh ..."

I explained, "Based on my own experience, I think 1 cc is just starting to hurt; at 2 cc you know you're getting a shot; by 3 cc it hurts about as much as it's going to – and not much more than the 2cc (except it lasts longer); and 4, 5, or 6 cc really doesn't hurt any more – in my opinion – but it hurts longer.

"If I injected you with 2.5 cc and left the needle in for 30 seconds, it would probably hurt about the same as if I had injected 6 cc over 30 seconds." I don't think Kelly wanted this level of detail ...

Having to give only a single shot enabled me to place it where it should go – in her upper outer buttock (hip), in an area above the Gluteus Maximus, allowing the 1.5-inch needle to reach muscle – as opposed to injecting her in the middle of her bottom, where the needle tip was still in fat.

I had read a clinical paper that said many people aren't really being injected intramuscularly – where the medicine will get into the bloodstream easily – but into the fat, as the population is getting more obese, and nurses are still using

1.5-inch needles for most patients – and not the 2 or 2½ inch needle that might be needed to reach the muscle.

While I thought all of this, I swabbed Kelly around the selected injection site on her right side, and held her skin taut between my thumb and second finger of my left hand, positioning the needle an inch or so above the injection site. I darted the needle in, pushing it firmly until the entire needle disappeared into Kelly's bottom, and then I checked for blood.

As this was Kelly's last shot – at least for the day – I decided to give it very slowly. While the 6 cc could be injected in about 30-35 seconds, I stretched it to about a minute.

I then broke our code of silence, and said, "Kelly, you are now fully injected. This is part of your punishment, and you will get a level-10 credit for taking 6 cc on each side. I doubt that you will want to get any more shots today." Kelly began shaking her head. "So, I'm going to leave this in for another minute." Kelly groaned. "Please give me a rating."

Kelly said, "I guess it's about a 15, Sir." I chuckled, not quite remembering what she had predicted earlier – written down on the form sitting on my desk – but I thought she had predicted that it would hurt a lot more.

Leaving the needle in, with the empty syringe – plunger pushed all the way in – seemingly attached to Kelly's bottom, I walked around the side of the table, and bent down, folding my arms on the exam table, and putting my head near Kelly's.

"You've been a very good girl, Kelly. In a moment, I'll take this needle out of you, and I'll bend over the desk for my last shot(s). You know what to do. Then, we'll take the butt plugs out, and go back into the playroom for your afternoon punishment session."

Kelly, her head turned toward me, resting on her arms, had been smiling, but now scrunched her face, closed her eyes, and nodded once.

I stood up and walked around the foot of the exam table, and pulled the needle out of Kelly, placing a gauze pad over the injection site, and putting mild pressure on it for a few seconds.

Then, I bent over the table again, picked up the die, and rolled it quickly. As it tumbled around the box, I just hoped it wouldn't land on '6' again! No, it was a '3'. That was OK. I wouldn't have minded a single shot, or maybe 2 shots ... but my bottom really was feeling like Swiss cheese!

I put my head down, and waited for Kelly to do her thing. She gave me the first shot near the top center of my right buttock. At 2 cc, it would take about 10 seconds to inject; the entire shot took under half a minute and hurt just a little. I got the second shot on my far upper right buttock, and it hurt a bit more. Then, the needle went in for the third time.

After another 10-15 seconds, I realized that Kelly must have already finished injecting me, and was leaving the needle in, as I had done with her. I inwardly sighed, and again thought, 'well, fair is fair ...' as the injection began hurting more. I don't know how long she left the needle in, but finally it was removed, and I heard Kelly dropping the spent syringe/needle into the sharps container.

I stood up, and asked Kelly, "How do you want us to take out the butt plugs?"

She thought for a moment, "I would have said we could just bend over while we stand here ... but I'm remembering the pain when it finally went in, so I think it might be best if I got up on the table in a knee-chest position again." I had been thinking the same thing, but wanted her to do the logic and make the decision.

"That sounds like a good idea. You, or me, first?" Kelly laughed, as she climbed onto the table, and got into a knee-chest position, moving the pillow to the head of the exam table, and holding her head up.

I positioned myself behind her, and grabbed the thin disc of red tightly attached to her behind. "Take a couple of breaths and, when you're ready, let me know, and then I'll count 3, 2, 1, and you can give a good push. It will come out very quickly, and won't hurt as much as going in."

Kelly glanced back at me with a skeptical look, and then looked ahead, and I heard her taking a few deep breaths. She said, simply, "OK."

I gripped the thin disc, as well as I could, as it was slippery with KY and pulled very close to her with only a narrow lip to grab. I called out, "Three, two, one, PUSH!" Kelly gave a good push, and I pulled and, as the butt plug's widest diameter popped out of her, I heard only a quick yelp from Kelly.

I slid the butt plug fully out of her, and said, "Stay in position a minute," while I turned to the sink, and quickly washed the butt plug. I then took a couple of tissues, and carefully wiped the KY from Kelly's peri-anal area. Kelly chuckled. I stepped on the pedal of the covered trash bin, and when the top rose, I dropped in the tissues.

Kelly was still in position, so I took her buttocks in my hands, and examined her widely dilated anus. There was some red, but probably not more than I had, due to the irritation of the butt plug – even the narrowest part – distending our anuses for so long.

I exchanged places with Kelly, and she repeated the process with me – even washing the butt plug and wiping me, which I had not anticipated.

At this point, I realized that – with my 'package' hanging down, and Kelly viewing me from behind – I was only slightly turned-on, expanded a bit, but not very hard. I had a quick flash of Kelly masturbating me in the chair, but snapped out of my thoughts when Kelly said, "I guess we're done!"

I got off the table, and hugged her without asking; she returned the hug, and I kissed her softly on the cheek. "Thank you, Miss, for administering the punishment that I earned at lunch – and deserved. Again, I apologize. I will try to use my brain a little faster and my mouth a little slower, in the future!"

Kelly first gave me a stern look, and I wondered what she would say, but then put on a submissive look, batting her eyelashes and looking at me with her big, hazel eyes, "And I thank you, Sir, for allowing me to take a substitute punishment. The enemas, and physical exam, and shots were ... interesting," and looking down, she followed-up quickly, "and they certainly didn't hurt as much as the spankings you've given me."

I hugged her again, and said, "Let's go back to the playroom."

I took Kelly by the hand, and led her into the playroom, and across to the desk area, both of us totally nude – and totally comfortable with each other. As I walked, I glanced down, and realized that I was entirely flaccid now, although I had initially gotten turned on by just seeing Kelly; I was thinking back to our first lunch, when I saw her bounding across the street, waving at me. I felt very serene and satisfied. Well, mostly satisfied.

This young, beautiful, intelligent woman walked self-confidently next to me, a brightness in her steps, her breasts bobbing, and holding my hand in a firm, but tender way. We reached the desk, and I told Kelly, "Assume the standing position, young lady!" Kelly did so immediately, and had a cute smile on her face, as her ponytail hung nearly to her waist, swinging back and forth behind her.

I brought the drink tray to the bar, dumping the iced tea, and putting fresh ice in the pitcher, before refilling it with mango iced tea I had stashed in the bar fridge. I put the pitcher and two fresh crystal glasses on the tray, and brought it back into the office, placing it on the desk. I sat down in my executive chair, and looked up at Kelly, who was in perfect standing position, with a grin on her face looking back at me.

I thought a bit, biting my lip, and said, "Kelly, before we continue your afternoon session, let's take a few more minutes out of our roles, to discuss the punishment plan. I'm going to let you sit down, but could you please first run to the bathroom, and get a hand towel from the shelf and bring it back here, please?"

Kelly didn't nod or say a word; she just turned, and ran across the playroom, her bottom bouncing. It was a great sight. I hadn't meant to imply literal 'running', but now that she was doing it, I was pleased.

When Kelly returned from the bathroom, holding the towel up questioningly, I told her to put it on the chair before sitting down. I saw a relieved smile, as she put the towel on the chair and sat down. I doubt that many Americans are knowledgeable enough or considerate enough to put a towel down, if they are going to sit, nude, on hotel furniture.

But in Europe, where there are beautiful spas with saunas, steam rooms, hot and cold pools, 'rain' showers, and chaises around the flowered grounds, populated by friendly people – all of whom are nude, nobody would ever think of sitting or lying down without putting down a towel first. It's just the hygienic thing to do!

I offered Kelly some iced tea, and poured some for myself; I didn't want either of us going into the afternoon session dehydrated.

We sipped our tea, as we sat there in silence, looking across the desk at each other. I had the feeling that we were both seeing different people in each other than we had seen this morning, when Kelly had first arrived.

CHAPTER 12: AFTERNOON SESSION

I sat back in the executive chair, and looked at the ceiling, "Let's see ... You've had a level-10 OTK spanking, then a level-10 tawsing, and a level-10 paddling this morning. Then, you had a second enema and a physical exam, which I'll rate as a level-10. And finally, you got a level-10 of shots (12 cc of intramuscular injections). So, you're at a level-50 now ... halfway towards the 'level-100' punishment that we planned for today."

I looked at Kelly, and saw that she was fidgeting. "Sir, I'm not complaining ... but do you think my bottom will take another level-50 of spankings?"

It was a good question. Of course, I knew that her bottom would take it without undue damage ... and, I thought she was strong enough to take it mentally ... but at this point, I wasn't sure *I* was strong enough to complete Kelly's punishment, and watch this beautiful girl cry.

As I had repeatedly told Kelly, I'm not turned on by hurting someone or seeing them cry – that is just a by-product of the spanking scenario, where I get to see someone willingly submitting to something they feared.

"Kelly, I have no doubt that your 'bottom' can take it. As I recall, you weren't even too sore to sit down on the couch, after your morning spanking session. And I promised your father that you wouldn't be able to sit down for a week, after I completed your punishment ..."

Kelly laughed, and I could see her entire body relaxing into the chair. I continued, "And, while your bottom is warmed up, I would like you to feel some of the other spanking implements – probably not the slipper, but maybe the spoon, certainly the hairbrush, possibly the switch, maybe a few strokes of the board ... and certainly the cane!"

Kelly slumped down in the chair, and sipped some iced tea. She was slowly shaking her head. She looked at me, and a crooked smiled formed on her face; I think she probably had seen a sparkle in my eyes, as I decided on how the afternoon session would proceed.

"To be honest – and this is why I wanted us to get out of role for a few minutes, and sit down to talk – I'm not entirely comfortable with giving you another level-50 of punishments today." I saw Kelly frown briefly, and hoped that I hadn't disappointed her – perhaps she secretly *wanted* to receive a full level-100 punishment today?

I wasn't sure how this next part would go, so just decided to wing-it: "So, I will make you an offer."

Kelly suddenly laughed, and said, "Is this where you break down and have wild sex with me?"

I laughed too, but briefly considered that she said 'have wild sex' and not 'make wild, passionate love' ... I wasn't sure if this was good or bad, but it created a nervous feeling in my stomach. "No, but it's something that will take more trust – from you, and from me."

Now, Kelly was curious, cocking her head, and staring at me. I looked into her eyes, and said, "Let's work together to see how far we can get with your afternoon spankings – I want you to really try. But I'll be willing to 'let you off easy' this time ... IF you will promise to return to take the rest of your punishment another time ... within the next 30 days ... but you will get another level-1 of punishment for each day beyond that."

I thought of giving a limit to Kelly – such as 60 days – but decided that she would cooperate, and come back as soon as she could ... or perhaps decide to never to return at all. I realized that I might be risking never completing her level-100; and I certainly hoped that this wouldn't affect our long-term relationship, even if only business-oriented. Which meant that whatever we did in the next few hours might be the last things we ever do together.

What a terrible thought! I didn't want to admit that I might be falling in love ... but I had tremendous feelings for Kelly, and really enjoyed her company ... and I didn't want to risk losing her by pushing too hard; I guess the 'pushing' so-far hadn't been too hard ...

Kelly looked up with bright eyes and a beautiful smile, "Sure! That sounds like a good idea. Sir."

My mind was already wandering to what we might do the next time. I made my decision, "OK. We will see how far you get this afternoon – you'll get a *minimum* of a level-10 of the spoon and/or hairbrush, and level-10 of the switch and/or cane. That will get you to a level-70, altogether, leaving a maximum of level-30 for your return visit ... unless you delay the visit, or unless we decide together that you need more."

I was already thinking of things that we would do that would be fun, but *not* be considered a 'punishment'. Then, I decided something else: "AND, I want you to agree to come over next time for an entire weekend ... and ideally a 3-day weekend."

Kelly arched her brows, "And THAT'S when you'll give in and make love to me?" Now, Kelly was saying 'make love'; I wasn't sure exactly what I was feeling, or how far I wanted this to go – including our relationship, and the limits that we were setting.

Assuming a serious look and tone, I said to Kelly, "We'll have to see about that, young lady. First, I need to complete the job that I've been commissioned to do!"

Kelly smiled, and said, "Sir, I would be happy to spend a weekend with you. And, as far as this afternoon, I will cooperate to the best of my ability, and help you get me through more punishment."

Now, *my* eyebrows arched. What was she saying? I had to ask. "Kelly, it's a wonderful turn-on for me to hear you say that. But I'm not sure if there are any hidden meanings that I should pick-up on, so I'm going to remind you of your agreement to be honest with me.

"I'm not sure how to ask this, so let me ask in several ways: What do you want, today? How far should we go with your punishment? Do you 'secretly' want me to give you a severe thrashing?" I stopped, and wondered whether the 'honest' approach would help or hurt, in this case.

Kelly pondered the question, picking up her glass and taking a swallow of iced tea, and then putting it back on the tray.

She looked up at me, and said, "Sir ... I'm not sure how to put this, either. You know that I got turned-on this morning ... even though you made me cry. I don't want you to hurt me ... what I mean is, I don't really want to feel pain. I think. But I'm turned-on by the idea of it. And, I can understand now how you could get turned-on by being either the 'top' or the 'bottom'."

This sounded like real honesty, and I was surprised and impressed that Kelly had used the proper terms, even though I had mentioned them earlier. She went on, "And, you have been wonderful at letting me get turned-on, and helping me to satisfy myself. You are ... a 'gentleman' – but a considerate, sexy, and interesting one ... especially after all of the 'studs' that have tried to get into my pants ..."

I just listened (for once). "And, I know I could get turned-on this afternoon, if you beat me," I gave her a stern look, and began to interrupt. "Sorry, Sir. I mean cane me ..."

Here was another revelation: After I had mentioned all of the implements I could think of, she had now mentioned the cane — certainly, the most intimidating implement, if not actually the worst. I had a few 'school canes' and other thicker devices ... but only planned to use the thin, whippy First Year cane that stung like hell, and left marks, but didn't bruise the bottom. Kelly seemed to be turned-on by the more severe implements ... or at least, the threat of them.

Kelly roused me from my trance. "But, I'm afraid. Even after you've given me some spankings ... I guess, *especially* since you've given me those spankings, I'm not just nervous, but really afraid of getting hit with the larger implements."

Again, I started to interrupt, but she continued, "I know that it's your responsibility to protect me ..." She gave me a mischievous smile, "while you're beating me," she looked up at me with her big eyes, but then turned more serious, "But, you're asking for me to somehow overcome my primal fears ... I don't know ... I can rationally understand that you won't really hurt me, and I know I'll get excited by the experience, but it's just hard ..."

I presented my fatherly smile, "Of course, it is, Kelly! That's part of the challenge for you ... and for me. You do need to let go of your primal fears, and have implicit trust in another person. You need to accept the pain you will receive, knowing that it is only temporary, and a small price (I hope) to pay for a potentially seismic orgasmic experience." I looked at her. She was deep in thought, trying to understand all of this – primarily the feelings she was now having about pleasure and pain.

I said, "Kelly, this has been, and will be – for a couple more hours – an intense experience. It is supposed to elicit emotions." I said this as if I was the world's expert ... but I'd actually only had one 'real' experience of this type previously – with Liz.

"And the hope is that the emotions lead to an overall positive experience – one which provides you with a different perspective, that may serve as a seed for ideas you may have in the future regarding your sex life. Or, to an experience that – although you may not want to repeat it – confirms your own self-confidence, and – perhaps – leads to a new, close friendship."

We sat across the desk from each other – both nude, but both in thought about the morning's activities, what we wanted from our sexual lives, what limits we were willing to set, and what trust we might have for someone so new to our lives.

I had deep feelings for Kelly and, I'm sure, she for me, by this point; but these feelings may have been just the result of our intimate activities, and earning each other's trust, rather than about any longer-term relationship.

It is well known that the people participating in various 'touchy-feely' group seminars tend to bond closely, within a day, or three, of meeting each other. Kelly and I had not spent much more than a dozen hours together. But they had been very 'close' hours ...

Kelly was looking down, still in thought. I felt compelled to remind Kelly, "This day is partly about seeing how 'far' you can go, Kelly; how strong you are physically and mentally." I knew that would have an effect.

"And you've proven yourself, as far as I'm concerned. But, if you will let me take you through a few more experiences, perhaps you will reach a new 'level'. And, please remember that you can always use your 'safeword' to end the scene today. In that case, we could have some wine (if you like), and I will still take you to dinner ... if you would like that."

Kelly looked up, and seemed close to crying, "Sir, I don't want to use my safeword, and I don't really want our session to end."

I finally took some definitive action: "OK, Kelly, here's what we're going to do. In about 5 minutes, your afternoon punishment session will begin. I will give you the punishment I feel you need – probably at least the level-20 we've already discussed ... and perhaps more.

I'm not going to be 'hard' on you ... but I will expect your cooperation just as before. I think you should behave as if you were going to get the full level-100 punishment today.

"I will, of course, monitor you closely, and adjust the punishment to your needs, capabilities, and condition. I will push you to complete additional punishment. You still may have to use your safeword. I will understand, and never hold that against you – it is always your right to stop the session; it will not re-start today, but your use of the safeword will not affect any future 'play' we mutually decide to do."

Kelly was still looking down, seemingly about to cry. I softened, a bit. "I've pushed you quite hard today, Kelly, and you've done a great job cooperating (maybe 'coping' is more accurate?) with me. I'm very proud of you. I want us to be friends, even if you decide you hated this experience. Maybe we could work on your pirate fantasy, if you were interested?"

I concluded, "In any case, when we decide that you've had enough today, we'll stop, get cleaned up, have a debriefing session (so I can better understand your reactions to the day), and then we'll go out and have a nice dinner."

Kelly finally looked up and laughed, "Thank you, Sir. I agree with your plan. And, as I said, I will try to take as much punishment as I can, and trust you to not get carried away." She gave a half-smile.

"And, regardless of the amount of punishment I take today, or 'owe' you, I would be happy to spend a weekend with you ... and 'play' some more." She smiled further, and then chuckled, "when my bottom has healed."

I was very happy to see her change in mood. She said, "Now, I'm wondering how much more you can come up with! What else is there to do?"

I just smiled, trying to control myself. I was concerned that I might be running out of ideas – including, for example, what her afternoon session corner times should be. But I also knew that there was a world of sexual perversions ... I mean fetishes and fantasies ... most of which I'm not much interested in ... if only Kelly knew!

Or, perhaps she did! Now, my mind was wandering, and I had to exert great control to stop my fantasizing, and respond to this 'real' woman sitting in front of me.

Kelly may have been awaiting an answer, but I commanded, "Enough of this small talk! Assume the standing position, girl!"

Kelly's eyes went wide momentarily, and there was a slight delay until the change in roles sunk through, and then she jumped up, and quickly got herself into the standing position, facing ahead, and looking quite serious. I walked around to the corner of the desk, and picked up my t-shirt and running shorts, putting them on, while Kelly kept her eyes forward.

I asked, "Do you need to pee, before we start your afternoon punishment, young lady?"

Kelly glanced over at me, smiling and said, "Yes, Sir."

Then I was smiling. "OK, you may go to the bathroom. Then, please fetch a large towel from the shelf next to the shower, and meet me by the bed." Kelly headed across the playroom, and I opened the credenza behind the desk, selecting a few items, and then walked to the bed at the far end of the playroom.

A couple of minutes later, Kelly walked, then skipped, and then ran the last few steps to the bed, taking the standing position, looking straight ahead at the unusual headboard, and reporting crisply, "Yes, Sir! Here's the towel, Sir."

I took the towel, and spread it smoothly on the bed, draping it over the end. I stood up and looked at Kelly.

She said, "I'm ready for my punishment, Sir."

I smiled, and told her to get in the over-the-end-of-the-bed position, which she did, quickly and quietly. I pulled the pillow down from its decorative position at the head of the bed, where I had put it earlier, placing it under Kelly's arms and head. She smiled up at me, and then put her head in the pillow.

I picked up a long wooden spoon, which we used to cook with, and wiped the convex side with an alcohol swab. Kelly waited patiently, with her upper body flat on the bed, and her legs extending down over the foot of the bed to the floor, her toes just touching the carpet.

She suddenly stirred, and I could see that her left hand was reaching beneath her ... to spread her labia (she finally remembered!) before bringing her hand back under her head. And, she brought her body toward the edge of the bed a bit, and pushed on her toes, bringing her bottom up, and separating her buttocks for a fine view of her well-dilated anus.

"Well done, Kelly!" I said. Then, I put on my sternest tone, "Young lady, you have had your break, and now you will feel the full benefit of my punishment service. Many of the implements I use – some of the most severe – are normal home products – the hairbrush, the back of a wooden scrub-brush, the plastic rod used to adjust the blinds ... and this wooden cooking spoon. We will begin with a level-5 spanking on your bare bottom with the spoon. That will be 60 strokes." Of course, it all depended on how hard the strokes were ...

At that, Kelly raised her head; it looked like she was about to speak, but she put her head back down, closing her eyes. I continued, "The spoon is small, so it takes several strokes to equal one swat with the paddle. I will need to cover your bottom and upper thighs ... so we may need to extend this to a level-10 spanking."

Kelly shook her head slightly – I'm sure it was carefully calculated so that I would notice, but not so blatant as to require corrective punishment. Then again, it could have just been a spontaneous reaction. I sat down on the bed next to Kelly – might as well get comfortable for this! I said, "I want to hear some deep breaths, and I'll start when I think you're ready."

Kelly took in some deep breaths through her mouth, releasing them more slowly through her nose. She got into a rhythm, and on the fourth breath, I brought the spoon down very hard on the middle of her right buttock. The flesh rippled outward from the spoon, and as I raised it, I heard a grunt emanate from somewhere deep in the pillow.

I then began in earnest, raining hard strokes of the spoon all over Kelly's bottom; giving her several on one

side, then on the other, then alternating for a while –
always keeping her off-guard. I kept up the 'spooning'
giving her 2-3 licks per second, and moving the spoon
around to cover her entire bottom, from just below the top
of her gluteal cleft, down to the gluteal fold (crease between
her buttocks and thigh) ... and then down and around her
thighs.

Kelly bucked a little, but kept herself reasonably in
position. She started to make little yelping sounds with
each stroke, but I continued until the full 60 strokes had
been delivered.

Kelly sobbed quietly, taking a deep breath every few
seconds, and keeping her head in the pillow. She was in
the proper position, with her legs spread and toes touching
the ground, but her bottom was quivering, and bounced a
little whenever she sobbed.

I stood back and admired my work: her entire lower
bottom and upper thighs were red, with a mottled
appearance, but I knew this had not been a very difficult
punishment ... yet.

I told Kelly, "Thank you for cooperating, young lady.
But I can see that we're going to have to do better than this,
if your father is to accept this punishment as the final one."
I heard a couple of sputters from Kelly.

"I will continue your punishment – to a full level-10; in
other words, another 60 strokes." Kelly groaned, but
stayed in position, not even moving her head from the
pillow. Then, I added, "but your second half will be done
with your corner time started."

I picked a small baggie up from the floor, and shook it.
Now, Kelly's head was up, and she was looking back at me.
I poured the contents of the bag into my hand, with a lot of
clicking sounds. I then picked up the loop at the end of the

thread, and lifted the entire device out of my other hand, for Kelly to see.

Hanging from the loop was a thick black thread, on which were three gleaming stainless steel balls, each about an inch in diameter. They were spaced so that there was about an inch of thread between each ball.

Kelly squinted her eyes, then widened them, first a questioning look, and then a look of comprehension. She closed her eyes and, dropping her head on the pillow, she moaned (or groaned?).

I said, "Yes, Kelly, these are 'anal beads'. I will insert them until only the looped thread remains outside your anus. Then, we will continue your wooden spoon spanking." I leaned over her, and separated her buttocks a bit more, holding them in place with my left hand, as my right held the last stainless ball on the string, and put it up against her anus.

Kelly flinched a little, and then relaxed her anal sphincter, as I pushed the first ball inside her. All I heard was an 'Mmmm ...' so I continued with the second ball. Having inserted the large butt plug in the exam room, Kelly was ready for these beads, and her body took them in without complaint.

I proceeded to insert all of the steel balls, making sure the looped thread hung several inches out of her. I then released her buttocks with my left hand, and with my right I roughly shook her reddened globes from side to side.

Kelly let out a loud, "Oooh!"

I picked up the spoon, placing it on her left buttock, and said, "Prepare yourself, girl: The rest of your punishment will begin shortly."

Kelly did some deep breathing and, without being asked, requested her punishment. "I'm ready for the rest of my spanking, now, Sir."

I smiled, and brought the convex side of the spoon down on her bottom hard and quick, moving from side to side, from bottom to legs, and back to bottom. I pulled her buttocks upward, toward her head, with my left hand, and thoroughly covered the area between her buttocks and thighs with the spoon.

Kelly was quietly weeping again, swaying left and right, her toes bouncing off the floor with each stroke ... but she held herself in position.

After 30 strokes of the spoon, I stopped briefly to rub my hand over her bottom and thighs, feeling for welts, or any sensitive spots, while Kelly calmed. I then picked up the spoon again, and continued her spanking, until all 60 additional strokes had been delivered.

When I stopped, Kelly was still bucking, breathing hard, and sobbing. "You've done well, young lady. You have just completed another level-10 spanking, bringing your total today to level-60." I put the spoon down, and began softly massaging her back, starting with the evident tension in her shoulders, proceeding downward, to her waist, and then to her red bottom.

Kelly's sobs turned into soft moans, as I rubbed her buttocks with both hands, swirling my strokes, and bringing my hands down her upper thighs, and around her legs. As I continued rubbing lightly with my left hand, I slipped my right under her.

She repositioned herself slightly to give me better access, and my hand moved up and over her clit, and then back down, and then up once more, between her lips, confirming that – once again – the spanking had resulted in some excitation of Kelly's private parts.

I pulled my hand out, Kelly groaning quietly, and wiped the juices off with a tissue. As I did this, I thought about how this would be written in an erotic romance novel

– certainly with me licking my fingers and savoring the fine taste of Kelly's secretions.

However, that would – of course – be in total contradiction of our rule not to transfer body fluids. Even so, I couldn't help but wonder what she tasted like, and whether I would ever have the opportunity to find out.

I got up from the bed, and walked around behind Kelly, looking at her now well-spanked bottom. She was lying there silently. I left her and walked over to the office area to check the displays on the panel behind my desk. Yes – the recorders were still running, and I had plenty of disk space left on my multi-terabyte disk array.

I took a swallow of iced tea, and walked back toward Kelly. Then, I diverted slightly, grabbing the straight-backed, armless chair next to the small table by the wall, and pulled it out into the room, diagonally facing the bed.

"You may stand up now, Kelly." She slipped off the bed fully onto her feet, and stood up, suddenly groaning (or moaning?), as the steel balls found their lowest position in her rectum. Kelly managed to get into the standing position, and faced me – about ten feet away.

"Please come over here," I requested, as my inner smile broke out onto my face, and Kelly frowned as she complied – walking delicately, as the steel balls rattled inside her. Kelly finally took her standing position about three feet in front of me.

"How do you feel?"

She tried to smile, but managed only a lopsided frown, "Well, Sir, my bottom is very sore, and those things you put inside me feel really strange. I feel like I have to poop!"

I smiled, and nodded, "Yes, Kelly, they put pressure on your rectal wall, and they are sitting on the inside of your anal sphincter." Enough anatomy lessons! "Now, we will complete your corner time."

Kelly stared at me with a 'you've-got-to-be-kidding' look; her mouth opened then closed, and I was again reminded of a fish out of water.

"Kelly, as you are part of a sports family, I'm sure you must know how to do jumping jacks?" I watched Kelly's expression turn from questioning, to dawning, to horror, and then to resignation. Even after almost a full day of 'playing', I was still able to elicit a chain of emotions from Kelly, as I introduced her to another new experience.

Kelly cautiously said, "Yes, Sir," and just looked at me with an amazingly blank (or maybe dazed) expression.

I said, "Let's first review the basics, and have you do one part at a time. Please do these things as I call them out. First, you jump up, and spread your legs and your arms."

Kelly complied, and I could hear the balls clicking as she landed on her feet. She was now standing in front of me, totally nude, with her feet widely apart and her arms out horizontally to each side of her.

I said, "And then, you jump up again, and bring your feet together and arms together when you land." Again, Kelly did as I said, and again, her face scrunched as she landed, the stainless steel balls clicking in a muted way.

"Very good, Kelly. I think you're ready for the rest of your corner time: I'll only ask you to do 20 jumping jacks, but they must be done correctly, and you need to really jump off the ground, or I will make you restart the exercise. We can both keep count. You may begin now."

With only a slight frown – realizing what was coming – Kelly began doing jumping jacks, grunting or 'Oooh'ing' or 'Aaaah'ing' with each landing. She was trying to do it slowly, one at a time, so I told her, "You have a dozen more, and I want them faster – at a regular speed."

Kelly closed her eyes as she continued her jumping jacks, somewhat faster than before. When she had completed 20 jumping jacks, she got back into the standing position, breathing heavily. I told her, "OK, young lady, get back over the bed."

Kelly waddled over to the bed, and got back into position. I debated whether to try one more thing, or hold it until her next corner time ... but I decided to save it, and not satisfy my urge to indulge in some instant gratification. Unfortunately, Kelly's gratification would have to wait a little longer, also.

I walked over to the bed, and told her, "I should probably leave those anal beads in you during your next punishment, but as you completed the full level-10 spoon spanking and the 20 jumping jacks, I will reward you by removing the beads now."

I picked up the baggie from the floor, and then leaned over Kelly, again spreading her buttocks apart with my left hand.

I told Kelly, "You've had a few rectal insertions today, but this should be a different experience." As I said that, I began pulling on the looped thread, until it was taut. "Just relax, now."

I pulled harder, and a shiny metallic dome appeared in the center of her partially dilated anus, growing larger, until the ball popped out of her. Kelly squealed, and I continued pulling the thread until the next ball appeared.

I told her, "There are a two left. You will say "Ready!" each time you are ready for me to pull another ball out. Are you ready?"

Kelly resignedly said, "Yes, Sir. ... Ready!"

I pulled and the next ball popped out of her. Kelly took a breath, and said, 'Ready!' again, and I pulled the last ball out of her.

I lowered the beads into the baggie and sealed it. I then spread Kelly's cheeks, and did a quick swipe with a tissue to remove the excess KY that had come out with the balls.

Kelly giggled into the pillow, and I took the tissues, swab, baggie, and rest of the trash into the bathroom, disposing of everything except for the beads, that I quickly washed, leaving them on the counter next to the sink, where several butt plugs now sat lined up in a row.

I walked back into the playroom, and admired Kelly's backside positioned over the foot of the bed, her head not visible from this angle.

I stepped over to the desk and grabbed a couple of thin birch switches that were stored inside the credenza, and walked back to the bed. On the carpet near the corner of the bed, there were still a couple of alcohol swabs, and a small felt bag.

I debated on changing Kelly's position for her next spanking, but she was positioned so well right now; I decided to ask her. "We will now move on to your next level-5 punishment, young lady: the switch." Kelly didn't make a sound, but wagged her bottom left and right a few times; I didn't know whether she was 'settling in', or teasing or tempting ... or mocking me.

I ignored this and continued, "Normally, I position the spankee differently for each level-10 punishment ... but you're actually in a pretty good position for the switch as you are. However, if you like, you may select another position for your switching."

Kelly said, "Mmmm," and I interjected, "You could bend over the side of the desk, bend over the back of the chair by the coffee table, or even get in a knee-chest position on the bed, if you prefer."

Kelly chuckled as she thought of these options, but raised her head from the pillow and said, "I'm OK staying in this position, Sir, if you don't mind."

I smiled, "Not at all, Kelly. This position will do just fine." I opened an alcohol swab, and swabbed the switch, and then repeated the process with the other switches, opening a new swab each time. This wasn't really necessary, but also didn't cost much or take much time.

Kelly glanced back, and my careful preparations of the switches built the tension she was now feeling. Once the switches were wiped down, I put two of them on the towel next to Kelly, picking up the third, and placing it across Kelly's bare bottom.

I wasn't quite ready to begin, yet, but left the switch in position, sliding it back and forth across her bottom, to continue building tension. I told her, "The switch was a common punishment in early American days, with the punishee often having to cut it from a tree, and prepare it by whittling off any side-branch protrusions with a sharp knife.

The switch is not as brutal as the cane, but is very 'whippy' and really stings. I think you'll find it a different kind of punishment than you've felt so-far."

I further explained, unnecessarily, "An extremely severe punishment is sometimes done by tying a bunch of these switches together, and soaking in brine. The punishment is then called a 'birching'."

I continued, "A level-10 switching requires 50 strokes. Let's start with 25, and see how you do. I have half a mind to begin your corner time now, and administer your switching with the insertion in place." Kelly groaned, but I smiled, as she didn't know what insertion was coming next.

I continued, "But I will give you a break, and leave your corner time until after the switching. Are you ready to receive your next level-5 punishment, young lady?"

Kelly cleared her throat, and said, quietly, "Yes, Sir."

I pulled back the switch, and let it swoosh onto Kelly's bottom, with the impact sounding somewhat like someone snapping his fingers. Kelly let out a yell, and then said, "Sorry, Sir. That felt like a hot poker across my bottom!"

"That was a mild demonstration stroke," I said, although it had been fairly hard. "I'll count that as the first stroke, so you will receive 24 more. I'm going to give you six strokes at a time, and then wait until I think you're ready for the next six. After each six strokes, you will count the set, and say 'Thank you, Sir.' Do you understand?"

Kelly just pushed her head into the pillow and nodded.

I assured her, "I know you can do this. The switch leaves thin red stripes across your bottom, but won't cut or bruise you."

I raised the switch, and brought it down hard on Kelly's bottom, and she yelped and bucked, leaning sideways, but got herself back into position quickly. I continued, with about one stroke every 5 seconds, and Kelly squealed as each stroke landed. After six strokes, I stopped and waited for about 5 seconds before Kelly remembered.

"Set one. Thank you, Sir!"

I smiled, and watched as she calmed herself and steadied her body; she was sniffling, but after half a minute, I decided that she was ready to continue. "Next set!" I called out, and then continued the switching, with the strokes coming about every 4 seconds. It was all Kelly could do to keep her position; it had to be especially difficult to keep her hands in front of her, while she felt the cuts across her bottom.

Kelly gave a loud 'Oooowww!' as each stroke landed, and by the sixth, she was in tears. "Set two. Thank you, Sir," I heard quietly coming from somewhere deep in the pillow.

"Good girl," I commended her.

Kelly continued to sob, and her bottom was quivering again. I lightly ran my hand over the switch marks, and stepped back. I looked at my watch, and waited a full minute, and then placed the switch across Kelly's lower buttocks. "Next set!" I said, and with no delay, I gave her the six strokes, one every 3 seconds.

Kelly yelled loudly after each stroke, starting with 'Ooww's', then a couple of 'Noooo!'s, and finally a couple of unintelligible utterances – the meanings of which were clear enough. Despite the pain Kelly was receiving, she did not use her safeword.

After the loud 'SNAP!' of the sixth stroke had faded, Kelly said, quietly, "Set three. ... Thank you, Sir."

I sat down on the bed next to Kelly, and lightly rubbed her bottom; she flinched a little, so I removed my hand, and asked, "Would you like to rub your own bottom, now?"

Kelly said, "Yes, please, Sir."

I laughed, and said, "Go ahead. When you're ready, put your arms around the pillow again, and I'll administer the last set. We will stop at 25 strokes: That will be a level-5 switching."

Kelly drew in a large breath, and sobbed a couple of times, "Oh, thank you, Sir. I think I have a good idea of what a switching feels like."

I thought, 'I better not misbehave, or Kelly will return the experience, and my bottom will have thin red stripes across it, also'. I let Kelly rub her bottom, and then decided. "Kelly, you may have thanked me too soon. For your last set, I'm going to do the insertion, and you'll have to hold it in, while I finish your switching."

Kelly groaned. She had her head on top of the pillow, turned to the side, away from me. I reached down and picked up the bag from the carpet, and dumped a similar set of steel balls into my hand; these were somewhat smaller, but there were six of them. I took the stainless ball on the end, and reached under Kelly, separating her labia, and stuffing the ball into her vagina.

Kelly let out a surprised howl, as the ball felt cold, but she settled quickly into a low moan, as I continued stuffing the smaller balls into her, leaving another looped thread hanging out of her.

She was still sobbing a little, but turned her head to the other side, toward me, and said, "I didn't know you meant *that* kind of insertion!" Kelly stopped rubbing her bottom, and brought her arms up and around the pillow.

I stood up, laughing, and said, "I guess, if you're joking with me, you must be ready for your last set, now."

Kelly watched me put the switch down and pick up another, then turned her head into the pillow. I said, "It's going to be fast. Hold your position. Here we go!" I let the switch fly six times, very hard, and about 1-2 seconds apart; the set was done in 10 seconds.

Kelly managed to hold her position – more or less – for the 10 seconds, but when it was done, I knew there was no possibility that she would be able to call out the count and thank me. She was bawling, her tears flowing freely, and soaking a good portion of the pillow.

I lay down on the bed next to Kelly, my legs angling down to the floor like hers. Her head was turned toward me, and her crying morphed into soft sobbing, as I reached over and stroked her hair, then down her upper back. I snuggled closer to her, putting my right arm around her waist.

"Kelly, when your corner time is completed, you will be at a level-65 punishment so-far today. I think your stamina and self-control has surprised both of us." I took my hand from her waist, and began softly stroking her hair and back. Shall I rub your bottom for you?

Kelly, still in tears, nodded and tried to smile. I lightly rubbed her bottom, covering all of the thin red stripes created by the switch. "When you're ready, we will finish your corner time. My suggestion is that we postpone the rest of your punishment for your return visit ... but that I give you a small taste of two severe implements: the hairbrush and the cane."

As predicted, Kelly groaned. I continued, "Nine strokes of the hairbrush would be a level-2.5, and 3 strokes of the cane would be a level-2.5, so if you can finish those, you will finish the day at a level-70."

Kelly closed her eyes, and wiped the tears off her face with the edge of the pillowcase, "OK, Sir, I'll try."

I smiled, "That's what I wanted to hear, Kelly. In return for your agreement to try, even with your bottom still sore, and your crying barely over, I am going to make an executive decision: I will give you only six strokes of the hairbrush, and 2 strokes of the cane ... but I will give you full credit for two level-5 punishments. Does that sound, OK? I don't want to short you, if you want your full punishment ..."

Kelly tried to laugh, "I don't think you're shorting me, Sir. Anyway, it would be 'shorting' my father. So I appreciate the 'discount' on the last level-5 punishments, Sir."

I laughed, too, then said, "Now, let's get you up, so we can finish your corner time. You'll be getting a 'special' corner time after your final level-5 punishment."

Kelly struggled to get up off the bed, and I heard a sarcastic 'Great!' after my comment about a special corner time. But I still had to maintain the tension, until the very end of her punishment. I went over and sat in the straight-backed chair again, and asked Kelly to come over and stand in front of me.

She wasn't exactly waddling, but she had to clench her PC muscle to hold the stainless steel balls in her, while she walked. It was actually good Kegel training! She stood in front of me, and assumed the standing position. I told her, "Now, you're going to do another 25 jumping jacks ... this time, with beads in your vagina."

Kelly winced, and said, "I'll try, Sir ... but I don't know if I can hold them in."

I laughed, "All you can do is try, young lady," and then under my breath, just loud enough for Kelly to hear, "and take your corrective punishment, if you fail." Kelly just shook her head.

I assured her, slightly getting out of the role, "Kelly, you may remember that I told you I would be hard on you – in terms of corrective punishment – at the beginning of your session today, but would be easier on you, as you proved that you could cooperate through the harder punishments.

"You've done that, now, so I don't intend to give you corrective punishment ... unless you really screw-up!" Kelly gave a nervous laugh.

"You may begin your jumping jacks any time, young lady."

Kelly took a couple of breaths, and then began another set of jumping jacks – this time, with a different, but equally as challenging insertion. When Kelly had finished the jumping jacks, she again took the standing position, breathing harder and awaiting my next instruction. "It doesn't appear that the vaginal beads turned you on much, Kelly."

She looked serious, "No, Sir, they didn't turn me on ... I was concentrating too hard on keeping those balls inside me."

I laughed, and said, "We're going to have to do something about that." I quickly walked over to the small table, and grabbed something in the top drawer and, sitting back down in the chair, said, "You may relax, now, and come over here, please."

Kelly approached me, and I had her turn around, and straddle my legs, then sit in my lap with her legs over mine, and her lower parts suspended off the chair, between my legs. I held her around the waist, as she adjusted her position– rocking back and forth, her bottom against my groin, having the effect of waking my sleeping member.

I then took the blindfold I had taken from the drawer, and slipped it over her head, making sure it covered both her eyes.

As I wrapped my left arm around her and held her under her breasts, I reached down with my right hand, and moved it slowly over her mound, then further down, until it was over her clit and labia. Between my fingers, I could feel the thread coming out of her.

Kelly moaned softly as I stroked her with my right hand, which focused its attention on her clit – moving up and down gently over it, and then with my fingers around it, putting increasing squeeze pressure between my fingers, and letting my trailing fourth finger move between her lips, parting them, and riding just inside them, as I continued moving my hand slowly.

On one of the downward strokes, I surreptitiously inserted my little finger into the thread loop. A few more strokes, and Kelly's breath caught: She was ready for her orgasm. I held my hand so that her clit was between my second and third fingers, which moved infinitesimally, but faster and faster, now more vibrating than moving.

That did it. Kelly threw her head back (another inch or two, and my nose would have been broken!) and at that moment, my right hand left her, as my little finger pulled on the thread, and the stainless steel balls came out of her, one after the other.

When the balls were out, I dropped them on the carpet (I'll get it cleaned later!), and placed my hand over her once-private parts again. Kelly came and came, moaning and moving herself on me, a lap dance that continued to turn me on, as well. This had turned out to be an interesting position.

As Kelly came down from her exquisite natural high, I removed the blindfold, dropping that on the carpet, also. I put my arms around her, now holding a breast in each of my hands.

I cupped my hands, and held her, as I imagined a crazy scene where a slave trailed behind the princess, who wore a long dress, but was bare on top ... with the slave being her 'personal bra', as his arms encircled her, and his hands cupped her breasts, while he followed her around the castle.

Now, *that* wasn't one of my usual fantasies! I leaned forward, putting my mouth near Kelly's right ear. "How are you doing, young lady?" I kissed her ear.

Kelly started crying. I turned her head to ask what she was feeling, but she suddenly wriggled off my lap and turned around to face me. Maybe I *had* pushed her too far, now; maybe I had blown it? I didn't think so, but her sudden response did not seem promising. With tears streaming down her cheeks, she frowned at me ... and then climbed onto my lap – again straddling, with her legs outside mine – but this time, facing me.

She wriggled herself up my legs, and I put my hands under her bottom, lifting and pulling her toward me. I had to reach down and adjust myself, lifting my hardening shaft vertical, and pulling her close to me against it.

I then took her head in my hands, and asked, "What's wrong, Kelly? Did I spank you too hard? Did I do something else wrong? Did you forget your safeword?"

She flicked her eyes down, then back up, and said, "No, silly. I didn't forget my safeword. You won't trick me into saying it, but it has 11 letters, and starts and ends with an 'H'. You didn't do anything wrong!"

I had to think a moment about her safeword, realizing that she had known it all along, but was too strong – or stubborn? – to use it. Now, I was becoming confused. I asked, "So what is making you unhappy or sad, right now?"

Kelly answered by leaning forward into me, and hugging me tightly for nearly a minute. The room was silent, and I heard both of our breaths, my heartbeat, and – I thought – her heartbeat, as well.

It was another surreal experience, adding to the already amazing day. I still didn't know what Kelly was thinking, but she seemed to read my mind, leaning back, and looking into my eyes, with tears still in hers. "May I be honest, Sir?"

I was nonplussed, "Of course, Kelly. We've gone in and out of our roles all day. And you know that one of the rules is that you *must* be open and honest with me – about your thoughts as well as your body."

I couldn't help glancing down, and saw a rounded wall of breasts, squashed against me. Someplace further down, invisible to either of our eyes, was my almost fully erect penis, which Kelly – knowingly or unknowingly (it only took an instant to know that it was knowingly) was rubbing against with her mons, which was positioned perfectly to do the job. She had known it, and I was just realizing it, as I wondered how this new 'lap dance' would end.

The rubbing slowed, and Kelly looked more serious. She held my shoulders as she leaned back, and looked into my eyes again. I knew she wanted to tell me something important, but I had no idea what it was. I wondered if she knew – or remembered – what it was.

Kelly was at once a small child and an experienced, sexy woman, both alluring, and down-to-earth. She was comfortable to be with, and I thought about her thoughtfulness and intelligence.

But she was living on a dangerous social edge – accepting the invitation of an older man to bare her, spank her, and 'ravage' her ... and either naively taking his word that he would not have sex with her, or actually desiring sex so much, that she was willing to accept pain, and perhaps some embarrassment to further our relationship.

All of these thoughts passed through my mind, as Kelly looked into my eyes, undoubtedly seeing them glaze-over.

CHAPTER 13: CONFESSION

"Sir, are you OK?" she asked, both surprising me out of my daydreaming, and surprising me with the question – her concern for me, at a time when she was clearly upset about something.

I nodded, and said, "I'm just concerned about you. Please tell me how you're feeling, right now, and what I can do to help make you happy, again." Then, Kelly began speaking slowly, quietly, in a stream-of-consciousness style, and I was mesmerized – by her story, and by the raw beauty of the woman sitting naked on my lap.

"I am an adopted child – I don't think you knew that." She looked me, and the evident shock on my face confirmed her supposition. "I loved my birth parents, and had a wonderful life – at least the parts that I can remember. But my father left me in a car one time in a parking lot, and the police found me – I was fine, working on a coloring book. I couldn't understand what was happening, or why.

"They dressed me up a lot, and we met some judges – I remember their robes, and having to look up to see their mean faces. We went to court a lot of times, and I was taken by an old lady who told me that I would be better living another place. I remember screaming and crying, fighting her, but I was eventually dragged away from my parents, who were also screaming and crying.

"I still really don't understand why this all happened – they had left the windows down and the doors were locked. I was eight years old at the time, felt safe, and they were only gone for a few minutes. Anyway, I eventually ended-up living with Dave and Darlene.

"When you saw me those Saturdays all those years ago at the soccer field, you may have noticed that it was my brothers who got all of the attention; Dave was only interested in sports, and he didn't consider 'girls' worthy of the team sports he admired so much.

"Maybe that wasn't the reason – perhaps it's because I never showed any interest or aptitude in sports … until much later – and then, not to make my adoptive father happy, but to prove something to him … I guess."

For a moment, the mesmerizing situation ended, and I looked around the room, and then back at Kelly. I had been so much inside her story, that I had lost track of reality.

I mumbled, "Yeah, my wife and I noticed … but it didn't seem strange, at all: We, also, didn't really care for sports – but for social and educational reasons, we had to make sure our sons joined various teams, and participated with their neighbors and schoolmates. We know how demanding Dave is, and you seemed quite capable of playing by yourself. What were you, about 11 at the time?"

Kelly thought, and said, "Probably between 10 and 13 … although I think your sons stopped playing when they got to high school, so you might have only seen me when I was 10 or 11."

I nodded, amazed that Kelly remembered any of this stuff – which I wouldn't have remembered, unless reminded, most likely by my wife. I drifted again, memories of her with our sons, on the PTA Board in elementary school, driving them to Tae Kwon Do, and her doing a multitude of other activities flashed through my mind. Suddenly, I was becoming depressed – both with Kelly's story, and with my own.

Then a very definite image came into my head, one that could not have been a photograph that I had taken: My wife and I standing at the edge of the soccer field, cheering for our team, with Dave very upset about something, and punching the air.

Somehow I remembered Kelly as a young girl, playing under a tree, about 50 feet from the edge of the soccer field. I remember a certain sadness about this, but couldn't really figure out why; I had not thought about it for more than a decade.

Kelly continued her story. "Dave and Darlene are nice people, but they're not my 'real' parents, and I purposely looked for any dis-similarities, rather than similarities. My glass was always half empty.

"As their sons left for college, they paid more attention to me, but my response was to 'show' them ... and I entered my 'wild' period. I've since swung the other way, and got rid of all of the body jewelry; fortunately, I never got a tattoo."

She thought a moment, and chuckled. "My parents didn't know how to react – their sons had been 'perfect angels', never doing anything wrong, and here I was in full rebellion, circumventing most of their prior experience in child-raising."

Kelly looked down, and took a few deep breaths. She pulled herself closer to me. I realized that I was flaccid again; that I really was mesmerized by this unexpected story. I looked at Kelly's face – her nose and lips, for evidence of a prior piercing, but didn't see anything. I still had no idea where all this was leading, or how it related to what we were doing earlier. I listened intently.

"I made an art of finding my parents' 'buttons' – mostly by trial and error, and 'pushed' them, as often as I could. I didn't care what happened to me, anymore. I had tried running away a few times, drank from Dave's liquor cabinet, and played loud music at 2AM.

"Although Dave was a 'rough and tough', macho man, he left most of the parenting to Darlene – especially when it came to me. He never spanked me, or even threatened me; I remember him walking away from me, shaking his head, resigned to the fact that I would never amount to anything, and leaving the punishment to my mother.

"By this time, she was bored, and also drinking from Dave's cabinet, so she tried to ignore the things I did, bringing me little presents, trying to 'win me back', rather than disciplining me – which might have shown that she cared. But, she didn't care, either.

"There's a reason why you haven't been invited by them to a party in so long ..." Her voice trailed off, and my emotions went out to her, as she mentioned the lack of discipline, the lack of care – and probably basic respect – by at least one, and perhaps both, of her parents.

Then, I thought of what Kelly must think of men: her original father causing the problem that led to her losing her parents; Dave's sports-mania orientation, and lack of consideration and respect, let alone love and discipline for her; and her boyfriends, that sounded like a bunch of jerks – although I had to take into consideration their age, and what I would have been doing at that age.

I realized now that Kelly was beautiful and intelligent, but deeply emotionally disturbed by her past. Amazingly, she seemed to be a rational, strong-willed, active woman – getting her Master's degree – and beyond her understandable 'wild' period.

When I thought about one of my key 'buttons' – trust, I thought that, perhaps, she had never really trusted anyone – especially men – since the incident with her parents: Her birth father, the policeman, the judges, then Dave, and finally her recent boyfriends.

My hopes for building a relationship with her alternately faded – thinking that she was about to tell me why she couldn't trust men; or brightened, thinking that perhaps I was giving her something that she knew she needed.

And, I didn't mean a spanking, I thought. What my Psych 1A background told me she needed was someone in whom she could trust, and share her feelings; a friend who she could be open with; someone who would respect her, listen to her, and fulfill her sexual and emotional needs.

The pieces seemed to be falling into place. But it seemed that Kelly was far from the end of her story. She was getting heavy – both in the content of her story, and the weight on my thighs, so I reached under her buttocks, and lifted again, re-settling her higher-up in my lap.

My eyes cleared, and I realized that Kelly and I had been staring at each other, neither of us seeing the other, but images from our past ... or future.

I gave Kelly a sad smile, and she shrugged. "So I stayed away from both of my adoptive-parents, as much as I could."

She thought a moment, and added, "And that includes leaving home (aka 'running away') a couple of times, hanging out with quite a few guys, and trying almost every drug. I even started smoking, but quit after less than a pack, since it only made me more nervous, and I hated the taste and smell."

I smiled: She believed acid and coke were OK, but cigarettes were evil. I guess that was as it should be;

perhaps the legally enforced tobacco disclosure ads were actually making a difference.

Kelly looked down, to our joined laps, and then back into my eyes, "I was really screwed-up for a while. I'm happy that I can tell you I never tried to commit suicide ... although I had thought about it a few times, in a drug- or alcohol-caused stupor."

I looked into Kelly's eyes, and said, "I'm glad, too." Kelly gave me a small, quick smile, and looked down, continuing her story. "With all of the boys I was with in those years, none of them ever gave me what I needed."

Kelly paused, thinking. "I've had a few close girlfriends – and I still see some who I went to high school with – like Julie and Linda, and a couple who take courses at the university I'm attending."

She continued, "I haven't had any long-term boyfriends. I think, at best, I could describe them as entertainment. Some were pretty fun – we did some crazy things, like trying to beat a train through a railroad crossing in a souped-up car, and we had basic sex, as I told you. But after each 'date', I always thought back and realized how unsatisfying it had been."

Kelly looked into my eyes, then closed hers for a moment. When she opened them, her mouth twisted into a slight frown, and she said, "I don't know what I was looking for. I don't think I knew then. I had friends, did wild things, had an active sex life, was doing well in school (and not dropping out of high school, pregnant, like some of the girls); so what was wrong?

I'm tempted to blame it all on being taken from my parents or the treatment I received from Dave and Darlene ... but I'm not sure."

Kelly looked into my eyes again. I may have been holding my breath, again mesmerized by her story.

She said, more positively, "But today has given me a few new insights. I'm going to make an effort to understand myself, and what I really want from life – and a relationship. I've never been able to 'see' myself as others see me, or analyze my feelings or thoughts rationally."

I wasn't sure whether to hold Kelly tight, or give her space; whether to say something in response, or just listen; to empathize or sympathize with her. I just sat there.

Kelly started to talk again, but tears came to her eyes, and she looked down and sniffled. "I feel like today might make a difference in my life, or mark a turning point. But I'm not sure how or why.

"I know the psychology nuts would say that I was craving some discipline from my father ... and that may be a small part of it (although I never once had a desire for Dave to spank me) ... but it's much more than that."

She looked at me. "Through most of my spankings today, I have thought about our conversation when you told me what turned you on." I tried to recall exactly what I had said, but she went on.

"Maybe it's some combination of the openness, honesty and trust – that resonated with me, because I can't remember anyone in my life who I could say provided those values. Or, maybe, in some crazy way, it's the submission."

Kelly sniffled again, "Or, maybe, it's *you* – the fact that you are actually living all of these ideals with me ... at least for the day."

She suddenly brightened, and looked up at me, "And, before you get yourself into more trouble by telling me how young I am," I winced, "I *know* that I should be looking for younger men. I'm not concerned about marriage and kids, but it would really be nice for someone in my 'social group' to understand some of these things, and try to live them."

She thought a moment. "Some of the men I've met are very nice ... but *you* are a 'gentleman'." I winced again, exaggerating my mock discomfort at hearing this. Kelly tried to clarify, "And I don't mean in the 'nice' way ..."

Now, I was confused. I was a gentleman, but I wasn't nice? How could she call me a gentleman, in the first place, after I had spent the day spanking her and sticking her with needles? We were both very tired, and probably not thinking straight. And, after all her oration, I still didn't know where Kelly was going with this.

In a more confident tone, she tried to explain, "What I mean is, you have values you believe in. I don't necessarily agree with all of them," I made a mental note to ask her later what she didn't agree with, as she continued, "but they make sense to you, and you stick by them. You're a 'gentleman' because you have shown me respect, even though I came here for a spanking experience.

"You could have acted mean to me – with the role as an excuse, or because maybe you really were a sadist, and wanted to hurt me. Or, you could have treated me like a slut, with disrespect. But you have been incredibly 'gentle' with me ... at least when you weren't spanking me."

She chuckled, remembering some of our earlier 'play'. "You have been very considerate, making me lunch, asking if I needed to pee, and even letting me spank you – something that I would never have imagined you doing.

"In my pirate fantasy, I am not treated nicely, but as a piece of property." She glanced up at me, and back down, adding quickly, "But I think I'm turned on by letting myself submit, until he takes me down from the mast, and presumably – as you suggested – makes wild passionate love to me. So it's not about the lashing or being treated badly, but the 'reward' of tenderness and love for submitting."

She breathed deeply, "Although I never seem to get as far as the lovemaking part. I know all this sounds ridiculous – it doesn't even make sense, as I'm telling you this!" Kelly was quiet for a few moments, and I wiggled my body slightly, to re-adjust Kelly on my legs.

Kelly then looked up and said, "You've treated me the exact opposite of the pirate in my fantasy! You have been kind and considerate to me as the starting point, and then spanked me hard. Of course, you've also been pretty nice to me after my spankings."

She looked up and batted her eyes at me, then turned more serious again. "So, you did give me my 'reward' after I submitted to you spanking me." She reasoned, "I suppose it's not that different from my fantasy, after all."

I made a decision. "Kelly, I would like to use my prerogative to end your spanking session now."

Kelly let go of my shoulders, and almost fell off my lap. "WHAT? I think you have misunderstood what I've been saying." She just looked at me incredulously. Some random thoughts of still taking the hairbrush to her bare bottom flitted through my mind, but we had done enough spanking for one day.

Perhaps I really was misunderstanding, and Kelly still craved the pain and resolution of her level-100 punishment? Maybe, I had given her exactly what she wanted, and now that she was opening up to me, I was backing away from her. But that would be a very incorrect impression, as I felt closer to her than I ever had – or thought that I could have.

"Kelly, let me explain. In my 'professional spanker's' opinion, your bottom has had enough punishment for one day. The last two implements that I had in mind – the hairbrush and the cane – are very severe, and I don't want to see you hurt (in pain, maybe, but not 'hurt').

"As your 'top' for the day, I can say that I have been thoroughly impressed with your behavior: Your cooperation and self-control has fulfilled more of my fantasies than I could have imagined. Well maybe not 'fulfilled'."

I chuckled, and Kelly looked at me with a sparkle in her eyes – and no more tears, as I explained, "I could get turned on by continuing this, or other types of 'play' – whether a 'punishment' or not. For example, maybe you would let me make a corset on your back with 'needle play'."

Kelly cocked her head and opened her mouth a little. "Or maybe you would like to be the 'school marm', with me the 'bad boy' student. It would be fun to play with you, and I'm sure we can think of some things to do that would be interesting for both of us." I gave Kelly my most serious look, and stared intently into her hazel eyes.

"But even more than 'playing' with you, Kelly, I would like to be (and remain) your friend. Just the experience we've had today has made us 'closer' in many ways ... you opening up to me, just one of them.

"And your story has been very emotional for me; I want to hear all of it, and be able to understand you better ... and perhaps help you to understand yourself."

I looked down, and thought about how I wanted to proceed. "Kelly, here is what I would like us to do – if you agree. I would like to hear much more about how your life evolved over the past decade ... but I'd rather do it while sitting on the couch – or out on the patio – than with you sitting like this, cutting off my circulation. I don't mean to be selfish, but ..."

Kelly's face relaxed, as if a huge load had been taken off her, but she had a curious half-smile, and I could not gauge what she might be thinking. So I continued laying out my plan, "So I suggest that we first hug each other."

I hadn't meant immediately, but Kelly pushed against my chest, her head in the crook of my neck. My arms were around her back tightly, and her arms were over mine, and draped over my shoulders. We lost ourselves in each other for the next several minutes.

Kelly sat up, and her serious expression became softer. "What would you like to do next, Sir?" I laughed at the sudden transition from quiet romantic interlude to bright, business-like discussion.

"Let me lay out the plan, and then we can discuss it – and hopefully agree – and *then* we'll do it. OK?"

Kelly smiled, and said, "I know you didn't really mean to hug then, Sir, but I couldn't resist. I have a lot more to tell you, now that I have started, and my mind is full of new thoughts."

I smiled, "Well, that's exactly my point! I hadn't planned on having time for this today, but let's first bathe each other quickly,"

Kelly raised her eyebrows, and interrupted, "Quickly, Sir?" I laughed again; this girl … woman … was again melting my heart. And forcing me to have feelings that I had only experienced a couple of times in my life. Feelings I hadn't believed I would ever have again.

"Yes, Kelly. Our first shower should really just be a rinse … but after our day's efforts – sweated up and gooped up – I think we should bathe each other fully … before going in the sauna."

Kelly jerked her head up and smiled now. I continued, "I don't want to take too much time with our first shower, as we will need to get in and out of the shower a few times in-between our saunas. If you haven't done it before, I'll show you some of the traditional old Finnish customs."

Kelly gave me a 'look', and I added quickly, "I didn't mean those customs ... but we'll have to see. My idea was that two or three 10-12 minute sessions sitting together in the sauna will give you time to continue your story, and complete some of the thoughts you said you had – which I'm looking forward to hearing."

I smiled, "I'm not sure how your bottom will do in the sauna, but you can consider it a 'corner time' for the entire day – your red butt on display, and enough ongoing pain that you won't forget you were punished." We both laughed, and Kelly reached down with her hands, rubbing her bottom, as I held her around her back.

"We will take another shower afterward – although I would be OK, if you want us to bathe ourselves – I have double controls and multiple jets, so we can watch each other bathe ... or bathe each other again ... whatever you like." Kelly just smiled, and tossed her head, making the ponytail fly across her back

"Then, we will get dressed, and I'll open a bottle of champagne to celebrate your 'First Experience' – or, a nice bottle of red or white wine, if you prefer. I have some nice wine crackers that we can munch on –to soak up the alcohol, so we can still make it to dinner."

Kelly laughed at this, and said, "The plan sounds nice, Sir. So far. No ropes, or chains ..."

I said, "Well, maybe doing it with *you*, I *could* get interested in bondage ..." We laughed so hard, that we were almost crying – another close duality, I thought briefly.

Kelly got control of herself and, looking into my eyes, said, "And then ... Sir?"

I was still laughing, but choked out, "I'll take you to a nice dinner, and then I'll drop you off at home."

Kelly howled. "You can't do that, Sir – I drove here, so we have to come back."

I couldn't resist, "To pick up your car?"

Kelly was nearly hysterical, "I wasn't thinking of that, Sir."

I lifted her from my lap, and she stood up; I wasn't sure if my legs were working any more, as the blood had been cut off for so long. As I tried to stand, I said, "Ow!" and fell back into the chair. I looked up at Kelly and said, "Pins and needles!"

Before she realized that I hadn't meant it that way, Kelly squealed, and said, "More? In the bottom?" Then she cracked up. I was finally able to get out of the chair, but decided not to stand up, quite yet. I took Kelly's hand, and pulled her down to the carpet, where I hugged her, and we – literally – rolled around on the floor laughing.

After few minutes, we were both getting exhausted with the laughter, and we separated our bodies, and lay back on the soft playroom carpet, parallel to each other, panting heavily, and staring up at the ceiling.

I looked over, and Kelly's eyes were closed, but she had a huge smile on her face. If I had taken a picture, this could easily be passed off as her fantasizing and masturbating. Then, I realized that I had plenty of 'pictures' – at least 6 million high-resolution video frames worth! I had no plans to play it, let alone edit it into a story.

After another couple of minutes, I turned to Kelly and remarked, "This would be a great time to do an hour of Yoga," She turned her head toward me, and smiled, then frowned. I continued, "but we have other plans now, so that will have to wait until another time."

Kelly beamed, her head sideways with her left cheek against the carpet, and nodded, "When I return for the remainder of my punishment." I laughed a little, but realized that she was quite serious.

CHAPTER 14: SAUNA

I hopped up and offered her a hand, "Let's go take a shower and get in the sauna!"

Kelly grabbed my hand, and easily pulled herself up; she quickly got into the standing position and, saluting me in an exaggerated military style, she said, "YES, Sir!"

As we turned toward the hall, I slapped her bottom, and she jumped. Then, looking at me over her shoulder, and realizing that the next spank was only seconds away, she ran across the playroom, and into the bathroom.

When I got to the door, she was on the toilet peeing. She looked up at me, with her big eyes, and said, "Sorry, Sir. I had to go."

Sure! Kelly was really a funny girl. I slipped off my running shorts and t-shirt, dropping them in the hamper, and turned into the shower room. I walked over to the small control panel on the outside of the sauna – which crossed the far end of the shower room.

I had kept the sauna at about 150 degrees, but it needed to reach nearly 190 for the full effect. It was a good idea to start at relatively low temperature, so Kelly's bottom could get used to the heat gradually; I was pretty sure it would burn, anyway, even with her sitting on a towel.

I walked into one side of the shower, and turned the faucet for the large 'rain shower' head – a disk with hundreds of holes, where large drops of water fell as in a heavy tropical downpour. There was a separate temperature control, which was already set to normal shower temperature. I would need to lower it for our in-between sauna refreshers.

I started rinsing, as Kelly came into the shower room, and joined me under the rain shower. I squirted some body wash onto my hands, and turned her around, so her back was to me, and then began a light massage of her shoulders and back, then washing her arms, and slipping both my arms around under her breasts.

I washed her breasts from the back, kneading them, and bouncing them around, as I pressed my front up against Kelly's back. I reached down, and lifted my slowly growing manhood up, placing it along her butt crack, stepped forward, and held her, putting pressure between our bodies from nearly head to knees.

As I stood pressed against her, I continued to wash Kelly's breasts from behind, and then brought both of my hands down, swirling my soapy fingers over her belly, and down to her 'extended' Bikini wax, and washed her everywhere, from the tip of her trimmed black triangle up.

Kelly moaned, and pressed back against me, wagging her bottom, which had great effect on my now hardened member.

I stepped back, and kneeled, bringing my hands carefully down over her buttocks. Kelly gave a little laugh, "I might not be able to sit down for dinner, tonight."

I hadn't spanked her *that* hard and, in fact, she would be sitting in the sauna in just a few minutes – her bottom possibly in slight pain, not due to the sauna seating, but to the heat.

I gently washed her bottom, sliding my finger down the middle, and into her relaxed (and still dilated) anus. I did a few 'ins and outs', and proceeded down her legs. She held my shoulder while she lifted each lower leg back, nearly to her butt, so that I could scrub the bottoms of her feet, which were quite dirty – I guess due to walking on the patio during lunch.

I turned Kelly around, and did another 'once-over' of her front, ending, finally, by sliding two, and then three fingers into her vagina, bringing plenty of water with them, but avoiding the suds.

Kelly's eyes were closed, and she moaned, as I finished on the inside, and brought my hand up and over her clit. I suggested, "I could get you off in the sauna, rather than here ... or we could do both, if you like?"

Kelly kept her eyes closed, and responded, "In the sauna sounds good ... assuming I don't pass out from the heat." I turned Kelly around a few times rinsing her thoroughly under the rain shower. Then, I said, "We'll do our shampoos later, after the sauna. Would you like to bathe me?"

Kelly looked down at my erection, "I'd like to do more than that!" She squirted some body wash, and took my penis in her hands, wrapping her fingers around me, moving her flat hand along the underside, and then making the 'OK' sign with her right hand, and stroking me, as I had taught her.

As I started breathing more heavily, I asked, "May I make a suggestion, Kelly?" She continued holding me, and nodded. "I would like to come by rubbing myself on your pubic hair. You can use the thumbs of each hand to guide me."

Kelly stood, and I stepped up against her, bringing my erection vertical against her pubic hair, and lower stomach. She put her hands on either side of me and, as I had suggested, used her thumbs to guide me, pressing in slightly every time I slid myself up, the sensitive underside of my penis grazing her trimmed pubic hair.

It felt wonderful. I held her breasts, as I continued the ever-increasing motion of my lower body. With her hands fixed between us, I took her head in my hands, and stroked her hair. I lifted her ponytail over her shoulder in front of us, and stroked it, just as Kelly was stroking me, with my fingers wrapped around it, and my hand sliding down its length.

By this time, I was ready, and looked into Kelly's eyes. I was surprised to see that they were open and watching me closely. My breathing got ragged, and Kelly responded by squeezing harder from the side, as I slid up her, finally pressing against her, and sliding myself over her pubic hair, as I spurted my hot fluid up between her breasts, where it dripped down over her stomach.

Kelly took her hands out from between us, and we hugged each other tightly.

I was still panting as I stepped back, and said, "Sorry – I'll wash your stomach again." At this, Kelly laughed and we both squirted body wash into our palms, and washed each other.

Kelly washed my front, and then turned me around, and washed my back, quickly but thoroughly. At the end, she slipped her soapy finger into my rectum, pressing against my prostate, completing my release..

I said, "You see, those lessons today are already paying off!" Kelly turned me around, and we both continued laughing as we rinsed off. I turned off the shower, and handed Kelly a large towel from the shelf, taking one myself, and opening the smoked glass sauna door.

We slipped inside the dark, warm cave, and I quickly shut the door behind us. We stood for a moment to allow our eyes to get used to the dim red light, and then I spread my towel over the second tier of seating, letting it drop to the lower tier, where I smoothed about six inches of it, and then sat on the towel, with my feet on the small strip of towel on the seat below.

Kelly watched, and then did the same, and after a little adjusting, we were sitting next to each other on the sauna bench, both naked – as a sauna requires, and looking through the smoked glass door into the shower room. I turned to Kelly, and said, "How are you doing?"

She smiled at me, and said, "I'm fine." She adjusted her position again, and said, "But my bottom is hurting." Kelly felt the wood of the seat next to her, and then the wood walls of the sauna. "It's a good thing the towel is protecting my butt from the heat of the seat!" We laughed again.

I said, "That reminds me of the old high school 'physics' formula: 'The angle of the dangle is directly proportional to the mass of the ass, provided the heat of the meat remains constant'." Kelly broke into a laughing fit, and it was great to hear her so happy, despite the spankings and her sad life story.

I turned the hourglass on the wall, and a stream of fine sand began falling to the bottom portion. We sat there a few minutes, getting used to the heat; the thermometer was already up to 165, and rising.

I asked Kelly, "Would you like to continue your story, now?" Kelly looked down for another minute, and then brought her legs up, and sat cross-legged on the upper seat, turning her whole body to face me. Kelly looked up at me, and wiped a few beads of sweat from her forehead. "It's hot in here," she said, fanning her face.

I laughed, "Not yet, but it's getting there. My preference is around 183-187 degrees."

Kelly looked startled, "What? We can't survive in that heat!"

I laughed again, "'Survive', no. But we can certainly last ten minutes or so. Then, we'll get under a cool (or maybe cold) shower. Your skin will tingle, and we'll take a few minutes to walk around – maybe even outside – and then go back in for another sauna session."

Kelly rolled her eyes, not really believing that the temperature could get that high; but the beads of sweat now started appearing all over her body. I especially noticed the glistening of the sweat beads on her breasts ... thinking briefly that I should do a photo session in here, sometime.

"Now, tell me your thoughts. How does your story relate to what we did today? It still sounds like you craved or needed punishment – perhaps for upsetting your parents during your 'wild' period, even though they were trying their hardest with you."

Kelly shook her head, and looked up at me, with a large drop of sweat forming on her nose. One more shake and the drop dropped from her nose to somewhere in the dark area between her black triangle and her crossed legs.

She wasn't smiling: Her face was contorted and her mouth opened and closed, once again behaving like a fish out of water. I could see that she was struggling with her thoughts, but I had no idea what they were. Then, she just looked down into the blackness of her lap, silent.

I hoped that I wasn't the cause of making her situation worse; I hadn't known about her history, and had no idea whether the punishment experience helped or hurt, even though she clearly wanted it. Or, at least, wanted to try it.

It was getting hot in here. I looked at the thermometer, and it now read 175. The hourglass said we had been in the sauna about 9 minutes. I turned back to

Kelly, and said, "Lie down, and it won't be quite as hot. Let's just relax for another few minutes, and then we can cool off for a while."

I stood on the lower bench and put my towel horizontally on the upper one, then took a small wooden wedge from the corner, putting it under the end of my towel. I then lay down on the towel, with my knees up and my feet close to the bottom of the towel, while my head rested on the towel over the triangle of wood.

Kelly, in her birthday suit, followed suit, lying down, looking up at the wood ceiling, closing her eyes, and taking deep breaths. By the time the hourglass had registered 12 minutes, we were done.

"Kelly, let's get some fresh air!" We got up, taking our towels with us, exited the sauna, and walked into the shower room. Hanging our towels on a hook, we stepped into one side of the shower, where I set a misting jet to 75 degrees, and turned it on.

A fine spray of mist floated down over us, cooling us gradually. I then set the lower jets to 70 degrees, and turned them on – surprising Kelly with 12 jets that were aimed at our legs.

We turned around and around together – almost like dancing – before I turned on the rain shower, set to 80 degrees. Now, we were surrounded by water that felt cool, but not shockingly cold. Every minute or so, I lowered the rain shower by 5 degrees, and after a few minutes, we were getting chilled.

I turned off all of the jets, and we wrapped ourselves in the large, soft towels. There were pairs of sandals and flip-flops in a shoe rack in the wall connecting the bathroom to the shower room under a narrow built-in cabinet, and I pulled out a pair for each of us.

I then led Kelly upstairs, where we grabbed a pitcher of ice water with a wedge of lemon from the fridge, and a couple of heavy plastic glasses, and went out to the patio. It was now late afternoon, and the sun was glistening through the rustling leaves of the trees, dappling the backyard in a mottle of light and shadow.

We sat at the table, sipping water, and looking out over the pool and greenery. I told Kelly, "I don't have all of the various amenities that European saunas have – for example a cold pool, or a foot-bath – but I'm getting there." Kelly nodded, and I saw a shiver run through her towel-clad body.

"Are you cold?" I asked. It had been a warm day, but the afternoon still had the chill of late spring, and we had just been sprayed with cold water.

I turned to Kelly, "We can fix that, easily!" I got up, and Kelly followed me across the patio to the pool, and we climbed a few steps next to a rock waterfall, then put our towels on a replica old-fashioned wrought-iron park bench, and stepped into the Jacuzzi.

It was only lukewarm, at about 95 degrees, and the jets were off, but the combination of warm water and cool breeze caressed our bodies, and we both began to really relax, for the first time today.

"I like sitting in the Jacuzzi, no jets – just quiet, late at night, looking up at the stars, and watching for meteors." Kelly just smiled, put her head back, and closed her eyes.

After several minutes, Kelly opened her eyes, looked around, and moved slowly around the Jacuzzi, her legs bent and water almost to her neck, her breasts bobbing on the surface.

She looked over the edge to the pool below, black-bottomed, and looking more like a lake, with boulders serving as the edge of the pool in some places. A huge area of green grass spanned the hundred feet from the edge of the small aggregate walk that surrounded the free-form pool, to the planters that fronted a multitude of tall trees. It truly was a park-like setting.

Kelly asked, "Can you turn the jets on for a while?" as she continued around the large Jacuzzi. I reached over to the air switch recessed into the deck and pressed it, the jets coming to life a few seconds later.

Kelly watched for a minute, as the waterfall started flowing, and then pushed across the spa over to me, and maneuvered herself onto my lap – just as we were in the playroom a half-hour earlier ... but now with the water relieving the pressure on my thighs.

I kissed her on the cheek, and several times on the neck, and then we hugged. I felt stirrings below – how could I not, with our bodies conjoined from our thighs to our chests?

Kelly and I looked into each other's eyes, silently, and I thought I saw hers cloud over, and start to tear, but at that moment, she leaned forward, wrapping her arms around my neck, and pulled me to her.

We stayed in that position, the warm water swirling around us, for a long time. A cool breeze hit us, and Kelly wriggled off me, lowering herself deeper into the water.

"Shall we return to the sauna for one more session?" I asked. Kelly smiled, and nodded. Again, I thought I saw tears, but it was probably just the Jacuzzi water being splashed onto her face by the action of the jets.

We stepped out of the spa, and into our flip-flops, quickly wrapping the towels around us, and hurrying back through the French doors into the house. I grabbed the water and glasses as we passed the patio table, and brought them with us downstairs.

We re-entered the shower room, and I placed the pitcher and glasses on one of the shelves built into the wall opposite the shoe rack. I poured two glasses, and we nearly emptied them before hanging our towels, and getting under a 95-degree rain shower.

It was only a quick rinse, and at the end, I lowered the temperature every few seconds, until we were both getting chilled again. Then, we took our towels and re-entered the sauna, which was now at 185 degrees Fahrenheit.

I told Kelly, "We can sit or lie down on the upper bench to get warmed up a bit, or sit for a while on the lower bench, where it's cooler."

Kelly said, "Let's get warmed up," and she put her towel in the corner of the upper bench, and sat cross-legged, facing out into the sauna. I decided to warm us up quickly, so I dipped a wooden ladle into an old-style wooden bucket, and poured water over the hot rocks. A slight scent of pine wafted from the wall-mounted heater.

I climbed up onto the upper bench, next to Kelly, and sat cross-legged on my towel facing her. It was quite hot at this elevation in the fully heated sauna, but we were still chilled from the outside air, and the cool rain shower, so the heat felt good. I reached over and turned the hourglass over, re-starting the timer.

Looking at Kelly, I smiled, and remembered, "I guess we never got to the wine and appetizers ... but it's probably a good thing: Alcohol doesn't mix with the sauna, and I want us to make it to dinner."

Kelly turned herself toward me, still cross-legged, so our knees were touching. "I'm having a pretty mellow time right now, without the wine. Sir." she commented.

I laughed, and told her, "You don't have to address me as Sir, any longer, Kelly. 'Sam' will do fine." Kelly looked into my eyes, and said, "I like calling you Sir, Sam." We both laughed.

Then Kelly grew more serious, and said, "I want to share my thoughts and feelings with you ... but I'm not sure what my feelings are, or how to organize my thoughts, and I don't want to give you the wrong impression."

Kelly looked down, and subconsciously wiped the beads of sweat that were now forming on her legs.

Kelly finally looked up again, and said, "Sir, I do think it's you." I wasn't quite following after our long break since the playroom, and gave Kelly a quizzical look.

She continued, "I've known a lot of guys, and many of them have been very nice to me. I don't have it in for all men, as you suggested earlier. But, as I told you, I've come away from most of my male friends – and sex partners, although I would not call any of them 'lovers' – very unsatisfied.

"I said earlier that I was not satisfied sexually, but I'm now realizing that it goes far beyond sex. These men may have gone through the motions – giving me flowers or candy, taking me out to dinner, or to a movie, or taking their time to undress me and do some kissing before moving to their prime target.

"They may have been considerate in the mechanical sense – for example, opening the door for me, but most of them were not considerate in the caring, feeling way that you have been today."

I looked up, somewhat startled by Kelly's comment. I was now getting quite hot, and briefly wondered whether I was having heat stroke, and not hearing Kelly correctly.

Kelly explained, "It's not just about how you have acted but as I said earlier, some combination of your ideals, your unique moral sensibilities, your intellectual prowess, your strong masculine – but not macho – control, and your experience and interest in sharing it with me. It's difficult to explain."

Kelly looked at me, then put her head down and pulled a corner of her towel up to wipe the sweat off her face. "I may be falling in love with you ... I know that's not what you wanted to hear ... but that isn't the problem I'm having – although I realize I might get hurt later." Kelly looked up at me, and I wasn't sure if I was more or less confused than before.

She continued, "I guess it's the fact that what I've been exposed to, here, today, is a higher standard – of everything. From your hospitality, to the intensity of your spankings, from your closeness and emotions, to the fine line you draw regarding 'sex'. It's the intensity of the pain, and the intensity of the love, that I'm feeling.

"It's the possibility of having an intensity of *life*, that I had not known could exist, before. You've opened my eyes – or at least started to pry them open – to new experiences and feelings. As I said, our experience today seems to have triggered a process of self-introspection."

Kelly looked at me and smiled, "I'm not trying to get technical – I barely understand what is happening myself. But I want to explain to you how you – and this whole day – have made me feel."

I tried to lighten the conversation a bit, "You mean your sore bottom?"

Kelly laughed, and said, "You know what I'm talking about. Sir! And it's not just the role playing, or the spankings: As you explained to me at our first (or was it the second?) lunch, it's about letting go, and giving yourself to someone who you can trust, someone who you respect and, especially, someone who shows respect for you."

Kelly wiped more sweat off, and – after seeing that the hourglass had already registered eight minutes – I suggested, "Let's sit on the lower bench for a while." We moved down to the lower level, re-situating our towels. Kelly sat with her feet on her towel, knees up, and her legs apart. The view of her beaded and dripping body was magnificent.

"There must be other things that can result in those deep emotional feelings, but I guess pain is pretty effective – and I admit that the pain you gave me was done more safely than many other kinds of pain I can think of.

"And my submitting really wasn't part of my 'pirate' fantasy ... but letting go is – and somehow, in my fantasy, I always knew the pirate wouldn't hurt me badly ... and I knew – because it was my own dream – that the pirate would make love to me at the end – even though my fantasies didn't get that far."

Kelly looked at me mischievously, and said, "And I never had to 'walk the plank'." We laughed, and were now both dripping.

"I hate to interrupt, but would you want to get out of this heat, and take a cool shower together?"

Kelly batted her big eyes at me in a very sexy way, wiped sweat from her body in a pretty gross way, and then started laughing. As we exited the sauna, Kelly said, "That was fun, Sir. But you forgot to tend to my needs, as you said you would do while we were in the sauna."

I stopped in my tracks, and cringed: I had forgotten ... just when Kelly was telling me about men who did not satisfy her needs. I turned to Kelly, ready to get down on my knee and plead for forgiveness; she had a stern look, and her hands were on her hips. "I'm really sorry, Kelly. I guess I got carried away with your story ... and I certainly didn't want to interrupt – until it got too hot for us to stay in there without getting roasted."

Kelly just looked angrier, and I had a feeling that I knew what she wanted. "Look, Kelly, I really thought we were done today ... but my forgetfulness, just when you were telling me about men who didn't satisfy you, is inexcusable. I've been trying to take good care of you, and now I forgot what had I promised."

I knew that she would want to switch me, or strap me, or ... I didn't know exactly what. Kelly had now been trained, only partially, but well enough to make me squirm.

As I concentrated on the stock-still, stock-naked form before me, Kelly suddenly threw up her hands, and broke out a huge smile; her hands clapped in the air, as she laughed hysterically, having to bend over and hold her knees, as she almost started choking. I couldn't believe she had tricked me so smoothly!

"Well, young lady, I guess I'll have to pat you to stop that choking", at which point I gave her a couple of hard slaps on her bottom. She jumped up, but continued laughing, and finally, I was laughing too.

As soon as I had started laughing, Kelly quieted, and said, "But you *know* that I'm going to punish you for that, young man!"

I frowned, "I'm not 'Sir' anymore?" We laughed some more, as I took the towels and dropped them into the hamper. We turned on all the jets, and rinsed off under the cool water. I left the leg-jets spraying cool water, as I adjusted the rain shower to a lukewarm level, then Kelly and I bathed each other.

I offered to help Kelly masturbate in the shower, but she coyly declined, and said I would 'owe her one', and that she would also delay my punishment until the next time she came over to 'play' ... and receive the rest of her own severe punishment. After we had shampooed each other's hair, and rinsed off, we turned off the jets and took new towels from the shelf, helping each other dry off.

We both folded the towels lengthwise, and wrapped them around our waist, then I grabbed the pitcher of water and glasses, and we walked together – both 'topless' – into the playroom.

I poured the water into a glass, and handed it to Kelly; she drank the entire glass within a few seconds. I started to pour the other glass ... and stopped, looking down at the inch of water left in it. I was sure I had drunk my entire glass before going back into the sauna.

I started getting upset, then burst out in laughter. Kelly stared at me, waiting to hear an explanation for my outburst. "Well, Kelly, the best laid plans ..." I almost choked on this, "in a manner of speaking." Kelly was getting 'curiouser and curiouser', so I ended the suspense and explained.

"Kelly, I hate to tell you this ... or maybe not ... but, by my definition, we just had sex."

Kelly stood there, absolutely still, her mouth hanging open, and her eyes blinking for a few seconds, before looking down at the glass, then smiling and holding it up.

"Yes, Kelly. Somehow, We didn't pay attention to which glass was which, and I'm pretty sure you have now been 'orally inoculated' with a dose of my germs." I then poured water into the glass I was holding, toasted Kelly, and drank most of it in a few seconds.

Kelly laughed, and then became more serious. "Sir, you took my medical history and examined me, but I never did the same with you. Do you have any contagious or sexually-transmitted diseases that I should be worried about?"

We had been joking – and my discovery of our 'having sex' actually gave me some ideas about how we might 'bend' the rules, but I had to answer seriously.

"No, Kelly," I reassured her. "I'm perfectly healthy – as far as I know. But I guess I screwed-up again." I smiled at her. "Maybe I shouldn't have included oral-oral contact in our definition of sex."

Kelly smiled also, "Then why not also allow oral-genital contact?" I began wondering why I had set such limits, anyway.

"Let's talk about that over dinner." I was a little surprised that Kelly seemed to accept this. I would have to ponder these issues further, before I was willing to answer her question.

I led Kelly to the desk, and she folded the towel, and put it on the floor, then dug into her beach tote, and pulled out underwear, bra, and a light dress. I looked at her standing there, and had a thought of how I could spice up the dinner ... but then decided to save that idea for another time.

It did give me some additional fantasy fodder, though, and I had to chuckle. And, it reminded me of something that I *did* want to bring to dinner for Kelly's ... and my ... further entertainment.

Kelly put on her bra first – the purple one, hooking it in front of her, and then pulling it around so the cups were in front, and finally putting her arms through the straps, and straightening them on her shoulders. She smiled at me, picking up her panties and putting them on – they were cute cotton bikinis, white, with a small deep purple flower pattern covering them.

Kelly then put on the dress, and turned, so that I could zip her. She turned again to face me, and held out her hands, giving me a questioning look.

I said, "You look beautiful, Kelly. I love the dress." It was a pink chiffon, plunging a bit on top, and with a hemline above the knee; perhaps a bit too light for the cool evening, but perfect for a summer party.

I was still wearing the towel, and asked her if she would like to do her hair or put makeup on in the bathroom, while I went upstairs to get dressed for dinner. Not that she needed any hairstyling or makeup to look beautiful.

Kelly declined, saying, "You got to watch me dress. Now it's my turn!" She gave a stern look, then started to crack up, barely getting out, "Let's get along to your bedroom, young man, so I can dress you properly for dinner." She pulled my towel off suddenly and, before I realized what she was doing, she gave me two hard slaps on my bottom.

I jumped, but muttered, "Fair is fair ... I guess." We laughed all the way upstairs to the master bedroom, which Kelly entered cautiously, and with great curiosity. I turned to her, and said, with my best mock-French accent, "Come with me, to my boudoir!"

I had always wanted to say that in a real-life situation. Although I still couldn't believe this was 'real' life. Maybe it was a dream. I thought about asking Kelly to pinch me, but decided better of it now, as I'm sure it wouldn't be just a 'play' pinch. We walked through the bathroom into the big closet, and Kelly looked around at the clothing hanging on double racks.

"Are you going to model your underwear for me, Mister?"

I arched my brows, and smiled, "If you would like me to." Kelly leaned against the closet door, as I pulled open a drawer.

When she saw the contents, she exclaimed, "You wear *those*?"

I laughed, and said, "Well, the only time anybody sees me in my underwear is if I'm in Europe, going to a sauna, and in a mixed (co-ed) changing room.

"Most of these come from a small shop in Amsterdam, around the corner from Dam Square, or from another small shop in Barcelona."

Kelly arched her brows, mocking me, and then she giggled. Kelly had already relieved me of the towel, so I tried on the first pair.

"They are all 'bikini'-type underwear, mostly from 'Hom' and other European brands. As you can see, most are black, and are a lot more fashionable than American underwear.

Kelly giggled again. She looked beautiful, standing there in that dress, her skin lustrous from the sauna, and her hair falling naturally down her back – without being restrained by the tie.

I tried on several more pairs for her, and then left on the ones with the double strings at each side, and proceeded to take down a sports shirt, and black slacks.

I considered giving Kelly the choice of clothes that I would wear, but knowing the staff at the restaurant made it difficult for me to relinquish control – and potentially have Kelly select a silly, non-matching outfit.

On the other hand, I would be submitting to her will, giving her control, and accepting her decision ... *trusting* her to make an intelligent choice, and not embarrass me. On the third hand, I had given her at least 75 reasons why she might want to 'get back' at me.

I dressed, as these thoughts flowed through my mind, and Kelly looked on – her own thoughts flowing, as perhaps were some juices down below. She had declined having me help her masturbate in the shower, and we had both been focused on her story, when we were in the sauna.

After I had put on my pants and shirt, I reached for a belt on the hook; I hadn't thought of this but, as my hand went up to take a belt down, my eyes surveyed the possibilities – each belt potentially being a punishment implement. This was just too good – I had to tease Kelly a bit more ... and hopefully, it wouldn't 'backfire' ... in a manner of speaking.

I lifted the heaviest and widest leather belt off the hook, and folded it in half, holding the ends with my right hand, and making a few swinging motions into my left hand. Even a mild slap of this belt really smarted!

Then I turned to Kelly, "OK, young lady, I can't let you go out to dinner without a little warm-up, so you'll be sure to feel your bottom when you are seated." I almost laughed, but controlled myself, and in a stern voice, said, "Turn around, bend over, and get that dress up!"

Kelly was startled. She alternately looked down at the belt, and back up at my face, gauging my seriousness; her own face morphed alternately from a smile, to a frown, to a slight smile, and to a slight frown, and then she looked into my eyes, and gave a little shrug.

Kelly turned around 180 degrees and, in one smooth motion, lifted her dress in back, bringing it onto her back, as she continued to bend down, and put her hands on her knees. I was impressed, and so was the hardening bulge being held in by my tight European underwear.

Kelly looked forward, and then said, "Ready, Sir!" I was even more impressed, and now had to consider what I would do – with this young lady's pantied rear in the air, waiting for the belt. I stepped up to her, and put my left hand lightly on her lower back. "You will receive your warm-up now, Kelly. Stay in position, please." I almost decided to let her off the hook, as she didn't 'deserve' to get any more punishment.

But she certainly wasn't complaining, and I knew this could be a turn-on for her. I swung the belt hard, impacting her underwear, and buttocks beneath, with a solid 'WHAP!'. Kelly yelped, and leaned forward, but immediately got ready for the next stroke.

I smiled, walking back to the hook, and exchanging the thick leather belt for the thin black one that I would be wearing to dinner. I turned around to view Kelly's behind, quivering a bit, but waiting patiently for the next stroke. "That will be all, Kelly. You may get up, now. There will be no more punishment this evening ... at least, if you behave! ... or, unless you ask for it."

Kelly got up, her dress falling back down off her back, and both arms reaching around under the dress, and rubbing her bottom. I finished buckling the belt, as she turned toward me, and I was gratified to see that she had a broad smile on her face.

"I didn't expect that, Sir: Neither the punishment in the first place, nor you stopping after only one stroke. That was kind of you, Sir."

I laughed, "It's so nice for me to hear that I am 'kind', after blistering your butt!" I took Kelly in my arms, and hugged her.

"Actually, Kelly, I hadn't planned it, but when I saw the belts hanging there I just couldn't resist seeing if you would cooperate – even now that your 'official' punishment experience is over. As I have explained, just the fact that you turned around, bent over, and lifted your dress was enough to convince me of your cooperation – and also get me turned on."

Kelly glanced down at my pants, but I didn't think my pants were noticeably bulging. "I did consider making you wait a while longer, bent over and waiting for your punishment, and then let you get up ... but your bottom looked so inviting, and I didn't want to disappoint you."

I arched my eyebrows at her, and she arched hers at me, then we laughed, as Kelly reached under her dress for one more rub, before letting it fall, and smoothing it down.

I steered Kelly out of the closet, and into the master bedroom, realizing that it was nearly time to leave for dinner ... but she suddenly turned around, and said, "Sir, do you think you could help me have that orgasm I didn't have in the sauna, or in the shower? After your little belt demonstration, I seem to be a bit tense ... down there."

I wasn't quite sure if she was serious or joking, but one look deep into her eyes, and I knew she wanted it. I made an exaggerated bow, and said, "At your service, ma'am." I pointed to the bed, questioningly, and Kelly nodded.

When we got to the bed, I was about to pull a couple of the pillows down to the foot, but Kelly looked up and said, "Do you happen to have a blindfold, in here? Sir?"

I wasn't sure what I was hearing, at first, but smiled, and said, "Yes, I was a Boy Scout - I'm always prepared." I went to one of the dressers next to the bed and opened a drawer, fumbling around inside it until I found one of the blindfolds provided on first class international flights. I shut the drawer, and returned to the foot of the bed.

I started to lift the blindfold into position over Kelly's eyes, and she gave me a strange look, "No! That's for you, silly. Let's get it on you, now, young man." I stood there, dumbfounded, as she carefully placed the blindfold around my head, and pulled it down over my eyes. She then said, "I'll help you get on the bed. I want you face-down."

Uh oh, this is not what I had expected. Was she now going to take the belt to me? I had to trust Kelly ... and I did. Kelly helped me lie down, parallel to the foot of the bed, probably near the middle (I couldn't see, but my left arm could just reach the foot of the bed). I was now lying on the bed, awaiting ... what? I felt something heavy on my bottom and thighs, and realized that Kelly had placed a towel there. I was even more confused. What had I gotten myself into?

Then, Kelly was on the bed, maneuvering herself over me, and lying down on top of me – her breasts pressed against my back, her groin over my buttocks, and her legs straddling mine. I could feel the mattress depressing, as Kelly placed her hands on the bed on both sides of my shoulders, lowering herself completely, so that her full weight was spread from my back to my legs. She adjusted herself several times.

It was a warm, dark and very sensuous feeling to be lying immobile on the bed, dressed in my slacks and nice shirt, ready for dinner, having this beautiful creature envelope me.

As my mind began to wander, I felt Kelly reaching down with her right hand, between my bottom and her front, inching its way down – presumably for her benefit, but this was becoming an incredible turn-on for me.

I didn't want to come in the European underwear I had just shown her, so I lay still, not rubbing myself against the bed – which I now realized I had been doing – but just relaxing. And enjoying the feel of a woman masturbating on top of me.

I quickly got the point, and it didn't take ropes and knots to keep me still. I let my own sexual feelings fade and, with the blindfold preventing me from seeing anything, my mind seemed to meld with Kelly's.

I was living Kelly's masturbation in my mind's eye – as if looking down from the ceiling, watching this beautiful woman who was engulfing a man, as a crab or octopus capturing it's prey before eating it. Or, a black widow spider ... My mind was wandering again, so I focused on what was happening above me.

Kelly was stroking herself, her legs moving apart and together in time with the strokes, her breath quickening, and her mons and hand pressing down on my bottom. Increasing the rate of her strokes, she started bucking – almost in waves, from her chest to her legs, causing a sensual ripple of my own flesh, under my clothing.

It was an incredible feeling. Kelly was writhing on top of me. She was panting her warm, moist breath on my neck, her legs squeezing in on mine and then splaying apart, her arms clawing the bed next to me, and her breasts pressing on my back.

I didn't know if she was oblivious to me at that moment, using me only as a platform for getting herself off – or if she realized how much of a turn-on it was for me, too.

Suddenly, Kelly jerked her head up, lessening the pressure of her breasts on my back, and moving her other hand quickly underneath her. She bucked, and panted, and continued rubbing, and then calmed, relaxing completely – her entire weight pushing me into the mattress, her legs entwined in mine.

She pushed herself down slightly across my body, and then relaxed again, her head now turned with her cheek on my upper back. I was definitely 'turned-on', but did not have an erection.

Actually, it was one of the strangest – and most beautiful – 'sexual' experiences I had ever had. I was still blindfolded, and realized that – at least for a few moments – I had 'given in', relaxed, and gotten into Kelly's head, rather than remain in mine. It was Kelly who'd had the orgasm, but I'd felt every moment of it with her.

It was a supremely 'open' way for a woman to be with a man ... and yet, we were both – more or less – dressed. No need to see anything, but literally 'feeling' the emotions of another person, who trusts you enough, and is open enough to do this.

Kelly hugged me from above, and said, "If you behave, I'll take good care of you when we get back from dinner."

I smiled into the bed, and thought about flipping us over – so that I was on top ... and perhaps having my way with her. But we were late for dinner, and Kelly's offer was irresistible, although I really did plan to send her home tonight ... and share a bed another time. Not pushing the relationship too fast.

Ha! That was a good one, after everything we had done today, on – what? – our 3rd 'date'? But we weren't dating: I was an older man who had offered to help her with her academic and career choices.

How a brief meeting in her father's kitchen, and two lunches could have led to this was still amazing me, as was this versatile, creative, open, and thoughtful girl. Woman.

CHAPTER 15: ENCHANTED EVENING

When we had gotten off the bed (and my blindfold finally removed), Kelly went down to the basement bathroom carrying her panties. She had said something about 'quick makeup' – which I thought an oxymoron, and she was more beautiful without makeup than most leading ladies with an entire staff of makeup artists and hair stylists at their disposal.

I went into the master bath to get straightened up (not in a manner of speaking – that would come later), and then made my way down to the basement to check on Kelly, turning on various lights along the way, as it was already getting dark.

She was standing at the mirror, her hair now brushed, doing some minor touch-ups, and turned to me, smiling. If I had brought down the camera and some studio lights, perhaps we might have skipped dinner. I realized Kelly might be thinking the same thing about skipping dinner, but not for the same reasons.

I walked through the playroom and into the office area, where I made sure the recorders were off, the computer asleep, and most things put away.

I also picked up a special item from the drawer, and put it in my pocket – I couldn't resist doing something 'with' Kelly during the dinner. Kelly's clothes were still in a pile next to her beach tote; I would have to remind her when we got back from dinner, and before she drove home.

I drove us to dinner, with one of the Romeros playing a classical guitar piece on the satellite radio. Kelly looked out her window, deep in thought. When we arrived at the restaurant – only 10 minutes late – our table was ready, and we were escorted to a corner booth, with a large round table – enough for six patrons.

The room had Victorian-style wood features, wallpaper, and light fixtures, and was fairly large – there were at least a dozen tables – but it was still intimate, with the lights dimmed, and the large, black tufted booths separating parties, offering some privacy. Exactly what we might need! As my mind started to wander – again – the waiter came, and gave us the menus and wine list.

"Hello, Sir, it's nice to see you again." Before I could say, "Thank you, George," Kelly cracked up. George and I both looked at Kelly, before I suddenly 'got it', and cracked up, also. I guess Kelly now realized that she wasn't the only one calling me Sir; but she was the only one I cared to 'play' with!

"Private joke, George. Let's start with a half-bottle of the Chateau St. Jean Chardonnay." George smiled, and said, "Very good, Sir," before walking quickly off in the direction of the wine cellar.

I smiled at Kelly. "So, what did you think of the day?"

Kelly looked down, and then those huge hazel eyes came up to meet mine; she batted her lashes coyly, and replied, "It was very interesting, Sir." We both laughed.

Actually, we had laughed a lot today – more than I had in a very long time ... and much more than I would have imagined for a 'punishment session'.

Kelly was relaxed, and easy to be with. She had the enthusiasm, energy level and curiosity apropos of her mid-twenties age, but also an experience level and maturity of someone older. I was still amazed that she had been willing – and enthusiastic – to do the things we did today and, far beyond that, she had done so with poise and good humor. She was a rare person, indeed.

"Kelly, I thought today was incredible – in many respects; and I thought you were incredible, too. I would really like to know more of what you were thinking during our experience, now that you can look back on it with a glass of wine in your hand."

I had seen George approaching, and as I ended the sentence, he quietly opened the bottle, and I took a quick taste – being quite familiar with this vintage. George poured our glasses, and left us to our quiet corner.

I raised my glass, and looked into Kelly's eyes, "Thank you for the day, Kelly. I hope it was a turn-on for you, too. And I'm really looking forward to playing with you again." I took a sip of wine, and clarified, "I'm sorry – I didn't mean it to come out quite like that. You know what I mean.

"Actually, I would like to spend more time with you – regardless of what we are doing. And, of course, I am interested in helping you with your career." I took another sip of wine, and couldn't help but add, "You know, this all started with you inviting me out to lunch to talk about biochemistry!"

Kelly chuckled. She sat back in the booth, and ran her finger around the lip of the glass. Finally, she looked up at me, and said, "It *was* an incredible day ... and I'm still not sure about some of my feelings. What we did today came close to some of my fantasies, and I did want to see what it would be like to be spanked, even though I didn't expect to actually like it. But there was so much more than I expected ... and less."

I arched my brows, "Less?"

Kelly smiled, "Yes ... I guess in two ways. First, there was less drama – no yelling, no anger; it wasn't like I had envisioned the pirate in the fantasy I described. It was very civil." Kelly took a sip of wine, then put her glass down and looked at me seriously.

"And, second, although I know you said there would be no sex, I could not have imagined how much less sex there was ... and how much more sex there was ... than I thought there would be. Maybe not sex, but intimacy. I'm not sure I can put it into words."

I smiled, "Kelly, this is exactly what I was trying to convey, during our lunch: It is the combination of letting go, allowing someone else to take control, being totally open with each other, and – at its essence – trust.

"When we have done these things, and learned to trust each other, we begin to care for each other – a relaxed intimacy, a closeness that has nothing to do with sex. I don't necessarily want to equate it with 'love', but perhaps it is a certain kind of love."

I continued, "And, I would guess, you now have some idea of how I could be turned on either way – by having you submit to me, or me submit to you. I think you enjoyed being the 'top' for a while."

Kelly laughed at this, "Yes, that was unexpected – both that you would let me punish you, and that I would get so turned on doing it. But it was much more surprising that I could get turned on by the pain of you spanking me."

Now, I put my wine glass down, "Maybe it wasn't the pain that turned you on, but your own submission?"

Kelly looked confused, "I don't know ..."

George came with some great sour dough bread and a plate of extra-virgin olive oil and excellent Balsamic vinegar, and gave us the menus. "George, I know you won't mind if we slow down our meal tonight – we have a lot of talking to do." George arched his brows and, out of the corner of my eye, I could see Kelly doing the same. I smiled at George, and he took his leave quickly and quietly.

"As long as they're here, why don't we look at the menus?" We opened the large leather-bound menus, which featured a great selection of classic French cuisine, although I had my favorites at this place. While Kelly made her selection, I perused the wine list, and picked out a northern Californian Zinfandel – flowery and light on the palate.

George saw that we had put down the menus, and returned to take our orders – the scallop appetizer and duck breast with port sauce for Kelly, and the escargots and veal Oscar for myself. "Actually, George, I think I'll have the paté tonight," I said, and he took the menus and quietly took his leave again.

"Kelly, what were the high points of the day for you?" Kelly declined my offer of bread, so I took a steaming piece, and dipped it in the Balsamic and oil, as Kelly responded.

"Well," and suddenly she was laughing, "probably masturbating on top of you in your bedroom." I laughed too. That wasn't quite what I had expected, but it *had* been an incredible experience.

Then, Kelly continued, "And, when I put you across my lap and spanked you ... and stuck you with needles." I just nodded. Kelly was getting excited, now. "And our role-playing when you introduced yourself as a professional spanker."

Kelly chuckled, "And, I liked our shower together after the sauna. In fact, I liked our lunch, and our dip in the pool, and our fun in your closet ..."

I smiled, "It sounds like you had fun. What about the spankings?" As Kelly was thinking about this, our appetizers came. And so, almost, did I, when I remembered what I had put in my pocket at the last minute in the office, when Kelly was getting ready for dinner. Maybe as an 'intermezzo' after the appetizer?

Kelly tried a scallop, and her eyes lit up, "These are really good!" My paté was very good also, and I was glad I had remembered how garlicky the escargots were – something I love, but that Kelly might not enjoy quite as much afterward.

As I picked up a cornichon, I reminded Kelly, "You were going to tell me what you thought of the spankings. Perhaps not the best dinner discussion, but we didn't get to do a debriefing back at the house."

Kelly just smiled, "You scientists!" Then, she became more serious, put her fork down, and wiped her lips with the linen napkin. She looked at me with a mixture of pride, curiosity and confusion.

"This morning, I was really scared. It started with your e-mail; I realized that our lunch conversations were about to be 'played' out on my bottom. It's not that I didn't trust you – in fact, I *trusted* you to do exactly as you said you would – administer a hard spanking." She swallowed. "Then, we spent so long discussing the Agreement, and I wasn't sure that I would be able to meet all of the conditions you required."

Kelly looked down at her hands in her lap. "And then, when I was in front of the desk, it seemed that I couldn't do anything right ... and I was really trying. I didn't realize what you meant, when you talked about 'corrective' punishment and 'corner time'.

"But it was when you brought out those long needles, and told me you were going to stick them in my bottom, that I wasn't sure I was doing the right thing."

I reached over and held Kelly's hands in mine. She looked at me and continued, "You were right when you said that I would be surprised at some of the things we do. I couldn't have imagined many of the things we did. You gave me an enema, and then sat on my lap while I expelled it into the toilet. You made me roll dice, and gave me the number of shots indicated by the dice. You inserted large butt plugs in me, and then tawsed me. And you examined my 'private parts' in more detail than anyone but my doctor."

Kelly withdrew her hands from mine, and reached for the glass of wine; she suddenly seemed to have more confidence, more energy. "But even though the spankings really hurt – at the time – they weren't that bad ... my bottom is hardly sore at all now."

I laughed, "Well, if I had completed your punishment – with the hairbrush and then the cane – I'm not sure you would be sitting here now. Perhaps kneeling ..."

It was Kelly's turn to laugh. "I'm serious!"

I laughed more, "So am I! You'll see next time, when you really won't be able to sit down. I had to save a few things for the next time, you know." But I wanted to hear Kelly's thoughts regarding the spanking, so decided to shut up. Kelly finished her chardonnay, and I hoped that the wine wouldn't dull the evening prematurely ... in an antonymic manner of speaking.

Kelly explained, "I didn't think I could take the pain ... but I did. In fact, the whole experience today was surreal." Ha! That's what I had been thinking all day! Kelly continued, "Everything is opposites ... a real Yin and Yang."

I had no idea what she was talking about, but wisely kept quiet. "You were harsh and you were gentle. There was pain, and there was pleasure. You told me what would happen, but you surprised me. We didn't have sex, but I had a couple of the best orgasms I've ever had."

Fortunately, the sound of those amazing words had faded as George approached to remove our appetizer plates and open the red wine. I tasted and nodded, and George discretely left us.

"Kelly, I am so pleased that you found the day interesting, and a turn-on. I would like to continue hearing your feedback, but – like a certain computer mogul used to say, 'There's just one more thing ...'. I'm sure you knew that I would do *something* to surprise you during dinner."

Kelly's eyes blinked, and her mouth fell open, "What?"

I chuckled, "Well, I'd like to keep you just a little unbalanced ..." The color drained from Kelly's face, as she just stared at me ... and then a small smile formed on her lips. "OK, what is it?" She laughed, and sat back on the tufted black leather, quite confident in her ability to handle anything I threw at her.

I pulled a small box from my jacket pocket, and put it on the table. "I thought of a few things we could do here at the restaurant."

Kelly blinked, "*Do*?"

I continued, "But this is something simple, and might be interesting. At least, I can guarantee that it will keep you awake, if you start feeling the wine." Kelly's face contorted in confusion. "Will you submit to me?" I asked, in a mock-serious tone.

Kelly quickly looked into my eyes and said, "Yes, Sir."

I opened the box, and took out the small oblong metal item, which looked a bit like a small mouse with a tail.

After checking that nobody was coming down the aisle, I told Kelly, "Please pull up the front of your dress, and pull aside the crotch of your underwear. I'm going to have you insert this, with the small wire hanging out, like a tampon."

Kelly stared incredulously at me. However, it only took a few seconds for her to realize that this was another submission test, and that she would do as I asked.

I watched as she gathered the front of her dress to her waist, darting her eyes around the room to make sure nobody was watching. As I had instructed, she pulled her underwear aside, and inserted the device.

I asked, "Shall I check, or do you think it's fully inserted?"

Kelly laughed, "You may check if you want, Sir, but I've put it in as far as it will go."

I just smiled, and said, "OK, put your things back into place, and we'll continue our conversation."

Kelly gave me a funny look, but adjusted her underwear, and smoothed down her dress. I said, "I considered having you insert that in the car, or perhaps have you go into the bathroom and insert a small butt plug."

Kelly scrunched her face, "Thank you, Sir, for not doing that."

I laughed. Kelly didn't know what I *had* done, yet. "Kelly, you were saying that some of the things we did turned you on?"

Kelly smiled, "Yes, Sir."

That was concise. "Would you like to elaborate?"

"I don't know … the whole experience was a turn-on for me. Maybe not while it was happening, but as it evolved. It was partially the excitement of fear – mainly of the unknown (it didn't take me long to realize that you would continue to surprise me). But it was largely due to the way you approached it – the role-playing, your calm attitude, not turning it into just having sex."

I looked questioningly at Kelly, "*Just* having sex?"

Kelly smiled but didn't laugh, "You know what I mean, Silly. I mean, 'Sir'." This time she giggled. "And I really liked your 'fairness' – especially letting me punish you a little. That was certainly a turn-on ... but I was already turned on by other things ..."

I arched my brows exaggeratedly, "You mean, I let you spank me and stick me with needles for nothing?"

Kelly was shaking her head, ignoring my joke. "No, it was part of the whole experience – basically, having you punish me, and treat me respectfully at the same time. That may be what I needed from my new father ..."

Our dinners arrived, and George poured the wine. The crystal glasses refracted light from the candles on the table and fixtures on the ceiling across the tablecloth, and onto Kelly's face. George looked up at Kelly, as he poured her wine, and asked, "How are you doing so-far, Miss? May I get you anything?"

Kelly smiled at him, and said, "Maybe just a glass of water, please."

George smiled, glad that he could do something useful for Kelly, "Certainly, Miss!"

After George left, we toasted again, "Kelly, I have a few toasts to make." Kelly held the glass, and batted her eyes at me. "First, here is to your dissertation, finishing graduate school, and starting a successful career. I hope I can help a little bit with that." We took a sip of the wine – lighter than I normally would have chosen, but appropriate to the occasion, I thought.

"Second, I want you to know how proud I am of your 'performance' today. From the time you knocked at my door, to the time you bent over in the closet at my whim, you have been absolutely perfect in the role of a submissive – but still feisty enough and creative enough to surprise and excite me."

I took a sip of wine, and remembered, "And I wanted to tell you – having you masturbate on top of me was one of the most intimate sexual experiences I have had ... and I didn't even get an erection, but I was incredibly 'turned-on'. You have been totally open, and have not complained when I did some things you didn't expect – like giving you shots and enemas."

I smiled sincerely at Kelly, "So, here's to your 'First Experience' in submission!" We sipped more wine. I was now thinking that perhaps Kelly *should* sleep over, as we were going to be wasted after the big dinner and all the wine. The issue of having sex probably wouldn't 'arise' (Ha!) until the morning.

"And fourth, I want you to know how much I care for you ... I like you very much. Actually, more than that ..."

Kelly put her wine down and looked at me, her skin glowing in the candlelight, her long hair flowing along each side of her, and her eyes larger than ever. Now they were sparkling, with reflections of the flickering flames from the candles on the table.

I continued, "I'm sorry, Kelly, if I've overstepped. I just feel very close to you. I want to be with you more. I *need* to be with you more. Whether we 'play' or just spend 'normal' time together. I have discovered your inner beauty – as well as your obvious external beauty – and I have re-discovered something in myself that I have only felt a few times in my life, a very long time ago."

I looked at Kelly, but couldn't read her expression. "And, we seem to have hit it off well together; I don't remember laughing so much in years." Kelly smiled, and nodded. I concluded, "So, here's to the future of our relationship!" Kelly picked up her glass, and we 'clinked' the crystal together before drinking our wine in thoughtful silence.

Kelly put her wine down again, and smoothed the napkin in her lap. "Sam. Sir. I feel very much the same as you've described. I realize it's probably mostly the things we did today, but I feel really close to you, too. I thought I trusted you before, but after what we've done today ..." Her voice trailed off, and her eyes became glassy, as she recalled the day.

"I thought you were kind, considerate, playful, and took seriously your responsibility to take care of me. And, you're right – I haven't laughed this much in a long time, either." Kelly looked down, and then into my eyes, "I would like our relationship to continue ... and grow. You'll be stuck with me for at least another session, and then ... who knows? Maybe I'll grow tired of playing with you ... but I'm pretty happy at the moment."

"Well, that's a good start. Let's eat!" We dug into our meals, sipped our wines, and thought back on the day. I could not imagine a more perfect first submission experience for Kelly, nor could I imagine a more perfect play partner to help make my fantasies come alive.

I finished the last morsel, poured the last of the wine into our glasses, and sat back in the coziness of the large, but dark and enveloping booth. I reached into my pocket and fiddled with a small keychain remote, and asked Kelly, "Did you enjoy the meal?"

Kelly wiped the last crumbs of the meal from her lips, and beamed, "That was incredible! You can't eat like this all the time?"

I laughed, "Hardly, but it makes for a nice special occasion ... like tonight." Kelly sipped the last of her wine; I had to wait a few more moments, or risk the possibility of staining her beautiful dress.

As she put the glass back on the table, I said, "You know, you got off easy, being able to sit here on your barely-sore bottom, rather than having to squirm to avoid the fire from the welts of a cane. But, I didn't want to let you off the hook completely ..."

Kelly gave me a curious look, and then frowned, looking down to her lap.

"Yes!" I pushed the first button on the remote, and Kelly nearly jumped out of the booth.

"Oh my! I knew you had something planned with that thing, but I didn't know it could do this!" I had triggered the low-frequency vibrations from the vaginal device, the retrieval wire also serving as the antenna for the wireless control.

I laughed so hard I had to put my wine down. "It's one of my little inventions. You know how I love to tinker in the basement."

Kelly looked at me seriously, and then 'got it', and cracked up. I took the opportunity to trigger level 2 on the remote. Kelly squealed, and I had to stop the vibrations, lest the entire restaurant become involved.

Kelly's face was flushed, and she had her hands on her stomach, as though they could quiet the vibrations within her. I laughed again; this was so much fun!

The busser cleared our plates, and George returned to clean the crumbs from the tablecloth, and give us the dessert menus. He asked if we would like a coffee or after-dinner liqueur. Kelly requested a cappuccino (although that is generally not regarded as an after-dinner drink, at least by the Italians), and I ordered an espresso with Grand Marnier.

George left, and I was just about to continue the conversation with Kelly, when she suddenly looked pale, frowned, and then smiled broadly, as two other young women – about Kelly's age – came out of the adjoining room, and passed our table on their way to the exit.

"Kelly! What a coincidence to see you here. You remember, this is Linda's birthday!"

Kelly was flustered for a moment, and then remembered, "Oh! Happy birthday, Linda! I had forgotten it was tonight. Well, I told you that I had other plans."

The two girls looked at Kelly strangely, then at me, and back at Kelly. Kelly jumped in, "I'm sorry, this is Sam – he's an old family friend, and a researcher; he has offered to help with some career guidance."

I just couldn't resist: I tapped the second button on the remote – very briefly, but the effect was immediate. Kelly nearly howled, and her friends looked at each other, and then back to her. Kelly coughed, and said, "Sam, this is Linda and Julie – we all went to high school together."

I said, "Pleased to meet you! Kelly has been telling me a bit about her 'wilder' days." Kelly coughed again, and I tapped the #1 button on the remote, and Kelly squirmed: A true 'tit for tat'.

Again, Linda and Julie looked at each other, now with a bit of concern on their faces. Julie said, "I hope she didn't tell you too much!" Kelly looked uncomfortable.

I felt compelled to continue, "Well, she did mention Linda's birthday, but not that you guys would be here. Would you like to join us for dessert? Then, maybe, I should give Linda her birthday spanking?" All eyes were suddenly on me.

"Excuse me?" Linda said, with more of a laugh in her voice than a serious tone. Kelly just closed her eyes and shook her head.

Linda seemed confused, so I looked at her, while speaking to Julie, "Or, if you don't want dessert, we could do Linda's spanking now?" Kelly slunk down in the booth, and I had to push the #3 button to bring her instantly back to sitting attention.

Kelly jumped in, "Sam and I were just talking about corporal punishment. I told him that you guys had been paddled in junior high school, before you moved here from the South."

Julie laughed, "Yeah, they're real civilized down there. But if I was caught smoking, playing hooky, or wearing inappropriate clothes, I would rather take a lickin' from the Girls Vice Principal, than from my Dad, any day."

Linda was nodding, "It wasn't so bad, but it was embarrassing when you went back to class and couldn't sit down; everyone knew you had been paddled good!"

I was amazed at the turn of the conversation, and again offered the girls dessert. Julie said, "It would be fun, but we're stuffed, and I'm taking Linda to a movie tonight." Too bad.

"Well, perhaps another time," I said, eyeing both girls, who were relatively 'fit', and cute – albeit in very different ways. Julie was trim and had light brown hair that was cut straight across, a few inches below her shoulders, while Linda was heavier, with darker hair, wide hips and a very 'spankable' bottom.

"I'd be happy to give Linda a 'rain check'." All three girls laughed nervously.

Kelly, Linda and Julie said their goodbyes. Kelly got up, and my timing was impeccable as I tapped the #3 button on the remote just at the moment when Kelly gave each of the girls a hug.

Kelly was giggling, and when she got strange looks from her two friends, she just shrugged, and said, "I'll tell you later." I watched Linda and Julie depart, and noted the suitability of both their bottoms for a good spanking.

Kelly sat back down, and slid over next to me. "That was terrible! How could you do that?"

I tried not to smile, "What?" Kelly slapped me on the arm, and said, "I can't believe you mentioned spanking to them!"

I shrugged, "Why not? It is Linda's birthday. What a great excuse! In fact, I was hoping that you might work with me to get them to come over for a little birthday celebration." It was interesting that Kelly was more upset by my mention of spanking than my 'goosing' her with the vibrator in front of her friends.

I continued, "You know, you're going to have to explain to your friends what happened here tonight. You could tell them 'privately' that I'm a professional spanker."

Kelly cracked-up, "I can't do that! ... But it would be fun ..."

We thought of the possibilities, and smiles grew on both of our faces. "Let's discuss it, and I'd like to hear why you were so nervous about me mentioning your 'wild' days – I assumed they were there with you?"

Kelly nodded, but I jumped in, taking Kelly's hands and saying, "But first, I'd like to ask you a serious question." Kelly's smile disappeared, and she looked at me seriously. I said, "Kelly, I've told you how enthralled I am by you, and I know you've been frustrated by some of the limits I've placed on our relationship."

Kelly arched her brows, but wasn't sure whether to smile or frown. I continued, "So I'd like to know ... if we could have sex." Kelly's jaw dropped, and her eyes looked deeply into mine. I added, "I mean now. Right here in the restaurant."

Kelly's jaw dropped further – if that were possible – but suddenly I saw a gleam in her eyes, and the beginning of a smile forming on her otherwise-serious face. I couldn't help smiling – at least a little bit, "Yes, Kelly, I'd like to know if we could share a dessert."

Now, Kelly took her hands from mine and put them over her mouth; she was suddenly in a fit of hysterical (no feminine sub-meaning intended) laughter. I calmly explained, "You know, we mixed up our water glasses earlier, so there's a 50-50 chance that we've already 'had sex' ... but I would like us to make a decision together whether this makes sense."

Kelly continued laughing, and attracted a few looks of people turned around in their booth. I could barely keep from laughing myself, but had to continue. "After all, we've already had so many calories, with all the food, and the wine."

Now, Kelly looked up, and cracked-up anew. I laughed, "And neither of us got much exercise today; well, my arms got some exercise ..."

I slid over a bit in the booth, and snuggled with Kelly, and then sat up, taking her face in my hands, and asked, "Kelly, may I please kiss you?"

I think this made Kelly laugh more, but I was serious. I leaned toward her, and Kelly suddenly calmed, as we kissed – long, slow, and intense. The feelings of the day came to the surface for both of us, and we held each other for what seemed like several minutes, oblivious of anyone else in the restaurant. I kissed Kelly quickly on the tip of her nose, and slid back to my place.

George discretely appeared at the table, and asked if we wanted to order desserts. I looked at Kelly, and said, "You pick."

Kelly looked at the dessert menu and suddenly hiccupped ... except that it turned into a laugh. She looked at George and confidently ordered the molten fudge brownie á la mode, with cinnamon ice cream. George took the menus and retreated, while Kelly looked at me with sparkling eyes.

She explained, "I know you're uncomfortable with 'fluid contact', but I'm very glad you kissed me. And, if we're going to share our saliva, then let's do it right – with flowing ice cream over flowing chocolate – not some cake that can be eaten neatly and separately."

Kelly thought for a moment, becoming more serious, but still with a big smile on her face, "So what does this mean for the rest of our relationship ... or at least 'play'?"

I sat back in the booth, "That's a good question! But let's not get ahead of ourselves; we're just sharing dessert." Kelly chuckled. I steered the conversation back to the original question, "Tell me about Julie and Linda."

Kelly took a sip of her cappuccino, and sat back in the booth. She closed her eyes, and consciously relaxed her body. Then she opened her eyes, and looked into mine. "Julie and Linda moved here when we were all entering high school. They didn't – don't – know that I was adopted, but we all had problems, and they tended to get into trouble – and get me into trouble – more than anyone else in our class."

She continued, "There is a third friend and trouble-causer who was in this group – Kathy. She was also invited to the birthday party tonight, but is currently somewhere on the coast of Mexico, vacationing with her parents."

Kelly took another a sip of cappuccino, and glanced sideways at me, with a mischievous smile. "I've always wanted to get back at them for some of the things they got me into. They got good grades, and so did I, but we did a lot of 'extra-curricular' activities. Including drugs."

I had to ask, "Did you ever inject drugs?" Kelly was surprised, "Oh, no! The first time a needle has gone into me other than in a doctor's office was at your house, today."

I breathed a little easier, and Kelly continued. "We smoked a lot of grass, dropped acid a few times, and ended-up doing coke. Linda's parents are wealthy, and they didn't know how she spent her 'clothes money'. But while I was basically anti-social, Linda and especially Julie, actively *tried* to get into trouble – all the time." We sipped our coffees.

Kelly continued, "They got into college, but didn't make it a full year – except Kathy, who is studying art. It was about that time that I began to see that there was more to life than sex and drugs ... well, at least drugs," we laughed.

"So we pretty much parted ways. Julie is a beautician, and Linda works for a publisher in an administrative assistant position. They still get into trouble all the time. I wouldn't be surprised if they dropped acid before going into the theater tonight."

I laughed, "And they seemed so wholesome."

Kelly nodded, "It's that southern style – they dress nicely, and are polite ... but they can be a terror."

The germ of an idea formed in my mind. "How do you think Julie and Linda would have done today – if they had been in your position (so to speak)?"

Kelly thought about this. "I really don't know. I don't think they would be too bothered by it. But I don't think you could have expected Linda to get across the lap of a total stranger."

George brought our dessert. It looked fantastic – for a few moments. But once we had dug in, the melted ice cream and molten chocolate mixed on the plate, and it wasn't as appetizing – at least to me.

Kelly took a spoon of cinnamon ice cream, and said, "Yum!" She took a taste of the molten cake, and her eyes went to the ceiling, "This is incredible!"

I turned to Kelly and remarked, "It feels so good! ... I mean, tastes so good!"

Kelly smiled, but didn't laugh. She said, "I'm glad to see you're starting to relax a little. Maybe I can help to break down your inhibitions."

Now, it was my turn to laugh. The tables had turned: Kelly was obviously more open – in many respects – than I was. But fair is fair: I was OK with my inhibitions being broken down – especially by Kelly.

We finished our dessert, and the combined effect of the activities of the day, the food, and the alcohol resulted in both Kelly and I being exhausted.

CHAPTER 16: NIGHTCAP

I drove us home safely, glad that the restaurant was less than 10 minutes from the house. We went inside, and I reminded Kelly that she had clothes downstairs.

"You're not going to make me drive home in this condition, are you?"

I knew where she was going with this. "I would be happy to drive you home, Kelly."

She led me downstairs, and scoffed, "You're not in much better shape than I am. I'm staying here tonight." As we got downstairs, Kelly said casually, "Can we take this thing out of me, now, Sir?" I chuckled, "Only if you don't want it to be part of your orgasmic experience."

Kelly arched her brows and laughed, "Let's try that another time."

I directed her into the exam room. "Get up on the table and lie back. I'll take care of it." Kelly gave me a glance, and said, sarcastically, "Gee, that's very kind of you, Sir." But she got onto the table and lay back.

She lifted her legs, and pulled her knees almost to her chest. I put my finger under the thin fabric of Kelly's panties, and drew the crotch aside, as I separated her labia and located the retrieval string. "Are you ready?" I asked.

Kelly stared at the ceiling, and said, "Sure."

I pulled the device out of Kelly, and replaced her crotch into position. I quickly washed and dried the miniature vibrator – and my hands – in the exam room sink, and put it in a Petri dish on the counter. I then asked, in my best 'doctor's' voice, "Do you need any other exams or procedures tonight, Ma'am?"

Kelly lifted her head, and looked at me, "You're joking. Well, maybe you're not. I guess it's OK, if you want to take my rectal temperature, or something."

I laughed, "Or something? Let's see ..." Kelly lifted her head from the exam table and gave me a 'dirty' look. We both laughed.

"Thank you, Kelly. You remain open and cooperative, and have a good sense of humor, even after all we've done. But I think we're both very tired, so I suggest we get to bed pretty soon."

Kelly's eyes lit up, "So you've changed your mind about making love?"

I really wasn't sure what was in my mind, at the moment. "Let's go into the playroom, and we can talk."

Kelly got off the exam table, muttering, "I was hoping we would do more than that!"

In return, I muttered, "I was hoping Linda and Julie would come over ..."

Kelly made a slight detour into the bathroom, and I quickly went back into the exam room to clean up a few things, and lock the door. I stood in the doorway, as Kelly washed her hands. As she walked past me, she smiled, and led us into the playroom.

We sat on the couch, and I gave Kelly a big kiss – actually, a delightfully long and deep kiss, somehow eliciting in both of us all the emotions of the day. When I sat back, Kelly had a tear on her cheek. "Is something wrong?" I asked.

Kelly looked at me, and said, "No, everything's fine. I really enjoyed the day, and am glad you're letting me stay over. But now that you've broken me down, I'm afraid you're not going to give me as much of yourself as I want. Need."

I stared at Kelly, and a crazy thought ran through my head. "I could say the same thing, Kelly, although what I might want may be asking much more of you than you are of me." Kelly looked confused and, I admit, with the alcohol, I wasn't sure if I was making any sense. "Actually," I told her honestly, "I'm not sure what I want."

Kelly nodded, and said, "Me too."

In my current state, and having spent the incredible day with Kelly, my thoughts wandered. The image of 'Kelly, Sex Slave' came unbidden to my mind's eye. But I had an unconventional idea of what a sex slave might be ... certainly providing sex, but more of a 'royal subject' than a slave. I shook my head, and stood up from the couch.

Being my hospitable self, I suggested, "I would offer you a drink, but we've probably both had enough alcohol – at least if we're going to do more than just go to sleep. You can over-rule me, if you like; I do have some nice wines, and a collection of liqueurs." Kelly shook her head, "No, I've had enough liquor for one night."

I followed-up, "But I can get you some guava juice, or iced tea, or Diet Coke?"

Kelly nodded, "Diet Coke sounds good." I went to the bar and poured us two crystal glasses of Diet Coke, and returned to the couch. Kelly drank almost her entire glass, and I was about to get up again, but Kelly put her hand on my arm, and said, "I don't need any more Coke right now. In fact, I'm feeling fine. How are you doing?"

I sipped my Coke and thought about it. What a day it had been! Kelly and I had been together nearly 14 hours now, and had done some amazingly intimate things together. Kelly had shown her strength, her enthusiasm, and her humor, while cooperating with whatever I had thrown at her: Spankings, paddlings and tawsings, spooning and switching; medical exams, enemas and shots; and a lot of 'close' time, including in the sauna and our showers together.

We had both had several orgasms by the hand of each other, including my phenomenal 'out-of-body' experience with Kelly masturbating on top of me, while I was pinned to the bed blindfolded. The day had certainly been more than I had ever imagined possible, and Kelly was more than I had ever imagined possible.

"Kelly, I'm fine, too. Just a little confused."

Kelly turned to face me on the couch, sitting cross-legged, the lower front of her dress mostly gathered in her lap, her underwear casually on display. She said, "This has been an incredible day, and I've enjoyed every minute of it. Even when you were punishing me." Kelly smiled. "And I think we both lived up to the commitment of the contract we signed."

I didn't recount all the terms, but quickly thought through them, and commented, "You took your punishment with a positive attitude ... and I think you had some fun. And I hopefully gave you an 'adventurous' experience, if not at least a little bit enlightening."

Kelly nodded again, "Actually, it was very enlightening. Although you had described the turn-on, and I had even fantasized about very similar things, it was difficult for me to really understand – until I had gone through it – how exciting it can be. I still don't really understand it ... but I experienced it." Kelly looked down, and I thought she was going to say 'But ...'

Instead, she looked up at me with those big hazel eyes, and said, "I think I want more of it. I think I need more ... of something. It's not just the spankings, but ... I don't know ..."

She looked down again, "Maybe it's the challenge of submitting to everything you want to do to me and, at the same time, having you take responsibility for me. It's the opposites we discussed earlier – your harshness and your gentleness, the pain and the pleasure."

Kelly reached for her Coke, and I quickly went to the bar, brought over another can, and poured some for her.

Kelly continued, "And it's the openness. It doesn't bother me at all to be open with you ... but I got surprisingly turned-on when you were open with me. For example, having you get into a knee-chest position, while I stuck you with needles." She was quiet for a moment.

"And it's the respect. You have not 'beaten' me, but given me a thoughtful and controlled amount of pain. I admit that I wasn't too sure I could complete the punishment, when you tawsed me, but I realized afterward that I could take it – that you had controlled the intensity to give me the experience, but not overdo it."

I smiled, "Of course, Kelly, you haven't felt the hairbrush or the cane, yet ..."

Kelly looked at me, "No ... but I'm looking forward to it." Her hands dropped to her lap, against the front of her underwear, and they continued a slight – but visible – rubbing motion.

She then stopped, and looked seriously at me, "And what about making love? Real sex. I have deep and growing feelings for you, and I want to give you more of myself."

Now, I looked down. I truly did not know what was in my head. While I had set restrictions for myself when my wife was with me, there was really no reason for them now. I could be as free as I wanted, although I did have some lingering fears regarding sexually transmitted diseases.

And, I still had reservations about going 'too far' with Kelly – the daughter of a friend, and someone more than two decades my junior. Perhaps this was artificial, also, as I wasn't very close to her parents, and age really should not play a role with respect to having a casual relationship with someone; or, if two people love each other.

"I don't know, Kelly. I certainly would love to make love to you. You're a beautiful and sexy woman, and I find you even more of a turn-on now that you have shown your ability to be open ... and submissive. Not that submission has to always be a part of our relationship ... but you know it is a turn-on for me."

Kelly just looked at me, "I think we have discovered today that submission – in some form – is a turn-on for me, too."

I nodded, continuing, "I also made a commitment to you this morning that I would ensure that we had our experience without having 'sex'. That was originally intended to make you feel more comfortable – that I wasn't 'just' after sex.

"But I think it backfired, and perhaps illuminated some of my own inhibitions. Not that I'm inhibited about sex, but I'm conditioned by the past 20 years of relationships while I was married, where the issue of sex did arise (so to speak) both for my wife, and for some of my female friends."

I took another sip of Coke, and put down the glass. "We've already shared saliva, and I'm not finished kissing you tonight." Kelly arched her brows and smiled at me.

"But I want to finish our day without sex – because this is what we both have committed to do. When you think back on today, I don't want our experience confused or confounded by your thoughts about sex."

I wasn't sure Kelly understood what I was saying, as I wasn't sure, myself.

Kelly smiled, "Well, then we can just wait about 30 minutes, and we'll be into a new day, so we can have sex then!" I laughed. I guess that was true. But there was still the potential issue of how much alcohol I had consumed; I was pretty sure I could 'get it up', but not sure I wanted that pressure for our first lovemaking experience.

I suggested, "How about this? Let's settle for oral sex while you're here tonight and tomorrow morning. When you come back next time ... and assuming you complete the rest of your punishment ... we can make love – if you are still in the mood for it."

Kelly smiled, and nodded, "That would be OK. But if you're not going to make love to me tonight, I hope you're pretty good at going down on a woman."

I laughed again, "You can let me know how I compare with your boyfriends in that department." I leaned over to Kelly, and gave her a quick kiss, and then got up, and held out my hand for her.

"Let's go have some fun in the shower, and then some more fun in bed!" Kelly took my hand and got up off the couch. I gave her a big hug and led her to the desk area, where we quickly undressed each other. I turned Kelly around and took a good look at her bottom.

"Well, I guess next time I'm going to have to do a better job; your bottom isn't even pink anymore."

Kelly laughed, and replied, "Next time, I will be ready for whatever you do with me. I know that you'll have me in tears ... but I also know it will be a turn-on for both of us." We walked across the playroom and into the bathroom, where I got the showers going, the room quickly becoming steamy. We stepped under the rain shower, and Kelly took control, quickly bathing my back and chest, and then focusing on my private parts.

Kelly stroked my growing member using her hands alternately with her fingers curled around me, and stroking slowly but forcefully. I was about to lean forward to kiss her, when she suddenly dropped to her knees, taking my penis in her mouth, and stroking with her lips, as she swirled her tongue over its head. She sucked and stroked, tongued me and fondled me.

I was now fully erect and only a few moments from orgasm ... when, still sucking me, she inserted a finger deeply into my rear, pushing and curling it into my prostate. The effect was immediate: I exploded into her mouth, as the shower poured on us, and water flowed in streams down our bodies. Kelly continued sucking for a few moments, and then looked up at me with a smile ... and a finger still inside me against my prostate.

I was suddenly very weak. I smiled back at Kelly and kissed the top of her head, smothering myself in her long, thick hair. Kelly took her finger out of me, and stood up; we held each other tightly, as the warm water continued to pour down on us, my arms encircling her and pulling her against me, as I buried my head in her neck.

And then I started kissing Kelly with little pecks ... around the neck, up her cheek, across her forehead, and back down to her waiting mouth. As she began to close her eyes and open her mouth for the long kiss, I suddenly dropped down, continuing to kiss her lightly – across her chest, on each nipple, and around her breasts, down her stomach, and to her mound.

I looked up at Kelly, who had her hands on her hips, and was looking down at me as if I were a small child who had done something wrong.

"What?" I asked.

Kelly replied, "Get up here, young man, and kiss me properly!" I obeyed instantly, caressing Kelly while we kissed long and deep, our tongues intertwining, and our breaths catching.

Then, Kelly put her hands on my shoulders and pushed me back a few inches. "Now, you can take care of me. But I would like it to be in the sauna, since you forgot about me when we were in there earlier."

I gave an exaggerated mock frown, "I didn't forget about you; I was deeply involved in your story."

Kelly laughed, "I know, silly. But if you'll do me in there, maybe I won't need to punish you for last time." I wasn't sure this made any sense, but it didn't matter. As I opened a narrow closet and pulled out a couple of thick towels, I muttered, "But I want you to punish me!"

And as we opened the door to the sauna and walked in, Kelly, whispered, "Don't worry, young man, I'll punish you plenty!"

I laid one towel nearly the length of the lower bench. Kelly didn't need any prodding, and sat back on the toweled bench, parting her legs, as I put the other towel, still folded, down on the sauna floor, and got on my knees in front of her.

I glanced up at her, and she gave me a hungry, sensuous, sexy look, then laid her head back and closed her eyes – the signal to turn my attention to her swollen lips and already-throbbing clit.

I went down on her with full enthusiasm, first running my tongue along her labia, with the tip of my tongue going deeper. I curled my tongue and thrust it into Kelly's vagina, as deeply as I could, my face against Kelly's pubes, and my nose happening to rub against her clit.

Kelly gasped, and I withdrew my tongue, and continued upward, flicking it underneath her hood.

Kelly writhed above me, as I teased her by continuing the trek of my tongue, up to her black triangle, and then back down over her clit, and along her lips again.

Kelly's hands took my head and guided me back into position, and I swirled my tongue over her clit as I reached my arms around her, and held her bottom tightly in my hands, pulling her to me. I continued to lick, and then began to suck on her clit.

At some point, I had to come up for air, and my eyes feasted on Kelly's beautiful form, her generous but firm breasts, her head back, eyes closed, and long auburn hair – now looking nearly black in the dim light of the sauna – flowing down to the towel on the sauna bench.

We were both drenched in sweat, and Kelly's body gleamed, as the sweat rolled down her. I slipped two fingers into her and she gasped again, before my head went back down, and I stroked her clit with my nose a few times, playfully.

Then my tongue – like a snake – took control, slithering up one side of Kelly's clit and then up the other, more and more forcefully, then swirling over her swollen knob, as she screamed, and my fingers were covered by thick secretions. I continued to lick, more slowly, more delicately, Kelly coming again and again, letting out high-pitched squeals, and thrusting herself onto my fingers.

I inserted a third finger, and Kelly began a low moan, continuing her thrusting, but pulling my head from her clit. Kelly's legs were over my shoulders, and she was lying back on the narrow bench.

I extracted my fingers, and swiveled both of us until she was able to lay down flat on the bench, and I could climb onto the bench and maneuver up her until my head was on her chest, her breasts under my neck, my stomach on her mound, and my once-again-growing manhood between her legs.

"I feel like we're in one of those Southern movies, with the naked bodies gleaming and dripping with sweat ..." I began.

Kelly laughed, panted a few times, and said, "Well this naked body is about to pass out, if we stay in here much longer!"

I got the hint and, before getting up, kissed each of her breasts, lingering long enough to swirl my tongue over them, and gently bite her nipples. We stepped out of the sauna, dropped the towels into the hamper, and turned on the showers. I adjusted the 12 leg jets for cool water, and the overhead rain shower for warm, as we rinsed off.

We quickly bathed each other again — was this the fourth time today? — and finally turned the showers off and dried off with fresh towels from the shelf. Kelly started to wrap herself in the towel, but I pulled it off and dropped it into the hamper, getting only a brief curious look from Kelly. I then reached into the narrow closet next to the bathroom, and pulled out two heavy terrycloth robes, holding one for Kelly to get into.

Kelly smiled and, once we were both in our robes, held me, and put her head on my chest. "That's what I mean!" I didn't know what she was talking about, but she continued. "It's the thoughtfulness, the kindness, the 'sweetness' that you show, along with the sensuousness and sexuality and, yes, pain."

I frowned, "What we just did wasn't painful, was it?"

Kelly laughed, "No, silly. But ..." She had a gleam in her eye, and I knew she had come up with something. "Well, I think I would like you to spank me one more time before we go to bed." I couldn't believe my ears! Kelly was really getting into the spanking mood, and requesting this after an otherwise romantic evening.

"Well, young lady, if you really want," I looked at her sternly, and she just smiled and nodded enthusiastically, "I could give you one last OTK. But you might have to take care of me again, afterward."

Kelly laughed, taking my hand and leading me back into the playroom, "I think that can be arranged!"

I pulled the straight-backed chair from near the small table along the wall and surreptitiously opened the drawer of the table and put something into the pocket of my robe. When I turned around, Kelly was in the standing position, nude, with the robe around her feet. I nodded, and sat down on the chair (positioning it under the light, even though the video recorders were off), and made a 'come hither' signal with my pointer finger.

Kelly quickly got over my knee, positioning herself so that her pubic hair was against my right thigh, and her breasts to the left of my left thigh. I knew she would hold her position without any help from me.

When Kelly had settled, I informed her, "You're going to get a quick level-5 hand spanking, and then another quick level-5 - that I think you've been wanting. As usual, you will hold your position, keeping your hands in front of you. Are you ready, young lady?"

I couldn't believe she was ready for this, after the day – and evening – we'd had; but I didn't want to disappoint her. I had to ask, "Kelly, are you doing this for me or for you?"

Kelly kept her head down, and replied, "For both of us … but mostly for me." I massaged her bottom with my right hand, and then let it settle in the middle of her right buttock.

"OK," I told her, and then began a very hard and very quick hand spanking, alternating sides, and covering all of Kelly's bottom, and the tops of her thighs. Kelly squirmed a little, and made some panting and squealing noises, but she controlled herself very well. Although I had not put my right leg over her legs, she did not try to kick them, and it appeared that her entire body was relaxed.

As she knew, a level-5 OTK hand spanking consisted of 100 spanks and then, usually, a corner time. I decided that if there were going to be a corner time, we would do it on the bed. I didn't hold back, the spanks becoming harder and even faster. I heard a few 'Ow!'s from Kelly, and some moaning; perhaps the endorphins of the prior punishments had made her forget the intensity of the pain, and she was just now rediscovering what it meant to be thrashed.

It didn't take long to reach 100 spanks, the sudden quietness shocking, after the continuous loud slapping noises on Kelly's bottom. Kelly panted, and I heard a couple of sniffles, but she composed herself and tilted her head back at me. "Thank you, Sir."

I smiled, and said, "You're very welcome, young lady. But we're not finished here. You are now going to receive a level-5 hair-brushing."

At this, Kelly gasped loudly, and I thought I heard the beginning of a 'Wha...', before she silenced herself, and let her head hang back down.

I pulled the hairbrush from my robe pocket; it was one of my favorites, with a smooth fine-grained and highly polished wooden back that was about three by four inches in size, and thick enough to bruise. I placed the hairbrush on Kelly's left buttock and, without further discussion, lifted it and brought it back down hard, her buttock rippling, and a loud 'Crack!' echoing in the room.

"Ow!!! That *really* hurts!" I lifted the hairbrush, and before bringing it down on her right cheek, I said, "Yes, I know, dear." Kelly screamed with the second stroke ... and the third, and the fourth.

Kelly's body hung loosely from my lap, and she sobbed quietly. "Kelly, I'm doing this for you ... and you can stop it if you want. If you decide to finish, the strokes will be milder ... but they will still hurt. If you decide to stop now, I will never hold it against you. You've done great today!"

Kelly continued to sob and sniffle. I looked at her, "I will ask you only one time: Would you like me to finish your hair-brushing?"

There was more sniffling, and then I heard a soft, but resolute, reply from Kelly, "Yes, Sir."

I was amazed. I really hadn't planned to do any more spanking after our nice dinner. I had thought we would be too tired for any of this ... but I guess we'd both had a 'second wind' – probably the effect of the wine fading.

Kelly had asked for it, and I would oblige. I completed her hair-brushing – another 14 strokes – without incident. I was giving Kelly mild-to-medium strokes, but at about one every second or two, the hair-brushing was finished in less than half a minute.

Kelly was bawling when we were done, her hair hanging down and completely obscuring any view of her face. She sobbed, with a few big heaves, as I rubbed her now-red bottom.

I helped her up, and we lay on the bed. I opened my robe, and spooned Kelly, wrapping the robe around her, and holding her tight. I felt her bottom quivering, and she was still sniffling.

We lay together and I caressed Kelly, as she calmed down. Then, I turned her on her stomach, and reached for the bedside drawer, where I had stashed a tube of soothing lotion. I smeared it around Kelly's bottom and upper thighs, and rubbed it in. I kissed her shoulders her neck, and her ears.

I got up, and quickly turned off the lights, except the indirect lighting over the bed, and a nightlight in the bathroom. I brought from the bar a couple bottles of water to set next to the bed. Kelly was dozing.

I pulled down the covers around her, and woke her enough to get her body between the sheets. I tucked her in, and she was lucid enough to give me a little kiss. She had a very contented smile on her face.

I climbed into bed and dimmed the lights with the remote. Kelly was already snoring, and I couldn't blame her: The day had been stressful for her, emotional for both of us. And with the big dinner and wine, and then the sauna and orgasms, sleep came easily.

This was Kelly's first experience falling asleep with a sore bottom. Perhaps it wouldn't be her last.

CHAPTER 17: VISIONS OF THE FUTURE

I had expected to lie in bed analyzing the day ... or at least having one last orgasm, but I was evidently as tired as Kelly, and asleep within minutes. I woke briefly sometime during the night, and realized Kelly was coming back from the bathroom; she climbed into bed and spooned me, and we were both asleep again.

When I woke again, it was around 6:30AM, and Kelly was sleeping soundly next to me. She was beautiful, even while she slept. Her luxuriant long hair on the luxurious satin sheets seemed out of a classic movie.

Then, my mind started working. I lay back, staring at the ceiling – at nothing – but my mind's eye replayed some of the events of yesterday. It was mind-boggling. Not necessarily that we had done so much, but that so many of my fantasies had been 'satisfied' so quickly by this strong young woman.

Fantasies that I had only developed over the past year or so, fantasies with a young woman that I had assumed could never be realized, but were now an indelible part of our lives. Of who we were. And who we were going to be.

I had been afraid that actually acting out my fantasies would make them less of a turn-on, as Kelly had suggested. But just thinking about a few specific things from yesterday caused a stirring down below, and my hand naturally began its autonomic action as I relived and then expanded the fantasy. I was hard, and my mind was swirling.

Suddenly another hand took over the task, and I turned my head to look into Kelly's bright eyes. She smiled, and I climbed on top of her, straddling her, and gave her a big kiss. "Good morning! How are you feeling today?"

Kelly smiled, and said, "I'm fine. How about you?" She looked down at me and laughed, "I guess I can see how you're doing!"

I kissed Kelly again, and moved up and down along her length, rubbing the underside of my penis on her pubic hair. I laughed, and Kelly looked into my eyes. I explained, "We used to call this 'making love *on* you' — something to do when you're having your period." My legs were straddling her body, and her legs were together.

"This is the 'safe' way: You know, the safest birth control pill is an aspirin ... held tightly between the knees."

Kelly laughed again. I then put my knee between her legs, which opened up to allow me to position myself between them — ready to make love. I said, "I'm going to make love *on* you now. Just use your hands to guide me, like you did in the shower yesterday."

Kelly did as instructed, and I continued to move, starting to pant, and asked Kelly, "Are you ready?" Kelly nodded, and I jetted semen between her breasts and up to her neck. She caressed me, as I continued thrusting.

I then kissed her, and rolled over to lie next to her on the bed. After a few moments, I said, "Just a minute ...", and I went into the bathroom, and soaked a washcloth in warm water, wringing it out, and returning to the bed. As Kelly had done yesterday with me, I carefully cleaned Kelly's front, and then dropped the washcloth on a tray on the bedside dresser.

Kelly climbed on top of me, putting her hand between us and masturbating; very similar to when I had been on the bed upstairs, but this time I could look into Kelly's eyes, and caress her breasts, her shoulders, her back, as she moved sensuously over me, and came with a high pitched squeal. She fell on top of me, and I held her, massaging her back, and then moving my hands lower to her bottom.

She flinched, and said, "Yes, I still feel that hairbrush."

We held each other a while longer, and then got up and put on our robes. "You can have the bathroom down here, and I'll get cleaned up upstairs. Then, I'll round-up some breakfast for us. When you're ready, come up to the kitchen, and we can talk."

Kelly arched a brow, "Talk? You sure like to talk a lot."

I laughed, "Well, we can *do*, also, but I have some ideas I'd like to bounce off you. Some ideas for the future." Kelly arched her brow again, and I just shrugged.

Less than an hour later, I had made coffee, heated some croissants, and put out the fresh orange juice I had bought for yesterday. I was prepared to cook breakfast for Kelly, if she was hungry – we had enough supplies for omelets, French toast or waffles.

Kelly came up to the kitchen looking radiant, wearing the jeans from yesterday, but a different top. Her hair was brushed and her skin glowed. We sat at the kitchen table, and I poured the coffee. "We had quite a day, yesterday!" was the only way I could begin.

Kelly laughed, and agreed, "Yes, it was an experience! One that I liked more than I thought I would." She reached back and rubbed her bottom.

I sipped the coffee and smiled, "Yes, you really got into the 'swing' of things (pun intended)." We laughed, and buttered our croissants.

I was thinking along many lines, but especially about a fantasy that had been developing over the past 12 hours: Having an experience with her friends. It was too bad that

Linda and Julie hadn't come over last night – so I could give Linda her 'birthday spanking'. I was sure that would have opened some lines of communications ... or closed them quickly!

How could I bring this up with Kelly? Would our relationship be diminished? Was there a way that Kelly could be turned on by that experience? I also had other ideas, but they seemed so outlandish that I forced them to the back of my head. I looked at Kelly, and could see that she was mulling something over in her head, as well.

"Sir," she said meekly, "I enjoyed playing the submissive role. But I'm not sure whether it's a role, or the lifestyle that I may have been looking for." I choked, and nearly sprayed coffee over the table, but somehow managed to keep the coffee in my mouth.

I was dumbfounded. The 'other' fantasy that had been developing in my brain was the experience of having a 'sex slave' – especially the training of the sex slave. This was not something that I really thought about, and would not have brought it up with Kelly at this point. I thought Kelly brave – and trusting – to broach that subject. She certainly seemed to be able to fulfill the role, if not the lifestyle.

I put down my coffee, and wiped my mouth with the napkin before explaining, "Kelly, that is one of my deepest – and, up to now, most secret – fantasies: To train someone as a 'sex slave'. At least, *my* definition of a 'sex slave.' But I think that is getting ahead of ourselves."

Kelly smiled, and said, confidently, "I think I would be a good 'sex slave' for some lucky man!"

I laughed, "I'm sure you would, Kelly. And I hope I might be that lucky man." She smiled proudly, and took a bite of croissant.

I continued, "But, there might be some things that you would not like."

Kelly didn't say a word, but her expression (although her hands weren't on her hips) cried, 'Try me!'.

I elaborated, "For example, what if I wanted to spank you in front of someone else? Or ask them to spank you?" Kelly looked down. I wondered whether she had already thought through more of the ramifications than I had. But now was a good time to test her.

"Kelly, I thought it would be fun for Linda and Julie to come over and, if Linda's as wild as you say she is, she should have no problem going across my lap.

"I would have raised her dress, and then offered to give her the full spanking on the bare bottom, or double the amount on her underwear – to see how she would respond. I think they might have taken it as 'good fun' with some harmless older guy."

Kelly laughed, then became more serious, "I really don't know how they would have reacted. She might have done it, but she would have had to trust my judgment that you weren't dangerous."

I smiled, and continued relating my thoughts, "So I was thinking how you could 'get back' at your three friends, and how we could get them to submit to a punishment experience."

Kelly just shook her head, "I don't think you could get them to do that."

Some flashbulbs of ideas were going off in my head. "Well, I could think of two basic ways. One is that we catch them doing something bad – illegal – where a spanking would be the 'lesser of the evils'. For example, if we invited them here and I left some cash out, and they took it, and we got it on video ..."

Kelly laughed, "That's a lot of 'if's."

Then I thought, "But you could be the 'ringleader' and, as far as they were concerned you were all being punished. They wouldn't know you were 'in on it' until much later."

Kelly laughed again, but shook her head 'No'.

"The other way might be to dare them or shame them into doing it. How do you think they would react, if we gave them a little demonstration?"

Kelly grimaced, "I don't know if I could do that."

Touché. I smiled, "But if you were a sex slave, you would need to do it, if I asked you. Maybe you're really not ready for that?" Kelly frowned, but didn't put up an argument; she was exhibiting less confidence, now.

I thought a bit more, "Perhaps we should tell them that you are being trained as a sex slave. And that for your friends, I would offer an easy introductory session ..." This was getting better and better. I could see Kelly's mind whirling, and knew now that if this were orchestrated properly, it would be a huge turn-on for Kelly. And, of course, for me.

"Let's think about it. But in the meantime, we can spend a long weekend together. If you're still interested."

Kelly looked up at the sky, "You *know* I'm interested. It's going to be difficult for me to leave today. I think I'm going to be doing a lot of fantasizing in the next couple of weeks."

Then, I remembered. "And we'll have to start planning something for your birthday. When will that be? In about 6 weeks?" Kelly nodded and, as her eyes glazed over, I had no doubt that she was thinking about her 'birthday spanking'. Kelly popped the last of the croissant into her mouth. We were both having visions of the future. And they seemed quite compatible.

Kelly asked, "Do you mean we're only going to see each other twice in the next six weeks?"

That was a good question. I replied, "I'd love to see you more than that. How would you like to have lunch with me again – maybe on Thursday?" Kelly's eyes lit up, and she leaned over and hugged me.

When she sat back into her chair, I said, "I'm not playing 'hard-to-get', you know. As I told you a while ago, I would rather keep you as a friend, than lose you as a lover – or submissive."

I thought about next Thursday. "Maybe we can have lunch every week until you come over? We can eat ... and 'eat', now that the restrictions on our 'diet' have been lifted."

Kelly laughed, and this time I leaned over to hug her. And give her a passionate kiss. Well, at least as passionate as it can be over a breakfast table.

"Shall we go down to the playroom and get you packed up?" Kelly reluctantly nodded, and we carried the dishes to the sink, and put the butter back in the fridge before going downstairs. I told Kelly to get her tote bag packed, and I went into the exam room, where I made one last preparation. I carried a small black bag back to the desk as Kelly was finishing stuffing her clothes in the tote.

I then stood next to Kelly, and said, "Please lower your pants."

She looked a little surprised, but immediately undid her belt, unbuttoned and unzipped her jeans, and pushed them down to her knees. She got up into the standing position, and I lowered her underwear to just below her buttocks. I examined her bottom: It was still pink, but there were no marks or bruises.

I left her standing there with her pants and underwear pulled down, walked around to my chair, and opened the box. "Kelly, you have done very well as a submissive: Beyond all my expectations. But I'm learning to expect much more from you. I think you know that I won't hold back on your caning and other punishments when you stay over next time?"

Kelly swallowed hard, and nodded. She had no idea where this was going, but was starting to get nervous.

"You are going to obey my commands ... but I am also going to be kind to you. You will never be a 'slave' – in the traditional sense. I want you to have fun, too. I want you to share your opinions, and help make the decisions. But I also know now that you need someone strong, who will make requests of you, and who will take care of you." Kelly nodded, blankly, still unsure of where this was going.

I took the 10 cc syringe with 1½-inch needle from the box. It had been loaded with 4cc of sterile saline. I also removed an alcohol swab, and a gauze pad. Kelly's face dropped. I don't think she expected this. And I *knew* she wasn't expecting what was about to happen.

I walked around Kelly and put the syringe, swab and gauze on the desk. I turned to face Kelly, and said, "This will be my last request of you for this introductory – 24-hour (!) – session."

Kelly didn't look happy, but she nodded slowly, "Yes, Sir."

I then went behind her ... and pulled up her panties and straightened them. Then, I pulled up her jeans, reaching around the front to zip and button them. Kelly remained in the standing position, but her mouth had fallen open. I quickly went back around her, then undid and lowered my own pants and underwear, and bent over the desk.

"OK, Kelly. You will be trained next time, but I will let you give me one ... or two ... last shots. Your choice." With that, I lowered my chest onto the desk, with my head in my crossed arms, and my butt presented well to Kelly. I did not look back, and said nothing more.

Neither did Kelly. I heard her fastening her belt, then opening the alcohol swab, with a quick tear. I felt her fingers on my right buttock, and then the cold alcohol being rubbed on my skin. I saw her pick up the syringe, and heard her pop off the protective cap. Then I felt her fingers stretching my skin, and the needle sliding into my tissues.

She did a nice quick insertion, so it did not particularly hurt. But it was uncomfortable as she moved the syringe around, trying to pull back on the plunger to test for blood. Finally, I felt the saline being injected, a pinching feeling, increasing to an uncomfortable but tolerable pain.

I then heard Kelly chuckle. "I've now injected 2 cc ... and I really do need the practice ... so I think I'll finish with a second shot." I wasn't surprised. As I had done earlier, she left the shot in my right side, as she prepared the left with the alcohol. I then felt the needle sliding out of me, and Kelly placing her fingers on my left buttock. "Are you ready?" she asked.

"Yes, Ma'am," I replied (mistakenly addressing her as 'Ma'am', instead of 'Miss' ... but my mind wasn't exactly sharp at this point).

With that, she plunged the needle into my left hip, and repeated the process, taking her time to inject the remaining 2 cc. She pulled out the needle, and set the syringe on the desk. Then, she opened the gauze pad, and held it against each side for a few seconds. "That's all. You're done, young man."

I stood up and turned to Kelly. We hugged each other, and she reached down to hold my hardening penis. I hadn't planned on anything else; I had just wanted to leave her with thoughts that might stimulate additional fantasies. I said, "If you get me turned-on, you might have to do something about it."

Kelly smiled at me, "That's what I'm counting on." She then pulled up a chair and sat down, while I stood before her with my pants and underwear around my ankles. She took me in her hands, and then in her mouth. The sensation was exquisite, and the experience – again – beyond what I had planned or imagined.

I came in her mouth, and she swallowed, wiping her mouth with the back of her hand, and then reaching down to express the last drop of semen, which she licked off me. She raised her eyes to mine, and gave me a sexy smile. 'Sex slave'. That could really be something.

I pulled up my pants, and carried Kelly's bag out to her car. We hugged again, and I said, "Thank you. I had a lot of fun."

Kelly gave me a peck of a kiss, and said, "Me too." She smiled, and ran around to the driver's side, opened the door, and slid in. I waved as she departed, and could only stand there shaking my head for several minutes, before I went inside.

As I began to clean up the playroom, my mind wandered, and I started fantasizing about what we would do when Kelly came over for the long weekend. By the time I got to the bathroom, I was fantasizing about 'playing' with Julie, Linda and Kathy. And by the time I had finished cleaning the kitchen, and retreated to my desk, I was fantasizing about having a 'sex slave'.

The possibilities. Oh, the possibilities!

###

Thank you for reading Book 2 of the Experiences series. If you enjoyed it, please take a moment to leave a review at your favorite retailer. And, if you liked this story, you'll LOVE the continuation in Book 3: <u>Weekend Experience</u>!

- Simone Freier

Discover other titles by Simone Freier:

Experiences Series Book 1: Origins of a Fetish

Experiences Series Book 2: First Experience

Experiences Series Book 3: Weekend Experience

Experiences Series Book 4: Birthday Experience

Experiences Series Book 5: European Experience

Experiences Series Book 6: Friends' Experience

Experiences Series Book 7: Island Experience

Experiences Series Book 8: Domme Experience

Connect with the Author:

Follow me on Twitter: http://twitter.com/SimoneFreier

Friend me on Facebook: http://facebook.com/SimoneFreierAuthor

Visit my Website: http://SimoneFreier.com

Favorite me at Smashwords: http://smashwords.com/SimoneFreier